Grounded

Out of the Box, Book 4

Robert J. Crane

Grounded
Out of the Box, Book 4
Robert J. Crane

1st Edition

1

Sienna
Minneapolis, Minnesota

They say blood is thicker than water, and while this is literally true, it's also really annoying. Take it from a girl who's cleaned up way too much blood in her time. When you take this expression metaphorically, however, it's actually even worse than laundering your clothes to get the red out, writing off that nice new pair of jeans because they're sodden with—never mind. I'm getting off point here. What is the point? The actual point? That blood, the people you're related to—the ties are thicker than with almost anyone else. Because the things you do for blood—for family—well, I think they cause most of us more problems than can be fairly called our share.

And the things you do for the people you call family who aren't blood … some of them are even worse.

I was in the training room on the agency campus listening to Ariadne vent her spleen about another of our director's aggravating decisions. It was an early Tuesday morning in the middle of June, and the heat of summer hadn't settled on Minnesota quite yet. It was lovely outside, and I wanted to get out there, maybe take a flight, clear my head. But when Director Andrew Phillips—asshole extraordinaire—made a pain of himself on the administrative side of our agency, which Ariadne ran, I listened to her gripes. Because in return, when he landed on operations, my side of the agency, I got to yell and throw things in her presence. It was a fair trade, most of the time.

But on a nice day, when I was just trying to get through my training so I could take a flight? It didn't feel fair.

Ariadne wasn't blood, by the way. She was other kind of family, the found kind, which … well, even I have those people in my life that I'd probably choose over the ones I got born to. She was that to me, like a surrogate sister/mother/all-around useful person whose lover I kindasorta killed and have still living in my head.

Rivers of blood in my life.

That's probably not a metaphor.

"If he could just …" Ariadne searched for words. Her pale face was inflamed, almost matching the color of her hair. Almost. I wasn't positive she dyed it, but she had just enough lines on her face that if she didn't, *damn.* Because that red hair of hers wasn't losing an ounce of luster.

"Stop being an ass?" I was gently working over a heavy bag. By heavy, I mean about a thousand pounds of compressed sand hung from the ceiling by chains. It was specially made just for me and suspended from bolts fastened directly to the steel girders that made up the bottom level of the roof supports. The head of the construction company who built it laughingly assured me that it would hold up to anything I threw at it or my money back. As soon as it was finished I gave it about a quarter of my effort in his presence and he cut a check that afternoon. I never saw him on site again after that, even though the project went on for another month. Maybe he died of shame, I dunno.

"I don't think Phillips will stop being an ass." Ariadne was pacing, wandering back and forth in her navy suit, the V-neck of her cream-colored blouse revealing more mottled skin. She was clearly livid and had taken off her heels to walk over the uneven canvas mats that lined the floor. I paused, a little worried she might turn an ankle as she strode ten paces, turned, came back, and did it again for the nth time. "I just wish he could see this like we see it."

"He's not supposed to see it like we see it," I said, giving the bag a jab. It was really pitiful how much I had to hold back on this thing. I felt like I was shadow boxing with a child, afraid to even let it have a tap. When I channeled the strength of the strongest soul I had within—a really nasty beast named Wolfe—I could hit hard enough to probably knock a train off its tracks. I hadn't tried that yet, though I kept secretly hoping some grandiose ass would jack a BNSF freight engine just so I could find out. "He's supposed to keep us quietly under the radar so that President Harmon can win re-election without having to answer for my various and sundry misdeeds."

"And a fine job he's doing of *that* lately." Ariadne froze in place, mid-turn, and looked straight at me. I could see the regret pile up in her eyes as I watched. Her red skin flared brighter for a second and then drained. "I am so sorry, Sienna."

I hit the bag and heard its industrial-grade, space-age material rip from the force of compression. Dammit. I hadn't even channeled Wolfe or twisted when I punched. I just got a little rough with a straight-on shot from the hip and …

A mountain of sand spilled out of the bottom of the bag. I yelped like I was the wicked witch and it was water and flung myself into the air. I hung there, about four feet above it all as the bag emptied, sand spilling out, billowing around me under the fluorescent lights. Ariadne coughed and covered her mouth, taking an involuntary step back.

"Dammit," I said once the contents were mostly emptied. I hovered, more disappointed in my failure of control than anything. The whole point of the bag, I had convinced myself, was to help me to control myself. If I really wanted to go out and just beat the hell out of something to show my strength, there was no shortage of trees in the Northwoods of Minnesota I could go smash. It helped toughen up my skin against future traumas, too. That was another quirk of Wolfe's power that I could channel.

I looked at Ariadne, and she just looked so damned … guilty. "Sorry," she said again.

"It's okay." I floated back to the ground, feeling the weight of gravity take over again, and landed on my feet far enough away from the mound of sand that I didn't have to fear slipping. Not that I feared slipping much anyway. "It's not your fault that every single person in the media seems to have a sudden, deep, insatiable yearning to cast me as the next …" I searched for an appropriate villain. "What's the governmental equivalent of Hitler, Stalin and Mao combined?"

"Uhh … I believe they were all government figures of some kind," Ariadne said.

"Right," I said. "I'm them, but with fewer atrocities, body counts and—oh, yeah, actual power to affect anything."

"Well, you're catching up fast on one of those," came a voice from behind me. I turned my head to see my brother—half-brother—Reed Treston, standing at the entry to the training room, hair back in a ponytail and a rocking a full-on grey suit. He had a few months of beard going on, too, which was really different for him but had cleared up his babyface issue. I had a feeling he'd done it so that his (much) older girlfriend wouldn't have to feel quite so aged in his presence.

Okay, I mostly hoped that last bit. Out of pettiness. (I still don't like his girlfriend.)

"The atrocities or the body count?" I asked, trying not to put too much care into it. Reed had been distant for months; we'd had a conversation in my room that had seemed to change the nature of our relationship. That had been in January, right after I'd destroyed half the campus while fending off a prison break/terrorist attack. We barely hung out anymore, talked pretty tersely when we had to work together, and had many moments of extremely awkward tension filled with a lot of passive-aggression. It was great, like being part of a real family. One with big, fat, honking issues.

Oh, right, I already said like being part of a real family.

"Matter of opinion," he said tightly, then unfolded his arms to reveal a manila folder clutched in one hand.

"I'd be interested to hear which it is, in yours," Ariadne said.

"No, you wouldn't," Reed and I both answered in unison, never breaking off from looking right at one another.

"Here to train?" I asked, gesturing to the heavy bag. He could, and did, use the bag without any problems. Well, until now. "Because I kinda had an accident."

"At least it doesn't require a change of pants," he said, shrugging it off. "I've got something."

"Kinda figured, since you're here and talking," I said, nodding at the folder. "What's up?"

"Atlanta," Reed said. "Atlanta is up. I got contacted by a police detective down there that I talked to a couple years ago about something they had going on, and I think they've got a meta problem."

"It's always meta problems and never meta solutions," I said, making my way over to him cautiously.

"You're supposed to be the solution," Ariadne offered.

"Make a Final Solution joke and I'll end *you*," I said to Reed as I crossed over to read the file in his hand. He didn't even show a flicker of humor. "See, it ties back to a whole Hitler, Stalin and Mao bit—"

"Yeah, that's just bad taste," Reed said, thrusting the folder at me. "A little over a year ago, Atlanta P.D. had an unexplained murder. A woman, Flora Romero, got shot. The guy who shot her, Joaquin Pollard, died seconds later from a bolt of lightning." He kept a straight face the entire time. "This was while you were in England tracking down that slice-and-dice group that was cutting through old Omega."

"I vaguely remember you mentioning something about this at the time, I think." I stared at the photos, which had been color-printed on regular paper and had some really ugly line effects that did little to hide the stark grossness of the murder scene. "Why are you revisiting this now?" I felt dirty even though I hadn't worked out hard enough to sweat and had dodged the outpouring of sand.

"The same detective that contacted me about it at the time called me again," Reed said, flipping the file to another page. "He had a witness to the lightning incident. A six-year-old that swore some guy in a hooded sweatshirt shot lightning bolts out of his hands and killed Joaquin Pollard. The detective, Marcus Calderon, Atlanta P.D., had to let it go. No other leads, and the six-year-old didn't get a look at the guy's face."

"Okay," I said, waiting for him to tie it all together for me.

"Last night, Calderon gets called to two separate lightning strikes," Reed said, going to the next page. "Roscoe Marion and Kennith Coy. Killed less than a mile from each other, within about fifteen minutes."

"Was there a storm in Atlanta last night?" I asked, looking at the grainy printouts of the photos. They didn't show much, but what they showed was gross.

"There was," Reed said and snapped the file shut. "A summer storm. Thunder and lightning. Nice cover for a killing if someone wanted to get away with it—"

"And could shoot lightning out of their hands," I agreed, folding my arms. "So, you want to go take a look, see if this is a real thing or just a coincidence? Lightning striking twice and all that?"

His face flickered, and I caught the first hint of uncertainty. "I can't. I'm scheduled on vacation. I'm taking Isabella to—"

"Right," I said. I'd already forgotten that Director Phillips had emailed me my brother's vacation request already approved, without even consulting me. Of course, Reed could have run it by me, too, and he hadn't, so …

Whatever. Fewer administrative headaches for me, right?

"You want me to go check it out?" I looked up at him as neutrally as I could manage. All this talk of lightning was making me wonder if I could hear thunder in the distance. Probably just my imagination.

"That'd be great," Reed said. "If I hadn't planned this trip with Isabella, I'd be there, you know that—"

"Absolutely," I said, and snatched the folder right out of his hand so fast he didn't even know it was gone until he looked down and saw empty fingers. That was the advantage of being faster, stronger and more dexterous. "I'll take care of it."

"Okay." He turned, nodding, his broad, suit-covered shoulders turning away from me. "If it gets to be too much, call me. I'll keep my phone on."

"I'll be fine," I said as breezily as I could manage. "Enjoy your trip."

He froze at the door, looked over his shoulder at me. He felt miles away already. "Thanks."

I gave him a little half-hearted wave as he walked out and closed the door behind him. I just stood there, still, stewing, until he'd been gone a good thirty seconds and a voice rang out like thunder behind me.

"What the hell was *that*?" Ariadne asked.

"Me doing my job," I said, holding the folder lightly between my fingers. I cast her a look. "What did you think it was?"

"The most tense, awkward sort of conversation I can possibly imagine between the two of you," Ariadne said, sounding about two steps shy of horrified. "How long has this been going on?"

"Since the night you killed your first person," I said, heading for the door. I may have thrown that out to mask the sting I was feeling. Actually, that was probably obvious.

"Sienna—" Ariadne said.

"Gotta go," I said, and held up the folder in my hand.

"Time and tide wait for no man, after all." I paused. "Wait, isn't there some cheesy cliché about lightning, too?"

"Trying to run from this conversation is the last thing you should be trying to do right now," Ariadne said, still a little grey in the face. She looked as serious as I'd ever seen her, pallor settled in where anger from Phillips's actions had been replaced by concern. For me. "Sienna, talk to me."

"Trying to catch lightning in a bottle," I said, "that's the one I was thinking of."

Her concern died, replaced by a settled look, one of disappointment but not surprise. "That's what it's like, isn't it? Trying to talk about something you don't want to—"

"See you later, Ariadne," I said, and walked out. Blood, water—who cared which, really? Either one would drown you if you let it pull you down. I took flight the minute I was out the door, ignored the sudden grey skies and rain, and went supersonic as I turned south, clutching Reed's file tight in my hand, knowing I'd figure everything else out as I went.

2.

Augustus
Atlanta, Georgia

My name is Augustus. Yeah, like the Caesar. I could make a rhyme about that, and I have, going with "squeeze her," "seizure," and "cheeser" for the next line. See, you gotta make the joke before anyone else does. That's how you survive coming from where I've come from.

Nah, I'm just kidding.

Well, I'm kidding a little.

Nah, I'm not kidding that much.

But it all worked out! Sure, I still live in a rough area—but it's my neighborhood. It's where I grew up. That basketball court where some guys threw down and had a shoot-out? That's where my dad taught me how to ride a bike. My family lives there. It's where my roots are. That's home.

And you don't gotta leave home to be somebody.

See, that's what I'm all about. Being somebody. At six feet tall and a little under two hundred pounds, I was just shy of being able to play well enough to get the college scholarship. And that's okay. And my grades? Hey, they were good. Just not quite good enough for the academic scholarship. But like I said, it all works out.

Because straight out of high school, I got hired on by Cavanagh Technologies when they opened their new, super-modern factory outside Vine City, and I've been there almost two years now. Assistant line supervisor, that's my job title. That's right. Not even twenty years old, and I was management, baby! I strolled down the line and the workers saw Augustus Coleman, rising star. One more promotion and I was getting college paid for by the corporation. It was all in the cards, and they were getting turned over this autumn.

Or at least they were supposed to.

But life's funny, and it takes its little turns.

I'll show you what I mean.

It started off like any other day and went off the track faster than you could smack an emergency shutdown switch. But that's okay! Like I said, life does that. But this wasn't an actual emergency shutdown switch-flip situation. That would have been bad. This looked good when it showed up. Real good.

Edward Cavanagh made Elon Musk look lazy and unambitious by comparison. That morning, Cavanagh came wandering down the factory floor in a storm of activity. Guy like him makes noise everywhere he goes—paparazzi, girlfriends, hangers-on, bodyguards, yes-men—yeah, he's got an entourage. If you were a billionaire-genius-playboy-philanthropist in the mold of Tony Stark, you'd have one, too. He was a medium-height, medium-build, heading-toward-middle-age white guy.

"Oh, damn," Lawton Evers said. Lawton was one of the guys on my line. I'd known him forever. Dude was three years ahead of me in school. "Big boss is here."

"Look who he's got with him," said Eduardo Tomas. I didn't know much about Tomas; he was new to my little fiefdom. (Yes, I think of my team as a fiefdom. Not like they're serfs or anything, but like … you know, there isn't really any favorable way to slice this. Carry on.)

I saw who Cavanagh had with him. Cordell Weldon, a.k.a the reason the press hadn't so much as whispered the word "gentrification" when Cavanagh announced that he was opening a new, clean, ultra-modern factory right in the middle of a heavily minority area. Weldon was City Council, a big wheel in the community, in tight with all the right pastors, in deep with the community leaders—the man was revered. He'd delivered more for people in the area than the USPS. (No, really, our service was terrible. Like they couldn't read street names or something, I don't know.)

"Man, the three full rings of the circus are moving this way," Lawton said, his voice in a drawl. "You think we're about to get a photo opportunity?"

I could see the camera flashes going off around Edward Cavanagh and Cordell Weldon. There wasn't any paper, news blog, website or Twitter feed in the city that wouldn't love to have an interview with pictures from those two titans of Atlanta. If the mayor had been present, I think the political universe of Hotlanta would have imploded right there from all the damned gravity in the room. Like the trifecta between money, influence and … uhh … more money and influence. I guess it's like a difecta.

And it's not like those guys were bad! They were good guys, who did good things. Cavanagh had scholarships all through the community now. (I missed them by six months when I was in school. But it's all good! He was going to pay for my college anyhow, now.) Honestly, I kinda wanted to be Cavanagh. Except for being white. Not really a trade-off I was prepared to make—home, family, all that. Not worth giving up, especially when I was convinced that I could make my own money. Maybe not billions like him, but enough that I'd be happy. That my family would be happy.

Yes, Mary, I was gonna make it after all.

What? TV Land played reruns at night, and when I couldn't sleep, I'd watch them. Mary Tyler Moore was cute, okay?

Cavanagh walked with a swagger, like you'd expect a billionaire to. I'll admit it: I watched YouTube videos, and sometimes, I might have practiced walking like he did. Maybe a little bit. Cordell Weldon walked slower, more measured. He was older than Cavanagh by a little, dark skin and all serious. Dude had a bald head, too, and rocked it like Samuel L. Jackson. He smiled for the cameras, but it was a serious smile. Cordell Weldon was all business, man with a mission.

And I just about crapped myself when they made their way to my line.

"Right this way," Lawton said under his breath. The whole line was watching. "They're coming right over here."

"Then you ought to be working," I said, surprising Lawton right out of his knuckleheaded rubbernecking. I mean, he wasn't doing anything different than anyone else, but the line was going. Things needed to happen. We'd pretty much halted production, and last I checked we were still drawing pay while gawking.

"Oh, yes, sir, Mr. High-and-Mighty," Lawton Evers said, deadpan. He did get back to work, though. Eduardo did the same, and the rest of my line picked it up as things started to move again, and just in time. The first crush of photographers and reporters got to us right then, and they found Augustus Coleman's line humming along, everyone paying attention to their jobs. Yeah, I can't really take credit for that one. No one wants to look like they're slacking off on camera.

I went to stand ready to greet Mr. Cavanagh and Mr. Weldon, fairly certain they were going to pass us right on by but not willing to risk snubbing them in case they didn't. I wiped my sweaty hands on my navy overall. Then again. You try and meet a community leader and your billionaire boss without showing some nerves. Yeah, I wiped my hands again and actually let out a quick prayer that they would pass me by because the moisture situation was not improving. Damned non-absorbent overalls.

I was almost convinced I was going to be safe when Cavanagh and Weldon turned to look at the line across from mine, but then I caught sight of him. Laverne Dobbins. He was about ten years ahead of me in school, but he left some serious noise behind him. University of Georgia, full-ride football scholarship. Six-foot-six, built like a brick shithouse. Made good, didn't turn pro, went corporate instead, and now he was one of the top VPs at Cavanagh. He was the advance man for Edward Cavanagh, the sweeping usher of doom—no, that's not right. He was the hammer; Cavanagh was the velvet glove.

Oh, and you knew he was tough because he went by his given name. Yeah. Laverne. And nobody ever said it to him like it was maybe more commonly a girl's name, I promise you that.

Laverne Dobbins came out of the crowd like he was breaking a thousand tackles from those fawning, mostly-white photographers and reporters. He wasn't, of course, because a) he would have crushed them all and b) they would have been too scared to cross him, but he came right out like he was walking out of the tide.

I felt my stomach drop, but my natural optimism picked me up. This could be good! A chance to press the flesh with my ultimate boss, hero, a local legend and man of no small influence.

"You," Laverne Dobbins said, and I swallowed hard, "Augustus." Holy damn, he knew my name. It was on my overalls, but … still! He took the time to read it. "Mr. Cavanagh would like a word, and a picture."

"Well … of course," I said, like billionaires and community leaders took pictures with me all the time. Sure thing, gentlemen, step right on over to my line and let's make this look good.

Laverne raised an eyebrow at me, like he was looking over every word of my sentence for sarcasm. "You just hold tight right there. He'll be with you in a minute."

I decided to just nod rather than fawn or add what could probably have been a considerable bit of drooling stupidity to the floor. Quit while you're way ahead, that's what I say.

Except I wasn't actually saying anything right now.

Before I could really do anything else, Edward Cavanagh broke away from the crowd and walked right up to me. Full head of slightly curly hair, a five o'clock shadow that looked more like it was ten o'clock at night, and he took my hand in a grip so commanding I almost made a very girly giggle as he shook it. "Augustus. I've heard a lot about you. How are you doing today?"

"Ah, very good, sir," I said, taking great care not to stammer. Okay, I mostly was lucky on that. Clean living. That's what I'm chalking it up to. Clean living and optimism.

"Good to hear," Cavanagh said, breaking eye contact with me. I followed where he was looking and got blasted by a thousand flashbulbs. I wondered how he saw through things like this. "Smile through the searing pain on your eyeballs, Augustus. You're doing great."

I spent a moment trying to decode that remark. Was he talking about my job performance? Or my ability to smile wide while the cameras were snapping away? Because I'd been waiting for this moment my whole life. I always dreamed it was gonna come in a football locker room when I was younger, and when that passed, I thought maybe by me inventing something, and finally settled on the day I stood before a bunch of cameras to announce all the amazing things I was going to do for my town, to make my city proud through my own business—

"Keep smiling, son." The low, deep voice of Cordell Weldon was unmistakable. I'd heard the man speak at dedications to parks, at school events, at my high school graduation—I'd shaken hands with him that day, waving my diploma up at my mom up in the bleachers. "You're a natural." The man breathed inspiration and encouragement. He and Cavanagh were like my binary universe—black and white inspiration all in one.

I realized at this point they were talking so low the cameras and reporters couldn't hear them. "This is Augustus

Coleman," Cavanagh said, raising his voice and surprising the hell out of me. I'd thought this was a photo op, something to make him and Weldon look good in the papers, taking pictures with nameless line workers. "He's one of our success stories since opening the plant here—a young man with a bright future, on track for management. Without people like him, and the countless workers we've hired, we couldn't be doing what we're doing here—plowing ahead with projects that will reshape the country, the world, and revitalize the area." Cavanagh pumped up. "And if weren't for my friend Cordell and his efforts," he reached across and punched Mr. Weldon in the shoulder, leaning across my body to do so—oh, dear Jesus, "I think we would have ended up setting up in Florida or Texas instead. Which goes to show you how much of an impact one man of real influence can have on a community."

There was applause from the press, and it was more than polite, it was nearly deafening. I was just standing there in the middle of it all, swept up by the feeling in the epicenter. It was like a nuclear blast went off, and I was a feather blowing on the currents above, untouched by the fire and heat. I knew I had a grin on my face because I saw it in the paper the next day.

"Keep up the great work," Cavanagh said as he smiled at me one last time and gave my hand one last pump.

"I'm expecting big things from you, son," Cordell Weldon said as he grabbed my shoulder with strong fingers and squeezed it again, his face letting just a hint of smile through his normal mask of seriousness.

And I just stood there as they moved on, the flashing lights of the cameras trailing behind them, the crowd like a mob moving with them in lockstep. I felt like I'd been swept up in a tornado and set back down gentle as could be. Like I needed to look down and make sure my clothes were all still intact. I did. They were.

As the noise subsided, I felt like my heart was glowing in

my chest, like it was about to explode. Not in a painful way, but from pride. Pride that all the work I put in that I thought would go unnoticed except by my immediate bosses didn't. I showed up early, I stayed late, I outworked any other person in that factory as best I could.

And they *noticed.*

The noise of the line came back to me as Cavanagh, Weldon, and the whole media frenzy surrounding them headed off through massive steel doors to another part of the factory. I just stood there like I could see them through the wall, though, just watching like they'd come back and give me another moment in the spotlight.

"Look at Augustus," Lawton said from behind me, drawing me back into the moment, "looks like he been touched by God or something. Yo, Edward Cavanagh is a man. He's your boss. Get your head out of your ass."

"You sound a little jealous, Lawton," I said, turning to him with a smile. That was the problem with a man like Lawton Evers, see—he's not a bad guy, he's just determined to find the cloud around every silver lining, especially the ones that aren't directed at him.

"I ain't jealous," Lawton said, making a face that said he was lying, obvious as hell. "I ain't no kiss ass. I don't got to impress anybody."

"Well, you kind of need to impress your boss to keep working," Eduardo said.

"Shut up," Lawton said, blowing it off.

For a man who didn't know shit, Lawton Evers sure did talk a lot of it. But that was just him, and I was used to it by now. I shook it off, and watched Laverne Dobbins make his way after the crowd with the rest of them, trailing behind, and I gave him a nod like I knew him or something. Very subtly, he nodded back at me before he disappeared. I thought that was cool.

I looked down at the factory floor and let out a breath, then blinked. Something was a little strange about what I saw

…

Dust blows through the factory all the time. Not a ton of it, but it gets in. Wind brings it in through the loading docks, and big, heavy fans that keep the floor cool move it around subtly throughout the day.

All that dust that usually spread out around the factory floor was in a neat little berm around my feet, a little line of dirt circled around me in a rough ovoid like it had been drawn in by magnetism.

I blinked, staring at the phenomenon, like it was some kind of strange coincidence. I moved my hand toward it and the dirt moved *with me.*

"Ah!" I jumped in the air a little as I stepped back, and it followed. I caught the looks of Lawton and the others as they stared at me, waving my hand in the air and jumping like a fool, and I smiled. You got to smile at a moment like that. "I just shook hands with Edward Cavanagh and Cordell Weldon!" I said, weakly triumphant. I was lucky it had happened just then, because any other day, I wouldn't have had anything else to cover my shock with.

"Yeah, yeah, we saw," Lawton said, like he couldn't even muster up the energy to rain on my parade. He went back to his work.

As for me, I just stood there until I was sure no one was watching. Then, very slowly, I lifted my hand and concentrated, and watched the dirt follow every single movement I made. Like I had … power … over it.

Power.

Metahuman power.

Whew-eee.

Like I said, I always knew I was gonna be somebody … special.

3.

Sienna

I left Minneapolis without anything other than my gym clothes, my wallet, phone, badge, and the Sig Sauer I had tucked into my waistband under my workout jacket. Okay, so I actually had enough to be getting along with. Frankly, the gun and the badge were enough for me. Western Union could always wire money from my accounts in Liechtenstein; I'd done it before in a pinch.

Still, flying off the campus in a rush was not my best planning ever, but by the time I realized that I was at least halfway to Atlanta and didn't want to humiliate myself by turning around or chancing a conversation with Ariadne. I also didn't really want to tell anyone else where I was going. Then my boss might have expected me to report in regularly or something.

I landed somewhere in north Georgia and bought some different clothes at a factory outlet mall. I tossed my gym clothes into a dumpster like Jack Reacher and took flight again, a little more slowly this time. The skies had been clear for the last few hundred miles, but I didn't want to mess up my suit before I met with Detective Calderon.

This part could have been tricky if I hadn't known exactly where Calderon's office was. Fortunately, I had Reed's file, and imprinted on the windblown pages was the department's address. Okay, it was actually still tricky because it's not like Google map view is designed for when you're flying a thousand feet above the city. The roads aren't labeled, so I had to sweep down and stare at them, then stare a little more, then hit a cross street. Finally I just gave up and looked for government buildings. Those are usually pretty easy to spot. I figured out the right one on my third attempt.

I walked into the police precinct where Detective Calderon hung his hat and took a slow look around the place. It wasn't in bad shape, as far as police precincts went. It had new paint, probably very recent, and a quiet hum of activity that wasn't too nuts for lunchtime on a weekday, but busy enough to tell me that the area it served wasn't Mayberry. Reception was a little backed up, so I subtly butted in line. "I need to see Detective Marcus Calderon, please."

The lady at the counter looked me up and down. "You look familiar."

I paused. "I was on a reality TV show once." That was technically true, in an annoying sort of way.

"Oh!" She looked me up and down. "Wait, are you Giada?" She frowned. "No, I'm sorry, you don't really look like her, do you?"

"Not really," I said. "Detective Calderon?" I flashed my badge.

She gave it a glance and then looked back at the line behind me. "Oh, he's through there." She waved at the entry doors past her. "Just ask anyone in there for help if you can't find him."

"Thanks," I said, and started past the counter.

"Were you on that one show where they match people up with the right diet plan—"

"No," I said and slid through the door, glad to be leaving that conversation behind. I'd only been on one show, for a few minutes, and it had been pretty much against my will. They had used my likeness because I'm a public figure, but it had been a still frame picture of me during a phone call. I was still really annoyed about it, and it hadn't done a ton to improve my image.

It just totally exposed what I had thought was a private conversation by airing it in public, that's all.

The room I'd walked into was a crazy frenzy, a police bullpen like other ones I'd been to around the country and the world. Cubicles, police officers, and the strong smell of coffee. It was a universal thing. "Marcus Calderon?" I asked a patrolman passing by, and he pointed me toward the middle of the room.

There was a guy in a silk shirt with dark skin. He had his badge hung around his neck and was standing up while talking on a phone, gesticulating like the person he was speaking to was inches from his face. "Maurice, so help me God, if you're lying to me on this, I'm gonna find you. I'm gonna come knock on your door—front and back, Maurice, front and back—and I know you're an idiot, so I'm gonna knock on the front first, leave a big ol' flaming—not even a little bag, but like a grocery bag, like a paper grocery bag, filled with like horse crap—I'm gonna light it on fire and just leave it for you on your front porch. Then I'm gonna drop 'round back and squat down while you're dealing with that front porch situation, and I'm just gonna leave you a little souvenir for the next time you step out back to smoke, okay? Unscrew the lightbulb out your back door so you can't see it coming. Squish! Maurice needs new shoes!"

I made my way over to him slowly. The hand gestures alone were screwing up my resolve to keep me from laughing.

"You know why I'm telling you this, Maurice?" Calderon asked. "Because now that I've told you, I'm going to have to come up with something *even worse* to punish you if you're lying to me. It's like my version of a promise, coming up with something worse than—yeah, you believe that. Believe that. Something worse. It'll happen, if you're lying to me." He pointed his finger in the air, like he was sticking it into the face of an invisible man just in front of him. "Promises, Maurice. You believe me?" He paused. "Damn right you do." He pulled the phone away from his ear, pressed the red button and tossed it back to his desk in a spin and looked right at me. "Well, I'll be damned."

"More like investigated, if you're dropping flaming deuces on the porch of your CI's," I said.

"CI?" He snorted. "Maurice is my brother-in-law. Idiot said he could get me tickets for the Falcons on the fifty yard line, lower deck, against the Titans this fall." He stared straight at me. "Yeah. Now imagine how my conversations with snitches play out."

"So much worse," I said, and extended my hand. "Sienna Nealon."

He looked at the hand with smoky eyes. "I know who you are."

"That why you're not sure you want to take the hand?" I started to pull it back slowly.

"Oh, no, I hear I could live a few seconds after shaking your hand," Calderon said, "I'm just so honored to be in the presence of American royalty, that's all. Just shocked. Especially since a year ago your office didn't give me the time of day, and now—now, miraculously! Here you are, like two hours after I sent your people the file." He folded his arms, made a little *hrm* noise.

I didn't get too many of these jurisdictional squabbles. Most of the time, if they'd seen what metas could do, rank-and-file cops were relatively happy to get these cases off their desks. "You want me to leave?" I stuck my thumb over my shoulder at the door. I wasn't trying to sound nasty, but I hadn't had the best morning. I extended the rolled-up file back to him like an offering.

"My case still not good enough for you?" He looked at the file like it contained what he'd threatened to leave on Maurice's porch. "I see how it is. You get a call from London, England, you're there in about a minute, tea with the queen and all that—"

"I did not have tea with the queen—"

"—but a working cop in Atlanta's inner city calls up with a story about killing going on that's right up your alley, you just pass it on by." He nodded his head, had his lips pursed. Attitude. He was giving me attitude. "Like I said, I see how it is."

I felt my eye twitch a little at the corner. "Do you, now?"

"Clear as day."

"Clear as out Maurice's back door at midnight once you've unscrewed the lightbulb, more like."

"Maurice is a gastroenterologist," Calderon said. "Lives in the suburbs. That brother has a pool with ambient lighting all the way around. Looks like something out of the Caribbean. He can see just fine." He blew air out of the corner of his mouth and put his hands on his hips. "Well, you gonna sit down or what?"

He hadn't offered me a chair, but since I got the feeling that Calderon was a prickly personality—something I had maybe a little experience with—I knew how to deal with it. "Sure," I said and then sat down on the air, using Gavrikov's power to eliminate the downward force of gravity on me. I put my legs up like I was in a recliner and just sat there in mid-air, staring back at Calderon, whose eyebrow had risen involuntarily. "You want to talk about the case?" I asked, totally nonchalant.

I watched his lips purse, warring with each other until a smile won out. "Damn, girl, you can't let anyone else win a round, can you?"

I smiled back. "Nope. Case?"

He made that *hrm* noise again and rolled his desk chair under him to sit down. "Your brother tell you the basics?"

"Yeah," I said. "Girl gets killed by gunman, gunman gets struck by lightning. This was all a year ago?"

"Last April," he said, pulling out a green legal file of his own with pictures that didn't have the digital blur that marred my copies. "So, a year and two months later, we get these guys." He pulled out much larger, autopsy-style photos of two bodies on morgue slabs, taken from above. "Kennith Coy," he pointed me to the guy on the left, whose dark skin was marred horrifically along his arm with burns, "and Roscoe Marion." He indicated the one on the right, who looked a little like the mob boss from the original Batman movie after the Joker had joybuzzed him. I could see bone and cooked flesh, and if I had had a weaker stomach, I might have felt ill.

"Any tie between these two?" I asked, staring at them.

"Not any obvious ones," Calderon said. "Mr. Coy lived in the English Avenue neighborhood, Mr. Marion was a little south in Vine City. Coy was on parole—small stuff, repeated larceny charges—and Marion was a factory worker, no past history in his adult life. Not even a traffic ticket."

"What else do you know about the attacks?" I asked, taking my eyes off the photos to look at Calderon.

"I can't even prove these were attacks," Calderon said, studying me evenly. "Last year, though, I had a witness on that one. These two are just a really nasty suspicion."

"So they could have been legitimately hit by lightning," I said, glancing back at the autopsy photos.

"We did have a rather heavy storm," Calderon conceded, "but there's no hint of damage on the ground from strikes anywhere else. I'm not exactly a weatherman, but … I don't know, it doesn't feel right."

I nodded. "Agreed. This is how it usually happens, too."

He looked up at me in surprise. "How what happens?"

"Kids with powers," I said, "getting into trouble the first times. They start small, testing things out. Seeing what they can do. Then they push the envelope for their own gain—rob a convenience store, shoplift 'til they get caught. They start to develop this sense of invincibility—not like teenagers need much help in that department." I feigned a light laugh that was matched by Calderon, though he had a little smile on that I realized was his very subtle way of reminding me that I wasn't that far out of my own teenage years. "They get bolder. Start to think they're special, that they can't be stopped. Ego run amok, really, because they're different and better than anyone else." I leaned back again. "Sometimes local PD disabuses them of that notion, hard. Sometimes I get to. Either way, it's probably like what you see; most people don't just randomly commit murder at age eleven. There's a build-up, a steady movement over the line, then over again. Metas are just better at getting away with it because they can outrun the cops."

"Huh." Calderon folded his arms, leaned back in his own chair to match my posture. "Seen that a bunch of times, have you?"

"More than I can count," I said. "Most of the time I don't get to them until they're so far up their own asses that they're beyond help."

"Maybe if you'd come a year ago …" he suggested, not so subtly this time.

"And done what?" I asked. "I'm not much of a detective, to be honest. Don't have the training. I'm apprehension. I'm the hammer. I've solved the occasional mystery, but I've also been fooled more than once by clever criminals who were smarter than the average. It's my good luck that most criminals, especially the meta ones, lean hard on their brawn and make dumb mistakes because they think they're better than everyone else." I shrugged. "Give me some ego-fueled thief that's hyped to be stealing because he wants to wear the fancy jewelry and drive the sports car and live the life, and I'll knock him down every time." I held up the file in my hand. "This guy, though? He scares me. He's quiet. He's playing a game that only he knows the rules to, and he's not jumping off buildings and having lightning fights in the middle of the street while trying to take a bank vault. He's been quiet for over a year, and no one's heard a whisper of him the whole time?" I stared at Calderon. "CIs? Snitches? Word on the streets?" He shook his head. "That's worrying. It means this guy isn't knocking over armored cars for cash in his spare time, isn't heisting casinos with a flash of lightning. He's just doing his thing, whatever that is."

"Killing people," Calderon said, hands behind his head, tight look on his face. "Seems like his thing is killing people."

"Yep," I said, staring down at the photo and tossing it lightly back onto his desk. "Seems like it is. And he's a patient killer, too. Which makes it personal, I would think. Worse yet, he waited for a lightning storm, which means he's going to try to cover his tracks. A hothead would just go off zapping people at midday, damn the consequences. So he's got power, brains, calculation." I leaned forward. "Tell me about the first victim."

"Mm," Calderon said. "Flora Romero. Worked at a homeless shelter."

"Not her," I said. "Lightning man didn't kill her. He killed her killer."

"Joaquin Pollard," he said. "Another man with a checkered past." He rooted around on his desk for a minute and came up with a thin file. "Priors, some known associates, none of whom would cop to knowing anything about what Joaquin was up to since his last stint, not that I had a lot to offer them. Whatever he was up to killing Flora Romero, it remains a secret."

"Maybe a robbery?" I asked.

"Joaquin had done some armed robberies in his time," he said. "Very possibly there were some that had gone bad in this exact way that he never got tied to. Hard to say for sure at this point."

"What did your witness see?"

"Saw Joaquin catch up with her after a run," Calderon said, face inscrutable. "Saw him hold her at gunpoint. She said something to him, but the witness—it was a kid, six years old, caught outside in a storm, scared half to death by the thunder—said he saw the shot, saw her fall. Pollard turned to leave and lightning man came out of the shadows and blindsided him with a flash. Kid just sat there, blinking it out of his eyes, and when he could see again, lightning man was gone."

"You trust this kid?"

Calderon sighed. "I've re-interviewed him twice. Story is basically the same. He'll never forget the night he saw some metahuman shoot lightning out of his hand." He stared at me with those smoky eyes. "You ever seen someone who could do that?"

"During the war. Name was Eleanor Madigan."

He raised an eyebrow. "It's not her, is it?"

"She's pretty dead, so I doubt it," I said. "Also, she was British, so unless your witness heard—"

"Witness didn't hear anything," Calderon said, and I caught a hint of defensiveness that told me he'd bonded with the kid. "Didn't see the face, either. There was a hood, and the flash pretty much blinded him. He saw the electricity fork, could describe it curving through the air in slow motion, but that was about it for the mystery man. Loud crack of thunder in the air at the time."

"Sounds like a dry hole," I said, sitting back up.

"There are one or two things you could look at," Calderon said, letting my perfect set-up pass. "I didn't get a chance to look in on Flora Romero's life very much last time. With her murderer dead and the department wanting to write off Pollard to a lightning strike, I didn't get to dig. You might consider starting there."

"You're not coming with me?" I asked, letting the trace of a smile play across my lips, a little invitation for Marcus Calderon to step into a different world.

Calderon didn't bite, and I saw him cautiously shut the door behind his eyes. "I'm kinda busy here, and I don't think I'd be able to get my boss to clear me to go on this fishing expedition. Also, some dude throwing lightning out of his hands? I pull my pistol and all I do is get a jolt that sends me to the ground, dead?" He shook his head. "No, this sounds like a job for Supergirl."

"I'm no Helen Slater," I said and stood, switching the gravity back on.

"No, but that girl you used to roll with looks a little like her," Calderon said, and I felt myself flinch a little as he went fishing. "Petite, blond hair, flavor of the month, on every magazine cover—" He paused, looking at me, and smiled. "So, you are human. Jealousy and all."

I tried to smile, but failed. "Metahuman, but close."

"Pssshhh," Calderon said. "Same ballpark. Don't let 'em get you down. It's all just real loud noise, that grumbling."

"Don't let them get me down?" I gave him a cockeyed look. "Weren't you the one running an orchestrated campaign to give me shit from the minute I walked in?"

"Yeah, but you heard me talking to Maurice," he said, almost apologetic, "I give that to everyone." He extended a hand. "If you need questions answered, I presume you have my number."

I took his hand and gave it a shake so firm his eyes widened. "Thanks," I said. "I'll be in touch." I paused, almost to the end of the row. "Where should I start with Flora?"

"She worked at a shelter," Calderon said. "One of the bigger ones in the area. It's in the file. I'd start there, if it were me looking things over."

"You're the detective," I said, and started away again.

"And you're the hammer," he said to my retreating back. "Try not to bust up anything important, now, all right?"

"There's a first time for everything," I muttered and headed back through the lobby to the street.

4.

Augustus

I was buzzing all the way home after work. I played with the dust subtly, careful not to get caught by anybody and all that, for the rest of my shift. That wasn't like me. People noticed, so I had to lay off a little toward the end, kept making like it was just the shock of Mr. Cavanagh and Mr. Weldon dropping by and saying nice things to me, giving me my fifteen minutes. I was all smiles, and I don't think anyone had any trouble believing that I was just about as high as a kite from that experience.

But it wasn't just that. I mean, I was still shaking with excitement from that, but this was even bigger. This was me, finding out something awesome. Something special. I mean, I always knew I was a special person in my own way, but I thought it was gonna be, y'know, my work ethic and perseverance that carried me to the top. Nah, though. I found something in myself that nobody else even saw.

I walked home from work, hot sun beating down on my back. I was sweating even though I'd changed out of my coveralls and put them in my backpack. I was in shorts and a shirt, and I was sweating after about ten minutes. I hadn't even noticed, though, because I was fooling around with the dirt the entire time. I could make a clump move now, like almost a handful. Some people might take that as discouragement—"Oh, hey, why don't you just pick it up with your hand and throw it?"

Not, me, though. I wasn't discouraged. This was the start of something big. I'd read about metahumans when the whole thing up north came out and the president made his speech. I read the papers, I read rumors, I read everything I could get my hands on. If someone had said that at midnight on Thursday, there was gonna be a long-form essay written on a bathroom stall about metas, I would have been there at 11:59 to see what was up.

See, a lot of people get jazzed about fame and fortune, forgetting how many people get washed up along the way. I wanted to be somebody, but I didn't just want to be somebody famous. There wasn't any glory in that. Everybody assumed that if you were famous, you were rich, and that was just bull. I did some research, looked around. Nobody goes broke as hard as a famous person goes broke. It's always spectacular, watching someone who makes millions of dollars lose tens of millions. Hell, I was barely managing tens of thousands of dollars, and I couldn't see how you could lose even one (!) million, let alone tens of them.

I was looking forward to getting my chance to try, though, and this afternoon's development had me even more excited about how close the possibilities were.

I nodded at people as I passed, like always. Got that mixed assortment of nods of my own, some hellos, a few "What is this fool thinking?" looks, too. Same as always. I didn't care. If they were looking at my face, they weren't looking at the sand I was dragging behind me, dust in the wind, following along like I had it on a string.

I had no idea what I was going to be able to do with this yet, but ... yeah. I was excited.

I walked in the door to my house about two-thirty in the afternoon. Shifts ran a little strange at Cavanagh. We started early, at six, and got done early, which I liked. That way, second shift was done by ten p.m., which Mr. Cavanagh suggested was better for them. I assumed he had research or something on the subject, but it really didn't matter either way.

This had been one of the first days in a long time that I hadn't stayed late, and when my momma heard the key hit the lock, she must have come running, because she was standing right there in the hall when I opened the door.

The thing you've got to understand about my mom is that she is a formidable woman. My dad, he was a nice guy. Got along with everyone. When we had his funeral last year, it nearly filled the church.

But my momma was the voice you listened to in our household.

"What are you doing home so early?" she asked, looking at me with a furrowed brow, eyes all dark. "You feeling all right?"

"I feel fine," I said, closing the door behind me, locking the heat outside. I could hear the air conditioner in the next room, running to keep up with the midday sun. "Better than fine."

"Why are you home early, then?"

"I get done at two," I said, a little coyly. I wasn't quite smiling. She cocked her head at me in that serious way that demanded an answer. "Uh, I had a great day," I hurried to explain. "Mr. Cavanagh himself stopped by my line and took pictures with me and Cordell Weldon—"

By this point, Momma's eyebrows were just about stuck to the ceiling. "Uh huh," she said, with that same air she'd had when I used to tell her that my brother, Jamal, had hit me and I hadn't done anything to deserve it.

"No, they really did," I said. "It's going to be in a paper tomorrow, I bet. I saw a reporter from the Journal-Constitution there—"

She just turned her head and walked out of the room without saying another word. This was something she'd started doing to me once I was out of high school. I figured it was her version of "You're too old for me to whap you over the head with something, and I'm too old to stand here and listen to your nonsense anymore."

She went back into the living room, and I followed. It wasn't like I'd given her any reason to doubt my word in the last few years. "You don't believe me?" I asked as she settled back into the chair in front of her TV. Momma was retired. Dad had left her enough insurance that after she paid off the house she didn't have to go back to work. Having me and Jamal paying rent to her for living here helped, though, and we both knew it.

"Oh, I believe you," she said, not looking up from the TV. "I'm just surprised your fool self is taking a victory lap right now when all you did was get your picture in the paper." She snapped her gaze over to me, and I could see the hint of disappointment. "We didn't raise you to get all complacent—"

"I'm not, Momma, I'm not," I said, settling down on the arm of the couch so I could look at her. "I'm not complacent. I just … you know, I left a little early today. I'll be in early tomorrow to make it up, and, uh …" I got distracted by the TV screen in front of her as a blond white girl in a bikini that seemed like it glowed green against her sun-tanned skin made her way, laughing, across the screen.

Momma snapped her fingers in front of my face. "Don't you get distracted. Not by some mountain you think you've climbed at work, and not by some …" she looked sideways at the blond girl on the TV, still laughing, hanging out around some pool in LA, "… some damned hussy. You got a good thing in front of you with Taneshia if you'd ever open your eyes and see it—then seize it."

"Momma, I got nothing going with Taneshia," I said. Taneshia French was our neighbor. Yeah. The girl next door. "She's … busy." That was true. Taneshia was going to Georgia Tech to get her engineering degree so she could design bridges. We'd been rivals, sort of—always competing for grades.

I never won that one, sadly, which may be why she was going to Georgia Tech and I was working my way through Cavanagh management training so I could go to school.

Momma glanced back at the TV, where the blond girl was just dancing around the pool, playing for the camera. "I'd say you're blind, but you plainly aren't."

"Hard to miss what's right in front of me."

"And yet you do," she said and then nodded at the TV. "That girl is an idiot."

"I'm not staring at her brains—"

"Augustus Coleman!"

"Momma," I said, serious and low.

"Why can't you be quiet and dignified, like your brother?" Momma waved a hand behind her, where through the hallway was a door with a DO NOT ENTER sign that had radioactive or toxic symbols—something like that—on it.

"Momma, Jamal's depressing as hell," I said.

"But I don't catch him looking at some idiot bony-ass white girl who probably already has her butt implant surgery scheduled."

"Well, then he's also lacking a pulse," I said. I nodded toward the TV. "Besides, it's your show."

She bristled visibly. "I just like to know what's going on in the world."

"Try the news," I said, and stood up, heading for the hallway. "Because this—" I waved a hand at the TV, and the thin, pretty girl with the lively eyes on it, "it's what they call schadenfreude."

Momma raised that eyebrow at me. "Come again?"

"It's when you enjoy the pain of others because—"

"Boy, I know what schadenfreude is," she snapped at me. "Don't be a smartass. And I'm not taking pleasure in her misfortunes, because that girl is not experiencing misfortune. She's living about as high on the hog as you can get without standing on its backstraps. Everything comes up roses for her. Hmph. Schadenfreude. Throwing your big German words at me." She settled back into the couch, leaning back with her arms crossed over her chest. "For your information, I watch her because she is dumb as a bag of hammers."

"So you just like to feel a little superior yourself," I said lightly and disappeared around the corner before she could answer it. There was a time when that might have gotten me a snap on the ears.

I headed down the darkened hall, maybe doing a little dancing—it had been a good day, after all. I was about to clear the corner when the door in front of me—the one with all the DO NOT ENTER warnings cracked, just a little. It was subtle. It was near silent.

And I heard it like it was a crack of thunder in my ear.

I looked into the dark beyond and could see a thin layer of an eye peering out. "Jamal," I nodded to him as I started to pass.

The door opened a few more inches. "Augustus," Jamal said, sticking his head out like it was February 2nd and he was a groundhog. My brother looked left and right all fearfully, like I was gonna take his head off or something. Truth was, Jamal and I hadn't had a fight in years. But we probably hadn't had a regular conversation in a year, either. He was withdrawn, quiet. Jamal was a computer programmer, did contract work or something at a distance from his employer.

"What's going on, brother?" I asked as I paused outside my own door. I didn't want to ignore him if he wanted to talk. Part of me thought maybe he was heading out to the bathroom as I was passing and didn't think he'd get caught checking. Oops. Now he might feel drawn into a real conversation with me, just to be polite.

I'm just kidding! Jamal never did anything to be polite. He was a programmer for a reason; talking to people was not in his job description.

"How are you doing, Augustus?" I saw Jamal fiddle with his glasses as he stood in the doorway, apparently resigned to talking with me.

"Just fine, just fine. How about you? Job treating you well?"

"It goes," Jamal said. He had a narrow face, a skinny body. Jamal was always the brains of our family, but the dude had zero confidence—not in himself, not in his smarts. He talked in a hushed whisper almost all the time, made awkward as hell jokes that left people staring at him wide-eyed, not really sure if he was serious or not (he was). My brother was a nerd, of the type you find in stereo, if you know what I mean. (Stereo-type, get it? I'm a wordsmith.)

"That's good to hear," I said, nodding my approval. I was aching to get into my room so I could play around with my newfound powers a little more, maybe do some cleaning up, if you know what I mean—moving dirt around WITH MY MIND.

Yeah, it was still cool.

"Is she in there?" Jamal asked, nodding toward the living room.

"Yeah, she's watching that new show she likes," I said. "You know, the one with the—"

"I know the one," Jamal said. His glasses caught the reflection of sunlight streaming in from the long, narrow, white-curtained window in the front hall.

"You been watching a little of that in your spare time?" I was totally kidding him here. My brother didn't show much interest in women. Not that he showed interest in any people, really.

"Not really," Jamal said.

"Because that Katrina Forrest girl is something else, if you know what—"

"Your boss stopped by your line today," Jamal said, glasses flashing as he looked at me. "With Cordell Weldon."

I blinked in surprise. "You see that on the internet?"

"I did."

I nodded, a little enthusiastic that someone had caught

my moment of fame—the first of many, I was sure. "Yeah, it was kind of a big deal."

"You looked good," Jamal said, and I blinked again. My brother didn't go in much for compliments, even when he did finally open his mouth and speak to others.

I felt my chest swell out with pride a little. "Well, you know, I've been working hard for a while, and it was just nice to get a little recognition of the fact—"

"Mmm hmm," Jamal said and adjusted his glasses again, a flash of reflected light hitting me right in the eyes. "Speaking of, I should get back to work."

"Yeah, all right," I said, feeling like I'd pushed the conversation past the reasonable point. "I'll … uh … let you get back to it, then."

He disappeared back into the darkness of his room without another word, the subtle click of the door shutting between us another reminder that my brother and I had almost nothing to talk about anymore.

"Hmm," I said and shook my head. That was Jamal. And I had things to do anyway. I shut the door to my room and started to clean the place for the first time that I could remember that didn't involve my momma threatening to beat me with a broom.

5.

Sienna

Flora Romero was described by her co-workers as one of the nicest, sweetest, gentlest people that the world had ever known, surely up for sainthood with Mother Theresa if the moment ever came. She'd not just worked at the homeless shelter I was visiting as a paid employee, she also volunteered extra hours without pay both there and at a local needle exchange, and possibly also had her hair braided every morning by the local birds in preparation for work while commanding a thundering musical performance in which she was the gentle, trilling lead vocal. I could practically hear her "I want" song, and it was centered around peace on earth and good will toward men.

After ten minutes of talking to people around the shelter, I realized that Flora Romero was pretty much my exact opposite number; everybody loved her, everybody liked her, and I guessed there were buckets of tears shed on the day she died because I saw more than a fair few shed right in front of me while talking to people about her. I'm not saying emotion makes me uncomfortable, but—oh, hell. Yes, I am. Visible displays of emotion make me uncomfortable, and about ten times in the last five minutes I had wanted to fling myself toward the ceiling at full force, smashing through and rocketing into the sky until my eardrums popped and I couldn't hear any more whiny whimpering. Until my super-healing fixed it, I guess.

I didn't do any of that, of course. This was a serious bit of business, and I was a serious person, blah blah blah. I held my tongue, watched the older lady in front of me wipe a tear with her sleeve, and controlled my grimace as best I could. "She was just the best of us," Yasmine Colon said, her brown eyes blurred by the heavy amounts of water and slightly running mascara.

"Did she have a boyfriend?" I asked. I had a few questions on my agenda that I'd been asking of the three people I'd talked to so far. Coverage, just in case one of them knew something the others didn't. Yasmine had been pointed out to me as someone who knew Flora best, though, so if I didn't get something unique from her, there might not be anything to get.

She looked at me blankly, and a little droplet ran down her cheek as she blinked a couple times. "I don't think—wait, wait. Yes. She talked about a boy she'd met. A couple days before she died, she mentioned him." Her lips pressed into a hard line and she welled up again. I only narrowly avoided taking a step back. "She seemed so happy, like she was falling in love."

Finally, maybe all the tears I'd had to witness were going to be worth it. "Do you remember a name?"

I could see her agonize over it, trying to snatch up a memory of something almost insignificant from more than a year ago. "I don't, I'm sorry. It was so long ago. I've tried to forget." She sniffed.

"Fair enough," I said, then switched tacks. "Did you ever know a man named Joaquin Pollard?"

She shook her head lightly, her chin jiggling a bit as she did. "I don't think so. Was that her boyfriend's name?"

I stood there for a second, pondering that one. If Joaquin Pollard was her boyfriend, him killing her would have been … well, a fairly standard event, sadly. The motive wasn't a hundred percent clear in that case, though. "Did she show up to work with any unexplained bruises, looking like she was hurting at all, before she left?" Usually boyfriends didn't leap straight to murder, I didn't think. There was a buildup of abuse first, a pattern, though it was possible he'd just decided he was done with her and killed her.

"I don't think so," Yasmine said, "but …" She frowned and just stopped.

"But … what?"

"Things were crazy just before she died," Yasmine said. "She and I didn't have many chances to talk in the weeks before she died."

"Crazy how?" I asked, applauding myself for my Columbo-like persistence. Or something. (I'd never watched *Columbo*.)

"Oh, just the usual turnover at the shelter," she said, waving it off. "We had a bunch of regulars that left around the time that Flora died. Just picked up and moved off."

Now it was my turn to frown. "Is that normal?"

"Oh, yes," Yasmine said. "I saw on the news that some might have moved to Colorado because of the legalization. We get a few people that are badly ill, need the pain relief." She paused then shrugged. "And some just like it. Anyway, others moved on. That happens." She took a breath, composing herself. "We'll see people for years, get to know them, and then one day they're gone and we never see them again. It's hard not to get down sometimes, seeing all that we see. Flora, she was a special girl. She never let it all weigh her down. She had that quality of—of effervescence. She never got down."

I heard that bit echo in my head, about how it was hard not to get down sometimes, and I pictured in my head the morgue shots I'd seen this morning of the two guys that had been killed by lightning. I'd seen so many dead bodies in my time, they were just a couple more on the pile. I took a deep breath. "Thank you for your help, Ms. Colon."

"You're welcome, dear," she said, all matronly. I wondered if that was how Flora Romero had seen her, too. I felt a little more weight settle on my shoulders. "I am a little curious why you're here asking about her now, though. When she died, they said the man who killed her died a few minutes later from a freak lightning strike."

"Yeah," I said.

She stared at me then snapped into comprehension. "Not a freak lightning strike."

"Nope," I said, turning to walk down the hall of the shelter. It was plastered with PSA-type posters advertising different programs. "Just a freak. Like me."

"You shouldn't call yourself that, dear," she said, her voice chasing after me. "People have been talking about seeing you in the sky all day. The news is reporting on it. It's very exciting."

I could see the bright sunlight streaming out of a door only a hundred or so feet ahead. I could be there in a second if I chose to, if I just left everything behind and shot for it. I wanted to; it was a call in my blood, but I didn't. Because I had a responsibility not to act like a total jackass everywhere I went, blasting papers off desks and knocking posters off walls as I blazed along so fast I would stir whirlwinds behind me with every movement.

Responsibility. Phillips. Reed.

Yeah, it was hard not to get down about everything sometimes.

"I'm glad people are excited," I said, coming up with the only positive angle I could think of as I moved, slightly faster than human, toward the exit. "But if I were them, I wouldn't be so excited to see me coming." I made it to the door, stepped out into the light, and paused there for just a second. "I'm not bringing anything else to their lives but noise, the occasional sonic boom as I fly by."

And I took off before Yasmine Colon could offer any wisdom in reply, darting north a hundred feet above the street, heading toward my next destination, and thinking all the while that anyone who saw me coming would actually be much wiser to fear my approach than to be excited—because I couldn't recall ever bringing anything but death and pain to anyone caught up in my wake.

6.

My eyes were stinging a little bit as I took a turn toward my next destination: Flora Romero's last residence. I doubted I'd find anything there since she'd lived alone and her place had probably gone up for lease to someone else months and months ago, but it was worth a look, and it was pretty close to where she'd been killed in any case, which was another point of interest on my tour.

I slowed my flight a little, letting the heat of the sun work on me. I'd ditched the suit coat after the police station and was a lot happier for it. Honestly, in this weather I'd rather have been working in shorts and a t-shirt, but I had a sense of propriety and a preference for frumpiness that didn't allow for me to do that. I wasn't exactly tall and willowy, as had been noted on more times than I could count by various commenters on the internet by this point, so I figured it was best I just kept as covered as I could, even in swelteringly hot conditions like this. My arms were bare, though, and that felt damned good.

Something about Flora Romero's story was getting to me. I'd investigated a few murders in my time, and yeah, there was this tendency to sanctify the victim afterward. I call it the eulogy effect, but someone else probably has a better name for it. It's the idea that you don't really want to speak ill of the dead, because if you were the one dead it'd be kind of shitty for someone else to speak up during your eulogy and go, "Yeah, he was a broke-ass drunk that was mean as hell even when he was sober, he owed everybody money, and he'd have stolen a nickel from his mom for a pack of smokes." No one wants their foibles aired, and certainly not after death. We all imagine our funerals and think of the nice things people would say, things that they would never say in life. I dunno. Maybe that was just me.

I'd been listening to a lot of people talk crap about me lately, though. Lots and lots. I'd had a lot of—in my view—unfair comparisons to another metahuman who had jumped full into the spotlight recently. It was enough to drive me bat-crap crazy, too, because I was still full on fighting the fight and she was … not. It's a lot easier to talk sweetly about a celebrity whose sole focus is fashion and trendy causes and all that rather than someone who has to get her knuckles bloody single-handedly taking apart a crew of Russians and mercenaries in a hostage crisis. Without powers.

And, oh, had they talked, those heads on television whose sole purpose was to fill the air with opinions enough to cause the sturdiest tree to die of CO2 poisoning. "Sienna Nealon is simply a vicious savage, a product of a bygone age." "She's not an appropriate face or voice for our government, and she shouldn't be representative of a minority group like metahumans." "She's a thug, plain and simple. She should be in jail, and the people she's put in jail should be free."

I'd give you their contrast with the flavor of the month who's making me look like Himmler-with-a-machete by comparison, but I think I'd develop diabetes if I tried.

It had been six months since the incident with the Russians on the campus, with Simmons and the YouTube video beating that had hung around my neck like a millstone, and after every single news cycle, when things would get slow, there would be another five minute comparison hatchet piece talking about how much I sucked and how much Katrina "Kat" Forrest ruled.

It was like all my nightmares had been fed radioactive

growth hormone, all my teenage insecurities had been sniffed out, found and broadcast to the galaxy at large. There was no channel I could watch to hide. Every pop culture referential show made jokes about me, like a quiet sucker punch at the least convenient moment. I'd be watching a sitcom and suddenly the line of dialogue, "You keep talking and I am going to slap you so hard you'll think Sienna Nealon just got hold of your ass," jumped out at me with a slap of its own. I was beginning to fear that even *Game of Thrones* was going to somehow work a reference to a flying girl with a shitty attitude into an upcoming episode. Of course she'd die horribly, because it's *Game of Thrones*, and everyone would laugh and laugh again, at my expense.

I was pretty sure I was developing a complex.

Reed turning cold hadn't helped, nor had his having a girlfriend that couldn't stand me. Phillips taking over as boss hadn't been of much benefit to me, either. I'd lost my job in a very public, very obvious way, one that had resulted in plenty of discussion and speculation once things had started to turn, and it had provided lots of fuel for the fires of insecurity that were already chewing their way through me.

It made it harder for me to empathize with saints like Flora Romero, watching what had happened to me the last few months while Kat got built up into a star. Kat was flawless, she was the favorite, she was graceful, always sweet, uproariously funny, and beloved. A popular content-trawler website ran a page on her talking about "Why we love Kat Forrest more than anything," and detailing how she'd visited sick children in the L.A. hospital cancer ward. With her TV show cameras running, of course, because she didn't go anywhere without them.

At this point if I walked into a cancer ward, small children would scream and try to escape, probably getting tangled up in their IV lines in the process.

Flora Romero was a saint. And Joaquin Pollard had killed her. It was at that point that I wished someone would go ahead and make sure that Kat became a saint, too, because it required the person to die first.

Harsh, I know. I didn't really mean it.

Probably.

What stung was the betrayal of it all. How she had—

Aw, hell. I slowed rapidly, almost missing my turn. I'd gotten so wrapped up in feeling sorry for myself that I'd overflown the intersection by a hundred feet. I turned, sweeping around, remembered I didn't really have to follow the streets, and drifted back toward the road I was looking for. I was high enough up that I could hear the calls and cries below as I passed overhead, but not close enough to hear what they were actually saying. Which was probably good, because if anyone had said something along the lines of "Hey, there goes the Goodyear blimp!" I would have pretended I was a meteor and crashed right to earth on top of them. Which would not have improved my image.

The sun was starting to get closer to the horizon but was still hours from setting, and I started looking for my next turn. I wasn't far off, I knew, three streets and then a left. I slowed, letting myself drift.

It's okay, Sienna, Wolfe said.

Greatness is never appreciated by the weak and pathetic masses, Bjorn added.

Sadly, my greatest encouragement these days came from the murderers locked inside my head. If you don't find that worrisome, I think you should get your own head examined, because hearing voices was totally normal to me and I was alarmed every time they stepped in to provide affirmation and moral support.

"I'm fine," I lied. We all knew I was lying, but it was always 50/50 whether they'd call me out on it. They only did it when they felt like I was strong enough to handle the criticism.

Okay, Wolfe said, and silence followed.

Dammit. That said nothing good about what those

closest to me thought of my present state of mind.

Saint Flora Romero. I wasn't even really investigating her murder. I was investigating the murder of the pond scum who had killed her, in hopes of finding a link to another criminal who was killing people. That was convoluted. Still, it was Saint Flora and Sinner Sienna. Is there a demonic equivalent to saints? Devil Sienna, maybe, to hear the nice people at CNN—or my brother—tell it.

I slowed on the last curve, leading me to a row of houses with wildly differing lawns. The houses were brick with white accent on the gables and trim. One looked like it was completely overgrown with ivy, the next was beautifully manicured and well kept. The next house was no wider than a trailer, and the next after it was set back further than the others, the lot completely unkempt and spotty brown, with a massive shade tree covering a house that looked to be falling apart.

I surveyed the whole thing from the air, more than a little curious about the wide variety and the story it told, but I shrugged it off. I had somewhere to be, questions to ask, so I dipped toward the street and landed about three houses down. There were people out on the porches in rocking chairs, jaws dropping as I came in for my landing. It wasn't anything dramatic, like an airplane; I just slowly inched back to the earth and set down, starting to walk again as I landed as though I'd just come down a staircase's last step. I nodded at the folks who were gawking, and they nodded back politely through their incredulity. "Did you just see a little white girl step down out of the sky, or did the pharmacist mess up my medications again?" an older lady asked her companion. She received a shushing in return.

I gazed at the nearest house numbers and found the ones for my destination just across the street. The street itself was considerably narrower than the main street or even the branch I'd just followed. I guessed it had been built in the thirties or forties, maybe even earlier, part of the city's early growth. The houses varied in size, too, maybe built during different time periods. Some of them looked gorgeous and well maintained, but I saw one down the block that was boarded up and abandoned, too.

There was a white van just sitting on the curb in front of Flora Romero's old house, one of a half dozen cars parked up and down the street. It really narrowed the available lane space, and I guessed people had to swing hard around it because there were barely two lanes to this road—maybe more like one and a half.

"Is that Sienna Nealon?" I heard someone ask from somewhere behind me. I turned my head instinctively—and quickly—to look in the direction of my name being called. It stopped me for just a beat as I stepped off the curb, just like anyone else, trained to look at someone when they spoke my name.

The person who called my name probably saved my life.

The quiet street erupted into something else so fast that even with my meta speed, I was barely able to process it. Gunfire filled the air, the sharp crack of weapons discharge on full auto, the discordant blast of the chemical reactions pushing lead down barrels, the hard shockwaves reverberating into my heart.

A round hit my shoulder and I went down defensively, my back hitting the sidewalk, head snapping back against the concrete. I lay there, dazed, staring at the blue sky above, puffy clouds of white drifting overhead, my ears ringing, the smell of gunpowder wafting into my nose, blood filling my mouth and pumping out of my shoulder. Warmth spread, pain radiated, and my fingers found the wound and came up crimson. I stared at the red on my fingertips, the blue sky above, blinking, stunned, and the sound of gunfire snapped ever closer around me, concrete spraying next to my head from a shot just inches away as someone pressed their advantage in ambush, moving to take me out of the fight once and for all.

7.

Augustus

I had every speck of dirt in my room all up in the air, balled up tight in an area about the size of my forearm and fist, when I realized—damn, maybe Momma was right—I do need to clean this place more often. I was actually trying to shape it into a forearm and a fist, though, so it was good that it was turning out like I planned. I'd only had these powers for a few hours, after all, and the fact I could do this already was a good sign, I thought.

I pulled my hand back and forth and the dirt fist moved with me in a gentle sway that matched my movement. I stopped, then concentrated in my head, trying to see if I could move the dirt fist without moving my own. It took a few seconds, and then it moved, slowly. I almost let out a whoop but covered my mouth with a hand at the last second before letting out a little *squee* while biting my knuckle to suppress the sound.

I'd seen the hero movies. I knew what they did, always jumping right into the middle of trouble without really knowing what they could do. They were boneheads, always counting on a soft landing to break the fall when they leapt. Me, I was smarter than scripted characters. I wanted to do some practicing, see what my limits were, get really good and efficient, maybe work up a costume or something with a name—Sandman was taken, in more ways than one. Dirtman and Earthman had no flow to them, and I'd worked with what I had enough to know that I was basically empowered over dirt. Not regular dust; that didn't respond. I'd tried to move a dust bunny with my mind before remembering that it was human skin or something. I'd tried moving a few other things, too, just to rule out blanket telekinesis (like one of the X-Men or something—how cool would that have been?), and I knew by the end of the experimenting that it was earth-based powers, for sure.

I had a rock on my shelf, an old piece of amethyst I'd gotten after taking this summer program for kids at one of the local schools—I think it lasted one summer, but I liked it—for geology. When I made my moves toward it, it rattled off the shelf obligingly, spinning in the air like I'd lifted it with my own hands and was playing with it.

I was combining the dirt fist with the amethyst when the knock came at the door. It was sudden, insistent—Momma all the way. "Taneshia's here," she said, and I froze, my dirt hand and amethyst completely forgotten. They both fell to the floor in a moment of shock, the amethyst cracking down and skittering sideways like it had been kicked, the hand just dispersing into a mess in a shaggy carpet in front of the bed.

"Oh, hell," I said, leaping off the bed to scramble for the amethyst. It was kind of stupid in retrospect since I now had the power to control it with my thoughts, but hey, c'mon. I lived nineteen years thinking I had to pick stuff up to move it physically. Give me a break on not remembering that after six hours.

Momma opened the door, and I caught her peering down at me. There were no locks in Momma's house, which had been very, very awkward as a teenager. She stared at me on my hands and knees on the floor, amethyst in my grasping and extended fingers as I looked up at her, probably looking more guilty than if she'd caught me naked as a jaybird on my bed.

"What are you doing?" she asked, in a tone that told me she wanted to add, "fool boy," to that last part but lacked a justifiable reason to do so.

"You surprised me and I dropped my amethyst," I said, getting to my feet and holding it out. "I was, uh … tossing it around."

She cocked that eyebrow at me like I was lying to her. Which I wasn't, really! I had been tossing around the amethyst. With my mind, but still. "I said Taneshia's here."

I looked straight at her. Taneshia showing up was not an unusual thing. My momma collected other kids in the neighborhood like some people collected—I don't know, cigarette packs, or old cars. She saw something in everybody, and she tried to be encouraging, be like a momma to them, too. That got tougher as time went by and a lot of us got older and crept off the kind of paths Momma approved of. I remember one of my friends from when I was young took to dealing when he was … I don't know, twelve, maybe? He said hi the next time they passed, and she gave him a look that sent him about running. Never gave him the time of day again after that. Momma could write you off quick if she was of a mind to.

Taneshia was definitely one of my momma's collection. She still came over a couple times a week, even though she had long days at Georgia Tech. It wasn't far or anything, like twenty minutes or less to walk.

"She's here for you, though, right?" I asked, staring at her, a little baffled.

Her head dropped a little so she could look at me while appearing to roll her eyes up. "Get out here, boy." She closed the door with a thump.

I straightened myself up quickly, gave myself a once-over in the mirror. I tried to affect the look of a man at leisure. I didn't change clothes or anything for her, because that would have been too … uh … contrived? Needy? Desperate?

Augustus Coleman is not a desperate man, all right? I'm

careful. I'm selective.

And I'm single because I live with my momma and she would kill me if I brought a woman home. Full on kill me. I had my first time at eighteen in my girlfriend-at-the-time's backyard because I was scared witless that someone would see us go into her house. Instead we did it on a picnic table out back while I was watching the top of the fence around me with paranoid intensity, sure someone was going to see me and tell Momma. "What was that?" I asked, jerking my head around. Damned squirrel. To no one's shock, not even mine, that girl broke up with me the next week.

So was Momma pushing me to one of her favorites? Because if so, this was somewhat new. As demonstrated by my gawking at her little blond television star earlier, Momma preferred not to allow me to think of sinful thoughts related to women. I suspect she thought it corrupted me in some way, took me off the important focus of my ambitions. Which, hey, that's a reasonable criticism. Maybe taken a little to the extreme by her attitudes, but … everybody has their hobbies. Hers was wrecking my love life.

I walked out into the living room to see Taneshia sitting there next to momma. *Beyond Human*—that's the new hotness, the metahuman reality TV show featuring flavor of the month Katrina Forrest (I'm guessing her flavor was Very Very Very White Non-Mocha with extra sugar) was still playing on the TV. Must have been a marathon.

Taneshia wouldn't have come back to my room even if Momma hadn't been here. That girl had pride or morals or something. She stood up when she saw me and took a couple tentative steps forward for an awkward hug that I returned, all very gentle and proper. Momma wasn't even looking at us. "How are you doing?" I asked.

"Doing well, Augustus," she said, not really looking at me. Taneshia was short, like close to five feet. She was rail-thin, though, with the body of a runner. She was wearing her glasses, though they weren't as obvious or thick as Jamal's.

Her skin was dark, her features petite. She was real pretty, though she seemed to try to go to some lengths to hide it. "How are you doing?" she asked. "How was your big day?"

I froze, my hands stiff by my side. "Big day?" My head raced laps, and not one of them led to the memory that I'd been photographed with a couple of my heroes just a few hours earlier. Knucklehead.

"I saw the photos of you with Cavanagh and Weldon," she said, holding up the giant face of her phone. It was dark, but the meaning was obvious—she'd seen them online. "Thought I'd stop in and see if you'd gotten done shaking yet."

"Ha ha!" I said, nodding my head. Cordell Weldon and Edward Cavanagh. Hard to believe a day like this could be eclipsed by something even bigger. "Can't believe little news like my brush with greatness would make the front page."

"Oh, it's not the front page," Taneshia said, shaking her head lightly. "That's all clogged up with news about how Sienna Nealon is flying all over Vine City right now."

I blinked. My heart—did it stop? It felt like it stopped. What does heart stoppage feel like? Because I think I had some of that. "Wh ..." I felt my lips twist while my brain tried to find the ability to spit out the question that was turning it over. "What's she doing here?" I paused, thought it over, and added something. "You aren't just kidding, right?"

She kind of blinked back in mild surprise, like she was perplexed. "No, I'm not kidding. It's all over the local sites. Sienna Nealon's here, she's been flying around this afternoon. Even if half the reported sightings are fake, she's still in the Atlanta area and they got pictures of her flying over Lowery Boulevard."

"Huh," I said, my brain jumping to catch up. I always heard that metahumans were faster and stronger than normal people. I wondered if I could jump really far now. Should have tried that out, though it'd be a dead giveaway that something was going on with me, way more suspicious than playing with dirt and rocks in my room. "I wonder why she's here."

"Girl's the police," Momma said. "Probably here for one of them." She waved her hand at the TV.

"I haven't heard anything about a meta criminal," I said, frowning at the TV. Katrina Forrest was in a bikini again. Again. Red this time. I dragged my eyes away forcibly, back to Taneshia to find her looking at me, slightly angled, the red bikini reflected in her lenses. That worked out well.

"Couple guys got struck by lightning last night," Taneshia said. "Could be a meta."

I stared at her. "Say whut? Lightning?" I thought about that for a second and my voice fell to a whisper without me even thinking about it. "They can do *that*?"

"You ever see this girl grow a plant out of a seed?" Momma said, still looking at the TV. She didn't even need to try to eavesdrop on our conversation. Listening in was her natural state and we all accepted it. "They can do anything."

"Hmm," I said, nodding along. I wondered pretty quickly along a certain track that was—well, it was uniquely Augustus, I think. It went like this: *What if she's here for me? But how could she know about me? I didn't even know about me until today! What if they have a machine that detects metas from a distance?*

And then my mind exploded with that possibility, and my eyes must have gotten really big, because Taneshia cocked her head at me like she was wondering what I could possibly be thinking.

Unfortunately, she didn't get a chance to ask the question that followed, because the sound of gunfire popped loud and hard from somewhere behind us, and every single one of us was on the ground in about a second. I found myself nose to nose with Taneshia, her glasses askew and giving me a wonderful view of her dark brown eyes, though they were wide with fear. The reflection of the TV, still blaring next to us, was there in her pupils. Red bikini. Damn.

"Dammit!" Momma called. "Jamal!" Like he would hear

her but not the shots. Actually, scratch that, it could happen. The shots sounded like they had some distance. If they'd been farther off, we might have been able to mistake them for fireworks. At a distance it was easier to hear them and just sort of freeze, listening hard. These sounded like they might only have been a couple streets away, though.

The hard pops continued, unabating. We heard gunshots sometimes, it was true, but they were usually quick. *Pop pop pop pop* and done. These went on, strung close together, like multiple automatics ripping out in the day. This was not usual.

But then, neither was I, anymore.

I wanted to be somebody all my life, and now I had powers. I felt my hand shake as I lay there on the floor. I looked down at the dark skin on my knuckles, saw the shake stop, steady out. Something was going on out there.

And this was the moment I'd been waiting for.

I jumped to my feet and ignored my momma's calls. I listened and heard the shots coming from somewhere behind our house. I felt my balance steady and I leapt forward toward the hall, racing toward the back door. I could feel the change, the speed, the power at my fingertips. I unclicked the deadbolt and had the door open in a shake. I paused for just a second, looking out into the dying light, realizing that this was the moment—the one I'd been waiting for—and then I jumped over my fence like it was nothing more than a small hurdle as I ran off to be a hero.

8.

Sienna

"Wolfe," I whispered, my back hard on the concrete, the curb jutting into the base of my spine. It was hot, the pavement burning my arms where they touched it, warm through my black pants and on my face. I was still holding up a bloody hand, staring at the red on my fingers from where I'd been shot. Again.

Why was I always getting shot?

Go, Sienna, Wolfe whispered in my mind, and I felt my head snap back into wakefulness. I took a hard breath and rolled, ditching gravity as I moved, feet first, into the air, coming up about seven feet off the ground in a hover.

"Gavrikov," I said, looking at the scene before me. The van that had been parked on the street had spilled open, the side panels thrown wide and three men with guns staring up at me, tracking a little too slowly for their own good. At the rear of the van, the double doors were open there as well, and three more men with guns were doing their damnedest to acquire me as a target.

I was fast. Faster than any human being and most metas. But I couldn't outrun a bullet, and if one hit me in a place like the brain, I'd still be dead, because I wouldn't be able to summon the mental ability to draw on Wolfe to heal me. Right now I had six gunmen drawing a bead on me, and I could only hope that if they got off a shot before I took them out, it'd be a body shot, because that I could fix.

I twisted my fingers as I thrust both hands up. I peered down each digit like a gunsight, my right hand on the guys at the rear of the van, the left pointed at the open doors up front. To hit these guys without giant, beach ball sized blasts of flame? That was not something anyone had seen from Sienna Nealon before.

Fortunately, it was something I was practicing every single day in preparation for a moment just like this.

Fire, Gavrikov said, probably without any appreciation for the literal truth of his statement. Gavrikov was kind of like that.

Long, harsh tongues of fire lanced from the first three fingers on each hand like bullets oozing contrails of flame behind them. With the power of Wolfe working through me and speeding up my reflexes, it almost seemed like they were moving in slow motion to my eyes.

They each hit in succession, left hand shots landing first. They caught the men—all dressed in black, in tactical gear—where the hell do my enemies keep getting these guys? Mercs 'R Us? Anyway, the flames hit them right in the chest. As previously mentioned, this was something I'd been working on—superheated balls of gas that I shot like bullets of my own.

As the flames hit the tactical vests, which were presumably armored in some way, they sailed right through like they'd gone through paper. The impact was relatively minor, because they didn't have any real mass or knockdown force to them.

The real secret to them was heat transference, and that took a second or two to work its magic.

By the time the shots from my right hand had begun to land on the guys at the back of the van, the first three were starting to feel some serious consequences from my attack. I hadn't exactly measured the temperature from the attack during practice at any point, but I had a pretty good idea from Gavrikov's previous experience what would happen.

The first guy's mouth popped open and he coughed a whiff of smoke. The blood vessels on his face turned an angry red under the skin, and I counted my blessings that he keeled over onto his face right then, because I heard some serious popping under the layers of tactical clothing that indicated he probably wasn't going to look much like a human when someone turned him over again.

I watched the next guy wordlessly fall to his knees as the superheated gases lodged inside him. I wanted to avert my eyes but couldn't, instead turning them to the next guy in line, then the next. My shots were dead on, not that it was super hard to hit a target aiming over your finger at fifteen feet. I hadn't thrown the gases that hard this time; Gavrikov's power gave me the ability to propel them with a little more gusto, but I hadn't wanted to chance them breaking through my foes and hitting the houses behind them.

Smoke filled the air, and so did a horrible smell of cooked meat mixed with something extra foul. I had killed these guys, there was no question in my mind as I watched the last guy in the line, keeling over as smoke poured out from under his helmet, his plastic tactical glasses fogging up as something burst violently inside them, spattering the inside of them with something wet and red.

I had a pretty tough stomach, but this was grossing me out. I was also fully aware that in my haste to not die, I'd just killed all six of the opponents that were actively threatening me, and in a manner that was going to make identifying them … problematic.

Oops.

I touched back down on the curb and saw movement inside the van, in both the passenger and driver's seats. Oh, lucky me. Survivors.

"Hey—" I started to shout, and then I saw it.

One of my bursts of superheated gas that was directed at

the first guys had burned straight through its target and was now sitting on the floor of the van like an ash that had fallen off a giant cigar. I caught a glimpse of it as the carpet flared around it, little flickers of flame around a fingertip-sized pellet of hotter-than-hell. As I stood there, it slipped through the floor of the van, presumably into the machinery below, including—I don't much about cars, but I knew this—a gas line.

Damn. That wasn't good.

It took a couple seconds, and they were seconds in which I was frantically preparing for the worst. *Gavrikov*, I called frantically inside my head. With his power, I could pull the heat and fire off the impending explosion, absorbing it into my body, but there was nothing I could do to keep the metal blown out of the van from becoming shrapnel that would drive into the air around me, possibly hitting innocent bystanders just sitting on their porches or huddling in nearby homes.

I hoped for a near-empty fuel tank.

I didn't get it.

The explosion lit off big, the van bursting with flame and force. I felt the shockwave start to billow outward, expanding as it blew. It was way too big for just a tank of gas; my attackers must have had some sort of explosives with them, because I watched the van's metal deform as I sucked the fire and heat toward me in a desperate bid to rip it out of the air before it could turn the van into a giant frag grenade.

It was like trying to hold the sun in the palms of my hands, like trying to draw the heat off a propane stove with a vacuum cleaner. The world slowed around me as the flames drove toward my fingers, coming out of the explosion just a little too late. I could see the seams ripping as the metal blew out in 1/16th time; the ripple of the flames, moved down to a gentle motion, gradually arced the fiery portion of the explosion from its path of least resistance and sucked it toward me.

It wasn't gonna be enough, and I knew that less than a second into the attempt.

There was no one on the planet good enough at absorbing explosions to draw this one out of the van without it shredding metal and sending it flying on its way out. Worse yet, if the metal hit me and killed me, the rest of the explosion would proceed without me drawing it off, making everything so much worse for the people who lived on this street.

Damned mercenaries. If I ever found out where these rent-a-assholes came from, I was going to personally pull a Gavrikov and nuke that place.

Something slid above the van, something like a dark cloud that blotted out my view of the fire. It sailed over my head and then paused there, joined by another piece, from another direction. Then another, and another, clouds of darkness that formed the upper part of a sphere. I saw motion out of the corner of my eye and another piece of—was that dirt?—rolled along the ground and broke into clumps that formed a solid shield between me and the explosion.

In another second, the van was completely covered with a cloud of dirt, and I was cut off from absorbing the heat and flame. I blinked, watching as the dirt pushed down, seemingly of its own will, tightening like it had been contracted over the explosion.

I closed my eyes from the sound of the explosion finally hitting me, a continuous roar that filled my ears and sounded like hell itself had grabbed a lobe and yanked me close, the better to bellow right into my canal. I couldn't help it, I averted my eyes and covered my face, like that would do anything.

The roar subsided in seconds, and I forced myself to look back. The dirt shield that had been thrown over the explosion seemed to be … hardened. I took a few steps closer, tentative, and I could feel the heat contained within. It had held against a bomb going off within it, keeping within its heart a furious storm of propulsion and heat. I pushed against it with a touch, and still it held. My fingertips came away dusty, turned almost red. I turned my head to look and saw giant, gaping pits in the earth around me on either side of the street where the ground had risen up to offer this earth as its sacrifice, protecting me and the entire street from what would have become an uncontained disaster.

My eyes fell on sudden motion to my right. Just off the street stood a young man with his hands in the air, mouth agape like his jaw had fallen down in total shock. His fingers were extended and he was shaking, a thick sheen of perspiration across his forehead, like he'd strained himself utterly to do what he'd done. As I watched, he fell back on his haunches on the curb, exhausted, and to my left the shield of dirt fell with him, crumbling back to red dust, the Georgia clay turned into brick by the heat and now too thin to be held together without this young man's help.

The van was scorched, roaring with flames, which I absorbed into an outstretched hand as I looked at this young guy who had saved my life. I took weary, faltering steps toward him, and he stared up at me as I approached, seemingly wary. Or maybe he was just about to pass out. He certainly looked the part.

I turned and dropped right next to him, more than a little sweaty myself. I was still caked with blood and I could smell it, but the heat and the strain of the last few minutes had left me exhausted, too, and I settled back on my hands as I heard the sound of sirens in the distance. I watched the van burn and knew that the last two guys had bought it in the explosion. Alas. Someone had tried to kill me. Again. Must be Tuesday.

"What's up?" he asked as I looked at him sidelong, nodding in greeting. He was still shaken, sweating profusely, and not just from the heat.

I sat there, covered in my own blood, glad I didn't have

sleeves on this blouse because they'd have been burned off by my heat absorption, and let myself rest, taking a deep breath and then letting it out. Smoke billowed out of my lips like I'd taken a big old draft off a cigarette, and once it cleared I coughed. "Not much," I said, returning his cool observation in kind. His eyes widened and quickly returned to normal at my casualness. We were both playing, I was just better at it than he was. Years of experience with this sort of thing. He was clearly new to the game. "Earth powers, huh?"

"Yeah," he said, looking at his fingers. They weren't shaking now. "I guess so."

I gave him a slow nod as I stared straight ahead. People were coming out of their houses now. A crowd was bound to assemble soon; they always did. I saw people pointing to us, saw them mouth my name. Heard a whisper from someone as they pointed to him. "That's Augustus Coleman," they said.

"Augustus?" I asked. He turned his head very slightly to me and nodded. "Nice to meet you. I'm—"

"Pfft," he said, and waved me off. "Like there's anyone who doesn't know who *you* are. You—you're somebody." And he said it with a certain reverence that—frankly—I hadn't heard associated with my name in a long time.

"Thank you," I said quietly, and he looked at me like he was surprised, or like he didn't know what I was thanking him for. "For the help back there."

"Got to do what heroes do if you want to be a hero," he said with a shrug. There was a long pause. "And you're welcome."

We both settled back and sat there in silence as the sirens drew closer, discordant music to my ears as I waited, and felt the warm heat of the sun on my skin.

9.

"It's not going to be quite what you expect," I said to him as the first police cars were pulling onto the street. Augustus and I were both there with our hands in the air as one does when the cops pull up to the scene of an explosion. I had my badge in hand and was prepared to identify myself. When they pulled up, though, they totally bypassed us at first, the first two cop cars on scene screaming up to the wreckage of the van and ignoring us completely.

"What's that?" Augustus asked, like he couldn't quite hear me.

"This," I said, trying to clarify. "This whole … this being a meta thing. Trying to help. It doesn't … it's never a smooth thing, without consequence or …" I just shook my head. "You know what? Never mind. I don't know what I'm saying."

He gave me a sidelong look. "Well, that makes two of us, because I don't have any idea what you're saying, either."

The first patrol officer came over to us then. I waved my badge at him and he nodded. His nameplate said Delaurio, and he was a big boy. "You see what happened—" He caught sight of the blood on my shoulder. "Jesus!"

"Not exactly," I said. "Sienna Nealon. The men in this van attacked me, and in the process of repelling their attack, I accidentally set off some explosives they were carrying."

"I gotta … call this in," Delaurio said, taking a few steps

back. I could tell he wasn't sure quite how to handle the situation. He eyed me again. "You need, like … an ambulance or something?"

"I'm fine," I said, letting my badge flop to the curb at my side. I looked at Augustus. "You need anything?"

"No," he looked at me strangely. He looked at Delaurio. "I'm fine, too."

Delaurio nodded toward Augustus. "This your sidekick?"

"I am *not* a sidekick," Augustus said, suddenly outraged.

"Concerned citizen," I said. "Hero, really. He just saved a lot of lives by helping me contain the blast."

Delaurio nodded. "Well, if you wouldn't mind waiting right there …"

"I got nowhere else to go," I said, shrugging. Augustus's lips pushed tight together. "What?" I asked him as Delaurio edged away, making a call on his shoulder-clipped radio in hushed tones. I could hear every word. "You got somewhere else to be?"

"I'd like to go home," Augustus said, and he shivered. It had zero to do with the weather.

"Crimes scenes make me nervous, too," I said. "Especially after a fight like this. You always wonder which direction the local authorities are gonna go."

He froze in place like I'd hit him with an ice beam. As a side note, I would like an ice beam. Should have absorbed Winter when I had the chance, I guess. "Could we … I mean … we were the heroes in this. We're not going to get arrested, are we?" he asked.

"Nah," I said. "And if we are, it'll get sorted out quickly."

This only seemed to increase his agitation. "I can't get arrested."

I shrugged. "Why not?"

He looked at me like I'd gone nuts. "Because I've never been arrested before, and it's a streak I'd love to keep going all the days of my life."

I snorted. "I broke that streak a long time ago. It's NBD,

as my brother would say. Don't sweat it, it'll all turn out all right, especially for you. You didn't even engage in the fight, all you did was shield the locals from a potentially hazardous outcome."

That didn't seem to settle him down much. "Maybe now I'm starting to get an idea of what you were talking about before, with things not going quite like I expected them to."

"The problem with being a hero," I said, staring straight ahead at Officer Delaurio, who was still speaking into his radio, "is that the system doesn't really know what to do with them when they're outside the traditional structure."

He gave me a look that asked for further elaboration, but an unmarked car pulled up and squealed to a stop before I could. Marcus Calderon popped out of the passenger side like a jack-in-the-box, leaning on the door and staring at me, shaking his head. "Your rep is clearly well earned."

"My rep?" I asked, more playful than I felt. "I haven't even done any reps today. Still got a workout in, though."

Calderon nodded at the van. "How many were in it?"

"Eight," I said. "Mercenaries or some type of soldier of fortune."

"Eight?" Calderon's jaw was a little slow to close. "That's hardcore, even for the Bluff. You get a look at them?"

"Not close," I said. "They were wearing tactical masks like a SWAT team. Carried HK submachine guns. Caucasian-ish, though, at least the ones I saw."

"Eight?" Calderon just shook his head. "That's seven too many for this area, statistically speaking. That's like an Aryan Nation meeting stumbled down here or something. I got enough problems here without importing white guys with automatic weapons to boost my stats."

"Let's just work on your closing ratio for now," I said. "That's a stat boost I bet you wouldn't mind seeing."

Calderon finally let go of the car door and sauntered over to me. He had a good look, and he was wearing a black fedora-esque hat. It suited him. "What'd you find out?"

"Flora had a boyfriend," I said, "according to a co-worker. I was on my way over here to check out her last address when …" I mimed putting my hands together and an explosion as I pulled them apart. "Ambush."

Augustus perked up next to me. "Wait, that was an ambush? For you?"

Calderon gave him a pitying look then turned back to me. "You get any idea where this is coming from?"

"Not a clue," I said. "Who even knew I was in town?"

"Everybody," Augustus said. "You think eight guys in a van dressed up like a SWAT team is weird around here? Try a flying white girl zooming over your house. All of Atlanta knows you're here."

"Random killing attempt?" I asked. "You think so?"

"No," Calderon said, rubbing an index finger on his upper lip. "Someone's nervous that you're poking around. Maybe jumped the gun a little."

"They frigging pulled the trigger while it was still in their holster," I said. "Blew off their own foot. Because now I'm thinking this is linked to Flora Romero and the lightning man, and I'm not likely to back off it until I've got answers."

"That's probably gonna put a little bit of a limp in their walk," Augustus said, drawing a look from me and Calderon. "Oh, sorry. I thought I was part of this conversation. I can just let you two get to it."

"Who's your junior partner?" Calderon asked, looming over both of us.

"Still not a sidekick," Augustus said.

"Local hero," I said. "Kept the explosion contained. Marcus Calderon, this is Augustus Coleman."

Calderon looked him over. "Got any lightning in those veins?"

Augustus gave him a weird look. "Is that cop slang for something I don't know about? Because I'm clean as a preacher's sheets, man."

"Maybe you know different preachers than I do,"

Calderon said, "because that's not exactly a protestation of innocence to me."

"If lightning guy was uneasy about me being after him," I said, "why did guys with guns come after me? Seems like it'd be smarter to stage a summer thunder accident than a merc hit."

Calderon gave me the eye. "You think we'd fail to notice a federal agent and high-profile meta getting struck by lightning on a clear day like this?"

"You'd think you'd notice me riddled with bullets, too," I said.

He looked at my shirt. "You do look like you might have been riddled a little."

"You just noticed that?" I asked. "Maybe whoever's running this play might have been safe after all."

He shrugged like it was nothing. "You seem fine. You feeling all right?"

"Right as rain," I said. "Minus the lightning." I sighed. "Something's going on here."

"Which is what I tried to tell your brother last year," Calderon said. He was only a little smug about it. "Flora's situation didn't feel right. But this? This is getting out of hand."

"You're so different from other detectives," I said, smarmy as hell. "Most of them are so grateful when I bring death and property destruction into their jurisdiction."

He smiled, and there was something unmistakable in it. "How grateful?"

I pursed my lips, deciding how playful to be in my response. "I—"

"I think I'm gonna go home if y'all don't need me for this," Augustus said, getting up and brushing himself off. "Because it's getting a little awkward up in here. Three's a crowd and all that."

"Give a statement to Officer Delaurio on your way out," Calderon said, not taking his eyes off me.

"I'm gonna want to talk to you in a few minutes," I said to Augustus. "Once they're done with me here."

Augustus leaned in and whispered low, "I don't think the detective is gonna be done with you until—"

I cleared my throat loud enough to shut him up. "We have things to discuss."

"Yeah, yeah, grownups talking and all that," Augustus said, drawing himself up. "All right, you can induct me into the fraternity later."

"In my case, it'd be a sorority," I said, "but I was just thinking we'd have a conversation."

"Like I'm Luke Skywalker and you're Obi-Wan?" Augustus paused, thinking it over. "You know, if we were both white dudes."

I frowned. "And *old*, in my case."

"Well, I got work early tomorrow, and I kinda, uh …" He suddenly looked a little grey in the face. "I kinda ducked out and left my … uh … aw, man."

"Statement to the officer before you leave," Calderon said. "He'll get your name and contact info so we can follow up if need be."

"I live two streets over," Augustus said, pointing behind us. "The house with the yellow mailbox."

"I'll be over in a little bit," I said, looking back at him.

"Sure," Augustus said, like he didn't believe me. "Whenever." He disappeared into the background of the steadily increasing chaos on the street. Fire trucks were pulled up now, sirens silenced but red lights flashing brightly all around us.

"You know him?" Calderon said, following Augustus with his eyes.

"Just met him a few minutes ago," I said, looking back to see Augustus talking with Officer Delaurio, who had a clipboard out and was writing on it. I glanced back to Calderon. "Are you taking my statement?"

"Just asking," Calderon said. "You said the kid's got

powers?"

"Earth-based, it looked like," I said, watching Augustus. He was just talking to Delaurio. He was trying to be a cool customer, but he started to describe something and really got into it, with faces and hand gestures. He caught me looking and broke off, got all serious again. He probably wasn't much younger than me, maybe two or three years. "He put a shield of dirt around the van as it exploded."

"Hm," Calderon said. "You sure he couldn't have lightning powers, too?"

"Anything's possible," I said, "but I don't think so. My read is that he's freshly manifested, just starting to get his feet underneath him. He wants to be a hero."

"Uh huh." Calderon was jotting things down in a little pocket notebook. "How do you think that works out, based on your experience?"

"Shoddy," I said, meeting Calderon's dark eyes. "Based on my experience. They love you, then they hate you."

"Not everybody hates you," Calderon said.

"Oh, yeah?" I leaned back a little. "Do you hate me?"

"I have a practiced indifference," he said, keeping a straight face.

"That's a real shame," I said, and caught his smile. "While you're here, maybe we should go check out Flora Romero's old place."

"You asking me out on a date?" Calderon didn't even look up from the pad.

What was it about law enforcement types lately? "If I did, I could probably pick somewhere more exciting than a murder victim's last known address."

"Such as?"

"God, you're about as subtle as a—"

"Bolt of lightning?" His grin turned to a cringe. "Sorry. That was …"

"A little much, yeah," I said. "I'd have gone with 'a hail of gunfire.' Very topical."

He gave me a slight nod of appreciation. "So she lived …" he turned his head around, and he pointed to the house just past the van's smoking remains. The fire department was swarming all over it, even though their job was clearly done at this point. "Over there."

"Yep," I said. "I was just heading that way when everything went straight to hell." I stood and followed him as he made his way across the pitted lawn, huge gouges ripped out of the soil where Augustus had torn earth free to suppress the explosion. "I—" I paused, looking down into the ground. Something seemed a little off, a shape sticking out of the shredded earth, jutting out of the dirt like a tree root.

Except Flora Romero's yard didn't have any trees in it.

"The hell?" Calderon muttered behind me, and I felt his hand on my arm, holding me back from walking any further. I would have stopped anyway, but the touch—light, gentle—triggered my conscious mind and caused me to hold back as I stared down, eyes working their way across the exposed pits until I found another uneven shape hanging out of the side of one of the pits. This one … was much less ambiguous.

It sprang free from the red clay at several points, like a curved boomerang hanging out of the exposed soil. There was another next to it, and another, and another, all joining to meet at the same point, where an obvious fracture broke them off from what should have been the natural join to a mirror image on the other side.

I pointed. Calderon nodded and pulled out his cell phone. He had the number dialed while I just stood there and stared. "I need a crime scene unit." He said more, but I lost it as he wandered off, behind me, all thoughts of our little flirtatious play gone by the wayside.

I just stood there and stared at the half-ribcage that had been exposed by Augustus's heroism, hanging out of the side of a gash in Flora Romero's lawn.

10.

Augustus

My head was buzzing as I made my way back home. I didn't go jumping back over the fences or anything. I walked around the front like a normal person—even though I was most definitely not normal anymore. Word had already spread, though. I caught the looks on the street as I passed people. Some respect. Some fear. People crossing to get away, but nobody crossing over to say thank you. That'd come later, I hoped. I'd just done one thing, after all, and it had thrown the neighborhood into chaos. Whatever I did next, that'd solidify my reputation one way or another.

I needed to keep being a hero. I guess no one really knew the numbers, but you'd think if there were hundreds of metahumans out there, there'd be some heroes stepping up besides Sienna Nealon and her crew.

And can I just say—Wow! Sienna Nealon herself. She was shorter than I expected. And a little reserved. But I did just save her life, so she was probably a little rattled. If she even got rattled by that sort of thing at this point. Maybe she was just tired.

I took a left onto my street. I could feel my pace quickening. I could move faster, no doubt. I'd felt it on the way to the attack, but now it was like I was hyperaware of it, like I needed to go somewhere and lift something heavy just to check that, too. I needed, like, a training montage.

Wait, she did say she was going to come over later and talk to me, right? And I said … did I really say I was going to work tomorrow?

Well, I had to. Momma would kill me if I quit my job. *College*, she'd say. And that'd be the end of the discussion.

Also, it is probably not right to quit a good job for some vague, half-formed idea of how to be a hero. How do heroes get paid?

I stopped in front of my house. It looked … different. Smaller, maybe? Or maybe I just felt bigger. I took a breath, trying to plan out what I was going to say when I went inside. Rumors were already spreading. For all I knew, somebody had already stopped by and broken the news that I was a meta and had gotten in on a throwdown. In which case I was about to get an earful when I stepped inside.

I stood on the sidewalk for another couple minutes. Planning out what I was going to say. Yeah. That's it.

When I opened the door I could hear talking inside. I closed it behind me loud enough to let everyone know I was coming. Their hushed voices were coming from the living room, and I eased down that way, making footsteps loud enough to announce my presence.

Momma looked up at me as I came in, wearing a scowl. "Fool boy. What were you thinking?"

"I—"

"You don't go running toward gunfire unless you're in the Army," Momma continued, still fixing me with that glare. "Did you join the Army and not tell me about it?" She turned her head toward Taneshia, who was sitting in the chair on the other side of me. "You hear if Augustus joined the Army?"

"No, I did not," Taneshia said, giving me an absolute flashback to the days when we were six and she'd parrot back to me exactly what Momma had said not to do that I'd gone and done anyway.

"So, you're saying I should join the Army?" I asked, and

watched Momma's expression get a little bit darker. "They got the G.I. Bill—"

"Oh, we got ourselves a smartass," she said.

"Better than being a dumb one," I said.

"Oh, you're that, too."

"What were you thinking, Augustus?" Taneshia broke in, voice soft and quiet. The TV behind me had aerial pictures of the fight scene already. Fortunately, they hadn't been there when I left. I could hear the chopper in the distance now, though.

"I was trying to help," I said.

"You were trying to get yourself killed," Momma said.

"Rushing into something like that …" Taneshia just shook her head.

"I just saved Sienna Nealon's life," I said, and waited.

I honestly expected laughter. I got pity instead. That was not a good consolation prize.

"I actually did," I said, looking at the two of them in turn. "I found out this afternoon that I'm a metahuman."

Momma's left eyebrow went way up. It does that when she thinks she hears something crazy. She tilted her head to look past me to Taneshia, like she was asking without asking, "You hearing this?"

Taneshia just looked … thoughtful. "Really." Filled with doubt. "What's your power?"

"I'm glad you asked," I said with a little enthusiasm. I took a couple steps toward the TV and pointed toward the holes in the ground, the clay under the topsoil visible onscreen. "See that? That was me."

Momma just stared. "My son, the human backhoe."

"First, you might want to be a little careful about calling anyone a backhoe," I said. "Might make someone a little hostile, you throw that at the wrong person. Second, I did that. With my hands." I put my hands up in a flourish.

"Make sure to wash good under your nails before dinner, then," Momma said, deadpan, angling to look around me to the television. "Was that really Sienna Nealon there?"

"I don't know," Taneshia said. "Why did they park the chopper on the side of the street that has trees covering everything …?"

I felt my lips press into a thin line out of pure annoyance. I reached out, put my hands out flat, trying to feel for what I was looking for in the carpet. I closed my eyes and concentrated, seeking out dirt and …

My eyes popped open. "Momma, did you vacuum in here today?"

"I vacuum in here every day," she said. "You should try it in that pigsty you live in some time, it'd do you a world of good."

I tried to focus on the positive. "That's all right," I said, taking a deep breath. "That's okay. I'll just use the lawn—" I turned my head to look out the window. If I ripped my momma's lawn to show her and Taneshia I was a metahuman, I was going to have to hope I secretly also possessed a power of extremely fast healing, because she was going to beat me all about my skull.

Wait.

I took another breath and reached out, lifting my hands and pushing them toward the arch. I could feel through the walls, could feel the dirt—small, like little grains. The flicker of the TV was the only light in the room save for the last faint strains of day through the half-closed blinds. I could feel a little dirt in my room, and—

Yeahhhhh.

I heard a *thunk!* as my amethyst smacked the wall. I cringed and saw Momma turn her head around, looking to see where that noise had come from. "Jamal?" she asked.

"No, Momma, that was me," I said, mentally trying to steer the rock around the corner with the threads of dirt just behind it. It was not as easy as it sounds, I promise you.

"Boy, you look like you need to excuse yourself to the restroom before something bad happens to your drawers,"

Momma said.

"I just need to ..." I strained, steering it all around the last corner. The drift of dirt came threading through the air, lit by the sun in the main hallway. I pulled it toward me, the amethyst leading the way, and halted it directly in front of me, letting it twist right before my face. The dirt I let settle into an easy spin around it, a neat ribbon oscillating in a circle. "See!"

"See what?" Momma was looking at me. "I'd like to see the TV a little better, but someone's standing his butt half in front of it."

"See this?" I made a hand gesture, all grand and theatrical, to indicate what I was doing.

Momma squinted. "You been practicing magic? What is that? You levitating a rock?"

"I'm—yes, I'm levitating a rock," I said. "No strings. See the dirt?"

"No, I don't see anything." She squinted harder.

"Momma," Taneshia said in a whisper. "He's floating the dirt and the rock."

Momma fumbled in the half-light, reaching up for the lamp that rested behind her seat. I heard her fingers trying to turn the little knob, and then it popped on, flooding the room with a dull orange light.

My little ribbon of dirt just spun there, waves rippling across its surface. I turned it with my hands, making it go vertical, so they could see it better, and set the amethyst to orbiting it. The planet orbiting the rings. Figured I'd try something new.

"Augustus," Momma said. Her tone changed in an instant. "Did you bring that dirt into *my* house?"

"Momma," I said, trying to get her to realize the point being made. "I'm making it *hover.*"

"Well, you need to make it *Hoover*, as in get the vacuum and get that mess out of here—"

There was a knock at the door that interrupted us, and I

strode over, keeping the dirt spinning while I entered the hallway. I opened the door wordlessly, and there was Sienna Nealon, still bloody, still a mess, but standing right there on my doorstep. "Come in," I said, motioning her forward.

"Thanks," she said. She looked like she was wearing a scowl, but she followed me in, pausing at the archway to the living room as I scampered back inside, ready to show off my last piece of evidence to Momma that her baby boy had finally—finally!—become somebody.

"Momma," I said, "Taneshia—meet Sienna Nealon." And I just stood there and waited. It didn't take long.

"This little white girl is about two feet tall! She doesn't even look anything like Sienna Nealon," Momma said, shaking her head at me. "How stupid do you think I am?"

11.

Sienna

It took me, Augustus and his—girlfriend? Friend? I never got a clear answer on that—a few minutes to convince his mother that I was who he said I was. She wanted to see my badge, so I showed her. It doesn't really look all that impressive.

"Metahuman Policing and—" She looked up at me over her glasses. "What is this?"

"We just call it the agency," I said.

"Why don't they just come up with a cool acronym for it like all those agencies in movies?" Taneshia asked. "Like S.H.I.E.L.D.?"

"That one's probably copyrighted," I said and turned my attention to Augustus. "We, uh … found some bodies."

"No kidding," Augustus said. "You burned those people up yourself, remember?"

"We found more bodies," I clarified. "In the yard you dug up." He was staring at me blankly. "I was coming to talk to someone at that house, and—whatever. Anyway, there are skeletons in the yard. Literal skeletons. CSI showed up and said they've been in the ground there for, like, a year."

"What are you into, son?" Momma asked with more than a little alarm. I don't normally call total strangers "Momma," but Augustus introduced her as such, and without another name to go by …

"Hell if I know," he said, and she reached out and smacked him right on the leg, presumably for swearing. Which was weird, because I could have sworn I'd heard her curse a little already. He took it in stride. "What *am* I into?" he asked me.

"Nothing, if you don't want to be," I said. "I came down here to investigate some people who died in a presumptive lightning storm."

"There's got to be more to it than that," Taneshia said.

"Of course there's more to it than that," Augustus said. "She had a bunch of guys waiting for her outside this house with machine guns."

"There appears to be more to it," I agreed, "but I don't know. There was a girl—Flora Romero—she got murdered a year ago and her killer was struck by lightning immediately after. There were two more suspicious lightning deaths last night, and a local detective has me looking into it. *Something* seems to be going on. Or else people are randomly trying to kill me, which …" I thought about it. "Actually, we can't rule that out."

"What do you want from Augustus?" Momma asked, viewing me with increasing suspicion.

"Some kind of meta apprenticeship, maybe?" Taneshia asked. "Sounds dangerous."

"Uh," I looked at each of them in turn, "actually, I just stopped by because I said I would, kind of a thank you—and to talk to him about his new powers. See if I could help while CSI is digging up the corpses." I frowned. Why did I have to keep conversationally discussing corpses? Was this normal? My money was on no.

Momma was frowning at me. "Well … I don't understand. Could he help you?"

I stared back at her. "Help me how?"

"You know," she said. "Work with you somehow?"

"Oh," I said, taken aback, "obviously, as you can see by

what happened today, my job can sometimes be inexplicably dangerous. I wouldn't want to expose your son to—"

"Well, that's a load of bull-crap," Momma said and glared at Augustus. "You should go with her."

"Weren't you the one yelling at me for being a fool and charging headlong into danger not an hour ago when there were gunshots going off?" Augustus asked.

"That was different," Momma said without missing a beat. "We didn't know you were special then."

Augustus looked daggers at his mother. "Momma!"

She patted him on the wrist. "You know what I mean, baby. You've always been special to me. But you should go help this girl. Look how short she is." I frowned and looked at Taneshia, who was even shorter than I was. "Especially if they're digging up bodies in our neighborhood." She shuddered. "That is just downright creepy."

"That was maybe the fastest turnaround I've seen since the time Malcolm Turner greased the cafeteria floor and told Mr. Davis that Sherice Storm was playing with herself in the corner," Augustus said. "You went from telling me I was a liar and a fool and an idiot to—" He folded his arms in front of him. "What if I go with her and die?"

I felt like the spectator for the most alarming argument ever. "That is a very real danger," I said. "People do tend to die around me." This was all happening very fast. Augustus had been extremely helpful in the van explosion, but I was under no illusions about my ability to retain people close to me. They either died—like Zack, Breandan, my mother; they left—like Dr. Zollers, Scott, Kat; or they flat-out turned their backs on me and walked away—like Senator Foreman.

Or like Reed was going to.

"What if he could help you?" Momma asked. "What if he could save your life again?"

"Oh, so you believe me about that, now, too?" Augustus asked, still looking pointedly at his mother.

"Momma, this is dangerous," Taneshia said quietly.

Thank the heavens, a voice of reason.

"Life's dangerous," Momma replied sharply. "Nobody gets out alive, last I checked." She turned her gaze toward Augustus. "All I hear you say when you talk about your future is how you're going to 'be somebody,' like that means something at all in and of itself. I been telling you—your father told you—told you and Jamal both that you need to 'be somebody' someday. But you left off the last part of what we told you—that you need to be somebody you can be proud of. Somebody to be counted. Somebody who stands up for what's right." She looked at me. "We see a lot of things in the neighborhood. Some wrong things sometimes, but we live here. We love here. This is our home. You come here and you tell me someone's killing people with lightning? Burying bodies in people's yards?" She leaned forward on her couch. "Can my son help you find this person? With his powers?"

My mouth fell open and an answer came tumbling out. "I don't know. Maybe."

"Then he *should* help you," she said and straightened up, like it was settled. Then she looked at him. "Provided it doesn't interfere with his work."

I found myself looking at him as he looked at me. "What do you do?" I asked helplessly, strangely reminded of my mother, but in a less threatening way.

"I'm a—" Augustus started.

"He's in management at Cavanagh Technologies," Momma said proudly. She launched into a description that I suspected had been repeated many, many times before, and I listened and nodded along, sparing only a look for Augustus, who seemed only slightly less embarrassed than he was proud at hearing her talk about him in such glowing terms.

12.

Augustus

"So how's this going to work?" I asked her as I walked Sienna Nealon to the door. My mother had talked her ear off about how great I was for, like, thirty minutes. To her credit, she only looked glazed over during the last five, and it hadn't exactly been thrilling stuff compared to a murder case involving a lightning-throwing person.

"You got a job, right?" she asked. I was almost used to her bloodied blouse by now. Almost.

Nope. Still weird. Who walks around in bloody clothes all the time?

"Yeah," I said. "Six to two tomorrow. I mean, I could call in—"

"Nah," she said, shaking her head. "Go to work, meet me when you're done."

"Okay. You got like a cell phone number I can call you on?"

"I—" she fumbled in her pocket and came out with an iPhone. "Looks like I still do, yeah." She punched a button and summoned up her own contact, complete with phone number, which I dutifully snapped a picture of with mine for later. "Clever," she said.

"Time saver and all that," I said. "So am I like … your partner on this?"

She gave me a very guarded look. I got the feeling she wore it a lot. "Let's call it an apprenticeship, since your mom kind of … talked me into it, and I don't really have any backup at this point." She dropped her voice to a level so low it was like she smashed through the floor for whisper and kept going. I was amazed I could hear it, because her mouth didn't open at all, it was like it was all in her throat. "You sure you want to do this? There are easier ways to make your mark."

"Mmmrawwwwmrmmmaaa—" I tried to do it like she did it then just went for a whisper instead. "You heard me before. I'm supposed to be somebody. I want to be a hero."

"Heroes have short lifespans," she said.

"Man, who wants to live forever?" I joked.

She just stared at me. "Most people would, I think."

"Could you imagine living your whole life not standing up for anything you believe in?" I asked. "Just sort of … letting things pass you by unanswered? Like a whole bunch of dead bodies? Especially when you could be doing something about it?" I stared her down, saw her eyes move just a little. "Power and responsibility, right? That's the problem with being powerless—you got no real responsibility, because what can you do? But the minute you got power … doesn't it mean it's time for you to step up and do what you can?"

"That's sweet," she said, a little condescending.

"Well, what do you do, then?" I asked. "I doubt you're in government service for the money. You just like shooting people with fireballs and busting skulls?"

She folded her arms in front of her. Lady was like a stone wall. "Maybe I love it. Maybe a little too much." She let out a breath and the arms unfolded. "Or maybe it's the only thing I'm good at."

"Well, maybe I'm good at it, too, and just don't know it yet," I said. I hesitated. "Not at busting skulls, probably. But maybe at, you know, solving mysteries. Helping the helpless and … whatnot."

"Being a hero," she said with a sigh. "All right, so the deal is, you follow along with me if you want. I'll let you watch what I do. If things get hairy, you take a step back, though, especially if I tell you to. We run into lightning guy, you make a shield around yourself, as fast as you can. I don't want to have to explain to your momma why her baby boy got bugzappered."

"I'd be more worried about lightning guy at that point," I said. "My momma would put on a full rubber suit and just drag that man's ass across a thick carpeting for days at a time until he begged her to stop. They'd be calling him Mr. Ex-static by the end of—" I paused. "How about we call him Mr. Ex-stat—"

"No." She was firm in her refusal.

"Everybody's gotta have a name—"

"This isn't the comic books," she said, and the arms were folded again. "We don't give people cheesy names."

"Like Sovereign?" I teased.

"I didn't name that jackhole," she said. "He named himself a few centuries before I met him, and he did it as part of an orchestrated PR campaign to make himself look like a badass and also to hide who he truly was."

"So you never thought about making a hero name?" I asked. "Like Fly Girl—or, uh … Super—"

"All the good ones are copyrighted and trademarked," she said. "It's actually a real minefield, I'm told by the government lawyers. They strongly advised that I not even try."

"Wait, you're serious?" I asked. "But … I was gonna be …"

"Don't," she said. "Just … don't. Be yourself."

"Well, that's half the fun gone right there," I said.

"Yeah, we'll work on taking away the other half tomorrow," she said, reaching for the door. She looked back at me, all seriousness. "I know it seems so cool now. Maybe you've seen my fights on TV, or you've watched …" there was a twitch in the muscles around her eye, giving her crow's feet that smoothed out perfectly a second later, "… other metas who sell a glamorous lifestyle. Those fights hurt more than anything you can imagine, and every other meta except for …" she twitched again, "… that one—"

"Katrina Forrest, you mean?"

"Except for that one, yes," she said, twitching again, "either live and work just like normal people or they're criminals working their way toward going to prison for a very long stretch. My life is not glamorous, and the hits you've seen me take on television and YouTube would kill even you deader than those fried guys in the van. This guy with the lightning? If he hits you, your heart will probably stop just the same as the last people he killed. You want to be a hero? Don't. Don't try. We're going to take this slow. We're going to investigate. People are apparently going to throw some resistance our way, judging by what we've seen so far. We will handle it carefully, not by rushing headlong, stupidly, into something that will get us killed." She seemed to relax a little, like something was weighing her down. "I don't want to get you killed. This is an investigation, not a 'super hero saves the world' story. So just … listen and take it slow and we'll be fine." Her eyes got hard. "And if I tell you to run, you damned well better do it. Okay?"

"Got it," I said, just listening.

"All right," she said. "See you tomorrow." And she closed the door without another word.

I heard something behind me and turned back to see Taneshia standing at the entry to the living room. She was leaning, looking a little weary herself. "You sure about this?" she asked, like it hadn't just been asked of me a few minutes earlier, like we hadn't just covered it in exquisite detail.

"It's all going to be good," I said. "We got this. I'll listen, and I'll make sure to pull my weight in a fight."

She looked at her feet for a second and started to shuffle forward. "You never were much of a fighter, Augustus." She headed past me toward the door then paused and gave me a kiss on the cheek. "Be safe," she said, and the door closed on me for the second time in as many minutes. This time the sound seemed a whole lot … lonelier.

13.

Sienna

When I got back to the crime scene, the yard around Flora Romero's house had been dug up a little more. Men in plastic suits were putting up tents and using small hand tools to excavate things. I saw bones, bones and more bones being slowly exposed, the layers of dirt being peeled back to reveal what someone had tried to hide. The smell of dust was heavy in the hot evening air, and the sun was on its way down somewhere below the houses to the west. It was a sticky feeling, and not just from the blood that was dried and crusted on my left side. Humidity had seeped in, making my skin feel like it was leaking just moments after I'd walked out of Augustus's house.

Calderon was in the middle of the crime scene, in the thick of it all. The activity seemed to be mostly taking place around him, though, like he was a giant stone in the middle of a stream, letting it all wash by. He had a heavy walkie-talkie clutched in his hand like it was a lifeline as he watched things unfold.

"What are we up to now?" I asked, easing up beside him.

"We haven't had a ton of time," he said, "since you went to go inculcate the boy wonder in the ways of the superheroes, but …" He glanced at me and made a sucking sound with his tongue and lip that expressed concern, "we've found at least four skulls."

"Wow," I said. "Coincidence?"

"They look like they've been there about a year," Calderon said, turning back to watch the investigators at work, "and when I came here to check out Ms. Romero's accommodations in the wake of her death, I recall there being some yard work being done. Sprinkler system excavation, I thought, or maybe a sewer line being dug. Didn't think someone was using it as a dumping ground for their misdeeds."

"So what are the possibilities here?" I asked. "Flora was in on some murders, got killed for it. Flora wasn't in on it but found out about them, got killed for it. Flora was an innocent victim and her place got used as a graveyard. Am I missing anything?"

"The bodies are unrelated to Flora's murder," Calderon said. "Unlikely, but a possibility, so long as we're listing them out." His fingers came up and rubbed the bridge of his nose, an expression of exasperation and fatigue that I was very familiar with. When I wasn't doing it myself, I was often the cause of it in others. "It kind of hurts to be proven so right about this case, because the way we found out is just … so wrong."

"If these guys were sent to stop me from finding the bodies," I said, "then this was the most ham-fisted cover-up attempt ever. They actually led me right to what we assume they were trying to hide and hinted at something way beyond lightning man. This is criminal conspiracy."

"Unless it's just lightning man deciding to cool his thunder and outsource his murdering," Calderon said. "I mean, we are spinning at this point, no idea which way true north is."

"But we've got so much to work with," I said. "We've got … uhm … remains of the mercenaries." Calderon gave me a pointed glare. "Well, we've got … some parts of them. Sorry. I did what I had to do. But we've also got bones, now, too, that link to earlier crimes. I mean, this was a clumsy hit—"

"That might have succeeded if you hadn't picked up a sidekick." He was on that again, and he was staring me down. It took me a second to come to a conclusion about that, and I called it out immediately.

"You jealous, Detective?" I asked, a little playful.

The corner of his mouth crooked up. "I don't know. Are you into boys … or men?"

"I'm into stealing the souls of the people I touch for more than about twenty seconds," I said, without a hint of suggestion.

"A dangerous woman," he said, sounding more than a little amused. "My mother told me to stay away from those types. Made it seem irresistible."

"Either you're heavy on the flirting," I said, "or you've got a death wish."

"Could be neither," he said, "could be both. I heard you've had boyfriends before. I guess I just figured maybe …" He sort of shrugged like it was nothing. "… maybe there was a little more to the story than the general line would indicate."

I brushed against his shoulder, leaning toward him. "Maybe there is. Maybe where there's a will, there's a way."

"Detective Calderon?" a voice called, and I saw Calderon grimace as a man in one of those rubber suits approached, big plastic goggles obscuring his face. "We've got something here."

"Another skull?" Calderon asked. That kind of took the air out of the moment. Once again, I found myself macking on a man at a crime scene. Clearly I was developing a type.

"Well, yeah, that too," the tech replied. "We're up to seven. But something else, also. Some of these bones, they're uh …"

"Be right there," Calderon said.

"Can't," the tech said, waving him off. "You don't want to walk over anything important."

"I got this," I said, and grabbed Calderon around the waist, lifting him up under one arm as I floated into the air.

"Holy crap," the tech breathed as I floated toward him with Calderon tightly against me, like we were just taking a spacewalk. No reason to rush, after all.

"How you doing?" I asked Calderon, who turned his head to favor me with a look that I had a hard time decoding. His dark skin didn't wrinkle at all in reaction.

"I'm being carried through the air by a metahuman," he said nonchalantly. "I think some of my boyhood fantasies might have just come true."

"So you don't have a problem with strong women?"

"Only if they drop me," he said with a smirk.

"You are kind of heavy."

"I'm like two hundred pounds of ripped steel. That's a lot."

I shifted him like he was nothing more awkward than a pillow. "Oh, yeah? I didn't notice."

We made our way over to where the tech guided us. He'd extended a tarp over his find before leaving. There were tents going up to preserve the area in case of rain, I guess, but the guys who were setting them up must have been on a long dinner break, because they didn't seem to have made much progress.

"This is something," the tech said.

"Something … what?" Calderon asked.

"Well, it's …" The tech just stalled. "Maybe you should just see for yourself." And he yanked back the tarp.

Bones. Bones. And more bones.

My eyes could see the shapes, the patterns, and I knew immediately that something was … off. I was getting used to seeing the familiar shapes, things I'd learned about from an anatomy textbook probably from the 1980s that my mother had purchased. Still, the shape of human bones hadn't changed over those years, and so when I looked at what the tech revealed from under the tarp, I knew immediately that something was …

… wrong.

The bones under the tarp were stretched. Distended. They weren't broken, exactly, but they looked like maybe they had been at some point and had grown back … strangely. Not like a clean break and healing, or something that a doctor might have found in an abused person. No, these bones looked like they'd been broken, and had been pushed apart so that they couldn't heal naturally, just to see if they'd … rejoin in strange ways.

And oh, they had. There was a femur that looked like it had an extra three inches of disjointed bone running at forty-five degrees right down the middle of it, a strange bridge like the bone had desperately tried to heal itself, contorting into a bizarre shape in the attempt.

But normal human bones didn't *do* that when healing.

Meta bones did. But only if someone had intentionally kept them from healing properly.

"What the hell?" Calderon asked, summarizing my thoughts perfectly. "What … is that?"

"A dead meta," I said, staring at the remains of someone who had been … tortured? Experimented on?

Murdered.

"Looks like you called the right person," I said, as a cold fury settled into my own bones, causing me to shake—just a little—as I floated there over the latest victim.

14.

Augustus

Work moved the slowest I could remember since … uh, the day before, I guess. I normally didn't mind work, but it was dragging now. I was counting the hours until I could be done, until I could go do my apprenticing thing. In spite of Sienna's "Scared Straight" approach to mentorship thus far, I was still excited. It was tough to dampen my enthusiasm. I mean, I'd been watching superhero stuff from a young age, and when the announcement had come out that superheroes were real, it had been like a dream coming true. I was glued to the television for a month straight.

Having what happened yesterday happen, that was a dream, too, but a different one. A crazy dream that I couldn't have hoped for in a million years. We live in a world of super powers, and I'd acclimated to that. But I didn't expect to join it, and that was the most pleasant surprise of all, one that could never be topped, I figured.

"Mr. Cavanagh is coming to see you," Laverne Dobbins said, looming over me as I stood next to the line with my clipboard in hand. He nearly scared the hell out of me, voice still deep and full over the machinery's light rattle. Cavanagh's factory was a lot quieter than most factories. He'd put time and research into muffling the machinery, decrying the effects of noise pollution on his workers' hearing.

"I … what?" I asked Laverne, who stood there like a big, imposing mountain, his expression utterly flat.

Laverne evidently didn't feel the need to repeat himself just because my brain was operating at half-speed. He just stood there until I saw a familiar face cutting through the crowd, though with less of an entourage this time—none at all, actually.

Edward Cavanagh worked his way around a piece of miniaturized assembly machinery and came toward me, smiling. "Augustus!" he called when he was in earshot. "You looked great on the front page this morning." He had a paper under his arm and unfurled it to show the picture of me sandwiched between him and Mr. Weldon. The headline read, "Local Hero." That was it. Big letters. And they'd cropped the photo to put me front and center, with Weldon and Cavanagh each losing an arm in the process. "Good timing on the pic, huh?" Cavanagh said as he came closer. He was grinning wide. "Seems like yesterday was a big day for you all around."

"I'm sorry," I said, trying to catch sight of the paper. A picture of Sienna in flight was in the left-hand margin, attached to the story I was in. "Does that say …?"

Cavanagh just grinned. "Your secret is out, and what a splash. Saving the life of the most famous meta in the world? Good way to get your name out there. I'm sure the papers were overjoyed that they just coincidentally had a fresh file photo of you on hand. First time I've ever been unceremoniously chopped like that." He moved his arm to hold it close to his side. "Well, if you and your new friend are looking for the one-armed man, I can assure you it was not me." He popped his hand out.

"I'm sorry about that, sir—" I started.

"Sorry about what?" He looked at me, almost incredulous. "I see nothing but good news all the way around here. You did something great for this community and—

okay, I guess the bad part would be all those bodies they found, but I mean other than—God, that just sounds bad, doesn't it?" Now he was grimacing. "I try to look on the bright side of things, that was all I meant by the—anyway." He just sort of shrugged. "I think your heroism is wonderful. Your powers—also wonderful. I'm endlessly fascinated by metahumans, just like everyone else is, and I wish we were in the biotech space, because I'd love to know more about what makes your powers happen. But in regards to all this—I just want to say thank you, for the community, from Cavanagh Tech, for being you, Augustus." He held up the paper again. "Congratulations. You're a hero. And it couldn't have happened to a more deserving guy."

I found myself more than a little stunned. "Thank you, sir. I … I … I've been so fortunate in so many aspects of my life … having this job, getting that opportunity and recognition with you and Mr. Weldon yesterday, and then finding out I had my powers yesterday."

Cavanagh looked like he was about to choke. "You found out yesterday? And saved Sienna Nealon last night?" He laughed. "You are every bit as ambitious as everyone says you are."

"I don't believe in wasting time, sir," I said. "I feel like we have a responsibility to do something when we have the ability to, you know?"

Cavanagh nodded. "I feel the same. I've built my whole company's philosophy around that idea. I'm just glad to see it shines through in all areas of the business." He clapped me on the shoulder and leaned in. "Can I … can you just … show me … real quick … what you can do?"

"Uhm," I looked and felt around me, seeing if I could get a grip on some dirt, something, in the area. I could almost feel like I had my fingers on a thread, and I tugged hard on it. I caught a glimpse of Laverne Dobbins, giving me a look as I strained, and something came floating through the air from the big, open garage door on the opposite wall.

It was a clod of dirt that must have been just … sitting there?

"Wow," Cavanagh said, nodding his head, impressed. "I heard you had earth-based abilities. I brought that in for you." He grinned again. "Didn't want you to think we just had clumps of dirt lying around. Janitorial might feel like they'd been smeared on that one." He slapped my shoulder again. "That's just amazing. I predict big things for you, Augustus. I hope you keep your talents local, because … let's face it … every town could use more heroes." He extended a hand to me and I took it, and he shook mine firmly. "You need anything from me, let me know, all right?"

I paused, thought about it for a second. "Well, there might be one thing, but I hesitate to ask …"

"Don't," he said, looking a little offended. "Don't hesitate. You can ask me for anything. Anything I can do to help you—money, resources, time—whatever. Ask. It's yours."

"I could … use some time off to help Ms. Nealon," I said. "She was going to include me in her investigation." I saw his eyebrows go up at that, and he nodded to Laverne.

"Make sure Augustus gets all the paid time off he needs for his hero work," Cavanagh said. "And give him my phone number, too, so he can call me direct if he needs anything else." He looked me in the eyes, and I felt his sincerity. "Really. Need a car, a plane, a helicopter—whatever. You or Ms. Nealon. Call and it'll be done. Okay?" He shook my hand one last time. "Take care, Augustus. Make us proud." With a last nod, he started away, that purposeful stride carrying him across the factory floor. Someone called his name and he headed straight for them, willing to give them a moment of his time.

Yeah, he was some guy, that Edward Cavanagh. I guess you don't get to the top without learning how to make an impression.

"Here's Mr. Cavanagh's private number," Laverne

Dobbins said, stepping up to me. His suit looked expensive. I felt a sudden desire to ask him if I could have one of those, too, but I figured I'd just take the card and save my requests for help for when I really needed it.

"Thank you," I said as I looked over the white rectangle of paper. It had a hologram in the corner, next to the Cavanagh Tech name, that made it shine like a silver-tinged rainbow as I turned it over. I was going to put the number in my phone right away, but the card? I was probably going to keep it forever.

"You can call any time, day or night," Laverne said and then started away. "Consider your PTO request approved. Please apprise your supervisor of any day you need off, and he'll forward that to me." I expected something from him about not wasting Mr. Cavanagh's time with trivial requests, or not to call about getting a free suit, but he didn't say anything. Just nodded and left.

I just stood there for a minute, staring around, looking back at my line like someone was going to jump out and yell at me for not working. Of course, no one would, because that was my job and that's not how I ever handled it. "Okay, then," I said, mostly to myself. "I guess I'll just … go and … be a hero."

No one answered, so after a moment more I started walking toward the exit, tentatively at first but picking up speed as I went. This being a hero thing was not turning out half as bad as Sienna had made it sound.

15.

Sienna

I've long ago given up trying to understand men. It should be a warning to me that anyone with half a brain in his head would go running, not walking, away from a woman who can kill with her very touch.

Most don't, though, which leads me to believe most men are out of their damned minds.

And very occasionally, I meet one with which that particular attribute doesn't bother me much at all.

I was lying tangled in Detective Calderon's—is it bad that I'd forgotten his first name? Of course that's bad—in his sheets. It was mid-morning, I was feeling lazy and quite contented, and he'd disappeared into the bathroom a while ago and not come back quite yet. It had been a busy night at the crime scene, and I should have been exhausted afterward, ready for sleep. But I hadn't been. Seeing craziness like this started a slow itch in the back of my head.

No.

Wait.

I don't think this craziness started it at all, now that I think about it. I think it might have started earlier, with Ariadne and Reed in the training room. Like a symphony, warming up. Bows across strings, discordant noises, horns blowing out of tune and time. It was that isolated feeling, that sense of being cut off from the world, from everybody, from having Andrew Fricking Phillips sending me hourly email requests, updates and orders.

Not having received an email from him in a while had been a nice change of pace. I'd "accidentally" disconnected my email account from my phone and couldn't remember my password. Whoops. I probably needed to call J.J. about that.

I don't think I'd even realized how stressed I was until I was hovering over that crime scene, Calderon pulled close to my side. He smelled good, even with that musk of sweat from a day's work underlying it all.

Marcus! That was his name. I remember it now.

All those thoughts of Kat, of what she'd done to me, all the media onslaught. The orchestra was done with the warm-up, was in the middle of the damned overture, and it sounded like cats howling in pain to me. There was other stuff, too—guilt that made up the supports beneath, kept it all from falling down on itself.

If this had been a normal night when I was at home, I think I would have retired early to my closet and shut the door, leaving the world outside.

But I wasn't home, and there was no quiet, safe space to hide in, and the symphony was playing so loud in my brain that it made my hands shake.

So instead, I'd just clutched tighter to the handsome man who had been pushed in my direction and shown him how someone who can't touch people with her skin has figured out oh so many different ways around that particular obstacle.

I didn't hear any complaints from him. Maybe one about slowing down once, but other than that …

My head sunk into a thin pillow. Calderon's place had the scent of masculinity about it—deodorants and shampoos and stuff that smelled unmistakably manly. Laundry soap that lacked any perfuminess to it. Straightforward, bare-bones, clean but not frilly or whatever. I liked it; it reminded me of my own personal aesthetic.

But it was still a little uncomfortable, and I hadn't slept super well. I didn't really love being away from my own bed, but under the circumstances, I couldn't complain. Besides, I always won the cover tug-of-war. I am meta woman, hear me rip cotton sheets completely by accident. Whoops.

"You coming out anytime this decade?" I asked the blank door to the bathroom. "I thought girls took a long time in the bathroom." I presumed he could hear me through it. Calderon had an apartment not too far from the crime scene, and it wasn't too big, but it was well kept. People were on the stairwells at midnight when we'd come in, and they cleared out at the sight of him. Or me. Probably him. I just looked like a bloody mess, that was all. He was just a cop.

Okay, it might have been me that caused them to flee.

"It takes a while to keep all this looking tip top," he said and cracked the door. He was shirtless, standing in front of the mirror but not giving it so much as a look. Dude was reasonably ripped, looked like he worked out. Only a light layer of black chest hair covered his dark skin, and he was fiddling with the phone in his hand. "Got the preliminary back from the scene."

I clutched the torn sheet (I'm super strong; it seriously happens) in front of my body, feeling the mood shift back to all business, and suddenly a little self-conscious about my lack of clothing. "What does it say?"

"A lot," he said, looking up. "A whole lot." His dark eyes were slightly wide, like they'd just taken in a whole heap of info in one big eye-chug. "Here's the biggest nugget: we have identification on two of them through dental records."

I sat up, keeping the sheet clutched tightly to myself. "Who are they?"

"David Murphy Griffin and Miguel Alonso," he said, looking up to meet my gaze. "Griffin was a Gulf War vet, Alonso was a former auto mechanic, according to social security administration. Both locals."

"Huh," I said. "That's not much to go on." I lay back on the bed, smelled a rush of Calderon's scent as I pushed my face into the pillow.

"It actually is," Calderon said, stepping forward, brandishing the phone like Exhibit A. "Because these guys have something in common that a cop would pick up on immediately."

I stared at him. "Well … so … what is it?"

He grinned at me. Nice smile. I still liked him in the morning, which was a good sign, right? "You glad you came to Atlanta?"

"I'll be gladder if you'd stop holding out on me and spill it, already."

That did not make him smile less. "They've both got records with infractions for loitering, urinating in public, vagrancy … bunches of minor stuff that all spells—"

"They were homeless," I breathed, jumping to the conclusion before he could spell it out. "And they were found in the yard of someone who worked at a homeless shelter."

Calderon cocked his head at me. "The coincidences just keep piling up, don't they?"

16.

It only took a call to the shelter and a quick chat with Yasmine Colon to confirm that the victims were former residents who had gone missing. That hacked and slashed straight through any possibility that it was mere coincidence. Yasmine said that Flora knew both the men in question, without doubt, and that they'd disappeared shortly before Flora had been killed.

I was in Calderon's bullpen at the police department, pacing back and forth in front of the little cubicle he called his own while he did a lazy half-spin around to watch me move. I wasn't restrained in my motions; I was churning at full meta speed, right along with my thoughts.

"You're gonna wear a hole in the carpet," he said as I passed him again.

I paused, my cell phone in hand. "This is big. This is really big. I don't know how you can just sit there—"

"We all get our twitches out in different ways," he said, looking cool as a cucumber. "And this isn't as big as you think. It's not like we have a name, someone we can go slap cuffs on. We've just got a little bigger web to troll for flies, that's all."

"Bigger web?" I stared at him, my mind racing. "Okay. I'm not exactly a seasoned investigator like you, so I'll bite. How does this not narrow the field?"

"Because there are still a lot of possibilities," Calderon

said, and started ticking them off on his long fingers. "One—an individual serial killer, praying on the homeless, experimenting on metas in their ranks—"

"What kind of serial killer hires mercenaries?" I asked, smiling.

"One that has money," he said. "One that's connected. Pretty much the worst kind, actually."

"I don't buy it," I said. "Too pat. Doesn't feel like a serial killer, does it?"

"Tons of homicide victims buried with less regard than most people give to disposing of their pets?" He raised an eyebrow at me. "That feels a little serial killer-ish." He paused, thinking it over. "Esque, maybe? Serial killer-esque?"

I ignored his word search. "Second possibility: a group of killers, working to … I don't know, slaughter people?"

"See, we need motive," Calderon said. "Means, motive, opportunity. Those are the legs of building a case and finding our villain." He gave me a second for that to sink in. "There's always the wild card possibility, too—a *conspiracy*." He said the last word with silly emphasis, like he was discounting it.

"So how do we figure out who has those things?" I asked. "Means, motive and opportunity, I mean?"

"Gotta investigate the victims," he said, hands behind his head like he was totally relaxed, the old pro at this. "You've delved into Flora Romero pretty well, but you haven't even touched on Kennith Coy, Roscoe Marion or Joaquin Pollard. Remember, they were the victims of lightning man, not whoever killed these homeless guys. Pollard has to be tied to Flora Romero—"

"But maybe Coy and Marion aren't," I said. "Different killings, different MO, different case?"

"The lightning man is the common link," Calderon said. "He's the thread that runs through the whole case—your mercs that tried to hide bodies of evidence, Pollard who killed Flora, and lightning man who wiped out Pollard, Coy and Marion." He spun a little in his chair, about ninety degrees back and then forth. "Like I said—big web. Lots of spiders."

"Okay," I said. "You take Pollard, and I take Coy and Marion?"

Calderon got a pained look on his face. "Can't."

"What do you mean, 'can't'? You've got a yard full of bodies."

He eased his way to his feet, still looking like he was in great discomfort. "Yes. Unfortunately … my boss isn't buying the idea of lightning man. He's actually, uh …" he searched for words again, "… well … the phrase 'head in the sand' comes immediately to mind. Makes me want to walk on over and give him a kick in the hind parts, correct his perspective."

"Bad boss?" I smirked. "I wouldn't know anything about that."

"Things are the same the world over, huh?" He gave me a smirk of his own. "So … much as I'd like to help, unless you want to call your boss and get him to move some pressure onto mine, I'm stuck investigating my current case load … and a bunch of skeletons that were dug out of Flora Romero's yard. I might be able to widen that to include Joaquin Pollard, since he did kill Flora, but other than that … you're gonna have to dig on Roscoe and Kennith all by your lonesome.

I felt my phone buzz and looked at the faceplate. I didn't have the number in my phone memory, but it said "Atlanta, GA" under the number. "Maybe," I said, and pressed the talk button. "Hello?"

"Hey, it's Augustus," came the voice from the other end of the line. "Boss gave me the day off. Where you want to meet?"

I covered the mic. "Give me the info on Coy and Marion, and I'll start canvassing with my new partner."

Calderon did not look super impressed. "You're really going to take junior along on this?"

"He's only a few years younger than me," I said.

"Uh huh," he said and picked up a couple files from his desk. "I'll copy these and be right back." I watched him thread his way around me, nearly tripping over a rut in the carpet as he went. He looked back at me accusingly, and I realized that … whoops, yes, there were some slight ridges in the carpeting where I might maybe have left some tread damage.

"Hellooo …?" Augustus asked from the other end of the phone. "You still there?"

"Yes, sorry," I said, watching Calderon's retreating back for a few seconds. "I'm at the cop shop at the moment. Calderon is getting me copies of files on some guys we need to investigate."

"Anyone good?" he asked.

"Lightning man's victims," I said. "What happened to your job?"

"I told you, boss gave me the day off," he said. "I guess he saw me on the news and wants to make a positive contribution to society."

I saw Calderon disappear into an alcove. There was a coffee pot sitting on a ledge just inside, and a microwave. "Who is it you work for again?"

"Edward Cavanagh."

That one perked my ears up. "Like … the billionaire?"

"The very same."

"Hm," I said.

"What?"

"Nothing," I said.

"You had that tone."

"What tone?" I asked.

"That tone women get when they think about a billionaire."

"Billionaires are quite hot right now," I said, "though I think most people miss the fact that very few look like Edward Cavanagh. Most of them look like Warren Buffett."

"What's wrong with Warren Buffett?" Augustus asked. He sounded a little cross, like I'd stepped on his toes.

"Nothing," I said. "I'm sure he's a perfectly lovely guy. But he's not exactly Christian Grey in the looks department, is he?"

There was a pause. "Who's Christian Grey?"

"*Fifty Shades* … never mind," I said. "Point is, billionaires are old guys, not young ones."

"Except for Edward Cavanagh," Augustus said. "Or Mark Zuckerberg. Or Tony Stark—"

"Tony Stark is a fictional character," I replied tautly, "also like Christian Grey and countless erotic romance heroes."

"Why are we talking about this again?"

"Because—" I stopped. "I don't remember now." Calderon started making his way back through the aisles toward me, the files and some sheets of paper in hand. "Oh, good, here comes my info."

"What are you expecting to find?" Augustus asked.

"A murderer, I hope." My stomach rumbled. "Also, possibly some breakfast." Calderon's fridge had been that of a bachelor. The only thing in it was expired ketchup. I could sympathize, having a very similar setup myself.

"Do you just, like, fly through the McDonald's drive thru?"

"I've tried," I said. "Pretty much every time, they try to call me a walk-up customer and make me come inside. It feels a little ridiculous—"

Calderon arrived, not bothering to apologize for cutting off my conversation. "Coy and Marion's addresses, employers, some other basics." He held out a couple of sheets of paper to me. "I withheld the lab reports so you'd have less to carry. Only thing of possibly any relevance was that Coy had some traces of THC in his system, which would have been a violation of his parole if he'd been caught." He pointed to a page as he handed it to me. "Number for Coy's PO is here. You might want to talk to him."

"What's a PO?" I asked.

"Probation officer," Calderon said.

"Oh," I said. "Anything else on Roscoe Marion?"

"Home address," Calderon said. "Looks like a buttoned-up guy from what I can see. I'd start with Coy. With his priors, he just seems like a more interesting character, and the criminal theme in his past might be easier to dig up. If Marion was connected to the seedy side of things at all, he did a marvelous job of hiding it. You'll have a tougher time cracking that one open, so I'd go for the low-hanging fruit first."

"And you take Pollard?" I asked.

"I'm going to try," he said. "If I can't, I'll get you his details later." He ran a hand over his head. "I'm gonna be up to my eyebrows in paperwork for a while anyway, I promise you that."

"Okay," I said. "Augustus, we're going to check out Kennith Coy first. His address is—" My stomach rumbled again and it was loud enough that Calderon looked at me funny. "Is there a Burger King near this?"

He shook his head. "A ways south, but not really close, no. McDonald's?"

"Dammit." I like Croissanwiches better than biscuits. "Okay. Augustus, meet me at—where is it?"

"Just—there's only one," Calderon said. "MLK—"

"I know where McDonald's is," Augustus said. "I'll see you there in a few." He hung up like someone from TV, not even saying goodbye.

"Be careful out there," Calderon said a little stiffly, like he didn't want to be caught acting unprofessional in front of his co-workers. I could fully sympathize with that feeling.

"Why?" I asked. "Because someone tried to kill me yesterday?"

His face twitched, and I could tell he was trying to mask feelings. It was cute. "Yes. That's usually a cause for concern in my world."

"Really? Because in mine it makes it just another day," I said, turning my back on him and striding out of the room. He didn't have a monopoly on playing it cool.

17.

Augustus

I decided to run to McDonald's, and it turned out to be a good idea because it not only let me figure out how fast I could run (really fast!) but it also caused people to shout and honk their horns at me as I blew past. It wasn't, like, Flash fast, but it was pretty fast. Fast enough that people noticed. Fast enough that if I watched later on YouTube (lots of people recorded me, I saw them), I was pretty sure it was going to look cool.

I was also hoping to beat Sienna there, because it's in my nature to try and impress the new mentor/boss—wait, I'm not getting paid for this—uhh … do you still call them a boss in an internship? I'd never had one.

Anyway, I made it to McDonald's to find her already there, in the booth next to the door, bag in front of her, look of utter disappointment painted across her face. I'm sure my own look asked the question, because she answered without me having to say anything. "It's after ten-thirty," she said as she trashed her bag and led me outside. "Lunch. Blegh. I was not in the mood for a burger."

"Early bird gets the worm and all that," I said. She did look a little bleary eyed. Also, although her clothes were different, I could tell by her hair that she probably hadn't showered. "You all right? You look like you might have swallowed the worm last night." I paused, and felt a mild surge of panic. "Like from a tequila bottle! Not from – oh, hell."

She gave me an inscrutable look for a moment before she reached into her back pocket and pulled out some folded papers. "I'm just peachy and not just because I'm in Georgia." She looked up at me with a slight twitch upward at the corner of her mouth. "Get it?"

"Georgia peaches, yeah," I said.

"You're not the only one that can make with the mildly amusing." Her momentary levity vanished. "Let's get to work, shall we? Kennith Coy used to live about … six blocks from here, I think?" Her feet lifted off the ground.

"Uhh," I said, "you know I can't fly, right?"

She dropped back to the sidewalk like someone had let her loose. "Dammit," she said. "Sorry. I'm used to going places with my brother, and he's finally figured out how to fly a little now."

I looked around, and saw some bushes sticking out of the planted gap between the sidewalk and the parking lot asphalt. "I could … maybe ride the dirt across the sky like they do in the movies?"

She raised an eyebrow at me. "Can you really do that?"

I shrugged. "Maybe? You want me to try?"

She seemed to think hard about it for a few seconds. "If you haven't practiced," she finally said, "probably not. The last thing we need right now is you falling out of the sky and going splat in the middle of the street. Because the way things are going for me lately in the press, I'd probably take the blame for that."

"'Sienna Nealon kills black sidekick,'" I said.

She blinked a couple times. "Yeah, that's pretty much how it would read, except they'd probably also scathe me for having an unpaid intern."

"Damn," I said. "I'll practice later, see if it works."

"Be careful, okay? For both our sakes." She started to

walk down the street then paused. "Wait, which way do we go?"

"You don't even know where you're going?"

"I can usually ..." she let out a sound of low exasperation. "I just fly around until I find the right street signs, or I use my GPS and just ..." She pulled out her phone and shook her head. "Never mind. Give me a minute."

I plucked the paper gently out of her hands while she looked at me in mild surprise. I'd clearly caught her off guard, because I'd seen her move and I don't think I was fast enough to catch her if she wanted to avoid being caught. I stared at the paper with the name Kennith Coy at the top. "That's like three blocks this way," I said, pointing.

"Lead on," she said and fell into step beside me.

I hurried but didn't run, figuring it was better to not get into a race with her. I also assumed she'd let me know if she wanted to go faster. She didn't really say anything for a little while, kinda had her head in the clouds—metaphorically speaking. I needed to make that clear because she was the only person I'd ever met that it could have been literally true about as well.

"What's my, uh ..." I broke the silence, feeling a little swell of confidence that shriveled as she looked at me with those bluish-green eyes. "What's my role here?"

She sort of blinked for a moment. "Very basic. Help me out. Help keep me alive."

"Sounds simple enough," I said.

"Trust me, it's not," she said. "People try very hard to kill me. Constantly."

"Personality like yours, I'm not finding it hard to believe that," I said, trying to put a little humor into it. I thought I might have missed the mark and backed it up a little. "You know that was a joke, right? That didn't cross the line, did it?" She looked at me evenly. "We're supposed to banter, I thought. That's how they do it in the movies."

"Banter's fine," she said after a pause that felt like forever. "Banter all you want. It doesn't bother me; most of the time I enjoy it. Besides, even if you pushed a joke a little too far, it still wouldn'tbe the least shitty thing said about me this hour, so take some comfort in that."

"I don't get it," I said. "It's not my imagination, right? People have kind of … turned on you?"

"It's not your imagination," she said darkly. "They love you one day and then hate you the next. What was that old Stalin quote? 'Gratitude is a disease of dogs'? The press is definitely on board with that philosophy, except maybe they think he was understating it."

"Which I don't get," I said, "because, like … you saved the world."

"Not according to *Time*," she said. "Or *Newsweek*. I mean, yes, at first, they thought so. But I've seen a few lovely pieces lately that call into question every word I've ever spoken. I kind of suspect that at this point if I said the sky was blue, they'd just report it as suddenly green and then issue a correction on page 48 in a little itty bitty text box six months from now."

"Wow," I said. "I guess I just … I don't know. It all seemed a little over the top. I was watching the news a couple weeks ago and …"

She lowered her head, her lips turned faintly like a little ghost of a smile was there—the joy was long dead, all that was left was the form. "You're talking about the sudden burst of spontaneous think pieces where they accused me of being the villain while Sovereign was actually a misunderstood reformer, aiming to change the world for the better?"

"Yeah," I said. "That wasn't …" I didn't want to be insulting, but at the same time I had a question. "None of that was true, was it?"

She shrugged and kept walking. "He wanted to change the world, all right. By wiping us all out, eliminating all armies and putting everyone under his boot heel. So, yes, you could call him a reformer, if you were a big supporter of Germany in 1938." She smirked. "Which *Time* magazine was, apparently."

"Ouch," I said. "So why'd they report it that way?"

"I don't know," she said. "We've got a PR flack named Jackie who says that she's never seen anything quite like this. Like the entire press corps' mood has just turned on me. She's tried repeatedly to turn it around using every trick she has, and … she's smart, I'll give her that, but …" she shrugged again, "… no difference. They're gonna keep coming at me." Her jaw tightened. "And now that they've got a new favorite—"

"You talking about Katrina Forrest?" That wasn't exactly a tough leap to make.

She seemed to speed up just slightly, pushing me to quicken my pace. "Was it that obvious?" she asked.

"Not a whole lot of big-name metahumans out there," I said. "You, your brother, Katrina, your ex … though you don't hear much about him anymore."

"Scott?" She shook her head. "He wanted out. He's in the family business now, out of the public eye as much as possible."

"So there's really not a whole lot of examples to point to," I said. "Once you get through that list, then you start getting into some of the nearly-nameless, like that guy whose ass you beat down in Manhattan—"

"Eric Simmons," she said, not looking all too happy.

"Those Russians you killed when they tried to take over your headquarters, the Italian guy from the Vatican thing—"

"Anselmo." Her voice was hard.

"You got like three-four heroes," I said, "and a list of villains, most of whom are dead. Doesn't give a lot of examples to point to when you're looking for heroes. I mean, *I'm* now on the list of high-profile metas, and I've been in this game for like … ten minutes."

She cocked that eyebrow at me. "Yeah, I'd watch out for

that if I were you. Just based on personal experience."

"You think Katrina would say the same?" I asked. Not quite banter, but it was a little pointed, I'll admit.

"No," she admitted as we turned a corner. We were walking pretty fast now, but not so fast we were outpacing cars or anything. "She seems like she has the world by the damned tail."

"Well, if it's like you describe," and I was having a hard time believing it was that bad—call me an optimist at heart—"then she'll probably catch the other side of that sword before too long."

"Shut up, Gavrikov," Sienna muttered under her breath, so low even I could barely hear her. "We'll see," she said, back to normal volume. "Kat has a tendency to skirt through things mostly unharmed. She's a little like Teflon in that regard. None of the bad stuff sticks to her."

"What about the good?" I asked.

"Seems like she's getting a fair dose of that, doesn't it?" she asked. "Who's she dating nowadays? One of the Hemsworth brothers or something?"

"I don't know," I said. "Does it matter?"

We fell into a silence that I could tell, just by looking at Sienna, was sullen as hell. "She lies about her age, you know," she said after a moment's pause. "She's not really that young."

"Whaaaat?" I asked. "Girl looks like … twenty, tops. With that body? Or are you saying there's some Photoshop going on there?"

"There's always Photoshop going on there," she said. "But no, I mean she's older than she says she is. We metas … a lot of us don't age like others."

"So … you're saying I could be like sixty and still look young enough to date eighteen-year-olds?" I felt my eyebrows rise. "Because that would be—"

"Don't creep," she said and then hesitated. "But, yes, you could do that. Possibly even at a hundred and sixty, you could do that."

"Oh, damn!" I actually covered my mouth with my hands. "You're serious, aren't you? Man, this just keeps getting better."

She got sour fast. "Yes, it's such a wonderful fringe benefit, constantly being able to sleep with young women under false pretenses while avoiding the discussion about your recent sesquicentennial and the embarrassing collapse of your birthday cake under the weight of all the candles. Don't be a perv, Augustus."

"Hey," I said, "you know, I just look at older women and I think … I'm not ready yet. I'm just glad to know that I have the option—"

"Ugh, ewww, ugh," she said, putting her hands over her ears. "Just … ewww. You're Janus in training."

"Oh, yeah, I forgot all about him," I said. "That dude was kind of famous for a minute, too, and then he went and disappeared. What was up with that?"

She pursed her lips. "He and Kat broke up, and he went back to England."

I felt my brow furrow, my whole face shrivel up in disgust. "That old dude hit it with Katrina Forrest? Ohhhhh, that ain't right!"

A glimmer of amusement ran through her eyes. "Just think—someday that could be you."

"Ohhhh, yuck. I take it all back." I held my head in my hands. "Damn, that just ruins my whole image of her."

"Because she slept with an older man?" Sienna scoffed. "Get over it. You could end up sleeping with a thousand-year-old meta woman without even realizing it, you know."

"She'd have to have a pretty damned hot—"

"Oh, just stop it," she said. "Are we close?" She nodded to the paper in my hand.

"Ahead on the left," I said, nodding at the house numbers. "Odds on this side of the street, so …"

"Okay," she said. "Watch out for vans filled with

gunmen."

"That's a conspicuous choice," I said. "You'd think they'd just convoy in, like, two or three sedans, try and blend in a little or something."

"Strangely enough, I wasn't expecting a van full of mercenaries when I crossed the street," she said, "so really, they did okay on maintaining the element of surprise, I think. The residents didn't seem to think anything was out of the ordinary either, except, you know, me crossing the street in front of them."

"Well, you kinda are a little white girl in a not-so-pearly neighborhood," I said, sizing her up. She really was short. Not as tiny as Taneshia, but thicker, too. I had to look down to talk to her face. "They probably thought you were up to no good if they didn't know you."

"I'm always up to no good," she said and led me up the driveway of a house that had really been let go. It had shingles hanging off, plywood in the front window. I'd seen foreclosures around that had this problem. Kids would come and party in the houses, fire off paintball rounds or just tag the hell out of the interior with spray paint.

Sienna paused for a second next to the old Buick in the driveway, leaned against it with a hand on the hood. "You been in this area before?"

"Just passed through," I said, looking up and down the street. "I don't have any friends on this street or anything if that's what you're asking."

"Close enough to what I was asking, yeah." She knocked on the door, which was pitted and scarred like it hadn't been replaced since the house was built and stood back, waiting for an answer.

We stood there for a minute. "You think he lived alone?" I asked.

"File said he lived with his mother." She looked at the door intensely, and for a minute I wondered if she could see through it somehow.

"Maybe she's refusing to answer because she thinks we're cops," I said. "You've seen that before, right?"

She shrugged. "Not really. I don't tend to do a ton of investigating in my side of the business."

"Yeah, I suppose you're mostly dragging people out of bank vaults and beating the hell out of them in restaurants," I said, going back to that banter thing. She actually smiled on that one, though. "Don't you have to find these people first, though?"

"Yeah, but I mostly get the dumb ones," she said. "Big egos, little brains. They're practically defying authority in an effort to get caught. It's like they've got daddy issues with law enforcement. Catch me if you can, and all that."

"Wouldn't it be 'mommy issues' if you're dealing with it?"

She shrugged. "Whatever the case, it's pretty straightforward. I'm not exactly a highly experienced investigator." She hesitated for a second, looking a little reticent. "But, whatever, we'll make it work."

I stared at her. "Did you just … did you just kind of, like … bluster your way through that?"

She looked a little wounded. "I didn't … I mean … I'm just saying that I'm not a detective by trade, okay? It's a weakness, but, y'know, it's something we can work around. It's not a big deal."

"You're after a murder suspect, aren't you?" I asked. "Shouldn't that be a big deal?"

"I didn't mean to say that the murders aren't a big deal," she said, slowing down her speech, "I mean … we'll figure it out and catch who's responsible. It's all good practice for me."

"So you're not exactly Sherlock Holmes is what you're saying." I leaned forward and pounded on the door. "That's not very reassuring."

"Well, if lightning man peeks his ugly face out at us, you'll find me reassuring as I beat the living daylights out of him."

"Does anyone actually use the phrase 'the living daylights'

anymore?"

She stared at me with a thin veneer of annoyance. "You're really leaning on this banter thing. Nervous?"

"I'm knocking on the door of a total stranger whose kid just got murdered by lightning," I said. "It's totally cool. I do this every week or so. It's not unusual or uncomfortable at all."

Her gaze softened. "Just stick with me," she said, and pounded the door with her fist again, this time with extra emphasis.

"How do you know anyone's even here?" I asked.

"Car's in the drive," she said. "Hood's still cooling off, which means it was parked recently. Someone's here."

I let out a little whistle. "You're getting the hang of this investigating thing, I think. What do you want to do?"

"I'll go around back and knock there," she said. "You stay here."

I got the feeling from the way she said it that there was more in her mind than she was letting on. "You're not about to force entry, are you? Because like I told that cop last night, I got a clean record, and I need to keep it that way—"

"I'm not going to break down the door," she said. "Just want the person inside to feel a little surrounded. Plus, if they haven't closed their curtains, they're going to feel stupid if I walk around back and catch them standing there pretending they're not home."

"What if they're in their underwear?" I asked. She gawked at me. "People do that, you know, when they're at home. They could be in the bathroom—"

"Just stand here," she said and started off across the overgrown lawn, disappearing around the back.

I just sort of stood there on the front porch, not really sure what I should do. There was a little peephole, and I looked at it for a minute before I decided to lean in and take a look.

I saw an eyeball looking back at me.

I let out a short, sharp "Ahhh!" and heard one coming from the other side of the door, maybe a little higher than mine. I stepped back and heard the deadbolt slide, then the door unlocked and a short woman with a scowl who looked like she came up to about my belly button was staring up at me, grey hair all done up in a bun.

"What do you want?" she asked, hand against her chest. "You just about gave me a heart attack!"

"Uhm," I said, tongue twisting around, "I'm, uh … Augustus."

She peered at me through her thick glasses. "Augustus who? That doesn't tell me anything. What do you want?"

"I'm here about, uh … Kennith?"

"You asking or you telling me that?" She took her hand off her chest.

"I'm here about Kennith," I said. "I wanted to ask you some questions."

"Who are you with?" That scowl made me want to take another step back.

"I'm with, uh …" I tried to remember the mouthful of jargon that Sienna's agency was called. "The, uh … metahuman police."

She gave me a look. "The who what?"

"The agency responsible for policing metahumans," Sienna answered for me as she came around the corner, floating through the air. "Ms. Coy?"

"*Mrs.* Coy," the lady answered, staring furiously at her, like her floating was nothing. "And don't you make any jokes about it, either."

"Oh, coy, like—" I started then stopped myself. "Well, you did refuse to answer the door for a while, so … maybe you shouldn't play it so—"

She raised a hand like she was going to hit me, and I stopped and took a step back. "I am your elder and you will respect me," she said. "If your mother didn't teach it to you, come a little closer and I will."

"Ma'am," Sienna said as she landed on the front porch, "we're here about Kennith."

"I heard him the first time he said it," Mrs. Coy said, staring her down. "What do you need to say about him?"

Sienna gave me a look, something in the realm of *This lady is going to be a pain in the ass.* "We're here about what happened to him."

"You mean how he died?" she asked, getting right to it. Even Sienna looked a little taken aback by her bluntness on that one.

"Uhh … yeah," I said. "That's right."

"Well, then why didn't you just say that?"

"It's kind of a delicate thing," Sienna said. "I didn't want to just throw it out there in case no one had told you …"

Mrs. Coy's head dropped. "You didn't think I'd notice my boy got struck by a bolt of lightning outside my own window?" She yanked the glasses off her head and thrust them out at each of us in turn. "How blind do you think I am that something like that would escape my notice?" She turned her head, showing us each of her ears in turn. "Do you see hearing aids here? Do you think I would miss the crack of thunder?"

"Was there a crack of thunder?" Sienna asked, and for a minute I thought Mrs. Coy was going to lunge right out at her.

"Of course there was a crack of—" Mrs. Coy's face got screwed up for a minute, and then she paused, like she was thinking about it. "Well, there had to be, didn't there? Of course there was. Thunder follows lightning, that's how it is."

"Thunder follows lightning because the air currents make that noise as the electricity is discharged from clouds or something, right?" I asked Sienna. She just sort of shrugged and nodded, all in one. "So if he was killed by someone who could shoot lightning out of their hand, there wouldn't be thunder, would there?"

"What in the blue hell are you talking about?" Mrs. Coy

asked.

"Ma'am," Sienna said gently, which sounded a little strange on her, "we think Kennith was killed by a metahuman who generates lightning bolts from their hands." She lowered her voice even further, almost to a whisper. "We think he was murdered."

Mrs. Coy put her glasses back on and squinted at us, smacking her lips together like she was thinking something over real hard. "You think he was murdered?"

"Yes, ma'am," Sienna said.

"By a bolt of lightning?"

Sienna looked to me again, and this time I could see the pained need for reassurance pass across her face in a flash quicker than the lightning we were discussing. I got it, because Mrs. Coy had one of those personalities like those clouds that make thunder—she made everyone want to wince and take a step back. "Yes, ma'am. We think so. We'd like to ask you some questions about Kennith because … we're trying to track down the person we think did this."

Mrs. Coy screwed up her face again, and then pushed her door wide open. "You can come in, then." And she backed away from the door slowly, shoulders hunched over, looking for the first time not like a force of nature hurling herself at us at the gates to her own castle but like a woman—an older woman—who had lost her son.

18.

Sienna

Mrs. Coy's house smelled of good food. We followed her down the hall into a living room that looked well-lived in, older furniture that had a stately aura about it—classy and aged well, kind of like the woman herself. The outside of the house might have been a little rough, but the inside was the domain of this tiny terror, and she clearly kept it completely in line, like her own personal kingdom.

"Y'all want anything to eat?" Mrs. Coy asked. "People from the church brought all manner of food."

"I just ate," I said apologetically. I watched Augustus catch her eye and shake his head.

"I can't hear your head rattle," Mrs. Coy said, eyeing him.

"Ah, no, ma'am, thank you," Augustus said, tripping over his words. I couldn't blame him; she had that effect on me, too.

"Would you like some iced tea?" she asked, passing through a small gap between counter and wall into a kitchen on the far side of the room.

"Uh, sure," I said. "Please."

"Yes, please," Augustus said.

She moved about the kitchen for a few minutes, preparing three big pint glasses of tea with ice. I watched her go about the business, slowly, steadily, until she'd finished pouring all three of them. When she got done, she sort of stared at them for a moment and I could see her conscious mind clicking away realizing what she'd just done, and how she didn't have enough hands to effectively carry all of them. "You," she said to Augustus, "come help me with these."

Augustus snapped to it, nice guy that he was, and he grabbed two glasses and hurried them over to us while Mrs. Coy took the third for herself and settled in on one side of her couch, taking up maybe three-quarters of a plaid-ish cushion. She held the iced tea glass in her hand, and I watched it start to sweat. It wasn't exactly sweltering in her house, but it was warm, and she was wearing only a thin cotton dress.

Augustus handed me a glass and I took it up, immediately taking a long drink. When the tea hit my lips, I froze. It was like no tea I'd ever had. I'd gotten used to the British version of tea. This was not that. This was diabetes encased in a glass cylinder.

It was sugared like a soft drink, with a hint of honey running throughout. I tried not to slurp, because even as my brain was protesting that this was way, way too sweet for me, my tongue was asking me for more and more. Also, in fairness, it was kind of warm, so a cold drink felt pretty good.

"What do you think happened to my Kennith?" Mrs. Coy asked as I pulled the glass away from my face. I didn't really want to pull it away, but I needed to stop before I drowned myself in this stuff.

"Ma'am, we don't exactly know," Augustus answered for me while I composed myself. He gave me a sidelong look like he knew the tea had captured me and was holding me prisoner. The secret ingredient may have been heroin, because all I wanted at that moment was MOAR TEA.

"Another man was killed the same night," I said, finding my voice again. "Roscoe Marion. Does that name sound familiar?"

Her eyelids fluttered as she thought it over. "I read his

name in the paper, but … other than that, no. I don't think so. I don't recall Kennith or anyone else ever mentioning him to me before."

"How was Kennith doing?" I asked. "I know he was on … probation."

"He was following the rules," she said. "He worked at the tire shop down the road. He didn't go out at night, just went to work and came home straightaway afterward. His parole officer came by a couple times a week at first, but we hadn't seen him in a while now." She shook her head. "I don't see how he could have been in any trouble, let alone enough for someone to want to kill him."

I made a mental note about the tire shop. "Did he ever have friends come by?"

She looked up at me. "Just that Darrick. He would stop by every once in a while. I never did like him."

"What was wrong with him?" Augustus asked.

"He had no respect," Mrs. Coy said, and she was off to the races again, animated and irritated. "He would honk his horn on the driveway until Kennith came out and talked to him, like an animal. No manners."

"What was Darrick's last name?" I asked.

"Cary," she said. "Darrick Cary. I'll write it down for you so you can beat on his door for a while." She puckered her lips and gave me enough of a look that told me what she thought about my tactics.

Augustus's lips went into a thin line. "Darrick Cary … young guy. About yea tall?" He held up a hand to around his chin. "Drives a little SUV?"

"He's in a fancy Corvette now, but that's him," Mrs. Coy said, looking at Augustus with more than a little mild irritation. "He a friend of yours?"

"No," Augustus said, looking more than a little offended. "We went to school together is all. I know of him."

"Can we talk about the night Kennith was killed?" I asked.

"I don't see anyone stopping you," Mrs. Coy said, just a little short of a snap.

"What can you tell us about that night?" I asked.

"Well, let's see," Mrs. Coy said, with more than a little irony dripping, "it was the night before last, so it might take me a while to remember since it was so long ago. How do these stories normally start? 'It was a dark and stormy night'? Yeah, it started like that." She was clearly annoyed at us. "Kennith and I were sitting on the couch watching TV—"

"What were you watching?" Augustus asked.

She looked daggers at him—big, fat, stabby ones. "What does it matter what we were watching?"

"We try and be as thorough as possible, Mrs. Coy," I said as gently as I could. Augustus, for his part, looked like he was going to stutter an answer out somewhere around 2050. This woman was extremely off-putting.

"We were watching that show with the boy and the girl that fall in love—" She shook her head. "I don't know, he picked. I was reading a magazine." She glared at Augustus. "You want to know what magazine it was? *People*, okay? *People* magazine. It had that little blond tramp on the cover, the one with the—" She squinted at me. "You know her. That little skinny-ass bitch."

This was the problem with being well known; Mrs. Coy had been holding out on me a little bit all along, at least. Normally that would have thrown up a cloud of suspicion, but I couldn't really blame her for being a little ornery two days after her son died. "I used to know her," I corrected.

"Anyway, if we can escape some of these details," Mrs. Coy said, "we were sitting there and the TV went out. Just the TV, not the power. It started spitting that white static. It was storming, so we didn't think too much of it, but then there was a noise outside and Kennith thought maybe a branch had fallen on the roof, maybe took out the TV."

"Don't they bury those cables nowadays?" Augustus asked.

"We have an antenna," Mrs. Coy said, pointing to the roof. She paused, waiting. "May I continue?"

"Sorry," Augustus muttered.

"So he went out and looked, and—let me wrap this up before either of y'all go interrupting me again—I heard something, then a scream, and by the time I got out there, he was dead in the yard. Burned all up."

"Did you hear thunder?" I asked.

She concentrated hard, thinking it over. "There was thunder earlier in the night, for sure. I remember hearing it crack, feeling it rattle the house. But … I don't remember it when he screamed, not at all. His scream was so clear, so much louder than the …" She swallowed, nearly choking on her emotions before she got ahold of herself. "… than the rain on the roof."

I couldn't look away from her. "Mrs. Coy … did you ever see a branch?" She stared blankly at me. "The one that made the noise Kennith heard."

She frowned, thinking again. "No, I did not. I suppose I forgot about it in the fuss afterward. But no, there was no branch, no sign of anything."

"Thank you, Mrs. Coy," I said, and watched her put her face on her hand. "We'll … let ourselves out if that's all right with you."

"Are you going to catch the person who did this to my baby?" she asked, looking up at me again.

"I'm going to try," I said. "They're not making it easy on me. Whoever it is, they're covering their tracks so well that we can't even prove for a fact that someone did it, at least not yet."

"I don't even know what to think," she said, shaking her head. "If you could please … just … leave me alone."

"Yes, ma'am," I said, and gestured to Augustus.

He paused, just a little ways off from the arm of her couch. "Our condolences, Mrs. Coy."

She looked up at him, all trace of sarcasm gone, replaced

by a twin track of tears glistening their way down her cheeks. "Thank you, young man," she said, and we left her to her grief.

19.

"What do you suppose happened with the branch?" Augustus asked as we closed Mrs. Coy's front door behind us.

"I think our killer jumped on the roof," I said, walking back down her driveway with a purpose. "Sat there and waited until Kennith showed his face, then nuked it off with a lightning bolt."

"Burned his face off?" Augustus asked, sounding horrified. "For real?"

"Eh, from the autopsy photos it seemed like it caught Kennith in the hand," I said. "But still, it wasn't pretty."

"Man, I am hearing all the grossest stuff with you today," he said. "Old men sleeping with pretty starlets—"

"Like that never happens."

"—people getting their faces fried off," he went on. "This is not as clean as factory work."

"Good thing you can use your powers to fix that problem," I said, halting at the sidewalk. "Who is Darrick Cary?"

Augustus stopped short, and I could see the hesitancy in his posture because he stiffened like someone had just rammed a stick up his ass. "Just some dude from the old neighborhood."

I just stared back at him. "You seriously expect me to believe that?"

He deflated. "Come on. You can't expect me to … snitch on someone."

"'Snitch' on someone?" I snickered. "Like a rat? What the hell is this?"

"You don't do that," Augustus said. "It … that's not right."

"Code of omertà? Nice. I don't care what Cary's doing," I said, "except as pertains to this particular case. But I need to talk to him, and if I go into that conversation without all the facts, someone might end up getting shot."

"That's a little extreme, don't you think?" Augustus asked. "And a bit of a leap, too—straight from, 'I don't have all the facts' to 'BAM BAM BAM' and cooking some fool."

"Here's what happens when I don't have the facts going into an encounter," I said, trying to explain it patiently. "A lot of times, they run when they see me coming, especially if they have the sort of checkered background that would prompt someone like yourself—a decent and honorable person, clearly—to hesitate before discussing their business. This flight to avoid me … well, it ends up pissing me off." I clapped him on the shoulder with one hand. "Tempers flare. Unkind words are sometimes exchanged, ones that can never be taken back. And somewhere, in the middle of all that heat, a gun is drawn. Maybe by him, maybe by me, but the point is—who do you think wins that exchange in the end?" I gave him my most serious look.

Augustus chewed it over for a minute, finally looking disgusted. "I didn't think you were going to be able to draw the line between points like that, but you went and did it, and made it almost seem like a reasonable person talking instead of a crazy-ass insane killer person."

"I like how you threw in the 'almost.'"

"He's a dealer," Augustus said. "Has been for a long time. Probably where Kennith got his abnormal narcotics results."

"Hrm," I said, pondering that one. "That's … hrm."

"What are you thinking?"

"I'm thinking we have to talk to him," I said. "That's our obvious link to Kennith's criminal past, after all."

"Yeah, but what if Kennith went straight?" Augustus said. "You know, after jail. What if he went straight, except for maybe a little indulgence in the herbal remedy for his glaucoma every now and again?"

"Then this is gonna be a short conversation with Darrick," I said, "and also, you know damned well he didn't have glaucoma."

"How are you going to know if he's telling you the truth?" Augustus asked. I sensed skepticism.

"If you break like … three, four major bones in their body and they still tell the same story, they're usually telling the truth," I said, absolutely deadpan. Then I smiled, nodded, and started to walk away.

"Oh, hell," I heard Augustus say. And then, after another few seconds, his footsteps hurrying to catch up with me. "You were joking about that."

"You asking me or telling me?"

"You have a dark sense of humor," he said.

"I have a dark sense of everything."

"That a new thing?" he asked.

I thought about it for a beat. "Not particularly, no."

I could feel his presence at my side, walking along with me, eyes boring into me as we walked. "You know, they don't really talk about your early life much."

"'They' don't really talk about anything factual in relation to any point in my life," I said. "Because 'they' are a bunch of assholes who are paid to speculate in order to fill dead spaces in airtime, magazine column inches, and bytes on the web." I quickened my pace, and Augustus hurried to keep time.

"You really got a powerful anger for the press, don't you?" he asked.

"I've done, like … two interviews," I said. "Two. That's all they really know of me, other than some YouTube videos that have me in action doing things like flying around and beating the crap out of the occasional person that deserves it—"

"I think like ninety percent of your YouTube videos are you beating the crap out of someone," he said. "I mean, everyone knows the New York one, but there's that one in Houston—"

"Dude totally deserved it," I said.

"—Los Angeles—"

"Super-duper-uber-deserved it."

"—that one in Montana—"

"I didn't even break any bones that time."

"—and wasn't there one in like … northern Canada someplace?"

"Yellowknife," I said. "Which was totally unfair because that was a bar fight that someone else picked and I just finished."

"Wasn't that person human?"

"Yes," I said. "And very drunk. Which is why he's still able to walk and has all his limbs still attached."

"I mean, maybe it's just my naturally sunny disposition talking, but," he made a pained grimace that showed me rows of even teeth, "if I wanted more people to like me, I might be a little … gentler. More restrained. I'm not saying 'be like Katrina,' but she's got the public persona down—"

I stopped, feeling a hard shudder run through my body. "I will never be like her." I whipped a finger into his face. "You know what Kat is like? Weak. She's weak. She flops around from place to place, person to person, unable to make a decision with spine for herself."

"That's harsh," he said. "I thought you used to be friends."

"Yeah," I said. "So did I. Until she broadcast a private phone call between the two of us on her show's premiere without my permission in order to boost her ratings on my name."

"Oh, shit," Augustus said, and his hands came up to his

mouth like it could cover his obvious surprise. "You didn't know about that?"

"No," I said, more than a little miffed. "And I sat there and talked to her after the Russian incident for … I don't even know. Forty-five minutes? Thinking she cared. That she was a friend. That she was … *worried*." I spat the word out with hard contempt. "But she wasn't. She was just worried about her ratings. Worried how she'd look if her little vanity project bombed. So she used me to look concerned, sweet, caring—they edited that call down to five minutes of me being a complete and total—"

"Yeah, I heard," he said. "It, uh … I mean it wasn't the New York video, but uh … it maybe didn't highlight your most flattering … uh … side? Personality? I got nothing," he said, finally giving up on trying to put a nice spin on it.

I waited a beat to see if Aleksandr Gavrikov would interject. He didn't say much about her anymore, which I considered a giant effing blessing. "I keep getting blindsided by people," I said.

"So why'd you take me on as a partner?" He froze. "Intern? Uhhh … charity project?"

I sighed, felt the weight of everything I'd just told him settle on me. "Really, at this point … why not?" I felt my eyes burn a little at that admission. "What do I have to lose?"

He was quiet for a moment after that. "Your job?"

"Screw my job," I said.

That just hung there for, oh, about two minutes, and he finally spoke again. "So … what should we do?"

"Find Darrick Cary," I said. "After we stop at the tire shop and ask Kennith's old employer a few questions."

There was a flash of confusion across his face. "I thought you said—"

"I know what I said." I straightened my shoulders and started walking. Any direction would do, because I was sure Augustus would correct me if I was heading the wrong way. Eventually. "But I haven't lost my job yet, and until I do …

I'll just keep doing what I have to." I felt an acidic taste on the back of my tongue, a disagreeable aftereffect of the tea. It reminded me of life: it had seemed sweet for a little while, but that had faded pretty quickly, leaving nothing but awfulness behind.

20.

Augustus

There were easier things than finding Darrick Cary in the midst of Vine City, especially when I didn't know where he lived or where he usually hung out. I'd known Darrick way back in the day. He'd dropped out at—sixteen? Seventeen, maybe? I'd heard the rumors here and there about him, of course—that he'd had a kid and actually got married and turned to dealing when economic prospects didn't turn out so bright for a high-school dropout with a couple of high-level possession charges. Just enough to go felony, I heard.

Walking down the street looking at random passersby wasn't going to do it, I knew, but I was really hesitant to just go all out and call someone I knew would know where Darrick was. I had loyalties still, and one of those was … well, you didn't do that sort of thing without a damned good reason.

Especially when the person asking was the sort of person who might—oh, I don't know—break his kneecaps for the hell of it.

"Where are we going?" Sienna asked, still wearing that hangdog look. Man, I expected this killer lady to be a total badass, but I hadn't exactly expected the level of bad juju coming off of her in the emotional toxic waste department. This girl had some issues, and not just the kind that stemmed from a bunch of crappy articles about her, either. There was something behind all this "betrayed by a friend, everybody hates me" motif. Something deeper, maybe? She had an anchor of some kind on her, and it was dragging her down, or burying her in quicksand or something.

"Tire shop," I said tightly. No, I just wasn't ready to throw even a low-down street hood like Darrick Cary into her path just yet. "Maybe they can tell us where Darrick is."

"You think that they'll know there?" she asked. "Why? Is the tire shop secretly a drug den?"

I thought about it for a second. It was one of the big national chains, but I couldn't remember which. "Probably."

We walked along in silence until we saw the glowing sign. They had that thing lit up in the middle of the day. I suppose once you've gotten past burning tires, conserving electricity just doesn't really turn the dial anymore.

"Hello?" Sienna asked, just walking right under an open garage door. I followed her a little more cautiously. There was smoke in the air and I felt myself frown. "Hey," she said, taking a sniff. "I think it actually is a drug den."

"I don't see a car." Some dude with no neck came walking up, tall as Schwarzenegger but eight times as big across. He nodded at both of us, and it was kind of a challenge. "Why are you here if you don't have a car?"

"I'm looking for directions," Sienna said. She did not even bother to be sweet about it.

"Try the diner on the corner," No-neck said.

"This is clearly not that much-vaunted Southern hospitality I've heard about," she said, easing toward him.

He just looked at her through jaded eyes, standing next to a sedan that was waiting its turn for service. "Get your sweet ass on out of here before I show it some hospitality with my—"

I cringed, already knowing what was going to happen. She didn't disappoint.

She had a hand on the back of his head and just slammed

it right into the sedan in front of him. It echoed through the shop, and I swear he hit so hard I saw stars on his behalf. I felt my whole face just make that pained look, like "OOH!"

No-Neck's head bounced back up, eyes rolling, legs looking a little rubbery, like he was going to drop. He was blinking furiously, like he was trying to figure out if he was awake or asleep. "Whaa …?" he managed to get out.

"What's your name?" Sienna asked. She'd taken her hand off the back of his head and just stood there a pace away, watching him wobble. He looked like he was going to pitch face-first into the hood on his own this time.

"T-Tony," he said finally, focusing in on her face. "Wh-who are you?"

"My name's Sienna, Tony. Do you know where I can find Darrick Cary?"

Tony focused on her. "D-Darrick?"

"Yeah," she said. "I need to pick up something from him. Where is he?"

Tony looked like he was losing that fight with staying awake. "W … who are you again?"

She just shook her head. "Tony … this is going to hurt you more than me."

"Wait!" I said, holding up both hands. "You're going to kill this poor bastard."

She looked at Tony, who was registering none of the conversation we were holding before him. "He was really rude a minute ago."

"I am not going to argue that," I said, still holding up my hands. "But does he really deserve to die over it?"

"I think he'll get a concussion at best," she said.

"You hit him like that again and Tony's going to lose the capacity for speech," I said. "If you want people to like you, maybe you ought to consider not beating the crap out of everyone you run across that offends you."

"Tell me where I can find Darrick Cary," she said, and there was a darker overtone as her hand found the back of

Tony's head again. He didn't even seem to feel it.

"All right!" I yelled. "All right, just let me call Taneshia. She'll know."

Sienna looked at me like I was an idiot and pushed Tony aside. He fell back on his haunches, dazed, and just sat there. "Taneshia? That girl I met last night? You think she's going to know where to find a drug dealer?"

"Yeah," I said. "Because she's been known to indulge from time to time when she's partying. Straight A student, too. You got a problem with that?"

"I told you that I don't care about the drugs," she said, and turned back toward the entrance to the garage door. She walked past a desk and rang the bell on it rapidly until a guy emerged from the back room with a pissed-off look on his face. She paused, gave him a 'don't give a crap' look and said, "Tony's got a concussion. You should take him to the hospital."

"Who the hell are you?" he asked. Dude looked like he was about to turn purple.

She was already gone. "She's a lady with a really bad experience with … uh … tires," I said, making up bullshit that didn't even sound sensible while trying to back out the door myself. "You should really get him checked on, though," I said, nodding at Tony. "Hit his head or something." I ducked out of the garage door and left the stifling smell of oil and rubber behind, wondering exactly who I was following at this point.

21.

I dialed up Taneshia on my phone as I walked out of the garage. I could see Sienna a little further down, near the sidewalk, a phone of her own held up to her ear. Taneshia answered on the fifth ring.

"What is it?" she asked, sounding a little panicked, a little out of breath.

"I need to ask you something," I said.

"What?" Panic went to concern, about two degrees lighter.

"I, uh … need to know where I can find Darrick Cary."

There was a pin-drop silence on the other end of the phone. "Say what?" Taneshia finally asked.

"Darrick Cary," I said. "He was, a, uh, friend of the one of the victims, if you know what I mean. I—I mean, we—need to talk to him."

The silence wasn't good. Neither was the answer. "You want me to give the name of a dealer to someone who's probably going to go over there and mess him up?"

"You know I would not do that," I said.

"Why are you all up in my business about this?" Taneshia asked. "Darrick is not an unknown person in the neighborhood. You could find ten people willing to drop on him for five bucks."

"Yeah," I said, "but, uh … I don't know any of them."

"You got to be kidding me," she said, and I could almost

hear the pained look leaking over the phone. "I was in class, Augustus."

"This is important," I said. "I wouldn't have called if it wasn't."

"I give you his name and Darrick ends up in the hospital, what am I supposed to do?"

"Send flowers?" I joked. "Kidding. He's not going to end up in the hospital."

"People know we're like family," she said. "If he gets messed up, they might get to the idea it was me that gave him up."

"Nah," I said, "they're gonna think it was some dude named Tony that works at the tire place down by—"

"What?" She cut me off with fervor. "What did you do? Augustus, what are you into?"

"Nothing," I said. "I did not do anything." I left off the part where I just watched a superhero smash Tony's head into a car hood. I knew Taneshia, and that was the sort of thing that would make her not so cooperative in handing over Darrick's whereabouts.

"Darrick's got a family to support," Taneshia said, almost pleading. "He's got a baby he takes care of."

I wanted to throw out a line about how he maybe should have finished school and got a job, but it seemed … counterproductive. "I know, I know," I said. "I will make sure he doesn't get messed up." I hoped. I mean, it was this or watch this lady go through the whole neighborhood like they were Tony. She wasn't going to find any shortage of people willing to be rude to her, either, because let's face it, this was planet Earth. We can't export them, so they just seem to accumulate here.

"You beat up Darrick, your momma's going to hear about this," Taneshia said, more than a little irritable.

That got under my skin. "You're going to tell my momma on me? How about I tell her how you buy from him? How do you think she's going to take that, versus me maybe standing aside and watching Sienna beat the crap out of him for a little bit?"

Silence again. I cringed. I'd let my temper get the better of me.

"That's hard, Augustus," Taneshia said. "Real hard. Not like you at all."

"I'm changing every day," I said, not really sure what else to say.

"Not for the better so far," she said.

"You got his address?" I asked, once I'd given that a minute to sink in.

"Yeah," she said, "but don't go see him at home—please. For his family's sake. He does his business out behind an old mall. Parks his car out there so he can move fast if he needs to. I'll text you the address."

"Thank you, Taneshia," I said, not really sure what else to say.

"Don't thank me," she said. "Not for this. Just … keep your promise and make sure he doesn't end up messed up." And she hung up without another word.

22.

Sienna

I was only a few steps outside the garage when my phone rang, buzzing hard against my back pocket. I'd had to buy new clothes this morning, and I'd gone with jeans this time. Suits just didn't go with the Atlanta summer, not at all—like peanut butter and engine oil.

I held up the phone and saw the number. It was agency, and the last four digits told me who was calling. "Hey, Jackie," I said as I hit the talk button.

"Hey, Sienna," Jackie said in her professional, clipped tones. "Got a minute?"

"As long as you're not calling on behalf of Phillips, I have all the minutes you need," I said.

"He's keeping his distance on this one," Jackie said cautiously. "He knows I'm calling, but he didn't ask me to convey anything."

"He didn't want to call me himself?" I mused. "That's interesting."

"He knows you well enough by now," she said. "He knows you'd just ignore him."

"He could call from your number," I said. "Apparently that would get through on the first try."

She just laughed, a light, airy tone. "Because you know I wouldn't call just to chit chat."

"No," I said, "you wouldn't. What's up?"

"Well," she said, "you're in Atlanta."

"If you're calling to give me geography lessons, you're a few years late. I may be dumb sometimes, but I know where I am."

"I know this," she went on, ignoring my interruption, "because I've got a whole heap of news articles that are piling up on my desk as we speak from the Atlanta area."

"Unfavorable, I presume."

"And filled with more lies than a self-aggrandizing war story told by a nightly news anchor," she said. "I'm trying to handle it, but there's a lot of speculation about what you're doing down there, almost all of it unfounded."

"When they call asking what I'm doing," I said, "you could try answering with 'Her job,' though they probably wouldn't believe it."

She chuckled. "That's a definite. They would not believe it. There's speculation from a few quarters about whether you're down there to have an unpleasant conversation with Edward Cavanagh."

"Cavanagh?" I glanced over my shoulder and saw Augustus on the phone, hopefully getting the last known address of Kennith Coy's dealer. It hadn't been pleasant, but my little stunt with Tony would hopefully pay a few dividends. "Why would I care about talking with Edward Cavanagh?"

"Because Cavanagh developed the suppressant that the Russians stole from the government and used on you back in January," she said. "A few outlets are wildly guessing that you're pissed at him."

I shrugged. "Why would I be pissed at him? I assume he developed it at the behest of some senator or congressperson—or the president." I put some loathing into that one. I was not the biggest fan of President Gerard Harmon at the moment.

"Well, that's good to know," she said. "I'll work on a

line—"

"I'm investigating a murder," I said. "A series of them, actually, linked to a meta by a local cop."

"Yeah, but they won't believe that, either," she said. "They're just going to keep digging until they find whatever they want to find. You know how it goes." She sounded almost apologetic.

"Yeah," I said sourly. "I know how it goes. Like a dog with a favorite chew toy, they just keep coming back to me for another gnaw."

"Sorry," she said. "I've never seen anyone take heat like this who wasn't a banker or head of an oil company. For damned sure not someone who saved the world."

"Just do what you can, Jackie," I said. "It's not like I have a good name left to sully, but I do wish they'd get off my ass at this point and just let me do my job."

"Just be glad you can fly away at a moment's notice," she said, "or the paparazzi would be hounding you every minute of the day."

I turned my head to see some guy walking by with a cell phone camera, just holding it up pointed at me. "Paparazzi? They're professional losers. Lucky me, I just get constantly photographed by the amateur kind—every douche with a cell phone."

"Could be worse," she said.

"Yeah," I said. "I could be Kat and have the brains of a guppy, let some asshole Hollywood producer do all my thinking for me." I saw Augustus end his call and start walking my way, so I said to Jackie. "Gotta go. My sidekick is coming this way."

"Wait, what?" she asked. "You have a sidekick? Is it that young black guy, with the—"

"I have to go, Jackie. Like, now."

"He's cute. I could come down to Atlanta, maybe help you both out with the press inquiries—you know, on site …"

"Bye." I hung up on her and watched Augustus coming

toward me. She wasn't wrong about him; he was cute. But he had this innocence about him that I found … disquieting. Not like Calderon. That guy had seen some of the same shit I'd seen and come to the same jaded conclusions. Augustus was a baby, really.

And I was making a man out of him, but not in the way that would have led to any kind of happiness for either of us.

23.

"You didn't have to do that to him," Augustus said as he walked up. Credit to him, he didn't storm, as some might have. He did, however, have a slight kicked-puppy look, that mix of resentment for the pressure I'd put on him and a sick sense of being used. I knew how that felt. It was basically how I felt anytime I looked back on how Erich Winter used every conversation we ever had to move me in some direction or another.

"Oh, I think we both know I did, Augustus," I snapped right back.

"Why?" he asked. "Why did you have to put that dumbass, nearly-defenseless dude into the hospital for saying something stupid?"

"Because you needed to know," I said and watched his jaw drop. "That wasn't about Tony. Tony's an idiot. I suspect he was born an idiot, and he'll slack-jaw his way through life as an idiot until the day he stands under a hydraulic jack as it fails and drops a car onto his comically oversized dome, and when he dies of skull trauma, the doctor responsible for the autopsy will make millions from writing ten research papers detailing how Tony survived so long without a brain in his head. This wasn't about Tony. It was about *you.*" I looked him dead in the eye.

"About me?" he asked. "How is you giving some dude bleeding on the brain about me?"

"Because you need to know what you're in for, if you're going to ride with me," I said. "You think you know. You keep bringing up YouTube videos of me beating the crap out of people like they're some joke, or something that happened on an off day. They aren't. They're what I do. I beat the bad guys, and I take the 'beat' part of that very literally." I stared at him. "I don't think you have the stomach for this."

"Man," he said, shaking his head. "When I was a kid, I used to read about superheroes in comic books. People who would strive for good, save the world." He stopped shaking his head, just looked askance at me, and I felt the wounding I'd just inflicted. "You? You're not like that at all."

"I never said I was." I folded my arms. "The whole world has been telling you I'm not a hero."

"I wanted to be like you," he said, so crestfallen that I felt like I'd kicked him square in the balls. I felt the pain of what I was doing to him, that gnawing heartache deep inside, but I held it down—like I always did.

"I hope you never are," I said quietly. "I hope nobody is ever like me. I'm not a hero. I'm a bulwark. A wall. The line. I'm this way so no one else has to be."

"And you wonder why you're lonely," he said, his words so quiet and devoid of accusation that they shouldn't have hurt.

They hurt like hell anyway.

"Where's Darrick Cary?" I asked.

"Behind an old furniture shop ten blocks up," he said, pointing. "Parks his car back there." I started to lift off the ground. "I guess you're going alone, then."

"It doesn't hurt me to be alone," I said. "Not nearly as much as you think it does."

"Yeah, I'm sure that's why you slept with that cop last night," he said. "Because it doesn't bother you at all to be alone."

"Kid," I said, more than a little menacingly, "you don't know me."

"I'm not a kid," he said, disgusted, "and I think I know you well enough after seeing that," he gestured back at the tire shop, "to see a few things about how you work inside. I may not know the whole deal, but I've seen wounded people before. I've seen damaged folk. You don't have the monopoly on a bad past, okay? You just maybe hold it in until it explodes violently better than most do, as if that's supposed to be a good thing. Do they give a gold medal in the Olympics for repressing all your feelings?"

"What about you?" I asked, letting myself drop to the ground. "You're so … so buoyant it makes me sick. Oh, there's always another way—a sweeter, kinder, gentler one. Darrick Cary is one of the good guys who should be protected—"

"I don't think he deserves to die or get concussed for what he does, no," Augustus said.

"You don't think anything should happen to him, clearly," I said.

"I'm not the police."

"Oh, but you wanted to be," I said. "You wanted to be a hero. What do you think a hero does? We're supposed to be the triumph of the rule of law that keeps us grounded as a society. We're supposed to be justice—"

"What part of bashing some sexist pig's head in reflects justice in your world?" he asked. "Is that the penalty for being a dick? Because I didn't see that codified into law anywhere. Must have missed that."

"Well, the U.S. Code is like 40,000 plus pages, so it probably is in there somewhere," I said, deflecting. "I'm trying to protect civilized society, okay?" I paused, realizing the absurdity of at least part of my argument and making a minor concession. "Except for the Tony thing. He did piss me off just a little."

"You're 'trying to protect civilized society'?" Augustus asked. "Well, you're going about it like that big, furry white dude."

I searched around for the answer for a moment. "The Big Show?"

"No, the cartoon one."

I tried again. "… Sergeant Slaughter?"

"No!" Augustus said, annoyed. "Are you obsessed with the WWE? I'm talking about the one that's all like, 'I'm gonna love him, and hug him, and never let him go!' And then he kills Bugs Bunny!" He paused and lowered his voice. "In this example, Bugs Bunny is a free society."

"I got that," I said. "I've seen *Winter Soldier*. My brother makes …" I paused, letting my voice drift off, "… used to make this argument frequently."

"But he got tired of it falling on deaf ears?"

"Maybe," I said. "Or maybe he just realized the futility of arguing idealism in a world where some people can explode with the force of a nuclear bomb, or force every single person with any weapon to turn it on themselves, or … the list goes on." I looked at him, and I felt a soul-deep sadness settle over me. "Laws … are for humans. And as annoying to me as Kat's show is, they got the title right. We are 'Beyond Human.' And I want human laws to apply, I really do. But there's no one out there who can enforce them … except me." I held my hands out. "Lucky me."

"I will never believe that the ends justify the means the way you've been doing it," he said. "I believe in heroes, in people doing the right thing, not getting dragged down by the expediency of shortcuts."

"That's sweet, kid," I said, condescending as hell. He looked a little pissed at it, and I couldn't blame him. "Don't lose that." And before he could answer, I flew off, heading in the direction he'd pointed, strangely content that I'd lost the argument with him, at least in his own mind.

Because it meant maybe he *could* be a hero.

And I'd long ago given up hope that I ever would be.

24.

Augustus

She just flew off, just like that. Not another word, not a hint that she'd like to stay there and argue all day but she couldn't, just a patronizing as hell bit of bull, and off she flew.

I dug my phone out of my pocket and called my momma. Sienna Nealon may not have been a hero, but she was right about one thing—I wasn't going to go losing my desire to do the right thing just because she did.

"Hey, Momma," I said as Momma picked up.

"What are you doing calling me during work hours?" Momma asked, already on alert.

"Mr. Cavanagh gave me the day off to help Ms. Nealon," I said, using last names and titles to show deference. If I hadn't and I'd been standing in front of her at the time, Momma would have smacked me winding. "So that's what I'm doing—helping. You got yesterday's paper nearby? I need to know the name of the other man that got killed in the lightning storm." I couldn't remember, honestly, if I'd even heard it at all.

"Sure," she said, and I already knew she did. She had a stack of papers next to her couch that went back at least a week at a time. I heard her rustling for a couple minutes, thankful for the distraction. "Here it is … killed in the evening … lightning struck two places in … victims were identified as Kennith Coy, 32, and Roscoe Marion—"

"Roscoe," I said under my breath, barely believing it.

"You knew that man?" Momma asked.

"I should," I said, staring up into the sky. Sienna was already gone, flown off to her next destination. "He worked at the factory with me."

25.

Sienna

I found the furniture store without much trouble. It was one of those big box chain retailers in a mall that looked like the recession hadn't been too kind to it. There were a few stores in the middle still open, but the rest of the strip had closed down and both big anchors on either end were shuttered. The hints of the store's name were still on the facade of the building, stained in place by years of rain over the sign above the doors. The windows were boarded though, and I drifted over a dirty, messy roof that was strewn with litter to find a car in the back alley behind the store.

I had to admire a couple things about Darrick Cary. First of all, he picked a good spot. The mall backed up to a small area of woods, and I could see some trails that wound off, probably coming out less than a block away. He also could run straight back or straight ahead in his car and the "alley" created by the mall was wide enough it would take more than a few cop cars to cut him off. I would estimate ten to twenty, assuming he didn't drive off into the woods and lose them in there somehow. It didn't exactly look like an expansive forest or anything, more like a half block of forgotten woodland in the middle of the urban area, but still.

The second thing I admired him for was his car. It was a brand new, cherry red Corvette, parked at an angle that would make it easy to tear off at any sign of approach. Cary had clear sight lines in either direction, and if someone came at him from in front or behind, he'd see them coming a hundred yards off. If they came from the woods, he'd have a good fifty feet of movement over clear ground as a head start. He'd also parked between two doors to the back of the mall, giving himself a decent fifty feet of clearance from the nearest one as well, which was a loading dock. Those didn't open quietly.

All in all, he had himself a little slice of tranquility to do his business. He'd probably scoped it out pretty well, making sure that he had an easy escape, and that any potentially hostile customers who might try to rob him would be guarded in their approach to him. It certainly wasn't a street corner where someone could come at him from any direction, and if I'd been limited to two dimensions in my approach, he probably would have been out of there before I could have asked him anything.

But I can fly, so I just dropped down in front of his hood with a terrible thump. It was a mark of my respect for Augustus that I didn't land on the hood, but even the dramatic entrance that I'd gone with scared the hell out of the man in the driver's seat of the Corvette. He jumped in his seat, letting out a short scream. I mean, I didn't land quiet. I used full Wolfe powers to heal the impact as it was happening, because otherwise it would have broken both my legs. It still hurt, by the way.

But as I looked into Darrick Cary's saucer-wide eyes, I knew I'd had the intended effect.

I shot around to his window in a jiffy before he could go for the starter on the Corvette and leaned in so I could look straight at him. "Hi, Darrick," I said sweetly. I think after all the press I've gotten, doing things that way is somehow even scarier than if I'd started screaming at him from the word go.

"Holy sh—!" He opened his mouth and closed it a few times, pressing his lips together like he could use them to push words out. "Wh-what do you want?"

I admit it, I let my brow rise in surprise. Most people don't get it together that fast when I get the jump on them. "Let's start with basics. I don't care about your business."

He just stared at me, one side of his face slightly raised—horror, I think it was. "Uh—what business would that be?"

"The one where you had Kennith Coy as a customer," I said. "The one where you helped him violate his probation."

"Hey, I didn't know he—"

"Darrick," I said gently. "I told you I don't care about your business. So let's cut the crap, okay?"

He blinked at me, twice. "O-okay."

"I need to know what else Kennith was into that would get him in trouble," I said. "Because I doubt smoking weed was what got him murdered."

Cary's eyes went wide. "M-murdered?"

I squinted at Darrick, wondering if he had a genuine stutter when a super-scary meta wasn't bracing him for information. "Yes. Murdered. Kennith Coy was murdered by a metahuman. I need to know what he was into that could have gotten him killed, Darrick."

"I barely knew that mo—" Cary caught himself just in time, like he thought swearing would bother me. "That … guy. Other than as a loyal customer once he got out."

"A loyal customer, huh?" I asked, watching him with my best cop look. "His mother said you used to drop by the house."

"Because he couldn't leave after he got home at night," Cary said, "and he didn't want to get in trouble at work. Dude liked his smoke, okay? Is that a crime?"

"Yes, I believe it is," I said, "which is why you're having this conversation with me in a back alley behind the mall instead of in a dispensary in front of it." I tapped my fingers on his car. "Other activities? I need to know what Kennith was up to."

"I know nothing about other activities," Cary said. "And

the dude is dead, so I have zero reason to be defending his honor or whatever, okay? I have told you all I know."

I frowned at him. "You seem like the sort of snake that keeps his belly low to the ground. What else have you heard?"

"About what?" Cary asked, clearly of a mind to put some distance between himself and me.

"Murders," I said. "Disappearances. Gossip. Anything."

"Uhm … mmm …" It was unfair to say it was amusing to watch him try to figure out what he could throw to me to make me leave him alone. "I … I don't know. I don't know anything about any murder that isn't gang-related, and it's been a quiet month even for that."

I thought about it for a second and decided to float something, see if it got a response. "You know a girl named Flora Romero?"

He stared at me blankly. "Should I? Is this Twenty Questions?"

"What about Joaquin Pollard?"

That time he reacted. "Okay, yeah, I knew *of* him. Dude got …" his eyes widened, "… struck by lightning after killing some girl. You saying this is related?"

"I'm not saying anything." I gripped his car door in my hand and rocked the car gently. By which I mean gently for me; he ended up going all over the place kind of wildly. "You're the one who's supposed to talk."

"Joaquin, Joaquin, okay …" He searched his memory. "Okay, he was working for … uhm … he'd been in gangs at some point, but I think he was … someone hired him, maybe? This was a long time ago," he almost pleaded.

"Who hired him?"

"Some …" He was scrambling furiously. "Some … damn … uh … I don't know. Seems like someone from outside the neighborhood approached him. Maybe he dropped a name to friends of his, but I don't think I ever heard. I didn't even deal to him, he was tied up with some boys over in downtown."

"Hrm," I said. "Flora Romero was the girl he killed." I waited to see if there was a reaction. "Any idea why he did it?"

"Maybe he was robbing her?" Cary asked, putting his hands up. "Maybe he was doing his job. I don't know. Can I go now?"

"One last question," I said, feeling like I'd struck out so it might as well be time to try one last fishing trip before I packed it in. "The homeless shelter that Flora Romero worked at ended up seeing some disappearances around the time she died."

"And this has what to do with me?" Darrick Cary was about two steps shy of full-blown panic. "I ain't homeless, obviously." He slapped the door of his car.

"Very fancy," I said. "You know the feds could seize this car if they caught you with drugs in it, right?"

"Which is why I would hypothetically keep drugs in *it*," he said, "rather than at my home, where my family lives. Police can have the car, it's just a car. I can get another if I have to."

I let out a low breath. "You're a class act all the way, Darrick."

"You making fun of me?"

"Would it matter if I was?" I asked. "Homeless people missing. Last question, come on."

"Look, I'll sell to whoever can afford it," he said, letting out a sad sigh. "Yes, I sometimes sell to homeless people. You got names?"

"Miguel Alonso, David Griffin."

He stared at me. "Griffin? He's dead?"

"Yes."

"By lightning?" This edged toward panic.

"No," I said, "torture and murder."

"What the hell?" he asked. "Yeah, I knew him. Used to go to the shelter over on … hell, which one was it? It was the one Cordell Weldon's bunch fund."

"Cordell Weldon?" I asked.

"Yeah, you know," he said. "Community leader. Upstanding citizen." He said it in a way that made me think he didn't carry that opinion himself. "That Cordell Weldon."

"I've heard the name," I said. "Kind of a loudmouth?"

"Heh," Cary said. "You could say that. Only time he shuts up is when he's sleeping, the rest of the time he'd knock his own mother over for a six-second sound bite on the local news."

"You seem pretty familiar with him considering he's a pillar of the community and you're, like, a …"

"Local businessman?"

"I was going to go with 'piece of crap,' let you counter with 'filler of needs,' and then settle on 'dirty, dirty drug-pimping whore,' but you've gone and tossed that out the window," I said.

"Hey," Cary said, "if I was in Seattle right now, I'd be living like a king instead of hiding behind a mall."

"Yes, you'd be living like a king in King County," I said. "But instead you're in Fulton county, where you're Full-of-tons—of shit. How do you know this Weldon guy?"

"I decline to say," he said, adopting a surly attitude and slumping down behind the wheel. "You wouldn't believe me anyway, and it has nothing to do with your search." He put his hands on the wheel at ten and two and just sat there, staring straight ahead. "Have I answered your questions satisfactorily?"

"Sure," I said, and stood up. "If you don't take your drugs to your family's house, what do you do with them at night? Because I'm guessing parking on the street with this ride would be an invitation to burglary and grand theft auto."

He turned his head slowly. "Is this an official inquiry I have to answer under threat of … whatever you're threatening?"

"No," I said, shrugging. "Just idly curious."

"Great," he said, and hit the starter on the car, "because I'm done being idle." He waited until I stepped back and then floored it, letting the Corvette's engine roar as he took off, nearly fishtailing around the corner as he went.

"Cordell Weldon," I said, saying the name out loud again. It sounded familiar for some reason.

26.

Augustus

While I was on my way to Roscoe's house, I examined my motives a little closer for why I was even doing this. I'd just had an up-close glimpse about how my supposed hero was not so heroic, bashing the hell out of a guy who probably deserved it, but … I don't know. I guess what bothered me was that it seemed like such a punching-down kind of thing to do. Heroes were supposed to take on the threats the rest of us couldn't take on. And then here was Sienna Nealon, the ultimate badass, and she smashes up some dude who said the wrong thing to her. Not that he didn't deserve a hit, but she could have whacked him in the gut and been done with it. No hospital visit needed.

It was excessive force, I thought. How much punch did he need? Less than what she gave him.

I made my way down the street like a normal person. I wasn't feel a lot of energy at the moment, and I didn't want to draw attention. I had business of my own to complete, after all.

I needed to talk to Roscoe Marion's family. And while I had a good idea of where he lived, it wasn't exact. Fortunately, the internet saved me on that one. Pulled it up on my smart phone in about two and a half seconds.

It took me twelve minutes to walk to his house. Twelve

agonizing minutes in which I felt like I was loafing along, trying not to think about what was on my mind, even while it refused to get off my damned mind. My head was like a merry-go-round, and the constant thoughts of what made a hero and how they might fall in my estimation was a ride I couldn't escape.

When I walked up to Roscoe's house I saw a couple cars out front. I didn't think about it being him that died, because I hadn't seen him in a while. And I must have missed the buzz of gossip at work because … well, the day after he died was the day Mr. Weldon and Mr. Cavanagh came by.

It seemed like a million years ago now, even though it was yesterday.

I walked up to Roscoe's front door and knocked, not too hard. An older lady answered wearing funeral clothes and I felt pretty out of place in my shorts and t-shirt. "Uh," I said, "my name is Augustus Coleman, and I used to work with Roscoe—"

"Come in," the woman said, drawing me into a hug that just about squeezed the life out of me. "Come right on in," she whispered in my ear as she turned me loose. "It's good of you to come."

"Are you Roscoe's momma?"

"No, I'm his mother-in-law," she said, closing the door behind me as I stepped into a front hall. "His momma died years ago. Ever since he and my Shelia have been together, I've always considered him like one of my own."

"I'm sorry I'm late," I said. "I just heard about it a little while ago."

She nodded. "Shelia's on through there if you want to give her condolences. Some of the ladies from my church brought by food, if you want some—"

"I'm not hungry," I said, "but thank you."

I walked through into a dining room where a younger woman, probably about five-ten years older than me, was sitting in a chair. She was all done up fancy, wearing a string of pearls around her neck. There were gold inserts between each pearl, and they gave the necklace a nice gleam.

"Mrs. Marion?" I asked, and her eyes fluttered as she looked up in surprise, like I'd snuck into the room and blown a bullhorn or something. "My name is Augustus Coleman, and I used to work with Roscoe. I came by to … pay my respects."

She blinked at me a couple times, and it was obvious as hell the woman was in shock. "Would you like to sit down?" she asked, voice almost dead.

"All right," I said and started to scoot out the seat next to her. She actually blanched a little, and I halted, moving around the table to sit opposite her instead. I figured maybe I got Roscoe's old seat, and I didn't want to bring up any bad memories.

"You said you used to work with Roscoe?" she asked.

"Yes, ma'am," I said. "I'm a line supervisor at Cavanagh."

"You're so young," she said, looking at me with eyes that could only be described as dulled. I suspected she'd cried all the emotion out of them in the last couple days.

"Yes, ma'am," I said. "Roscoe used to joke with me that I'd make line supervisor before he did. I used to be a floater when I started, and his work partner—Markeith—was always calling in sick, so he and I used to work the line together a lot."

"Oh, yeah, Markeith," she said, nodding. "I haven't heard that name in a while. I almost forgot about him."

We settled into an uncomfortable silence for a couple minutes. "I'm sorry to ask this," I said, "but … can you tell me what happened? No one seemed to be able to give me an answer, and Roscoe was … I mean he was a young man." He couldn't have been older than mid-thirties.

She just stared at me with those unresponsive eyes and nodded, like all the emotion of the experience had left her. "I don't entirely know. I came home late that night after working a long shift—I'm a nurse at the hospital, and I didn't get here until after midnight." She licked her lips. "Roscoe's car was outside, but I couldn't find him anywhere. The back door was unlocked, so I went out, figuring maybe he fell asleep on the back patio, under the umbrella." If she'd had anything left, this was the part where she would have welled up with tears. Instead, she just kept talking in a flat voice. "I found him out there, scorched all to hell, no pulse, no respiration. He was cold." She looked up at me. "I tried to … resuscitate, even though I knew he was gone. After … I don't even know … an hour? It was like my brain kicked back in, like I was dealing with any other patient. He was long gone."

"That's a damned shame," I said. "Just doesn't make any sense that he should be gone. He was a good man." He'd always been nice to me when we worked together.

"Yes," she said, voice hollow. She blinked a little, then sniffed like she had been crying even though she hadn't for a while, I guessed. "How long ago was the last time you worked with him?"

"Long time," I said. "I haven't even seen him lately. I didn't even know where he was working now. Was he still on the line?"

"Oh, no," she said, shaking her head, a little quiver of rueful excitement making its way out. "He got a promotion. He was being trained for something else, see."

"Did he move up to line supervisor?" I hadn't heard about it, but it could have happened. "Move into the office?"

"No," she said.

I made a little frown at that. In the Cavanagh factory, there was a pretty clear path to advancement.

"He was being trained," she said, "as a lab tech."

That one furrowed my brow. "I didn't even know Cavanagh had a lab down here."

"Oh, yes," she said. "It was off-site, though. Roscoe was so excited when he got the promotion. Said they chose him, gave him a fifty percent raise." Her fingers fell to the pearl and gold necklace. "He brought this home with him the day he told me. We were … planning on getting a new car now that he was on salary." This caused her face to squinch with emotion in a way that telling about his death didn't. Probably because now she was talking about their dreams for the future, and no one had asked about those like they had his death.

"It's all right," I said, and reached out to brush her hand with reassurance. "Please. We don't have to talk about this any more."

She slipped a little and then composed herself. She swallowed hard and held it all in. "It's all right. I'm all right."

What do you say to that? The woman just lost her husband and she was putting on a brave face. "I am so sorry for your loss."

She nodded. "It's going to be tough without him."

"I imagine it is," I said and stood. "Is there anything I can do for you?"

"No, I don't suppose there is," she said, looking up at me, eyes restored to their comfortable balance of apathy. I felt for her. I didn't know what to do; if she'd been a close friend I would have given her a hug and told her to let it all out. But I was a stranger, a man who used to work with her husband. There was no way I could approach this that wouldn't be desperately awkward for both of us. "Thank you for stopping by, Augustus Coleman."

I nodded to her and headed for the door. I paused, wincing inside, not really wanting to get out before I asked that last, nagging question that was eating at me. "Shelia?" I turned to see her looking at me with as close to a quizzical expression as she could muster with her subdued emotions. "Where was this Cavanagh lab that Roscoe was working at?"

She thought about it for a moment. "I don't rightly remember," she finally decided, and I could tell it was eating at her. "I don't know that he told me, just that it was a clean room and he was handling … samples and such. He had to take some classes so he could handle biological materials." Her face creased slightly with grief. "He joked he'd just learn from me, because I already knew how to dispose of sharps and such."

My first instinct was to freeze, because Edward Cavanagh himself had assured me this very morning—in an offhand comment, but still—that they didn't a have any bioresearch divisions. Hadn't he? It felt like a cold gut-punch, a chilling sensation that started at the stomach and spread through me, slow as a knife dragging across a frozen flank steak.

But I smiled at her, reassuring as I could. "Thank you. And I am so sorry for your loss." And I excused myself to let the widow Marion grieve—or not, given her current state—in peace.

27.

Sienna

As it turned out, Cordell Weldon was not a particularly tough guy to find. Which worked for me, because I wasn't necessarily convinced I needed to see him for the purposes of this investigation. If he'd been unlisted, tough to track down, shown up with an office in another state, I probably would have given that one up. 'Why bother?' would have been my mantra on that one. He just funded the shelter that the homeless victims came from, after all, and had had some aspersions cast on his good name by a drug dealer. None of that was necessarily anything other than a tangential connection to the case and an indicator that Darrick disliked his stance on something or another.

But when I performed a Google search, Cordell Weldon's name, picture and even his office address came up in about 0.000000046 seconds, and since the address ended up mapping out about one mile from where I was standing, I figured what the hell. I headed straight for him and found a nice little three-story brick office building waiting for me with the doors open.

There was muscle waiting all around, by which I mean bodyguards in suits. I'd taken a few seconds to read the profile on the way to his office, and I remembered him now. Cordell Weldon was basically a local community organizer with big ambitions. Current city council member, likely future congressman, etc, etc. He had the bona fides, and I counted on the first page of the search results no fewer than three glowing pieces that wondered if he'd be appointed to a recently vacated senate seat. He hadn't been, to the gushing disappointment of a fourth article that blamed the oppositional politics of Georgia's current governor.

I set down in front of the red brick office building under the watchful eyes of his bodyguards. They didn't make any sudden moves, but they were eyeing me pretty heavy. Every single one of them looked like they'd played ball somewhere, and not one of them had the physique that indicated their sport had been soccer or basketball. They were brick walls, thick with muscle from more gym visits than I'd had hot meals in my life.

"I'm here to see Cordell Weldon," I said, opening pleasantly. "Please." See? Best behavior.

The head mook looked me over. "Just a moment," he said and whispered into a microphone I hadn't even seen at first. "Mr. Weldon will see you now," the guy said after a moment's pause, and opened the door. "Third floor."

"Of course," I said and wandered in to find myself in a stairwell. This didn't look like a traditional office building. Had I accidentally wandered into the back entrance? I guess I hadn't paid attention.

I saved some time by flying up the stairs and found a young lady holding a door open for me at the top. I floated through and shot her a tight smile. "Thanks."

"You're, uh ... welcome," she said, her eyes wide as I made my way through. She scrambled to the next door, and while she did, I looked around. We were in a hallway with dim, beige walls. She scurried forth and opened the next door for me. I waited, trying not to get out of place and make a faux pas by pissing off my presumptive host until he gave me a solid reason to.

I floated through into the next room and found a

tastefully appointed office looking out at the Atlanta skyline. I came in through what was plainly a side door, as two wood paneled double doors waited to my left as I came in. There was a giant desk, and behind it was a tall man with zero hair on his head. He stood as I entered, but he didn't smile. He did not look like he had the humor or ingratiating demeanor of a politician trying to curry favors. His eyes were narrowed, the look of a man constantly assessing both friend and opponent, and when they settled on me, I stared right back. The ebony skin on his bald head gleamed from the light of the window, and he came out from behind the desk to greet me.

"Ms. Nealon," he said, his deep voice calling me forward. It wasn't inviting, per se, but it was commanding enough that I obliged. He extended a hand, which I took, and then the flash from my side jarred me. I hadn't even noticed that I'd been followed by the woman who showed me into the office. She had a camera in hand and was gesturing at me to move closer to Mr. Weldon, which I did only instinctively. I started to say something, but a plastic smile that only moved his lips a few centimeters had sprung up on his face. "Pictures first," he said.

His assistant took a half dozen snaps of us and then retreated out the big double doors without another word, without offering me a water, nothing. I could have used a water. It was a hot day. I was thirsty. Still, this wasn't quite rudeness of the level to warrant me beating Cordell Weldon's brains in, I supposed.

He gestured for me to take a seat across from him and then sat straight upright in his chair, leaning back maybe enough that his body was at a fifteen degree angle. I suspected that for him, this was lounging. "I'm not surprised you've come to meet with me," he said.

"Really?" I asked. "Why?" I figured I'd shut up and let him explain, since I hadn't known just fifteen minutes ago that I was going to be here.

He pulled his hands apart in a gesture that seemed to me to be either "Isn't it obvious?" or "Let's be honest," or maybe, "I am about to offer something to the rain god." He settled it for me shortly. "When someone has a public image as badly mangled as yours is, oftentimes they look for ways to do some damage control through outreach, by gaining a favorable endorsement. In truth, I'm surprised you haven't sought a blessing from someone in the black community sooner."

I just stared at him, wondering if I'd heard that right. "Wait … you think I'm here to … what? Kiss the ring? Why?"

"Your reputation isn't exactly glowing at the moment," he said, meeting me with eyes that had some serious thought going on behind them. "I've been hesitant to leap on the bandwagon and make things worse since I've had … other concerns … but let's face it, you're ripe for replacement."

"Excuse me?" I asked. I seriously blinked about a million times. "Replacement how?"

"Your record is terrible," he said.

"My … fighting record? The internet videos?"

"Those are no picnic either," he said. "But I'm talking your diversity record."

"My …" I just stared, willing him to finish what he'd started.

"When you had your team together to fight Sovereign," he said, "it was like looking at a country club luncheon. It was whiter than a Nickelback audience."

"What the hell are you talking ab—?" I halted mid-sentence. I had completely forgotten that Dr. Zollers had been left out of all the press coverage afterward because he'd carefully manipulated the minds of the reporters and photographers into shooting around him. At the time I'd found it a little objectionable and told him so. Looking back on it now, I wished I'd had him do me the same courtesy. "Oh. Right."

"Not a single African-American on your team," Weldon said. "Not one in a visible position in your agency."

"Well, our press flack is—"

"Now she is," he said, "when you're on the bottom of the barrel in terms of exposure. I'm talking about then, when you had some pull, some influence."

"I don't think you have the full story," I said. "I actually had two black men on my team at the time, but neither one of them wanted to be exposed to the limelight. And I doubt they were thinking we'd run into this particular sort of … difficulty when they chose to remain anonymous." Plus, one of them was now running for president of the United States and seemed like he might have a decent chance of winning, which would probably not be the case if everyone in the world knew he was a metahuman.

"That's awfully convenient," he said.

"Not for me," I said, "at least not at this moment, since you've just accused me of racism." This had gotten awfully uncomfortable, awfully fast. I wanted to clobber him now more than ever, though.

"I'm not accusing you of anything," Weldon said, templing his fingers in front of him. "I'm just trying to make you aware of something that's clearly problematic—and in your blind spot. Something that could be used to drive your nearly destroyed approval numbers further into the negatives."

"Seems like a legitimate complaint," I said, a little sarcastic. I had to admit, I was feeling it. I'd been attacked personally quite a bit lately, but this one was making me madder than most of the others.

"There are no 'illegitimate' complaints," Weldon said with a healthy sense of satisfaction, a man with the world as his oyster.

"Really?" I asked, sitting up straight. "Your actions are far too guided by the movement of Mars in Scorpio."

His expression darkened. "That is the most ridiculous

thing I've ever heard."

"But totes legit, according to you," I said. "What do you want from me?"

"Diversity, of course," he said. "Visible people of color working in your agency."

"Great," I said, "I'm all for it. Send as many metahuman minorities as you can my way, because we're hiring right now."

"I'm talking about in office roles, staffing positions—"

"Then you want to talk to the head of the agency," I said. "Because I'm just in charge of the portion that's responsible for law enforcement, which means people with guns and people with powers. That's who I have the power to hire."

His eyes narrowed at me. "Are you trying to be purposefully difficult during these negotiations?"

I felt my jaw drop a little. "'Negotiations'? Okay. Let's say I hired a sufficient number of, uh … minorities to satisfy your requirement. What else?"

"We should partner on some initiatives," Weldon said and stood up, adjusting his suit as he did so. The guy was tall and thin, but he looked like he had some power. "Things to provide opportunities for you get your face out there doing good works. Charitable events, things like that. Chances to repair any damage that might have been done to your name by … intemperate actions and poor hiring choices. Naturally, you or your agency will have to front the cost for these events, but pretty soon you'll find some more sympathetic press stories to help abate the current crop of … how shall we put it delicately?"

"Perpetual flagellation?" I asked. "Repetitive flaying?"

"That's not very delicate."

"Feels accurate, though," I said. "How much will this good press cost me?"

He smiled, but it was a thin, menacing line. "I can promise you it will be an amount commensurate with your agency's budget, and it will go to good causes that you can certainly promote your involvement in."

I sucked in a big old breath of air and then let it out again. "Wow. I had no idea this was why I was coming here. So interesting."

He frowned, three big creases showing up in his brow as he stood there. "Why did you think you were coming here?"

"Because Flora Romero was killed by a lightning-wielding metahuman, and she worked in a homeless shelter that one of your 'good causes' funds," I said. "I was just going to poke around and ask you some questions. I didn't exactly expect … this."

He didn't take his gaze off me, and it was a power look. I got the feeling that Cordell Weldon had stared a few people down in his time. "How would you describe … 'this'?"

"How should I put it *delicately*?" I asked. "Oh, yeah—a shakedown."

"That is false," he said, "and not at all delicate. I'm apprising you of a problem you're about to face, and ways you can correct it—"

"By giving you money and exposure," I said. "But I'm glad you brought up how you're doing me a favor by letting me know, because that's actually what I came here to do for you."

His eyes narrowed again, and I felt like he'd spent half the meeting looking at me like a mongoose looks at a snake. "Excuse me?"

"Well, here's something tragic you might not have heard," I said, "they started digging bodies out of Ms. Romero's lawn last night, and two of the skeletons matched with former residents of your shelter." I stood because I was so ready for this meeting to be over. "I'm sure you have nothing to do with it, but I thought I might mention it since it could be … problematic."

I could feel the steam coming off him when he answered. "Are you to here to accuse me of something?"

"Gosh, no," I said, holding my hand up to my chest and

feigning utter surprise. "Like I said, I wanted to warn you. I like how you jumped straight to that, though. It tells me a lot about you, even more than the shakedown—oh, I'm sorry—the 'warning about my blind spot.'"

He seethed quietly for a beat, nostrils flaring. "You should be careful what sort of accusations you make right now, Ms. Nealon. You're not in a very good position to be believed."

"I haven't made any accusations yet," I said. "I just stopped by for a chat and got … so much more than anticipated."

"I think you should leave," he said and gestured toward the door I'd entered through.

"I'm not allowed to go out through the front?" I asked, feigning hurt this time. "But we took pictures together."

"Yes," he said, "somehow I don't think those are going to see the light of day, seeing as you're probably about to vanish from public life. After all, it doesn't matter what you do—it matters what you're *seen* doing."

I raised both eyebrows on that one. "Are you threatening me?"

"I'm predicting your future," he said and stepped out from behind the desk. "You're disliked at the moment, inches away from losing your job. All it will take is one slip, one mistake that can be seized on by a gullible press who doesn't like you, and you'll be finished. Lord knows, the president's close to just letting your past sins all fall out, watching the chips drop all over the table, pardon be damned. The only thing saving you right now is the election. *When* it happens, when your past catches up to you," his eyes glowed with the certainty, "you won't want to be around humanity. You'll retreat somewhere quiet, maybe change your name, and become the hermit that your upbringing practically destined you to be." His eyes glimmered, and he practically crowed. "Oh, yes, I know all about you, Ms. Nealon. And the difference between us is that accusations made by you will fall on deaf ears while anything I say about you, no matter how trivial, will be swiped up like gold dust as long as it advances the narrative."

"The narrative, huh?" I asked. "I guess that makes you the storyteller." I took a step closer to him and watched his eyes widen slightly. I don't think he'd planned ahead before threatening me while alone in his office. "You know what another name for storyteller is?" I looked him dead in the eyes. "*Liar.*"

The doors behind me opened and I looked back to see the young lady who had shown me in, quivering like a leaf. I guess the bodyguards were still hoofing it up three flights of stairs. "I'll see myself out," I said and went for the side entrance, throwing it open with a delicacy that I certainly didn't feel at the moment. A snake like Weldon would use any property damage I caused against me, though, and I knew that in some reptilian, calculating part of my brain.

I met the bodyguards on the stairwell, almost to the door. All it took was a look and they stood aside, flattening against the wall with expressions that told me everything about the look on my face. I guess I've still got it.

28.

Augustus

A search turned up nothing on a second Cavanagh facility in the Atlanta area. I did another for Cavanagh bioresearch, and then did five searches for variations on that theme. I was walking the whole time, not really paying full attention to what I was doing, playing Edward Cavanagh's biography (which, incidentally, turned up first in the results when I searched for "Cavanagh bio") in my head as I went.

Edward Cavanagh was a mechanical engineering guy all the way, from his roots to his education to his corporation. Cavanagh Tech was a mechanical concern. They built processors, automation systems, they had software divisions in Seattle and Silicon Valley. Factories all over the world that built hardware, and server farms all over the country that provided storage. They even had facilities in Texas, Florida and California that were fighting it out with SpaceX and others for who was going to build the next big rocket. Cavanagh had his fingers in tons of pies because his fortune allowed him to.

But I'd never heard even a hint that one of his pies crossed out of his core competency, the world of mechanical engineering. And he'd even said this very morning something to that effect when he was throwing kind words my way about my new metahuman status.

But Roscoe Marion, murder victim at the hands of a metahuman, apparently worked for a Cavanagh lab where bioresearch was being done.

Or was about to be. That was a possibility.

Still, this made no sense. Why hide it if he was getting into that branch of the sciences? This was not a secret that would be easy to keep, after all. Edward Cavanagh's finances were under constant scrutiny, because people wanted to know what he was investing in so they could jump in with him. He didn't get to be a billionaire in his thirties by throwing his money around stupidly, after all. He got returns.

I tried to apply Occam's Razor to what I was seeing here, and came back with this: it wasn't out yet because he wasn't ready to announce it. If he had a biological research division, maybe it was a new acquisition. Maybe it was something that was about to go big, and he didn't want to jump the gun on it, let his thunder (uh, metaphorical, I hoped) get stolen before he was ready to let everyone know.

Yeah, that was the simplest explanation for why a man with that high of a profile would try and hold something back.

But it wasn't the only one. Especially since he'd just lied about it to my face.

I was halfway across a street when I got this little tingle that ran down my spine, telling me something was … off. I couldn't tell if it was the noise of the city, the smell of the exhaust of the cars passing by, or just a general sense of malaise, but it was like a finger run right down my back unexpectedly, a caress from the touch of a hand unseen, and I could almost feel the shivers run across my scalp.

I spun in a circle and took in the scene behind me. It wasn't good, and it was a total surprise.

There was a guy with a ski mask. All I could tell was that he was black, and big, and he looked like he'd been trying to sneak up on me. He almost made it, too, was about ten feet away when I turned and saw him. We both froze for a second, and I took in the details around him. He'd crossed the parking lot of a shut-down gas station to get to me, and there were five other guys dressed similarly coming up behind him with automatic weapons.

"Oh, hell," I said as he pulled up his hands—way faster than a human could have done it. My eyes followed the motion to a shotgun clutched in his massive hands and fired from the hip, belching fire and death at me from a mere ten feet away.

29.

Sienna

"What the hell were you thinking?" Calderon asked me, more than a little put out. I'd come back to the station to talk to him, to check up on his progress, if any, regarding Joaquin Pollard. I hadn't even gotten out so much as a "hello" before he unloaded on me. Apparently in the five minutes it took me to fly from Cordell Weldon's office to his precinct house, the crap had already rolled downhill from the mayor's office to the chief of police and straight through Calderon's door, sweeping him off his feet.

"I was thinking, 'Oh, hey, a lead, maybe I should follow this where it takes me,'" I said. "Apologies if I screwed up on that. Maybe I should have gone the other direction and thought, 'Maybe I should just bury this and never think about it again.'"

Calderon put his hand over his head, a perfect facepalm that I could tell he was using to stall while he formulated a response that didn't sound like complete bullshit dropped from on high. "You can't go after a city councilman like Weldon—hell, leave off the City Council part and just say he was a powerful wheel in the community. You can't just walk into his office and throw down on him like that."

"In fairness, I didn't actually accuse him of anything," I said. "But he got real defensive after the first part of our conversation went south. Enough to make me think he's guilty of something."

"Of course he's guilty of something," Calderon said, like he was explaining this to a child. "All politicians are criminals. You should know that! And you can't come to Atlanta and accuse Cordell Weldon of something like this—"

"I told you, I haven't accused him of anything!" I lost my temper a little in my response. "Well, other than being a shakedown artist."

"You accused him of what?" Calderon's eyes were as big as the bottoms of pill bottles.

"Well, he was kind of trying to shake me down," I said. "But it's not like I accused him of complicity in the murder of Flora Romero or any of the others."

"That's good," he said, and I could almost taste the sarcasm.

"I might have called him a liar, though."

He made a noise full of utter frustration, and his face went into his palms again, hiding his eyes from me. When he came out, he was just looking at me with a jaded look, like he expected nothing and was getting exactly that. "You don't even care whose toes you step on anymore, do you?"

"I tried to tread lightly," I said, "but he decided to be ungainly during our dance, so I stopped watching where I stepped."

"Well, you ended up stepping in *it*," he said. "I can't help you any more. The chief has pulled me off the case. I was already getting flack from my captain, but I was trying to shoehorn in a look at Joaquin." He tossed a file on the desk. "Now that's done. And you're persona non grata around here."

"You're going to deny a federal agent assistance that she's asking for on a murder investigation?" I looked at him with a dark look of my own, an icy chill running through my voice.

"I don't think I'm going to have to," he said, crossing his arms. "I suspect you're going to get yanked back to your headquarters by a hard jerk of the leash in less than an hour."

I almost snarled my reply. "This bitch don't wear a leash." And I turned away from him before I said anything else that might make the situation worse. I was really good at that, and I'd liked him, so I decided to quit while I was only a few miles behind.

"Sienna—" he started, and it suddenly sounded like every phone in the room buzzed at once, with a few rings thrown in for good measure. I spun and saw people ripping cell phones out of their holsters, getting to their feet.

Calderon finished reading his message first, and his eyes fell right to me. "Augustus," he said, sounding a little choked. "911 call—someone saw a guy getting shot at by masked men, and the ground exploded—"

I didn't even wait for him to finish, I just flew out of the bullpen at speed and twisted skyward, into the blue, figuring if the ground was exploding somewhere near English Avenue, I'd see it from the air. I went supersonic and felt my hair whip in the wind as I charged toward the fight without any thought but to save Augustus's life—something that I had probably put in danger.

30.

Augustus

The street exploded around me as the shotgun went off, and I hit the ground so hard that I didn't quite know what was going on at first. It took me a moment to realize that the reason I'd hit the ground was that the street had been pretty much ripped up underneath me, every single piece of gravel and rock and dust from the asphalt torn out of the tar mixture, like someone had peeled a layer of the road off. When it had come up it knocked me over and formed a hard wall around me in a semi-circle, a dense mix of the stuff all formed into a long rectangular shield that protected my front.

"What the—?" I heard a deep, pissed-off voice call out from behind the little wall I'd made. "Flank him!"

I was still down on a knee, staring at my impromptu shield, but I heard steps coming to my left and right. I reached out, this time consciously, and could feel the street around me, waiting my command. I tugged at it, and it fought back. The asphalt mixture held it down, grounded it, wouldn't let it go. I concluded that I must have absolutely lost it when I pulled it all up before. Panic aided my strength, clearly, so I panicked again and ripped at the asphalt around me, trying to swivel the shield I already had and pull it closer.

Gunfire flew all around me, chipping away at my impromptu shield. The force of the bullets sent fragments flying over my head. One of them hit the top of my head, and I could tell it drew blood. I was clenching my left fist, my proxy for holding the shield together in my mind, and it was working—for now.

It wasn't going to work much longer, though, because I knew that they were circling even now. Once they got around the side of my little half circle, I was gonna catch a bullet to the head, and that was fact.

I tried to rip more pavement up, but it was still resisting. I threw some fear into it, felt it give a little, heard the sound of concrete cracking around in front of me and to the sides. "Whoa!" I heard someone shout as the ground shifted.

"Hurry!" Someone else called back, and I knew I didn't have much time.

I reached down deep and pulled, feeling the strain. I could sense the dirt underneath the road so much more strongly than the fragments in the pavement. Those felt like arms in a straitjacket, while the dirt beneath just felt like it was tamped down a bit. It was a difference in muscle strength, too; I felt like I was trying to lift the world when I was pulling on the road. I might have done it when the gun went off, but it was all due to instinct, that was for sure.

But the dirt beneath? That felt like a muscle I could flex, like a lever I could use to lift.

I pulled hard on just a small section of it and felt things shift again. I stumbled on the remaining layer of blacktop beneath me, the next section of the peeled onion I'd started ripping apart without even thinking about it. I held my hand aloft, though, and felt that dirt beneath, rock mixed in, felt it cry out to be released. I was just helping it, really, helping it after it had spent so long trapped, confined, compacted—

And I drove it up from the weakest spot I could find … the already damaged pavement beneath my feet.

A pillar of dirt broke through the asphalt like a park fountain bursting out of the ground. I could feel the fragments of the pavement crack and I drove them out as the dirt lifted me skyward. I launched into the air on a column of rock and ground, dragging my shield along with me. I rose ten, twenty, thirty feet, channeling it out and around me to protect my sides and back. The ground spewed forth enough to carry me up, and then I could feel it lose its strength. I'd overreached, spreading it out too far. Now I could feel empty air beneath me, and all I could think to do was throw dirt beneath, holding it in place for a few seconds as I started to stair-step my way back to the ground below.

I heard shots fired underneath me and realized I must have looked like a dirt cocoon making its way across the air, trailing and losing particulate matter with every step. I could feel the hard impact of bullets under my feet, and I knew someone was right there, trying to kill me.

I may not have been skilled, but necessity being the mother of invention, I came up with an idea pretty quick that filled my necessity—which was to not get shot and to not hurt myself while falling back to the earth.

I hardened the ground I was carrying beneath my feet, holding it together, and just let myself drop without trying to fall slowly by using my little tricks. I didn't have enough control to shape the dirt into anything other than a blunt object, and I'm not sure I would have wanted to, in any case. Either way, I fell a good twenty feet straight down and landed on someone, hard. The dirt absorbed most of the impact for me, and my legs took the rest like it was nothing. Fall like that would hurt most people.

But I wasn't most people anymore.

I pulled my dirt shield up around me, tightened back into my circle. People were still shooting at me. Impacts behind me felt like a shotgun, the ones to my left and right felt harder, bigger hits. Straight on bullets rather shotgun pellets. One of them hit close and blew dirt in my eye from the impact.

"Oh, shit!" I cried out, a little bit of panic squeezing out. I felt myself squeeze my powers, too. The ground exploded somewhere outside my shield, and I could feel a dozen little impacts hit the wall of dirt and gravel I'd put up. The bullets coming from that direction just stopped, and I wondered if I'd taken them out or just knocked them down for a minute.

I felt the shooting resume from both the other sources, and I could feel the impacts from the other handgun doing the most damage to my shield. I tried to calm my nerves, but I had a plan for this one, too.

I threw every bit of extra dirt I could muster toward my shield in that direction, and I took off at a flat run toward the shooter. I didn't possess any amazing amount of control, but I figured if maybe I could put out a low, flat scoop, like a bulldozer, maybe I could knock the guy off his feet by running at him. I shaped the rock as best I could while I was running at top speed. I was all turtled up, shielded from the world in every direction but up, but I could tell I was moving fast. Then I hit something, and I heard a thundering roar from above, and it felt like when you hit a bump in your car. Barely felt, but enough to know it happened.

There was a shriek followed by the sound of a body hitting the ground. I heard the rattle of a gun hitting pavement, and then silence for a minute. No more gunshots at all.

I stood there, facing in the direction of the shotgun guy's last … uh, well … shot. I spread my dirt around the whole shield and brought it down a couple inches. In the heat of the fight, I hadn't even realized that it had been like seven feet plus tall, me walking around like I was rolled up in a giant carpet. That top dirt was all wasted, so I brought it down and shaped it around my head so that there was only about five inches of clearance and it wasn't like me looking out a gun barrel anymore. Blue sky was overhead, the granules of dirt swirling around my face as my shield spun, active, waiting for the attack.

"Hey," a voice called from above, and I almost panicked again as I looked up by instinct, ready to throw something, anything at whoever was attacking me.

It was Sienna.

"Oh, thank God," I said, feeling my body relax a little.

She circled and came in for a landing. "What have you got?"

"Dudes with guns," I called to her out of the top of my little fortress. "Still a guy with a shotgun out there, I think."

She floated above me for a second, looking around. "Must have rabbited. No one here but dead guys."

"D—*what?*" My shield dissolved in an instant, dropping to the ground like a sandstorm that had just lost all its fury. It all fell in a weak ridge, a small mound no more than shin-high in a circle around me.

And beyond it, I saw … dead guys.

One of them looked like he'd been run over, and I realized he'd gotten crushed under the bulldozer action I'd planned to use to knock him off his feet. Three others were bloody as hell, looked like they'd gotten blown up or something.

Except there were pebbles and dirt all mixed in with the blood and the wounds. Like they'd gotten hit with a rock shotgun.

"Holy hell," I whispered, and I stared at the last of them. At least this one I could take no credit for, though it took me a moment to cipher that out.

"Well, well, well," Sienna said as she landed at my side, so softly I didn't even hear her feet crunch in the gravel that was spread everywhere from my destruction of the roadway. "This looks familiar."

One of the gunmen was lying flat, in the middle of the zone of destruction I'd created, but he had none of the signs of being run over or plowed down or blown up in an explosion of rock and dirt.

This one had burns to his face and neck that made him almost unrecognizable, like someone had come along with a blowtorch and just cooked off half his face.

"Looks like you've just had a run-in with our infamous lightning man," Sienna said, staring at the blackened body before us, which lay there like a clue we hadn't expected. "And maybe, if we're lucky, he's one of the ones that didn't survive."

31.

Sienna

The police showed up and cordoned off the area a few minutes later. Augustus had completely torn up the road, leaving at least two potholes that would be enough to destroy an Abrams tank if it wandered into them by accident. I didn't feel compelled to bring that up to the guy, though, because he'd taken the news that he'd killed people while trying to defend himself … poorly.

I could sympathize. I could almost, barely, remember a time before I'd killed people, when I felt pretty decidedly against the whole thing. I'd gotten a taste of it at first, found it unpalatable, and then decided to go in the opposite direction until a frost giant named Erich Winter had pushed me firmly the other way. By the time the war was over, I'd done enough killing that I only held back out of expediency.

Now that my ass seemed to be perpetually in the fire for some perceived wrong, I wasn't feeling an overabundance of restraint when it came to all forms of violence. The Russian situation had carried with it an enormous body count, and that little factoid hadn't been used as anything other than a cudgel to reinforce what a relentless killer I was. But I didn't really care at this point. My soul was appropriately calloused by now, I supposed.

Augustus didn't have that. He was sitting on a curb with

his head between his hands while the cops and medics swarmed everywhere. I'd already ruled out the idea that lightning man was among the dead because they were all wearing cloth gloves and none of them showed signs of burning where electricity would have passed through, but I was holding back on telling him that, since he probably had enough on his mind.

The police lights were flashing all around us, and Calderon was making the rounds with a sour look on his face. He hadn't talked to me yet, but I presumed that was going to be a marvelous conversation, one which would lead anyone watching to the conclusion we hated each other rather than that we had really quite enjoyed each other's company less than twelve hours ago. Things moved quickly for me, I guess. Always in the wrong direction, but quickly.

I shuffled toward Augustus. I didn't mind complete silence when I was alone, but it sorta drove me nuts when I was standing in the middle of a crowd. And it was getting crowded, to the point where I could actually feel the souls of the people moving around me, like they were all within arm's reach and I could just reach out and grab them one by one.

Which was not a power I had, thankfully, but it did make me want to just start grabbing people and drinking them dry of their souls. Never a good sign.

"How are you holding up?" I asked him, almost as much to distract myself as to be nice. I was still a little tentative after our previous conversation, after all. Gun shy, I think you could call it. I doubted he wanted much from me at the moment.

"I just killed those guys," he said, shaking his head.

"First time's always rough," I said, standing over him and watching the scene. Calderon didn't even look at me.

"Oh, you remember that, do you?" He was appropriately snotty for the situation, I thought, so I didn't hold it against him.

"Somewhere in the recesses of my memory, yeah," I said.

He looked up at me. "What about you?" he asked, a little grudgingly. He genuinely was a nice guy, and he didn't even have to pretend.

"I've had better days," I said.

"Oh, yeah? Still stinging from our argument?"

I eyed him. "It was not my favorite conversation ever, but I've had two I'd class as worse since then."

He looked up at me and frowned. "What happened?" He nodded his head toward Calderon. "You and the brother over there have a tiff?"

I sighed. "It wasn't a tiff, okay? It had nothing to do with us sleeping together." I snorted. "Hell, if I could have told Cordell Weldon I slept with Calderon, maybe he wouldn't have accused me of being a racist." Nah. He still would have.

"Wait, whut?" Augustus's eyebrows rocketed skyward. "What'd you do to Mr. Weldon?"

"I didn't *do* anything to him—"

"That man is a community leader," Augustus said, about half a step from bawling.

"That man is piece of human excrement," I said. "He tried to shake me down."

"*What?*"

"He implied," I said, choosing my words carefully, "that if I didn't get some agency money and time and cooperation to flow in the direction of his organization, he was going to aid the press in vilifying me even further by saying I was a racist. I can't imagine what the next accusation to come my way will be. What's left? Bestiality?"

"Cordell Weldon did not threaten to paint you as a racist," Augustus snapped.

"I think he did," I said. "And he got really defensive when I even brought up the fact that Flora Romero's shelter was one that his organizations run, and that at least two of our skeletons were regulars at."

Augustus just blinked. "I can't imagine why he would be upset at that implication."

"He didn't get upset," I said, "he got irate and defensive, like I'd just tried to shake *him* down. And then he proceeded to call the mayor, who called the chief of police, who then crapped from his higher perch upon Calderon, and *et voila*, here we are."

"You are the cause of most of your own damned problems," Augustus said. "Didn't anyone ever teach you how to approach things with some subtlety?"

"Not really," I said. "But I fail to see what was subtle about Weldon suggesting to me that the 'race image problems' I haven't actually had yet could just be vanished away with some money pushed in his direction."

"Maybe you should hire more black people," Augustus snapped. "Just a solution off the top of my head."

I felt my eye twitch. "You want a job?"

"With you? Hell, no."

"Well, if you run into any more African-American metahumans, send them my way," I said. "Personally, I haven't had much luck locking down all three of those categories since the war, but then I've also seen a fairly big outflux of my white employees too."

"Maybe it's your managerial style," he said. "Did you learn it from Sun-Tzu's *The Art of War*?"

"Sun-Tzu actually had some pretty good advice in there, and no—no, I did not."

"I see you two are picking up where he and these clowns left off," Calderon said, stepping up to us right in the middle of our little quibble.

"We haven't started ripping up the streets and throwing fire at each other yet," I said, "so count your blessings."

"Have you had a phone call from your headquarters yet?" Calderon asked me, looking daggers in my direction.

I fished it out of my pocket. Twelve missed calls. "Probably a few," I said.

"Don't you think you should answer them?"

"I feel like I need a vacation," I said, smiling sweetly.

"Minnesota is so cold, you know."

"It's June."

"Yeah," I said, "it's like … 75 degrees there right now. Frigid."

"You aren't going to find anything else here but problems," Calderon said. "Your investigation? Has turned up nothing except a lot of corpses I can't get answers on. I would have been better off if you hadn't showed up. This whole thing is radioactive now."

"Good news," I said. "Radioactive doesn't bother me. Advanced healing takes care of it, see. Let me handle it all."

Calderon made a grunt of frustration and stalked off. "You really do bring out the worst in people, don't you?" Augustus asked as we watched him storm away.

"You should see me and my boss," I said.

"I don't think I want to," he said. "I live a nice, drama-free life. Or I did, until—"

"I showed up?" I suggested, heading that one off before he could get it out.

"Until I developed these powers," he said. "Without them, I'd be at work right now." He paused, and I caught a hint of uncertainty about something from him.

"What?" I asked.

He hesitated, like he was trying to decide. "I talked to Roscoe Marion's widow."

"And?"

"I used to work with him," he said, "on the line at Cavanagh Tech—the factory."

I waited. "Uh huh …"

"She said he was still working at Cavanagh," Augustus said, "but he'd gotten promoted. Trouble is, he didn't get promoted the traditional way, to, like, line lead or super. She said he got promoted to work in an off-site lab working with biological research."

I shrugged. "Still not seeing it."

"Cavanagh Tech doesn't do bioresearch. They're a

mechanical and software tech company." He raised his hands in an expansive shrug. "It's not listed on the website, and Edward Cavanagh himself said to me this morning that they weren't in the biotech arena."

It was my turn to frown. "You called him and asked him this?"

"No," he said. "He came over to my line and offered me help, gave me time off, complimented me and—I don't remember how it came up, but he said something like, 'I wish we were in the biotech business so we could'—partner on something, maybe. I don't know."

I felt a rising tide of surprise. "That's really interesting, because apparently the Atlanta press is speculating I want to meet Edward Cavanagh and beat his ass at the moment—"

"Is there anyone whose ass you don't want to beat?" he asked in exasperation.

"Yours, until just now," I quipped. "But listen—the reason why they think I want to beat his ass is because apparently Cavanagh Tech developed that chemical weapon that suppresses meta powers."

"That thing they used at your headquarters?" he said. "That thing the Russians stole?"

"Exactly," I said. "So tell me how your mechanical engineering company developed a bioweapon if they don't work in that realm? Because I doubt it was a printer toner experiment gone wrong."

Augustus held a hand up over his mouth, face locked in serious thought. "Damn," he said quietly.

"Damn, indeed," I said and noticed for the first time a thin puff of black smoke in the distance, to the west. It was a little pillar, stretching up into the hot midday sky. The sun was beating down on me, making me sweat, and that black smoke just seemed … out of place somehow. I took a sniff and it came home for me at once—something was on fire.

"Hey," I called out to the nearest cop, "what's up with the fire?" I pointed to the column of smoke in the distance.

"House fire south of 278," he said nodding his head. "Four alarm."

Augustus's head came up at that, and he launched off the curb like his ass was spring-loaded. "Where is it? Exactly?"

The cop just shrugged. "Not sure. Somewhere near Pelham, I think."

I saw Augustus's pleading eyes turn toward me, and he whispered only one word, one that told me immediately what he was thinking: "Momma."

I scooped him up with one arm and launched us both into the air, centering on that column of black smoke and racing toward it, hoping that what we found wouldn't make things even worse for him than they already were.

32.

Augustus

The wind rushed past my face, and I didn't even care that I was being carried along by a girl that was, like, five foot nothing. I could see the billowing smoke ahead as we shot across the sky, and the closer we got, the surer I was, until we finally came down for a gentle landing on the street in front of my house.

The place was engulfed, fire raging out of every window, black smoke clouding the air and making its way up in thick, continuous bursts. I started toward the front door, which was practically gushing flame, and felt a strong hand on my shoulder that threw me backward in something less than a courteous manner.

"Hold on," Sienna said, and she rose into the air as I watched, biting back a stream of curses and a desire to shove her in reprisal. She floated toward the fire and her hands came out. "Gavrikov," she whispered, so low it was barely audible over the howl of sirens and cries of the crowd.

The fire crackled and burned, a wave of heat coming off my home like I'd stepped too close to an open oven. Sienna hovered there for a moment, and then I saw what she was doing as her powers started to work.

The fire was sucked toward her like she'd grabbed all the oxygen in the area and fed it along a pre-assigned path. It shot toward her hands, blazingly fast, curling like fiery tornadoes as it made its way toward her, swirling into her palms and dissipating into smoke as it made contact with her flesh. Her hands burned like they were aflame as she drew it all in, every bit of it, and I watched a tongue of flame the size of a concrete pillar fork off from the rest and head toward her face. She breathed it in like a reverse dragon, drawing it to her and out of my home. It came from every window, from the roof, and she pulled every bit of it into her body as she hovered there.

Within sixty seconds, every bit of the fire that had raged in my home was gone, and all that was left was the billowing black clouds, which still came, but lighter now, deprived of their heat source.

The crowd was quiet, the roar of the flames was gone, and as Sienna fell to a knee on the lawn, I heard a different buzz start. It sounded like amazement at first, surprise, and it was and startled. It was a chorus of voices talking with each other, over each other, around each other, in a way I hadn't been able to distinguish before I got my powers.

"That's her—"

"—she put it out—"

"—you see what she did to that dude in New York?"

"—wouldn't want to cross her—"

"—she's a bad, bad bitch—"

"Why doesn't she do that more often? Seems like she could help a lot more people putting out fires than—"

"—read about her in that magazine, how she—"

"—but she sure doesn't look like Katrina Forrest, amirite?"

"Are you okay?" I asked, taking a couple steps toward her.

"I oughta be asking you that," she said, and then she coughed, a long, hacking cough that belched out black smoke from her mouth.

"I'm not the one who just inhaled a whole house full of

carcinogens," I said.

"I did not," she said, trying to get back to her feet.

"You realize that the fire was burning like—the cleaning fluid under the sink, the insulation in the walls, the treatment on the wood they built the house with? So … yeah, you kinda did."

She coughed again. "Should have just used the hands, I guess. Felt like breathing in the fire would dispel it faster." She looked at me. Her eyes were bloodshot. "What about your mom?"

"I'm over here," came Momma's voice from behind me. I spun and she was there, a blanket around her even though it was ninety degrees outside. "I'm fine."

I felt a quick rush of relief that was replaced by panic. "Where's Jamal?"

"Wasn't home," she said, shaking her head. "I checked his room before I got out."

"Where is he?" I asked, taking a few steps closer.

"I don't know," she said. "But he's not here."

I felt my legs give out, and I sagged to the lawn, felt the strange embrace of the dirt as I touched down. I could feel it, could feel it from inside as well as against my legs. My butt hit the ground hard, but the ground pushed back, cushioning my fall.

The firefighters and the crowd kept their distance, that same chatter rising now. No one could ignore it as it was, but when I looked at Sienna, she wore an expression of strange indifference. "Now are you all right?"

I put my head in my hands, in exhaustion and relief. "Man. Yesterday was the best day of my life. This one … it's the worst."

She ambled over and wearily sat down beside me. "Yeah. This …" she waved a hand to encompass the wreckage of my house. "It's … terrible."

"I don't think terrible quite covers it," I said, looking at the wreckage of my house. "We've lived in this house my whole life. This was …" I felt a prevailing sense of emptiness, a sick feeling in my stomach, as I stared at the smoking wreckage, "… this was my home."

"Yeah," I said. "It's tough."

"How would you know?" I snapped.

She raised an eyebrow at me. "You know when the press first filmed me? At my house, where I'd just had a climactic battle with Sovereign that ended in a gigantic hole in my childhood home from basement to roof?"

"Oh," I said, feeling a little deflated. "Yeah. Maybe you do know." I put my head down. "Is that even covered by insurance?"

She sounded pained when she answered. "Meta damage is currently being argued as 'act of god'—little g—and headed toward the Supreme Court next year, probably."

"Worst day," I said, moaning. "Worst. Day. Ever."

"You're alive," she said, still sitting next to me. "Your family is alive. And if you were looking to prove yourself a hero, you're certainly being given ample chance, and so far you've come up aces."

"Aces?" I raised my head to look at her with incredulity. "I just killed people!"

"You did what?!" Momma called from behind me.

"Nothing!" I shouted back.

"Faceless flunkies," she said, dismissively. "They always get killed. It's a rule, hard and fast, and I didn't make it up. Watch any action movie."

"Oh, come on," I said. "That doesn't make it right."

"All right, fine," she said. "Look … here's the thing about heroes and what you've got here … they're self-sacrificing."

"You say that like you know it from experience." I was about two steps from just curling up on the lawn in a fetal position and calling it a day. Let the earth wrap me in its tender embrace and rock me to sleep.

She seemed a little more reserved when she spoke again. "Look, I know who I am, and I know who you thought I was before you met me …" she sighed. "I'm not a hero. But I have worked with people who have those qualities. My brother. A guy named Breandan who died …" she got quiet, "… to protect others. And … my mom." She almost sounded like she choked a little on that bit. "Sometimes being a hero means giving of yourself in ways that you don't want to give. Your time. Your relationships." All that snark and irony she usually spit out with every word was gone right now. "Maybe even, someday, your life.

"See," she went on, "for most people, heroes are an empty vessel. You pour your highest hopes into your heroes. You carve the virtues in their soul that you wish were in your own. Which is why, when they fail to live up to those … it's easy to hate them." I could tell she was aiming for cool indifference, but failing. Her voice was thick with emotion.

"Not everyone hates you," I said. It was the only thing I could think of.

"It doesn't matter," she said. "I'm not a hero. That ship sailed long ago, and I chose to be a … I don't even know anymore. Not a hero. But you … you could be one."

I blinked. "Yeah?"

"You certainly have more of the go-to qualities than I do," she said. "You were actually trying not to hurt people, but you failed because of lack of control of your powers. Well, you can learn control. And if you accidentally kill a few people who are actively trying to kill you, that doesn't make you … whatever I am. You just need to work harder to be able to live up to your ideals."

I nodded slowly. She spoke an odd brand of sense. "So," I said, "what do you think you are?"

"Question for another day," she said, "because right now I'm just a superior troublemaker and a piss-poor detective, in that order, and neither one of those is going to help us get to the bottom of this."

"Seems like we have a cast of suspicious characters," I said. "Cavanagh. Weldon—"

She smiled lightly but didn't look at me. "So you believe me on that one now?"

"Man, I don't know what to believe," I said. "Heroes are villains, villains are heroes. Down is up, up is down. This world has gone crazy."

"Same old world," she said. "Now you're just seeing it the way it is, maybe."

"Don't give me that depressing crap," I said. "You really are secretly a crabby old white man, aren't you, Obi-Wan?"

"Alec Guinness didn't seem too crabby," she said. "Ewan McGregor kind of did at times, though. And Yoda was like the quintessence of cranky, so … I'll take it, I suppose."

"So you're not a good detective," I said. "What do we do?"

"Hell if I know," she said. "The problem with having all this power is that I thrive on a clear enemy. Mysteries suck because they always deprive me of an obvious face to punch. You can't punch the face of an enemy you can't see."

"Yeah, I wouldn't go punching Cordell Weldon or Edward Cavanagh unless you have some compelling evidence," I said, cringing at the mere thought. "And how does lightning man tie into all this? And what are those guys up to?"

"This is why I don't function well under the same rules as the rest of you," she said, pushing her hair back. "It's just so much easier to start breaking random legs until someone cops to doing bad things." She paused. "And kinda more fun, too."

"Let's start with some questions, detective," I said, trying to steer her away from that course. "Momma!" I called, and she wandered over, still with the blanket around her shoulders. "What happened here?"

She stared at me like I'd gotten hit upside the head. "The house burned down, you fool boy. What does it look like?"

"How'd the fire start?" I asked.

"Oh," she said. "I don't know, exactly. I was watching

TV, and I thought I heard someone yelling outside. When I went to look out the window, there was someone in a hood that shot lightning out of their hands and onto the roof. It happened so fast." She shook her head.

"Lightning man burned my house down," I said. "He is definitely on my shit list now."

"Watch your mouth," Momma said.

"I feel like you're a little late to the game," Sienna said. "He's been on my shit list from the beginning."

Momma scowled at her. "If I had my soap, I'd be washing both your foul mouths out with it right now."

"Like you never swear," I said, drawing a spiteful look from her. My house just burned down. I was emotional.

"We've got Cavanagh and Weldon," Sienna said.

"Best buddies, I might add," I said. "Weldon convinced Cavanagh to build his factory here."

"Weldon repays the favor by giving Cavanagh access to test subjects from his homeless shelter?" she asked.

"That's real dirty," I said, "but plausible, maybe."

"What did you just say?" Momma asked. "Did you just accuse Mr. Cavanagh and Mr. Weldon of something? Boy, did you not ever learn not to shit where you eat?"

"Language, Momma," I said with a grin that I could see just burned her up. She fumed. Momma did not believe that what was good for the goose was good for the gander.

"So how are Roscoe Marion and Kennith Coy connected to Flora Romero and Joaquin Pollard?" Sienna asked.

The smoke got in my eyes, making me rub them while I thought. "Flora Romero finds out what Weldon's doing, and threatens to blow the whistle. Cavanagh and Weldon send Pollard, a criminal on their payroll, to kill her, then cover the killing by killing the killer." I paused. "I feel tongue-tied after saying killer that many times in a row."

"Oh, Lord," Momma said. "I'm not hearing any of this."

"Reasonable supposition," Sienna said. "So how are Coy and Marion related?"

"Marion worked for Cavanagh at this new lab," I said, brainstorming. "Maybe he saw something he wasn't supposed to."

"And Coy?" she asked.

"Ex-criminal, like Pollard," I said, shaking my head. "I don't know. We're missing something."

"We're missing a lot of somethings," she said. "Like motive for Weldon and Cavanagh to experiment on those homeless guys. I mean, I know in the movies it's cool to just target the nearest rich guy or politician in a massive conspiracy, but here in the real world we need a stronger through-line for them to act like assholes if we're going to prove they're committing murder."

"Prove what?" I turned to see that detective, Calderon, standing there behind us. He just looked jaded as hell, shaking his head. "Some wild-ass conspiracy linking two of the most powerful men in the city?"

"We were just spitballing," Sienna said, suddenly sitting up a lot more attentively now that Calderon was here.

"I heard," Calderon said, shaking his head. "I heard it all, and I have to tell you … at least you've got a good grasp of how gaping the holes in that fantastical plot are."

"They are gaping," she admitted, "but since it's not you investigating them, I guess it doesn't really matter, because you're not the one who has to find the evidence to fill them."

He just looked tired and shook his head. "There is no evidence to fill a hole that big, and you're not going to have a chance to look for it in any case."

"You planning to obstruct my search for justice, detective?" Sienna asked, staring him down.

"I'm not going to do anything," Calderon said. "Except warn you that the mayor of Atlanta is having a press conference in an hour to announce that you're being asked to leave the city. The White House is going to have one of their regularly scheduled briefings about thirty minutes later, and when the question comes up, it'll be mentioned that you've just decided to not follow any orders sent your way by your head of agency." He turned his head, shaking it all the while. "Go home, Sienna. Go home before you get yourself fired. Or worse … before they get the governor to call the National Guard out to go head-to-head with you."

She was on her feet in a hot second. "This isn't right, Calderon, and you know it. Something's going on here, and Weldon is pulling every string he has a grip on to shut us down."

When Calderon turned around, he had the look of a man who'd just given up. "Maybe you're right. Maybe he is. But you've gone and stirred up such a hornet's nest that if there ever was proof for what you're accusing the man of, you'll never find it before it gets destroyed." He shook his head. "Good luck, Sienna."

"Good luck?" she snorted. "That's all you have to say?"

"It's all I've got to give you," he said and started away again. "And if you keep doing the same crazy-ass crap you've been doing … you're damned sure going to need it."

33.

Sienna

Calderon's words burned like the fire I'd absorbed earlier, took the feelings I'd been harboring inside—all the insecurity about not being a hero, about not being good enough to figure this out—and dumped gasoline all over it. I've been accused of being stubborn—an accusation which I've never denied—but in that moment, my motivation cranked from "I need to solve this mystery because it's important to maintain order and justice," to "Fuck you all, I'm going to expose this travesty and then cram it all down your throats like bad sushi just to watch you choke on it while it's going down and vomit it up later."

It might also have activated this tiny little part of me that thrived on spite, but we'll talk about that later. (It's not that tiny.)

"Darrick Cary," I said, and Augustus turned his head to look at me.

"What about him?" he asked.

"I had a conversation with him earlier," I said. "He seemed to indicate there was something about Cordell Weldon that I wouldn't believe if he told me."

Augustus eyed me. "And?"

"And like the *Ghostbusters* motto says, 'We're ready to believe you,'" I said. "I want to find him, and I want him to talk, and I want to take his words and parlay them into a spear with which I can gut Cordell Weldon and Edward Cavanagh in a public forum."

Momma's eyes got wide with panic, and I'll admit I'd forgotten she was there for a minute. "Oh, Lord, please tell me you're not being literal."

"She's not being literal, Momma," Augustus rushed to assure her. His eyes ticked back and forth in thought. "Probably. Probably not being literal."

"Oh, Lord," Momma said, and I worried for a second that she was going to collapse on the lawn. "Oh, sweet Jesus, deliver me from this, my hour of trouble."

"Problem is now," Augustus said, "how do we get to Darrick? Because I'm guessing after your conversation with him—if it went anything like the ones I saw you have with people—he'll be about halfway to Memphis by now."

"Hah," I said as I pulled out my phone, "you underestimate my skill with people."

Augustus just gave me a look. "I thought I was being fairly generous, to be honest. I know he drives a Corvette. He's probably actually halfway to California by now."

"Oh, shush," I said as the phone rang. I had to hope that my persona non grata-ness had not been fully communicated to my own organization yet.

"Hey, Sienna," J.J. said in that high voice as he picked up, "I heard you're, like, on the lam or something."

"Yes, I'm a veritable tzatziki sauce," I said, getting a weird look from Augustus. "I need your help, J.J."

"Of course you do," he said, like it was the most natural thing in the world. "Thing is, I'm not supposed to help you. I'm supposed to transfer your call straight to Director Phillips."

I stood there in the middle of Augustus's lawn with the scorched-out remains of his house in front of me, stink of smoke heavy in the air. "And are you going to do that, J.J.?"

"Hellz to the no," J.J. said. "As we speak I'm erasing all

trace of this phone call from your records and mine, though, just to be safe. I don't really *want* to lose this job, but if I get caught by the brainless trust around here, I so deserve it and have like, five way better offers lined up out in the private sector doing soulless work anyway."

I thought about that for a second and just went ahead and bit. "So, why do you stay with the agency then?"

"Because sometimes I get to do really awesome things that aren't really in the bounds of what is, strictly speaking, 'legal.' And my anus is just too tender and virginal to chance prison. So," he said, "what exciting bit of almost or complete illegality am I performing today?"

"I need to find a guy," I said. "His name's Darrick Cary, and he drives a brand new red Corvette."

"Uh huh, uh huh," he said, and I could hear him pecking away at the keys. "Is Mr. Cary going to come to a black-licorice-bitter end?"

I frowned. "Black licorice isn't really bitter. It just tastes like—I dunno, probably like your tender and virginal anus." That one earned me another "WTF," look from Augustus.

"I'm just asking," J.J. said, "because if he's driving a Corvette, they've got this security vulnerability that I can hack, and it could totally look like an accident when he plows into a telephone pole at sixty. Sometimes air bags just don't deploy. It happens."

"No!" I said, a little too fervently. "Ah … no, J.J. I appreciate the offer, but I don't …" I lowered my voice. "Did you just offer to kill someone for me? Because that's worrisome." Worrisome? There might have been a time when I considered it awesome, actually. What was wrong with me?

"Technically, the velocity would kill him," J.J. said, a little too breezy for even my taste, "but no, I wouldn't do it myself. I'd basically send you an app that would let you do it with the press of a few buttons, thus keeping my hands mostly clean of human deaths. I kinda prefer to empower others rather than do it all for them. Teach a man to fish and all that."

My head was spinning from the whole conversation and its implications. "Can you locate this guy for me or what?"

"I already did," he said. "He's like … hmm … two miles from your phone, to the east. I'm in his car's system. Want me to send him into a brick wall at a gentle twenty miles per hour? Activate his windshield wipers and make him think he's got a haunted … uhh … carburetor?" He lowered his voice like he was talking to himself. "I so do not know cars."

"Just tell me where he is and get ready to apply the brakes," I said and looked at Augustus, who was frowning at me. "But … gently."

"Wow," he said, "it's like a whole new you, but okay! I'm ready to apply the brakes in a slow, methodical fashion when you say to."

"Let's go, hero," I said, gesturing to Augustus, who warily stepped close to me. I threaded an arm around him like he was the little spoon and used the other to keep the phone to my ear.

"This is so awkward," he said.

"Think about how I feel," I said as we lifted into the air, "I'm face to back of the shoulder blades with you."

"Are you flying?" J.J. asked. "Never mind, I see it on the scope now. Wheeeee! Flying! I'm pretending I'm right there with you instead of sitting in my office, wasting away under the command of morons who don't like or appreciate me."

"You got a plan for this?" Augustus asked as the wind whipped past us. I maintained an iron grip on his chest as we arced toward downtown Atlanta's massive skyline. That cylindrical building right in the middle stood out to me for some reason.

"You know my plan," I said.

"Find Darrick and make him cry until he tells you every seedy thing he's ever even thought about?"

"Why mess with a strategy that works?" I asked, slightly

amused.

"Ooh, sounds fun," J.J. said over the phone. "He's about eight hundred meters ahead of you, going down an alley."

"This is not a man who likes to step into the light," I muttered.

"That makes him smarter than the average dealer," Augustus said. "Though his choice of car seems like a lightning rod for the police. That brother has to get pulled over all the time."

"Then let's make this traffic stop memorable," I said, catching sight of the red Corvette moving below. "J.J … apply his brakes. Carefully."

"Because you don't want to hurt him, right?" J.J. asked. "For the interrogation?"

"Also," I said, "it's a really pretty car."

I watched the Corvette come to a gradual halt, screeching a little as it jerked to a stop. I was only about fifty feet above him at that point, staring down into the car. I couldn't see him, but I imagined Cary's face as his car stopped responding to him. "Can you kill the ignition, J.J.?"

A hard laugh came through the phone. "I can switch his radio to play something appropriately eerie, too, if you'd like. You know, set him up for the intimidation to come."

"Go for it," I said and hung up. The Corvette was squarely in the middle of a long alleyway, buildings on either side. I dropped Augustus over the roof of one of them. "Stand back and watch," I said, "that way you'll have plausible deniability if anything goes wrong."

"Plausible whaaaa—AHHHHH!"

I dropped him the last ten feet and he landed in a roll. Clearly he still wasn't entirely used to his meta abilities.

"All right," I said and altered my course to take me right in front of the Corvette—again. Then I cut out my powers just as I saw the door open and came smashing to the ground hard enough that the asphalt shook a little from my impact. When I stood, I saw Darrick standing at his door with his eyes wide open. Again. "Tell me what you know about that asshole Weldon," I said without preamble.

Darrick just stared at me, open-mouthed. "Yeah. Okay," he said, nervousness written all over his face, while the Halloween classic "Monster Mash" blared out of the Corvette's speakers so loudly that they could probably hear it back in the neighborhood.

Damn you, J.J.

34.

"See, the thing you need to understand about Cordell Weldon is," Darrick Cary said, leaning against the hood of his car, "is that whatever he says he's trying to do to help the 'Community,'" he held up air quotes, "is really just cover for Cordell Weldon doing whatever he can to help Cordell Weldon. Any good for the community is secondary and takes a back seat to advancing his own interests. That man has ties, see. Ties to Heshie LeRoux—you know who that is?" I shook my head.

"Organized crime boss here in the ATL," Augustus said. He'd climbed down a standpipe in a stubborn refusal to sit on the sidelines for this. Maybe he didn't trust me not to break Darrick's legs or something, I don't know. Maybe he was just feeling chatty.

"If there's a dirty deal being done in the Bluff, Cordell Weldon knows about it and has a piece of it," Cary said.

"If that was true, why hasn't some enterprising reporter made his name by blowing a big fat whistle on it?" Augustus asked.

Cary looked at him like he was stupid. "Are you out of damned mind? You know how fast Cordell Weldon can wreck a fool?" He snapped his fingers. "You'd get mashed before you even went to press. He has friends on all the editorial boards, and they all line up to kiss his ass. Not the left cheek, not the right cheek, but right in the middle, and they smile all the while and ask him if they can do it again."

I exchanged a look with Augustus, who looked extremely sour. "I am familiar with the effect he describes."

"You were beset by an uncontrollable desire to kiss Cordell Weldon's ass?" Augustus asked.

"This is a man with all the power," Cary said, saving me from coming up with a suitably bitter reply, "and he can call someone racist and have everyone in the world thinking they're a Grand Dragon of the Ku Klux Klan in about two seconds."

"That's bullshit," Augustus said. "Why doesn't anyone in the neighborhood call him out on it?"

"Because just like everywhere else in the world, he's turned on the money tap and let the green flow into the right pockets," Cary said, clapping his hands together. "This is not some new type of scam Weldon is running. In the history of the world, this is the oldest racket in the book. He's preying on the powerless, making speeches, stirring up shit, steering everybody in one direction while he veers his ass in the other while no one's looking. You call file that sumbitch under Charlotte N."

I stared at him blankly. "What?"

"Charlatan," Augustus said, sighing. "You know anything about how he's tied to Edward Cavanagh?"

"Cavanagh pays that man money," Cary said. "Same tie as everywhere else."

"But what does Cavanagh get in return?" I asked. "Assuming you're right."

Cary just laughed. "Something you governmental do-gooders never learn because you're so busy being up your own asses about serving the people is … money makes the world go round. Love? Pfffft. I love my family, but plenty of young men around here love their families. That doesn't put any food on the table or a roof over their head. Money does that. I don't know for sure that there's money passing back and forth between your boy Cavanagh and Cordell Weldon, but if you see a white man bringing his factory down into the Bluff rather than taking it Mexico or China, I would make my bet there's money in there somewhere for him. That's just the way it is, and you're a fool if you don't see it."

I looked at Augustus; he looked at me. "The lowlife makes a valid point," Augustus said.

"Don't you get all high and mighty with me, Augustus Coleman," Cary said. "We can't all get jobs at your white master's factory."

"Why not?" I asked, just ignoring the insulting part of that statement. Augustus looked irritable about it as well.

"Some of us got priors," Cary said. "Kind of makes it a little difficult to get a clean slate when the slate's already dirty as hell, you know?"

"Yeah, spare me your bullshit," Augustus said. "Some of us managed to keep out of the trouble you somehow steered your ass into."

"Well, congratulations on having your no-stink shit together earlier in your life than I did in mine," Cary said.

"If Weldon is somehow connected to supplying Cavanagh with warm meta bodies," I said, "maybe they tested the suppressant on them during development?"

Augustus nodded. "Could be. If this stuff came out in secret, maybe that's how they cooked it up. Found a couple of unregistered metas hiding, homeless, and rounded them up to be test subjects. That FDA approval is kind of hard to get, I guess."

Cary's looked like he was about to choke. "Did you say … suppressant? That shit that causes you people to lose your powers?"

"Yeah," Augustus said. "What do you know about it?"

Cary blinked, and I could see him doing the calculus in his head about whether to say anything or not. I stared him down, and saw him make the decision quickly. "Someone asked me about it recently is all. Not related to your current line of inquiry. Please, continue arguing amongst yourselves."

"I think we'll make that decision," I said, edging closer to him, "whether it's relevant or not. Someone asked you about suppressant? Like wanted to … what? Buy some?"

"Yeah," he said, backing away and into his car, his thighs bouncing off the hood lightly. "Maybe a little."

"Who?" I asked. "People don't just go looking for suppressant for innocent reasons. It doesn't provide any kind of high—"

"How would you know?" Cary asked, looking a little defensive. "I've seen people smoke some crazy shit when they can't get hold of—"

"Give me a name," I said.

"These are my customers," he said, protesting a little impotently. "I can't—"

"Let me tell you something else you can't do," I said, cutting him off. "Fly without a plane. Want me to prove that to you?" I pointed up.

Darrick Cary looked at Augustus, like he was considering his answer long and hard before it came out. "Taneshia. Taneshia asked about suppressant. She … wanted to know if I could get my hands on it." Cary bowed his head. "She wanted some real bad, and she was willing to pay to get her hands on it."

35.

Augustus

I stood there, stunned, Darrick Cary's admission still echoing in my ears. "Was she asking for it for herself or for someone else?" The question that popped out without me even having to think about it.

Cary sneered. "Wouldn't you like to know?"

Something about the way he said it, about the way he'd been acting throughout our whole conversation just set me off. I grabbed him by the front of his shirt and dragged him over to the wall of the alley and slammed his sorry ass up against the brick. His eyes went wide again, mouth fell open into an O as he realized for the first time that maybe he should have answered that differently.

"Whoa!" Sienna called from behind me.

"I can see that you *would* like to know," Cary said, humbled, "and I am willing to tell you in exchange for you not breaking my … anything."

"Start talking," I said, "I'll think about it."

"Well, the truth is that I don't know," he said, and I believed him because he was looking straight into my eyes and seemed like he might need to change his pants. "I didn't want to ask. I told her I doubted I could get it, but that I'd ask, and that was the end of that conversation."

"Starting to get an idea of why she hesitated to give me

your name and how to get ahold of you," I said.

"She gave me up?" Cary asked, suddenly outraged. "Oh, I ain't selling to her no more!"

"Let him go," Sienna said gently from behind me. "This doesn't really change anything."

"You don't think so?" I asked, turning to look at her. "There aren't that many metas around here. Either she was looking to suppress me, or she knows someone else she'd like to take out of the equation."

"Lightning man," she whispered.

"I'm thinking maybe lightning *woman*, now," I said. "No one ever saw it was a him. Only witness was a kid, and we got zero description of a face, just a hood. Could be anyone under that."

"Man, if Taneshia is shooting lightning and killing people, I really need to leave town now," Cary said. "She's going to know I gave her up."

"Anything else?" Sienna asked, coming up behind me. She waited a moment, and Cary tried to shrug in my grasp. It didn't go so well, but the point was made. "Let him go."

I dropped him and he slumped to the ground, catching his feet and trying to adjust himself in a faint effort to salvage his dignity from being manhandled by me. "I don't even think I want to know this, but … what are you fools planning to do?"

I looked at her. She looked at me. "Find evidence on Cordell Weldon," she said. "Drag him out into the light of day."

Cary shook his head, like he was just giving up on us and life. "A man like Cordell Weldon does not leave evidence. He's too smart for that. Fat cat like that will always land on his feet. Little cat like me? I got to stay low, keep to falls I can survive. Man. Such a waste. You got all this power in the world and nowhere to point it."

"I can point it at him," Sienna said, menacing.

Cary laughed, totally fake. "No, you can't, and that's the

point. Even you can't stand with the whole world against you. And, girl, they are turning that way. This is a whole new level of heat, one you are not ready for. Try and imagine them gassing you with that stuff and dragging your ass off to some prison. Or worse, digging a ditch somewhere and just letting you disappear—"

"Never gonna happen," she said.

"Pfffft," Cary said. "You're going to die a villain. They're going to make it happen, you just wait and see. They're setting up for it. And Cordell Weldon is going to dance on your grave."

"He's going to have a bitch of a time dancing once I break his legs," she said and grabbed me around the chest. We shot off into the sky, straight up. The wind buffeted us as we climbed into the warm midday air.

"Where we going?" I asked.

"I'm going to drop you off and you're going to try and find Taneshia," she said, loud enough to be heard over the howl of the air, "and then I'm going to make a slight … detour."

"Detour? Now?" I asked.

"No time like the present," she said.

I waited to see if she was going to say anything else. When she didn't, I just asked. "What is so damned important that you're going to take off in the middle of the investigation?"

"I need to talk to an old friend," she said, pensive in a way I wasn't used to seeing from her. "Someone who might be able to shed some light on how we go about ripping people of power out into the light of day."

"What makes you think that this person can help?" I asked as she arced us across the sky toward the black cloud that I now knew was my house. My home. A smoking wreck.

"Because," she said, as we started to come in for a landing, "if we're lucky, he'll be the next president of the United States." And she dropped me off and flew into the sky, vanishing from sight with a sonic boom that shook the world around me, leaving the spectators still standing on my lawn with their mouths agape.

36.

Sienna

It wasn't a long flight to Raleigh-Durham, North Carolina. It was somewhere around four hundred miles, and I did it in less than half an hour, hauling ass until I saw the skyline. It didn't take much effort on J.J.'s part to get me a copy of Senator Foreman's itinerary and to find his hotel. It was a big one, after all, a giant tower that overlooked downtown.

I approached carefully, dropping in from the clouds at highest speed and stopping in seconds before I splattered on the roof. It wasn't a comfortable landing by any means, but it kept me from being seen by any but the most observant, and even then they'd pretty much just see a blur falling out of the sky. The sound was somewhat obvious, but I couldn't do much about that. Breaking the sound barrier rattles windows, and that's just the way it is.

I entered the hotel from the roof stairs and immediately encountered the U.S. Secret Service. I raised my hands, badge in my left and looked the surprised guards in the eye. "Federal agent. I'm here to see Foreman," I said and let them scramble.

I stood in the stairwell with a steadily increasing number of black-suited agents while waiting. I figured they'd eventually reach critical mass and run out of places to stand, but somehow they all managed to continue giving me a wide berth while piling in. I took utmost care to avoid any threatening gestures while they kept their hands on their weapons. I was actually fortunate they hadn't drawn down on me. I'm sure it wasn't exactly protocol to let a super-powerful metahuman close to a presidential candidate, especially one who was likely having the word "rogue" thrown about in relation to her name. They kept it cool and cordial, though, and I did the same, extending them the professional courtesy of keeping my hands up and where they could see them, which allowed them the illusion of thinking me innocuous. The fact I could smoke everyone in the stairwell—literally, thanks to fire powers—in seconds was probably lost on them. It was a brave new world, and bodyguard training hadn't quite caught up to it.

I realized after a moment that the chill, calm atmosphere of everyone in the stairwell was probably not entirely natural, and shook my head, letting out a little sigh. I was definitely feeling calmer than I had been upon approach. Even identifying that as an unnatural feeling in my head gave it a little less power but didn't eliminate it. I didn't really want to be irate, so I just went with it in any case.

"This way, ma'am," one of the agents finally said, after a burst of staticky voice in his earpiece gave him his marching orders. He was a tall, light-blond-haired guy with freckles. They made way for me, though I don't know how. There had to be twenty agents in the stairwell by that point, and it wasn't exactly wide.

We descended three floors and entered a room that was completely controlled by the Secret Service. I'd heard they took over entire hotel floors during presidential and candidate visits, but it lent the whole place an ominous aura. Most hotels have a quiet hum to them, even when unoccupied. This one had four visible suited guardians standing sentry at various points in the hall. It cast a little bit of a pall over the place with them standing there like statues. Statues whose heads turned as I came in with my escort.

"Do I need to search you?" my escort asked.

"I'm carrying a Sig Sauer P227 in the small of my back," I said. "If you want it, you can have it, but it's the least lethal weapon in my arsenal."

He made his displeasure obvious with both a disapproving grunt and a reddening of his fair complexion. "I'm not leaving you alone with the senator, then."

"Dude," I said, "skip the interagency rivalry. If I wanted to kill him, I would have blown up the hotel and flown away before you even saw me coming. I'm here to talk, that's all. I've known the senator for years, Agent ...?" I waited to see if he was going to give me his name or play dick.

"Faraday," he said, conceding. "You understand my job here?"

"Protect the candidate," I said. "At all costs."

He paused at the entry to a door and stared right in my eyes. "Are you going to make my job more difficult in some way?"

"Nope," I said. "Just here to talk about items of mutual interest."

"You sure?" he asked. "Because I've heard things."

"Things?" I asked. "Like ... rules of grammar? Laws of the universe? Rumors? That sound a tire makes as it's deflating?"

He gazed at me suspiciously. "What are you talking about?"

"I don't know," I said and sighed. "I'm trying not to be an ass and it's really difficult. I could have made a really kick setup line there about 'the sound your balls make as they explode from the impact of my foot' against them. I'm just so used to pushing back against people who give me any hint of resistance on anything."

Agent Faraday stared at me, like he was trying to decide if I was bullshitting him. I was not. "That sounds like a personality disorder."

"Great, so we've got that in common. Can I see the

senator now?"

He made a grumbling noise and opened the door. "I'll be right outside," he said, loud enough that anyone in the room could hear him, too. He closed the door behind me.

I stood in a hotel suite that was ridiculously lavish. The curtains were drawn, though, giving it a half-lit effect, with only a little of the late afternoon light making its way through the sheers, casting things in shadow. My eyes adjusted quickly and fell on a shape in the corner, sitting in a chair almost against the wall, head tilted to look out the white lace curtains.

"Hello, Sienna," Senator Robb Foreman said in a low, ponderous voice. "It's been a while."

37.

Augustus

As soon as Sienna dropped me off, I was stalking down the street, my phone in hand. I wanted to have a conversation, and I didn't want to do it in public or anywhere Sienna could hear me. I watched her fly off into the sky, and once I was sure she was far enough away, I dialed Taneshia and listened to it ring.

And heard Alicia Keys's "This Girl is On Fire" blare out somewhere in the crowd behind me.

I turned as I felt my skin crawl like it wanted to shed me, chills running up and down even as the sun beat on me. I caught a glimpse of Taneshia, a flash of jet-black hair as she shoved her way through the crowd assembled outside my house. I didn't have to wonder too hard about why she was hiding, why she wasn't sitting on the back of the ambulance with Momma.

I went after her. Not too fast, not too slow. I didn't knock people over, linebacker my way through them. I pushed gently, said sorry, excused myself. People parted for me after a minute, realizing I was making my way through. I heard the words they said, the hushed gossip. It was all kind, too, not like I heard them say about Sienna. They knew me here, I was of the neighborhood, and I didn't have months of bad press dogging me like the grim reaper to drag my name down.

I made it out of the crowd and caught sight of Taneshia making her way determinedly to the end of the street. Shorty was hauling, too, so I hurried to catch up, breaking into a run. She scooted around the corner and I hustled after her, watching her cut across a lawn and disappear behind a brick house.

I came around it in a hurry and almost ran right into her. She was just standing there, waiting, hands in her pockets and eyes down. One look at her and I knew she knew, that she'd realized why I was calling, why I was following. I stood there looking at her, she stood there looking down at the brown and scraggly lawn we were standing on, and finally I spoke. "Why?" I asked.

"You're going to have to be more specific," she said, still not looking up.

"Why didn't you tell me?" I asked.

She hesitated, like she was wrestling with something. "More specific still."

I frowned. "How much are you keeping from me? Just tell me all of it."

She let out a sigh. "I can't do that, Augustus. Some of the secrets I'm keeping aren't mine to give away."

"Are you a meta?" I asked, staring her straight down.

I saw her bottom lip quiver. "Yes," she said.

"You can throw lightning," I said.

She held up a hand, and I watched electricity flow through it. "Yes."

I took a step back and felt myself clutch onto the ground in my head. I didn't know if I could throw up a shield that could protect me from lightning, and certainly not if I could do it fast enough to protect myself from her, but I wasn't going to die blindsided, even by a girl I'd known as long as I'd known Taneshia. "Why did you kill Roscoe Marion?"

She looked like she wanted to cry but there was not a tear in sight in her eyes. That girl was hard of heart, like she had a stone in her chest. "I didn't."

"Man, don't give me that!" I said, shaking my head. "Someone killed Roscoe with lightning, all right? And just a little bit ago, someone saved me with some lightning, too—"

"*That* was me," she said. "I knew you were going to stick your nose in this and get yourself in trouble, and I came to help you." She put up a hand and covered her eyes. "I didn't mean to—that guy … I didn't intend for him to … but I did …" She pulled her hand away. "He was the first person I ever killed, I swear."

"Then who killed the others?" I asked, and took a step closer to her.

"I … I can't tell you," she said, shaking her head. "I just … I can't. It's not my place to tell."

I stood there straight, looking right at her. "Yeah. Right. Well, maybe you can point me in the direction of whose place it would be to tell—" I watched lightning run down her skin like goosebumps and blinked. "What?" And I heard it a moment later.

I turned my head in the direction of the commotion. Three vans were parked behind me on the street and men were spilling out of them. Men with guns. Men with masks. Men with …

Men with powers. I saw one guy growing to fifteen feet tall, just ripping out of his clothes as he grew to giant size. Another's skin glowed with fire as he stepped from the back of a vehicle. A third had the gleam of moisture on his hands, and others had the aura of energy building around them. I counted ten of them, the powered people, and they had at least twenty guys with guns as backup.

And they were heading straight for us.

38.

Sienna

"Yeah, it's been years," I said in reply to Senator Foreman's greeting, with a not-shockingly muted amount of sarcasm. "I imagine if you had it your way, it'd be even longer."

He stared at me, entirely from the shadow. He took his time answering. "Let's just say I appreciate your discretion in coming to me quietly, in private, rather than in public."

"I don't imagine you'd want to be seen with me in public right now," I said, turning to walk along the wall of the suite. There was a flowery picture hanging there, a watercolor of grass with long green shoots. "I'm probably approval rating kryptonite."

"You've been having a rough go of things lately," he said.

"My star is definitely not rising," I said. "I'm a falling star. Problem with those is, they tend to burn pretty bright right before they hit the ground. If they're big enough, they cause quite the mess. Seems I remember dinosaurs getting wiped out that way."

"If I was just listening to your words, I might hear a threat there," Foreman said.

"But you're not just listening to my words," I said. "You're reading my emotions, and you know I don't give a damn about threatening you. I'm not here to do that, and I *wouldn't* do that, in any case."

"The Sienna I knew wouldn't do that," he said. "But I'm not sure I really know you anymore."

"Oh?" I asked. "Do I seem too different to you?" I pressed fingers into my temple, pointing at my head as I stared at the flowery painting. "Up here?"

"Yes," he said. "You know I can't read your mind, but I can read your feelings—"

"Same difference," I said. "Emotions lead the mind."

"—and you're … bitter," he said, after a moment's pause for reflection. Or maybe he was just trying to find a way to say it that wouldn't enrage me. I don't know. "You seem less … I don't want to say 'stable', but … I don't know that there's a more apt word."

"You afraid I'm going to snap?"

"Not really," he said. "But if you keep going this direction I'm not sure you're going to end up anywhere you want to go. You seem … defensive—"

"Because I'm under attack from all sides."

"—isolated—"

"Because I'm alone."

"—angry—because of all of the above, I know," he said before I could.

"You know what's been happening to me," I said. "I'm getting burned in effigy."

"Being a politician, I wouldn't know what that's like," he said lightly.

"It's different for you," I said, looking over my shoulder at him. "You have supporters. A lot of them, according to the last poll I saw."

"I do," he said cautiously. "And it's kind of you to bring that up. But … strangely … not the reason you came, I don't think."

I bowed my head. "Why is that strange?"

"Because most people in your position—someone under siege, attacked, alone … they might look to someone comparatively popular thinking that person could 'save' them somehow."

I snorted. "You're not popular enough to save me. And you're just as subject to this circus as I am. The press is coming at you with kid gloves right now. They'll turn and bring the long knives out at any moment."

"Probably right after the convention, my advisors tell me," he said. "Though my campaign manager says it's been a pleasant change of pace that they've gone somewhat easy on me thus far. She's not used to that.

So what do you want?" he asked. "I assume you didn't just come to me to catch up on old times."

"Don't get me wrong, I could use the civil conversation at this point," I said. "But no, you're right. I didn't just come to chitchat." I looked straight at him. "I've got a problem."

"Just one?" he asked. "You're scaling back."

"A big one," I said. "A big fat mystery with really powerful, connected people sitting in the middle of it that are making my life even more of a living hell than it was before."

"Ahhh," he said. "So that's where this sudden increase of heat is coming from." I watched him lean forward in his seat, and for the first time I could see hints of his features beneath the shadows. "What did you get into in Atlanta?"

"You know Cordell Weldon?" I asked.

He made a grunting noise. "I know *of* him. We're not exactly friends, sitting roughly across from each other on the political divide."

"Thought I might have heard you mention his name unpleasantly on one of the talk show rounds you made after the war," I said. "His name came up with regard to an investigation I'm on. One of his orgs funds a homeless shelter where some residents went missing, ended up murdered, possibly experimented on for being meta. One of the workers who was looking into it turned up dead, too."

"Curiouser and curiouser."

"So I had a conversation with him," I said, "and he got a little defensive and threatening."

"Only a little?"

"Maybe more than a little," I said. "Definitely more than an innocent man would, I think. So I hunted down this other source, and he says Weldon's dirty as a pig pen, has deals all over the place on the down low."

"Of course he does," Foreman said. "But you'll never be able to prove that."

"Why not?" I asked. "You can't tell me there aren't people that have witnessed this."

"Tons of them," he said. "All in on the take or dead, most assuredly, if Weldon is halfway competent."

"Ugh," I said, letting my frustration creep out. "How do you even deal with slime like that?"

"How do I deal with scum like Weldon, or how should you?" He stood and adjusted his suit. "Because those are two different things."

I looked at him across the room. "How should I deal with him?"

"If we go by your press, you should choke him to death and drop his corpse in the North Atlantic."

I blinked. "Are you … serious?"

"Probably not," he said, and he sounded grave. "How do you deal with a cockroach like Cordell Weldon? I don't know. I've been dealing with people like him forever. He's particularly good at galvanizing enough support and paying enough of the right people to keep the consequences of his corruption from raining down on him. Whatever the press says about your methods of dealing with people, sometimes I find it oddly refreshing. You just … do. And the problem is solved." He looked straight at me. "That guy in England, for example. He could read the future, right?"

"Yeah," I said. "Cassandra-type. He could read possible futures or something, see the probabilities and how they ran."

"Guy would have been a nightmare to contain," Foreman said, and he folded his massive arms over his chest and took a few steps forward. "People would go back and forth forever, for years, debating what to do about him. Hundreds of thousands of man-hours of discussion. All the while he'd escape a dozen times, maybe get recaptured if we were lucky. Or, conversely—" He snapped his fingers. "Problem solved."

"Thank you for your late support on that one," I said. "But what you're suggesting here—"

"I'm not suggesting anything," Foreman said, holding up a hand. "You can't kill Cordell Weldon, as much fun as it might be for me to consider how much easier life would be without him. I mean, you physically could, obviously, but if you did it, you'd be in a mess that's probably not worth considering."

"What do I do about him?" I asked. "I've got a mystery, he's at the core, him and Edward Cavanagh—"

"Cavanagh?" Foreman asked.

"They're in it together somehow," I said. "Up to their eyeballs."

"Woooooo," Foreman said, like the air was being let out of him low and slow. "He's a major opposition donor. Major. I feel like you're teasing me with Christmas here, hinting that Weldon and Cavanagh are tied up in dirty dealings that you might be able to prove if you push at it."

I stared at him. "It did cross my mind that you might benefit from my work. I thought maybe if there was an incentive, you might be more willing to … I don't know, give me some form of aid."

"I'm a little limited in what I can do for you," he said. "I've got a bully pulpit, but if I try and use it on your behalf right at the moment—"

"Nothing's going to happen," I said. "The new head of the agency has zero loyalty to you."

"Quite the opposite, actually," Foreman said. "He's a hand-picked appointment of President Harmon and the administration, which makes him likely to react to any pressure from me by going in the opposite direction. I mean, I could dig a real nice trench and make a political issue out of what's going on in your department right now, but I'm not sure it'll do you any good at all. Might shine a little light in places you don't want it to go, I think."

"Yeah," I said. "They've already threatened to drag my past into the cold light of day if I continue to make a pain in the ass of myself."

"Hm," he said, and his hands went to his pockets. "I think it'd be pretty self-serving of me to suggest you continue your investigation on this one. I mean, I'm not going to complain if you keep going and end up overturning these two, but you might want to give some thought to the blowback from this one. It could be … considerable."

"I've thought about it," I said. "But I'm not ready to let this go."

"Of course not," he said, again lightly, "because you wouldn't be you if you quit when it was smart to."

"I get the sense you knew that."

Foreman sighed. "I've been around you long enough to know your mind. Not as well as Zollers, but well enough. All along, the people who tried to pull strings at the agency, the ones who I approached with the idea to put you to work running the war against Sovereign, they thought that what we had on you would make you a loyal guard dog on a chain, one that would bark on command and do their bidding without question."

I felt my eyes narrow at him. "But you didn't believe that?"

I could see him smile in the dark. "All along, I had the benefit of reading your emotional state. No, I always knew that what we had was a furious tigress on a real thin leash." He took a few steps closer to me, revealing more of his face. "See, there's a rage in you, just under the surface. It bubbles like a volcano, always there, seething and raw and furious, ready to erupt from whatever vent it can find. Sometimes it goes big, sometimes it goes small, but I never made the mistake they did and tried to act like it was something I could contain."

"Why didn't it bother you to know that?" I asked, staring at him. "Why wouldn't you run away, if it's that bad? Shouldn't you be afraid to, I don't know, get burned or see the leash break or … something?"

"No," he said, shaking his head, "because I never made the mistake of viewing you as a tool rather than a person. See, to Cordell Weldon or the president, you're just a cog in the machine rather than an agent in charge of her own life. You're useful insofar as you can get them something they want—power, money, whatever. I knew who you were inside all along, and while I certainly wanted you to help protect the world, I wasn't pushing you against your own aims. That sort of pressure could be … unhealthy."

"They're pushing now," I said. "Hard. Weldon's pushing every button he's got. I've had mercenaries come at me. The guy I'm working with had his house burned down."

Foreman blinked. "That's … interesting."

"What do you mean, 'interesting'?" I asked.

"A man like Weldon wouldn't move hard and openly unless you had him over a barrel somehow," Foreman said. "He's a cautious guy, lives in the shadows with his illicit activities. If you didn't have him on the run in some way, he wouldn't have come at you like that."

"But how do I have him on the run?" I asked. "None of this makes any sense at all."

"Mysteries seldom do until you get all the pieces in place," he said. "So … why did you come to me?"

"Power protects power," I said. "And I don't … I just don't 'get' power, not the way someone like you, who's in it, would. I think I was just … hoping you had some insight. Some direction I could go. Something." I lowered my head. "Anything, honestly. I'm kind of at the end of my rope."

"No friends, no public support, no family," Foreman

said, and there was a strikingly mournful quality to the way he said it. "Your merry war band is on the outs, and now you're down to pretty much yourself, it feels like, based on what I'm getting from you. You sure it's not the 'lonely' part that's eating at you?"

"It's the … 'entire world arrayed against me' part that's causing the most consternation at the moment."

"It's not the whole world," he said. "I know that sounds funny, but it's really not the whole world. It's the loudest voices shouting you down, though, because the press is against you, and I know that feels like the whole world, but it's not. You can't get the majority of people anywhere to agree on almost anything, so …"

"I know you were aiming for reassuring, but—"

"Not reassuring," he said, "I'm trying to help you. Not everyone is against you, however it might feel. You get out of the ivory towers of Manhattan or out of the beltway in D.C. and get down to the street level in a city or town, and there are plenty of people who still support Sienna Nealon and think she's a hero who saved the world." He cringed. "I might take it a little easier on the people you run across, though, because that support is fading, and there are only so many more logs you can toss on that particular fire before you run out of fuel."

"I don't mean to sound like an ass, but so what if some of the people are with me?" I asked. "That doesn't help me against Cordell Weldon. It feels like he's holding all the cards at this point."

"Well," Foreman said, "I can't offer much, but I can offer you this: if you can get even close to bringing him down, throw up a cloud of suspicion, I can promise you I'll put everything I have into kicking the hell out of him while he's kissing the dirt."

"You'd kick a man while he's down?" I asked, joking just a little.

"I'm a politician," he said, "I have no shame in kicking

my opponents while they're down, in the nuts, while simultaneously extolling my own virtues and making it seem like I'm doing the nation a favor. This is what we do."

"So all I've got to do is drag him down a few pegs and your self-interest will allow you to step in and do the rest," I said, feeling my shoulders slump. "I gotta tell you, though … it still seems impossible."

"It's not as impossible as you're making it out to be," Foreman said, and here I could see his smile. "It's not as if he's not a criminal, after all, and a nervous one at that. If you're right, he's made a half dozen illegal, desperate moves already." He held up a lone finger. "Desperate men act in haste, and haste doesn't allow a lot of time to cover tracks. And you just need to catch him one good time with his finger in the pie …" He shrugged. "I can call Governor Hill of Georgia. She's supposed to be campaigning with me in a couple weeks, maybe I can persuade her to climb on the opposite side of Weldon on this. I know she doesn't like him, but she doesn't really want to be tarred by him or his allies, either. She might at least be able to take the state-level heat back to a simmer. She's got no control over Atlanta, though. Weldon owns that town. I—" He froze, like someone had poked him in the back, and stood up, ramrod straight. "Something's happening."

"A lot's happening," I said. "Starting with my ass being in a big damned sling—"

"No," he said, and moved at meta-speed to the TV remote and turned it on. "My whole staff just responded to some external stimuli in shock. There's breaking news of some kind—" The TV screen coalesced into a news channel, and the picture stabilized into footage that took my breath away.

I recognized the scene. It was Augustus's street, and it was in chaos. The crack of gunfire filled the air even as the camera swayed wildly. Flames and water and lightning and earth all swirled madly in the background, an insane dance of metahuman powers that moved at such a speed that I could hardly tell what was going on. An Atlas-typed stomped his way through the urban battlefield at a height of twenty feet, like a giant striding through a playground. I caught a flash of earth formed into a shield as Augustus stepped into view for a split second, embattled, flame and water coming at him in tandem and destroying his line of defense as he hastily threw up another. Lightning shot past and hit somewhere offscreen, causing a flash that temporarily blinded the camera as the gunfire picked up again.

It was war, and Augustus was right in the thick of it.

I turned to Foreman, and I knew my face was probably as pale as it had ever been. "I'm sorry," I said.

He nodded, and I knew in that instant that he was fully aware of what I was about to do. "Go on—" he barely got out before I smashed through his window and flew faster than I'd ever flown before, hitting supersonic speed before I'd even cleared the broken glass.

39.

Augustus

I thought about signing up for the Army after high school. The G.I. Bill had been appealing, college paid for after a few years of service, but the job at Cavanagh had come along and the carrot of college being paid for by them without ever getting shot at in a war zone had been even more appealing.

That dream had died a nasty death earlier today when the dudes ambushed me in the middle of the street, but I'd say the final nail went into the coffin about two seconds after the damned war broke out on my street.

War was the only way to describe it, too, because man, they came at us full-force. Metas. Badasses, too, with enough fury to convince me they weren't here to play tiddlywinks.

Taneshia and I were separated almost instantly, with a fire-flinging guy driving a wedge of flame between us. She went right, I went left, and I only caught a glimpse of her through the flames as the heat seared my cheek when the line of fire shot past. It darkened the wall of the house behind me and flared upward, catching the roof on fire as it was refracted up by the ground and brick.

I instinctively threw dirt right out of the ground in a clump, like throwing a punch at someone who takes a swing at you. I heard the chatter of guns and ripped more ground up to defend myself before realizing that the gunfire wasn't pointed at me.

It was pointed at the cops down the street in front of my house.

Aw, hell.

I saw a giant man leering down at me from above, some hundred feet away. Dude looked like he was about to go storming through the neighborhood, wading into houses in order to cause some havoc. He threw something at me and I realized it was someone's barbecue grill as I dodged it. I'm not talking one of those George Foreman ones, either. It was a full-on patio grill, looked like it weighed a few hundred pounds. It shattered on the wall behind me as I moved the hell out of its flight path.

A blast of water caught three of my impromptu shields and splattered them out of the air. I ripped up some more dirt and tried to get the shields that had just been blown away back, but the water guy was carrying them away with his currents, and I couldn't seem to get enough mental grab on them to get them to buck the flow. The spouts he was shooting were going at what felt like a hundred miles an hour, I thought as one raced past me. I knew if I got hit with one, I'd be feeling it tomorrow.

The only good news was that these guys were coming at me and Taneshia in a bum rush. They didn't seem to be coordinating very well, which looked like the only break we were likely to catch. I'd never been in a fight like this before, but I had a theory that my only hope was to do this guerilla-style: keep moving, don't stop, and try and take them out one by one.

As far as plans went, it wasn't a good one, but it was all I had time for as I dodged a blast of ice from a big white dude with frosty blue eyes.

"Taneshia!" I called. "Keep moving!" She didn't answer, or at least I couldn't hear her over the sound of the gunfire down the street. It sounded like the cops were getting a full-court press, too, which was a bad sign. There hadn't been that many of them at the fire, after all, maybe a half-dozen. It was mostly firefighters and crowd, and that wasn't a good place for a war to break out. Lots of civilians meant lots of chance for casualties. I was torn on whether I should work my way in that direction or not. If I did, things might get worse because I'd be dragging however many asshole metas with me.

On the other hand, if I didn't … who knew what was going to happen over there. The mercenaries had the cops outgunned, that was for sure.

This sure had gotten hot awfully fast, I thought as another burst of flame came my way.

But screw it, I figured. Heroes didn't just beat the damned odds; they flew in the face of them. They fought against the odds, fought the enemies no matter how many—and they always protected the innocent.

Whatever else Sienna screwed up by punching down with full and furious force, she did protect the innocent. She just tended to hit the guilty like a runaway train was all.

Well, I couldn't hit as hard as she could, but maybe I could do my part until—God willing—she showed up to pull a cavalry and help save the day.

I started ripping the ground so that it would rise up to meet me with each step, little segments tearing off and throwing up a continuous shield as I sprinted back across the lawn of the corner house. I had about four houses to go until I got to mine, but right now those guys with guns were probably counting on their meta friends to put up a defense for them. If I got there, maybe I could sucker punch them from behind. It wasn't really a sucker punch when they had you outnumbered like twenty to one, was it?

Momma would probably say—

Aw, hell. I forgot about Momma. Oh, man. I hoped she was okay.

I ran about three feet off the ground, ripping up the ground at my side in a thin shield as I went, a spray of dirt and grass exploding out of the earth like a fountain effect, tracing a curtain of earth in front of me. It was sloppy as hell, and when all this was over, I vowed to practice like mad to get better at working with the powers I'd been given. I doubted it'd stop much, that thin shield I'd thrown up, but a spatter of earth from the impact of a bullet convinced me it was better than nothing.

I saw a flash of lightning rip past and knew Taneshia was still in the fight, somewhere behind me. I hoped she was giving them hell, but I was afraid for her life. These were the tough choices, trying to decide who to save first, where to go. The numbers against us were insane, but at least she had powers. Those people in front of my house had a whole lot of nothing working for them, just a few cops without nearly enough bullets for what was heading their way. Those mercs had body armor and rifles. The cops had handguns and a prayer. Their backup was minutes away. The mercs had superpowered backup that was ready to swoop in as soon as they'd finished mopping up me and Taneshia.

Something burst through my shield just in front of me like Kool-Aid Man crashing through the wall. It took me a second to dodge instinctively and a second more to realize it was a damned bear. Its giant paw slashed through my little shield and almost got me. I saw the head and massive body, shrouded in the earth I'd thrown up to protect myself.

"Ahhh!" I said before I got control of myself. I threw a hand at the ground below his feet and blasted it skyward.

It was like I'd launched that thing from an ejector seat. It shot into the air like Sienna taking flight, arms and legs pinwheeling as it turned back into a human being. I saw panic in those eyes for the half-second until he flew out of sight, scared about witless. He landed somewhere on the other side of the road, probably pretty hard, and I knew I was at least down one enemy for a couple minutes. Hopefully longer.

Also, I'd just figured out a pretty quick way to dispense

with enemies. Ejection seat! Boom. I was definitely going to need that. Along with maybe the asphalt shotgun thing I'd learned earlier. It may not have been pretty, but lives were at stake. I couldn't chance these dudes getting back up again with odds like this. It didn't make me happy, but on this I was with Sienna all the way. Protecting people was the most important thing. I didn't want to kill anybody, but if one of those dudes got up again and started ripping through a crowd of my neighbors, I don't know that I'd be able to forgive myself.

I was going to put them down hard from here on out. I wasn't going to kill if I could avoid it, but I needed to make sure they stayed down at the least.

I could see the big guy, Mr. Giant, leering at me from above my curtain of dirt. I doubted I'd be able to ejector seat him, assuming he was even standing on the earth. I doubted he was; he looked far enough away to be out in the street. He also looked … taller?

I saw him throw a car at me and I froze. I was fortunate that I did, because he was leading me with it and my sudden stop saved my ass from getting crushed under the van. It was one of their vans, I saw once it got closer, a white one that looked new. It had giant finger dents in it, I noticed as it flew about twelve inches from my face. The giant's clothes were gone, his mask was gone—all because he'd grown too big for them. I could see him, leering at me as he lifted another van and prepared to throw it at me. I felt a flash of anger that it was going to be like this. This wasn't a fair fight.

So I wasn't going to fight fair.

I sprayed a hard column of compacted dirt right into his face from a distance. I knew it wasn't going to do squat to hurt him, but I didn't even know how to go about hurting a dude that big. I just knew that like Sienna said, you can't punch someone in the face if you can't see them.

He let out a bellowing, agonized scream that sounded like one of those flying monster dragons from *Lord of the Rings.*

I'd let him have a good amount of that dirt, and I'd aimed it perfectly. *Now you see me, now you don't, asshole.*

A splash of water swept through my shield and punched into my side, knocking me toward the house to my left. They had some bushes planted in front of their windows. Prickly ones, I realized as I landed in them, branches gouging into my back on impact. The landing knocked the air out of me, and it felt like something cracked hard, like a rib or something in my right side. It hurt like a mofo, but I didn't cry out. I threw up a hand to drag as much of a shield up as I could, which turned out to be well timed, because another geyser of water came spraying at me, just over my head, washing down on me as I lay there in the bushes.

I didn't have long to assess my situation, either, because after a moment I realized the water wasn't going away. It was pooling, unnaturally, around me. I came to a quick realization—that this dude with the water power could control it like I could move dirt, and that meant he could control its boundaries. Apparently he was aiming to use it to create a water entombment for me.

I had a feeling I'd be able to sense him if I had a little better refinement of my abilities, but that wasn't something I had time for at the moment. The water was rising, and it seemed the pressure was on. It was harder somehow, like he was compacting the molecules together to try and crush me. I didn't have long, either. Once it had me in its grip, I was going to be done.

I reached out and could feel little droplets of water falling from his spray to the dirt all along the path of his jet. It was subtle, but it was there, and I could feel the place that it stopped. If he could control the density of his zone of water the way I could do it with my earth, it meant he was dragging that moisture out of the air and giving it form so he could do this, and it also meant … maybe I could do the same, messing with the density of my element.

And now I knew where he was standing.

I pulled earth from underneath him and made it surge out of the ground, swallowing him up to the waist like a monster coming out of the depths. I heard a sharp scream and then the tightness of the water pressure stopped suddenly, and the spray halted a moment after. I used that grip I had on him like a mouth and let it ripple, dragging him down further and further, creating a little chamber for him in the ground. It swallowed him right up and the screaming stopped. I kept myself from using the power of the earth to just straight-up crush him, though I knew I could have. I just dragged him down a good five feet and figured he could spend a little time digging his ass out of that.

I felt my strength fading even as I got my sopping ass up to my feet and started running again. I threw that same shield wall up, taking a look over it to see giant man screaming and rubbing his eyes in a futile effort to get over that blindness I'd induced. I needed to keep an eye on that in case he somehow figured it out, because that man could be a serious problem if left unchecked.

But I didn't have time to deal with him right now. I hoped Taneshia was faring all right, because if she fell, they'd be on me pretty quick, and I'd get their undivided attention. I'd taken out two, maybe three if the giant would stay occupied for the duration. I didn't have anything else to throw at him at the moment, though, because I was using every bit of my abilities to try and keep that wall going up between me and the men with guns.

A man on fire came leaping over my curtain of dirt, and I felt my heart stop as I caught sight of him. He landed and stood straight up, staring at me as I stared at him. His skin was gone, completely replaced by flames licking up his body. His mouth was a dark, black hole, agape in a nasty smile.

"Dude!" I shouted, "you're on fire!" I threw up my hands as he started to put his up in turn. I redirected some of my dirt right at him, hit him with a blast that I shot right out of the ground between us. "You need to stop, drop and roll! Let me help you with that."

My dirt blast turned his ass aflip. I mean that, really. He got hit in the face so hard he flipped. I kept up the pressure as he fell, just covering him up with earth and rock, hitting him like it was coming out of a pressure sprayer. It took a lot out of me, but I poured it on. I watched him as his face came up, coughing and hacking, and I just hit him again, harder. I covered him with it, taking away all the oxygen around him and giving him nothing to work with on igniting his flesh again. I got the ground below him in the act, using that same thing I'd learned with water man, dragging him down into the earth.

As soon as he was covered over, I started forward again, but slower this time. I could feel myself wearing out, like I'd run miles. My wall went slower this time, and lower. I had pushed myself past the bounds in the last few hours, and I was finding out that my abilities really did have finite limits in terms of energy.

I felt a bullet skip along my back, grazing me, and it forced me to twist in an uncomfortable way, triggering my rib pain and dropping me to my knees. It was like nothing I'd ever felt before; way beyond the pain of that time I'd broken my arm. This fight had gone on for maybe five minutes, and I felt like I was on the twelfth round, with my knockout impending. Or maybe a TKO, given I'd just hit the mat.

I kissed the damned ground when I fell, getting a mouthful of dirt. When I hit, I arched my back and hurt myself even worse. That rib was going to be a severe impediment to my ability to fight, and I knew it. It was a weak point, and it wasn't like I could just stop and cover myself in a cast and keep moving—

Or … maybe I could.

I pulled the ground up and surrounded my limbs with it, making myself a suit of armor out of the dirt itself. I packed it on an inch thick around my legs, then two inches, bulking up my fingers as I did. I came back to my feet as I let it circle around me. It felt strange, the grains of dirt against my skin, but it was working. I got back to my feet, a little more protected, and let my curtain wall drop. I hardened the dirt down to an inch-thick crust around me and felt the molecules slide as I moved. I packed them in tight around my chest, felt my rib crack back into place, and left myself two holes to look through for my eyes.

I have no idea what I looked like because there wasn't a mirror around for me to see, but it felt like I'd just discovered that I was the earthworks version of Green Lantern. I let the little wall drop from in front of me; I'd already stripped it for most of the dirt anyway. It fell like a sheet and left me looking across a battlefield at my opponents and gave them a clear look at me.

Hell yeah, fools. Let's get to this. That's what I was thinking.

Then that big dude with the icy eyes and frozen hands came thundering at me with a wolf at his side, and I had a moment of fear, I'm not ashamed to admit. That guy frosted up an icicle with each hand and turned each of them into a sword, and I created a shield with one hand just in time to absorb some of the impact. His icicle cut through and sliced off part of my shield, which wasn't exactly perfectly rounded to begin with. This turned it into a three-quarters circle with rough edges, and gave him enough room to swing his other blade around it and bury it into my side.

I had just enough time to harden that dirt where I saw the weapon going. I still felt it, though, and it hurt. I was lucky it wasn't my injured side, because he hit me like a meta would. I saw ice spread into the dirt and jerked away from him once his momentum was spent. I twisted and watched his sword tip break off. He grinned at me through his black mask and came at me again.

I heard the wolf come up behind me. I didn't have the energy to ejector seat him like I had his bear buddy—or was this the same guy? Not while I was using so much of my focus on the armor that was protecting me. I had to pick my shots, and I figured maybe I could take a wolf bite if I had to.

Then I took the wolf bite and wished I hadn't.

He ripped into my ass like he was tearing into a steak, giving that dirt everything he had. I felt it shred in clumps from his claws and mouth. I hoped he was getting a stomach full of hard earth, but—

The idea occurred to me right then that if someone was going to try and bite through my earthen armor, I should by all means give them a heaping helping of what they wanted to take a bite of. I used my earth to feel the next place he tried to sink his teeth, and I just let him have it in a spray like it came out of a fire hose. I stripped the whole rear of my armor off in one good blast, leaving me unprotected but him with enough dirt to choke his ass. I heard him, too, gagging and retching. I could feel the dirt, and I'd managed to sneak a ton of it down his throat. *Best be careful what you put in your mouth, fool.*

While I was distracted with him, the ice man cometh at me hard. He swung those ice swords like he meant to kill me, which, presumably, he did. He shaved off some dirt from my arm as I threw it up with a little extra shielding. I could feel my reactions slowing, though, and he was coming at me full force. One good connection and he might end up taking a limb, which wasn't exactly something I could afford to lose right now. Dirt streamed off me in little flecks here and there as my ability to hold it all together flagged under his withering assault. My hand came up over and over again, channeling more and more dirt between me and his insanely quick attacks.

The iceman's teeth were bared in a ferocious grin of victory. He had me, no question; it was just a matter of time. I reached down deep, trying to generate enough upheaval to launch him, but the ground beneath his feet didn't even stir. I felt maxed out, like the days when I used to work out hard and had nothing left in my arms. Like I'd squeezed the power muscle so tight for so long that I just couldn't come up with anything else.

He hit me with a battering overhand strike with one of those swords, and I felt sweat stream into my eyes, carrying grains of sand with it. My legs buckled and I fell under the impact. I looked through my eyeholes and saw that what he was hitting me with wasn't a sword anymore. Maybe he'd decided he didn't need finesse at this point. Now he had an ice club, massive and growing by the minute, and he raised it over his head. One good hit and my armor was going to be done.

Two was going to cave my damned head in.

I stared at him, trying to come up with a defense, any defense. I felt for the earth and came back with almost nothing. All I could feel was the dirt I had hard-packed around my body. It was like being in the dark, unable to see anything. My range was down to nil, my strength at an end. I stared up at him and knew I was gone.

Then a lightning bolt came crashing down from above and caught him right on the raised ice club.

The iceman jerked as the electricity arced through him. I watched him convulse in pain until his eyes rolled back into his head, hands scorched and smoking as he collapsed. He dropped onto his face and stared at me with dead eyes as my armor slipped away. I just couldn't hold it together anymore.

"Thank you," I breathed as sat there on my knees, unable to muster the strength to get up. "Thank you, Taneshia."

A shadow swooped down from the roof above, putting itself between me and the rest of the damned army that was still out there making war on my neighborhood. "Not Taneshia," a deep voice called out from beneath the hoodie. The figure in front of me was taller than Taneshia, but the voice—

Oh, damn. The voice.

I knew that voice.

The hood shot lightning from both hands in a flashing burst that made me cover my eyes. The electricity shot forth and caught two metas near the road right in the back. One of them looked like they had about a million bullets caught in some kind of gravity field in front of them while the other was throwing stuff ahead at the cops, who were under cover. Both strikes hit home and fried the people they hit, no question.

I'd found my lightning man killer.

He turned to look back at me and I caught the flash of glasses as he did so, the sun catching the light, and I felt my stomach drop. I knew the killer. I'd known him all along.

It was Jamal.

It was my own brother.

40.

"Jamal," I said, not wanting to believe it. "Why?"

"No time to explain now, bro," he said, and his voice was louder than I'd ever heard it before. Jamal was shy. Jamal was quiet. He was the meek that was going to inherit the earth.

And Jamal was a stone-cold killer who'd been rolling around town executing people for some reason.

"I could use your help here," Jamal said, and I struggled against fatigue that threatened to drag me into the earth. I wanted to just cover myself in dirt. Maybe it would renew me. Maybe it would kill me.

Either way, maybe I wouldn't have to deal with my brother being a murderer.

I looked over the battlefield. It was intense. Jamal let out another blast of lightning, this time right at the guys with guns who were shooting at the cops. It forked and hit about five mercs right in the guns. They blew back in a flash I had to look away from. When I opened my eyes, one dude's shoes were smoking right in the middle of the street.

I'd bagged on Sienna for being ruthless and taking no prisoners, but my brother was looking like he was all set to one up the hell out of her.

"Jamal, no!" I called, and staggered forward as he started to unleash another blast at the big guy who was still clawing the dirt out of his eyes. I tried to throw up a shield of dirt, but I watched the electricity blow right through my little sandstorm, leaving sparkling glass twinkling as it fluttered under the sunlight and fell to the earth.

"These guys are serious, Augustus," Jamal said, neatly batting away my hand as I reached for him. It stung a little. Jamal had never been a physical threat to me, not even when we were kids. His strength surprised me until I remembered he was a meta now. The slap was loud, too, echoing in my ears and reminding me that while we'd had a divide between us for years, I'd never even realized how little I knew my brother until the moment he'd saved me. "Cavanagh's thugs aren't playing. They mean to put us all in the ground."

"Might be I want to go into the ground," I said as I watched that giant guy fall down dead from my brother's attack. I saw the black scar on his temple the size of a softball, saw his enormous body pitch over as the ground shook from the impact. "Where's Taneshia?"

"She's fighting with another Thor-type around the corner," Jamal said. "You might ought to go help her while I mop this up over here."

"How long have you been like this?" I asked, having trouble getting my breath. I could taste the dust in the wind as I stood there. Even now, it didn't taste good to me at all.

"Years," he said. "A year. I found out the night—never mind. Go help Taneshia, will you?" He threw his head at me in a fierce nod. "We'll talk after. I need to take out the last of these gunmen." And he let loose another burst of lightning that ranged far, hitting a car and running straight through it to blast back some dude hiding behind it.

I wanted to argue. I wanted to punch him right in that smug-ass, cold, lying face. But I didn't have the strength for that. Instead I dragged myself away back the way I came. I limped along my trail of destruction. The yards were savaged in a line from fires that were still burning, trenches dug out where I'd made my defensive stands. I limped past the bush where I'd landed and saw a bloodied branch. I wondered where the blood had come from, but I didn't wonder too hard. My side was on fire, and I suspected I was bleeding from there.

I turned the corner and saw Taneshia and some other guy going at each other with an electrical storm square in the middle of them. It looked they were both just pouring it on, some kind of Harry Potter vs. Voldemort contest, or maybe more like the Emperor from *Star Wars* facing off with himself. I couldn't tell who was winning, and not just because it was insanely bright.

And then I remembered that I was there to help. I reached out with one good grab and made a dirt fist out of the ground behind the lightning dude, and just hammered him in the back of the head with a sucker punch. Dude dropped, unconscious, and I quickly buried him up to his face in the ground.

Taneshia let off the lightning as soon as I'd knocked him out and fell to her knees, breathing hard. "Thanks," she said.

"You should have told me it was Jamal," I said to her in return, with nothing but a deep and pure anger.

"I should have," she said, nodding. "A long time ago, before it got to this point. It all just sort of spun out of—" She stopped suddenly and coughed, blood spurting from her lips and running down her green shirt, dark spatters that looked like syrup they were so dark.

Taneshia staggered to the side and looked behind her, and now I saw one of those guys standing there. He was grinning, was a bigger dude, solid and broad-shouldered, looked like he didn't miss too many meals. His pale, bald head was freckled, his eyebrows and the goatee around his mouth were a light ginger color. "Oh, sorry," he said, not remotely sorry. He held up a hand that was red with blood. "Did I interrupt your tender moment?"

41.

I felt that deep rage that had been pointed at Taneshia get redirected in an instant to the ginger bald dude. I flung dirt right at him and watched his face go ghostly whiter, like it was fading, and the dirt just passed right through it.

"What the hell are you?" I asked, and he just stood there smiling at me while my stomach sank.

"You'll find out when I yank your brains right out of your skull," he said, starting toward me. "Right through the bone, just tug 'em out like there's nothing but air separating them from the world."

I blinked at him. He smiled menacingly and started walking toward me, his feet making impressions in the dirt that had been exposed by the lightning battle between Taneshia and her enemy.

I picked up a dirt clod and hurled it at the guy.

It passed right through him like he wasn't there.

But his feet were touching the ground.

I remembered an episode of *Star Trek* where two of the crew members got bombarded with some kind of space radiation and could pass through walls. They called it 'phasing.' It was a cool episode, and I liked it a lot, but something always bothered me about it.

Why didn't they go sliding through the floor just as easily as they passed through the walls?

I watched the bald dude take his next step, and I just

pulled the ground out from under him. Easy, just a foot or so down, a nice tug.

And I watched him fall, like he'd just missed a step.

"Hey!" he said, a little alarmed. His eyes got big, and I knew I had a winner.

So I rearranged another foot of dirt beneath him, sending it crawling out the sides of the little pit, and he tumbled down further. His arms scrambled for hold, slapping against the sides, so I pulled the dirt out around him to widen the pit by another five feet in every direction. It happened pretty fast, and since I wasn't lifting the dirt into the air or anything dramatic, it didn't seem to take much of my strength.

He was in up to his chest now and starting to panic. "Hey! Hey!"

"Can't hear you," I said. I dug another three feet underneath him and watched him fall. Gravity still worked on him, and I just kept taking more and more of the ground beneath him. "Too busy trying to protect my brains from falling out of my skull." I had full control of the dirt beneath him, and I was making it run up the sides of the pit like crazy, just digging him into the ground further and further. I had him down ten feet now, and he was starting to disappear as I filled in the earth behind him. He hit fifteen feet, then twenty, and I filled the pit in so that only a five-foot-in-diameter hole remained above.

"You can't do this!" he protested, and I could barely see him as I narrowed his personal tunnel as he hit a depth I didn't think he could get out of easily. This part of Atlanta didn't have tunnels underground, as far as I knew, but even if it did, he'd be a long time in figuring out how to get back out of the earth again. I sealed the ground up behind him at thirty feet and didn't care if he ever saw sunlight again.

"I think I just did," I said, and slumped to the ground, spent. I looked over at Taneshia, who was on the ground, just bleeding. "And I think I'd do it again if I had half a chance."

42.

Sienna

I was way late and I knew it by the time the pillars of smoke came into view behind the Atlanta skyline. I shot out of the sky with cannonball force and slammed into the ground in the wreckage of Augustus's front yard. The sun was going down, and there was a guy with a hoodie and glasses standing there with lightning crackling out of his fingertips.

"And so we meet at last," I said, staring him down.

"This isn't what you think," he said.

"Really?" I looked around at the scene of chaos. There were no civilians in sight, and the police cruisers and fire trucks that had been parked on the lawn were in flames, along with a half dozen other cars. The neighborhood looked like a war had come through, and Augustus's lawn was ground zero. "It's not a battlefield?"

He paused, like he was thinking it over. "Okay, maybe it is what you think. But I'm not who you think I am—"

"You're a lightning-wielding killer," I said and let my hands flare into flame. I let my gaze settle on the smoking ruins of a man with an assault rifle clenched tightly in his blackened hands. It looked like he'd been hanging onto his weapon for dear life when something (lightning COUGH COUGH) hit him. "I can see the evidence for it from where I'm standing, and it's looking pretty compelling."

"You don't know what you're talking about," he said, and he went from uncertainty to coldness in a flash as he realized he wasn't going to talk me out of beating his ass.

"Wolfe," I said. *Ready*, the voice came.

"It doesn't have to be like this," he said.

"I've kinda always wanted lightning powers," I said.

He let the first volley go and I barely dodged it. I went low to the ground and it surged past my ear and hit the ground. I could feel it run through my body and give me an instant headache as I caught the trailing edge of it. It made me want to puke, but instead I sprang up using Gavrikov's flight and flung myself at lightning man's jaw with a punch.

He was fast, I'll credit him with that. I wouldn't say he moved like lightning, but it was clear his meta reflexes were way up the scale. I altered course and slammed a forearm into his jaw, knocking him back. It was the sort of thing you could only do if you had some control over gravity, which—hey, lucky me—I do. Also lucky for me, most people don't really take that ability into account when fighting, since it sort of violates the laws of physics.

He fell over onto his back, and I was on top of him in a second. He channeled lightning through his fingers and I grabbed his wrist with a flaming hand. He screamed as I burned him, pinning his wrist to his chest. I could smell the charred flesh as smoke wafted up. I headbutted him and heard his nose crack, knocked his glasses askew and watched his eyeballs roll from the impact. He made a faint grunt, a noise like I'd taken most of the piss out of him, and I punched him again in the face for good measure.

It felt good to finally have a face to punch. *Take that, lightning man.*

I felt my powers start to work on his burned wrist, and I just held him there. I felt vaguely like I was doing something wrong. I hadn't eaten a whole soul in years. I'd been afraid to, really, afraid to add any more crazy to the circus of nuttiness already in my head. Afraid that the meta stigma against eating souls would reflect badly on me in my newfound fame.

But you know what? Screw it. Everybody already hated me. And I had always wanted to be able to throw lightning. That was a badass power.

I stared into lightning man's eyes as I felt the burn of my succubus power begin to work. I could hear his voice in my head as I caught the first hints of his soul, the first stirrings of him in there. He was screaming, crying out as I grasped at him. He was clawing to hold on, raging against the burn of my power on his skin, and I held him down and realized that no matter what I did, no matter how hard I tried …

… they were never going to love me.

… they were always going to hate me.

… Kat was always going to win in the end.

I was never going to be like her.

I never was a hero.

I was a soul eater.

And it was time to accept that fact once and for all.

I ignored the screaming, ignored the shouted pleas and cries, and kept my hands on his skin as his agony drew to a crescendo, ready to embrace what I was once and for all.

43.

Augustus

I practically crawled over to Taneshia on my hands and knees. She had a giant, fist-sized hole in her back and I started to panic. Blood oozed out of it. I wanted to freak out but tried to hold it all together. I let out a stream of curses.

I took a breath and realized I was about ready to hyperventilate. She was bleeding hard, and I didn't know what to do. I wasn't a doctor, I wasn't a nurse. I was a dude who was about to lose his shit because a girl he lov—errr … had known for a very long time was dying in front of him.

Then I realized … she wasn't squirting blood out. It was a steady ooze, and the bones the dude had broken when he had pulled his hand out of her back already looked like they were—very slowly—growing back together.

And there were scorch marks all around the edges.

"Shocked … myself," Taneshia said, speaking into the dirt. I could feel the vibrations in the soil, could barely hear her. "Tried to … cauterize … until my healing could kick in."

"You are smart, girl," I said. "Knew there was a reason you were the one that went to college."

"Damned right," she muttered. Her wound looked clear, but … did metas have to worry about infections? That was something I'd need to ask S—

I looked up into the sky as a sonic boom shook the world

around me. Sienna came jetting down in front of my house, and I saw her disappear behind the roofline, smoke hanging in the air above the street. "You going to be okay?" I asked Taneshia.

"Go if you need to," she said. "I'm a little … sleepy …"

"I'll be back," I said, staggering to my feet. I limped along, not because my legs were injured, but because I was just so completely wiped out from my exertions that I was having trouble putting one foot in front of another. "Just hang out here."

It took what felt like ten minutes to get to the corner of the house, and then I slid around it. The whole street was heavy with smoke now. Looked like the fire engines had caught on fire, along with the cop cars in front of the house. Looked like Mr. Cavanagh and Mr. Weldon—if they were the ones behind this—had done a real number on the neighborhood. Dammit, this was my home.

I wanted to drag both those bastards out into the light of day.

Instead I dragged my feet along, slow and steady, moving toward my house. I'd seen Sienna head that way, and Jamal had gone that way a while earlier. I'd almost forgotten about my murdering brother. I had no idea what to do about him. I could hear sirens in the distance as Atlanta's finest finally got around to organizing their response to this calamity. I couldn't blame them; this was disastrous. It wasn't like our whole area broke out into a literal war every day.

I crossed the second lawn, watching out for the holes I'd left. I looked to my right as I saw water bubbling up out of the ground where I'd buried the dude that shot the jets of water at me. I guessed he was still working his way through it. I used my hand to shift some mud down in that hole, block the bubbling. I didn't have the strength to fight anyone else right now.

My legs were hurting now, and I started to get the feeling maybe I'd skinned my knees at some point. My rib was killing me, my whole side on fire. I wanted to stop. To fall down. To just give up and let myself rest.

But I couldn't.

Sienna and Jamal were still in the smoke, somewhere, fighting the good fight against these guys. I couldn't let them soldier on alone.

I pulled myself over another lawn, and I knew now I was only two houses away.

The smoke got thicker, hung in my throat. I couldn't hardly breathe, and that bitter taste was just caught on my tongue. My eyes were tearing up, but I kept putting one foot in front of another.

And then the smoke started to clear, and what I saw nearly took what was left of my breath away.

Sienna Nealon was atop Jamal, hand clutching hold of his wrist. Jamal's mouth was open, locked in a silent scream, and he was writhing under her grip.

Her grip.

"Sienna!" I shouted. "No!"

When I thought about it later, I don't know what I was expecting. Her to ignore me, maybe. To shout back some argument. To double down and grasp him even tighter.

I didn't expect what happened.

I didn't expect her to fly into the air ten feet in an instant, dropping her hand from him so fast it looked like he'd flung her into the air. Her head whipped around and her body hung there, and I knew she'd done it herself, not because of anything Jamal had done to her. He was too busy clutching his arm tight to his body, sporting a sickening burn on his forearm that was blistered and charred.

"What?" Sienna asked, standing there, staring at me through the dusky smoke. "What is it?"

"I … didn't expect you to stop just because I said so." I said it because I was a little stunned.

Her answer came out kind of cross. "Well, I did. So … what's the deal?"

I nodded to Jamal. "He's my brother. You can't … do whatever you were going to do to him."

She kept her cool, but I saw a hint that she might have been rattled. "Oh. You know he's the lightning man, right?"

"Yeah, but he's not in league with Cavanagh," I said, stumbling closer to Jamal. "Are you?"

"No," Jamal said, shaking his head through gritted teeth. "I hate that man … now that I know it was him."

"Know it was him that … what?" Sienna asked. She floated closer to the ground.

"Killed Flora," Jamal said, still clutching his burn gingerly. "He killed Flora."

"Who was Flora to you?" I asked, offering him a hand. Smoke swirled around us, the wind picking up and driving it west as it billowed off the nearby fire engine.

He looked at my hand for a long moment. "She was my girlfriend," he said and took my hand. I pulled him to his feet. "She was my first girlfriend, Augustus. And your boss and his thugs killed her."

The wind picked up and blew smoke between us all as we stood there staring at each other. I looked at Sienna; she looked back at me and then at Jamal. "We should probably get out of here," she said finally. "Unless you want to try and explain what's going on to a very unsympathetic police force."

"We're sitting in the middle of a meta warzone," I said. "No, I do not want to try and explain this to the police, because anything I say is probably going to be used against me since I buried at least three people during this fight."

"Grab your brother," she said, "and hold on tight."

"We need to get Taneshia," I said. "She's around the corner. She's hurt."

"Fine," Sienna said and grabbed hold of me as I threw an arm around Jamal. "Any idea where we should go?"

"Where's Momma?" I started to ask in a panic, remembering now that we had no place to go, really, because our house had been burned down.

"I got her out," Jamal said. "It's why I was late joining the fight. I got her five streets away. She's at Mae Grubb's house."

I felt my feet leave the ground and Jamal followed behind a moment later. "Great," Sienna said. "One less worry on the mind. But that still doesn't leave us anywhere real convenient to go, unless you want to have what's bound to be a super interesting conversation right in this Ms. Grubb's house?"

"I know where we can go," I said and looked at Jamal. "I think Flora Romero's house is still empty."

He looked at me, and the sun hit his glasses right when we broke free of the smoke. There might have been just a little extra reflection behind the glasses, though, the first time I could really remember seeing any emotion from my brother in … years. "Yeah," he said. "Flora's house is empty." He pushed his lips together, and they twisted as he turned his head to keep from looking at me.

44.

Sienna

Flora Romero's house was an empty mess of broken windows and scuffed up floorboards. Plywood hung in place to cover up some of the worst, most shattered windows, and the glass was spread all over the floor in the kitchen.

The four of us were arrayed around the living room at the back of the house, staring at each other in the darkness as the light of day faded and the sound of sirens filled the air. Jamal was looking surly at me, Augustus looked pissed at Jamal. I was shooting occasional looks at Taneshia, who was unconscious on the floor in the corner, on her face, with a nasty wound in her back.

"Well, this is fun," I said.

"Yeah, a real barrel full of monkeys," Augustus said.

"What are you so sour about?" Jamal asked, voice extremely quiet.

"Uh, let's see—my boss is apparently trying to kill me, my girl—" He froze and looked at Taneshia. "Uhh … my friend has been seriously injured … my brother's a killer, we probably got the law after us, which is a first for me, and … oh, yeah, we still got no idea why any of this is happening. Pick one of those and it's a bad day. Throw in our childhood home getting torched right to the ground, and it's a full-on winner, man."

"That does suck," I said. "But hey, at least Momma made it out alive."

"Yeah," Augustus said, "now she can kill me and Jamal both when she finds out he's a murderer and I got our house burned down. Yay. Now it's the best day ever."

"You didn't get the house burned down," Jamal said, and pointed his finger at me. "She did."

"Me?" I asked, feeling a little dumbstruck. "I wasn't even there!"

"They were trying to draw you out," Jamal said, looking at me.

"Well, that was dumb," I said. "But then, they've been playing this dumb the whole time. We would never have dug up Flora's yard on our own," I waved my hand toward the yard outside, still in its excavated state, "if those mercs hadn't ambushed me there and Augustus forced the issue by turning up bones."

"They only ambushed you because I tipped them off you were going to find something," Jamal said.

I blinked. "Well. I guess we're the dumb ones, then."

"You did what?" Augustus was on his feet, only a thin veneer between him and full rage. I was feeling a little nonplussed myself, but controlling it better than him.

"I tipped off the next link in the chain I was following that Sienna was investigating Flora's house," Jamal said. "It had taken me to Roscoe and Kennith—"

"Whom you killed," I said. "Why was that, exactly?"

"They were working with the bad guys," Jamal said, sullen. "Joaquin Pollard got paid by Kennith Coy."

"Kennith Coy was on parole," I said. "He was working at a tire shop."

"Which makes a good question how he ended up with ten grand in his bank account that made its way to Joaquin, doesn't it?" Jamal asked. "You know what he said when I asked him?"

"Before or after you blasted him to death with a bolt of

lightning?" Augustus asked.

Jamal's expression hardened. "The man didn't talk after death, fool. I asked him before I let loose on him. He said I shouldn't be asking questions that were too big for me. And then he pulled a gun, so I lit him up."

"Really?" I asked. "Where did the gun go?"

"I don't know," Jamal said. "Didn't matter. But I assume some stooge of Cavanagh's or Weldon's picked it up since it could probably be tied to them. They own the police force in this town."

"How's it going to get tied to them?" Augustus asked.

"That big dude," Jamal said, "the one that works for Cavanagh. He's the point man on all the ugly illegal dealings."

Augustus blinked. "Laverne?"

I stared at Augustus. "Tell me he's got a back-up named Shirley."

"Surely you must be joking," Augustus said.

We both had a nice chuckle while Jamal stared at us like we were idiots. "I bet he gets that one all the time," I said. "Still, if Kennith Coy was a bagman or a money fronter, what about Roscoe? He was just a factory worker—"

"He was working in Cavanagh's new bioresearch facility," Augustus said. "What was he doing there?"

"Experimentation on human test subjects," Jamal said. "Like the residents from the shelter that Flora found out were missing. Cavanagh was pulling them off the street, figuring they wouldn't be missed." His jaw got tight. "And he was right—except Flora. Flora missed them, and she went looking. Found something, too. Found out enough that someone got touchy about it and sent Joaquin Pollard to kill her."

"If you knew it was Cavanagh all along, why didn't you just kill him instead of Roscoe and Kennith?" Augustus asked, surly.

"I didn't know it was Cavanagh until today," Jamal said.

"Roscoe and Kennith didn't give me squat. I had to do the research to trace things back. I still can't prove it. But Roscoe said something to someone that ended up online and I found it in an email—"

"In a random email, somewhere on the net?" I asked.

"Yes," Jamal said.

My eyes narrowed at him. "That's some serious hacking."

He held up a hand and his fingers crackled. "I haven't exactly been idle in the last year. I can use my powers with brute force, but there's some other stuff I can do, too. Finer things. Manipulate 1's and 0's. It's taken a lot of practice, but it's been worth it. I found the link that tied Kennith and Roscoe to Pollard and the experimentation, and then went to question them both. Kennith tried to get fresh with me, pulled a gun. Roscoe … he was a whole other thing."

"Yeah, well, don't leave us in the dark," Augustus said, then froze. "I didn't mean to do that pun, I swear. And I talked to Roscoe's wife. He was a decent dude, had his shit together—"

"He was a damned cruel, torturous bastard," Jamal said, teeth practically grinding. "You know why they picked him for the job? Because he didn't care what happened to other human beings. Roscoe Marion enjoyed watching other people suffer. It's all over his electronic record. You know what he did in his free time? Watched bum fight videos and worse. Cavanagh's people figured out Roscoe had a mean streak, and they put him in a place where he could use his sadism to their advantage. The email I intercepted? It was to a friend of his, reaching out with a possible employment opportunity because they were looking for more sick sons of bitches to be lab techs."

"This is off the scale crazy," I said, rubbing my forehead. "You're telling me one of the biggest big shot billionaires is running a torture-porn style operation for the homeless right in urban Atlanta, backed by one of the most connected figures in local politics … and no one's tumbled onto that until you and your homegrown, baby lightning computer hacking investigation?"

"You came down here looking for me," Jamal said. "Think about that. Flora's death would have been written off as a robbery gone wrong. The Bluff—Vine City and English Avenue—is the fifth-highest rated neighborhood for crime in the entire U.S. These men prey on the weak. The nearly invisible. And they've got an operation that's stitched up tight. So tight because guys like Laverne, Cavanagh and Weldon? They don't leave loose ends or things to chance. They even buried their dead in Flora's yard because, hell, no one was going to look there, and if they did, it wasn't going to lead anywhere but to Flora, really. Only someone with the ability to parse the darkest corners of the net would ever be able to dig up a fraction of a trail." He shook his head. "You could spin your wheels here for months, knowing it was Cavanagh and Weldon at the center of it, and you wouldn't even have enough to get a reporter to publish a piece faintly suggesting they had anything to do with it."

"There's a lab," I said. "There's got to be some proof in the lab."

"There might be," Jamal agreed. "But as near as I can tell, there's nothing that links Cavanagh to that lab. The payroll is done through a separate company that doesn't co-mingle funds with his, that isn't traceable to him as an owner, that he's never set foot in—"

"Yet the press seem to know he's in the biotech business," I said. "That he developed the suppressant."

"Yet another shell corporation," Jamal said. "But that one you can trace to Cavanagh. The lab that developed it is in … Arizona or something, I think. Not Atlanta, for sure. He owns, like, fifty percent of it through a holding company and another forty-five percent through a fund he's the primary investor in. Still, the water's muddy enough he could deny he knew anything about it, and if the press was feeling charitable about him—which we know they always are—they'd give him a pass."

"So, what was he developing in the secret lab that he needed meta test subjects for?" Augustus asked.

"I don't know," Jamal said. "There's no internet record or footprint for that site. The place is a black hole without so much as a telephone connection, and they generate their own power. My next step was to gain access, but …" He waved a hand in the direction of their home. The smoke clouds were still visible on the horizon. "This happened. Kinda distracted me. I was going to do it tonight."

"You know they're going to be on red alert now," I said. "We've gone and stumbled right through the middle of their sandcastle city like Godzilla through Tokyo."

"You can tell how pissed they are because of how hard they've pushed back," Augustus said. "I don't even want to know what the Atlanta news is saying about us now. They probably know we were in on the throw-down in the street back there."

"Fleeing the scene might not have been the best move," I agreed.

"There's no way Atlanta P.D. or the feds were going to let you walk out of there," Jamal said, shaking his head. "At minimum, they were going to send you home. You're causing too much stir. The White House is freaking out right now. You should hear the phone calls back and forth between the chief of staff and your agency. I had to turn down the volume on my computer."

I raised an eyebrow. "That's a neat trick. Can you listen in on Cordell Weldon's incriminating phone calls?"

"I did try to listen in on him, actually," Jamal said. "Since I started, he's said nothing out of bounds, but he did work really hard to bring every legal kind of trouble down on you after your visit. Keep in mind I was only listening for a few hours, and … now all my stuff is burned." He shook his head. "We've got nothing unless there's something in the lab, and I doubt there is. You don't go to the trouble of setting up a giant black site like that without taking the precautions of making sure it can't be tied to you."

"How'd you get Taneshia involved in this?" Augustus asked.

Jamal smiled faintly, but it faded quickly. "She introduced me to Flora. Helped put me on the track of Kennith through Darrick Cary—"

"That little weasel," Augustus said. "He didn't think to mention that."

"He noticed Coy had some serious bank for a parolee," Jamal said. "Taneshia was close with him and his lady, used to babysit their kid sometimes. Once she overheard Cary mention something about how Coy had suddenly come into a boatload of money. This was a few months back. It was enough to get me digging. I think she threw it to me to keep me from sulking, but … it turned into something." He spoke with quiet resolution. "She didn't know what I was going to do. Hell, I didn't know what I was going to do when I set out to talk to him and Roscoe." He lowered his head. "I just … they both … I miss her so much, and Coy, in particular was just … such a prick about it. I knew he knew something, but I don't really have good control over the bigger bolts. I've been working on the fine connections since I learned about my powers, and so when he drew on me, I just let him have it. Afterward, I was … shaking, enraged. I went after Roscoe and … that didn't go so well either."

"I think you might be understating that," Augustus said.

"So we're at an impasse," I said. "Without going into the lab, we're stalled."

"We go into that lab, we're probably going to be just as stalled," Augustus said. "I mean, can we even bring the law down on that place?"

"Sure," I said. "Someone breaks in and dials 911 from inside the building—"

"No telephone lines," Jamal said.

"From a cell phone?" I asked.

"Might work," Jamal said. "Certainly easier than getting a warrant, because that'll never happen."

"Why not?" Augustus asked and then answered himself a moment later. "No ties to anything."

"No probable cause to believe a crime occurred there," I said. "No witnesses, no legally collected evidence … just shadows and speculation."

"Man, for someone who championed the rule of law to me earlier," Augustus said, "you sure don't seem to believe it applies to you."

"This is how it always happens," I said. "I keep coming up against people with abilities, powers, or in this case—power, of the political and monetary variety—that insulate them from evidence. There's always a threat, there's always a killing, there's always a breakdown in the system that circumvents everything. Before Sovereign, it was the fact that the world of metas existed outside human law. Now it's the fact that human law and enforcement is still trying to catch up to metas in general. Cavanagh is doing something here that's dirty, and he's got enough money to spread around that when combined with Weldon, they've locked out anybody from even looking for the truth. Without a press that's willing to kill its darlings—or at least look at them as something other than flawless saviors—this thing is never going to see the inside of a courtroom."

I looked at Augustus, who had turned his gaze uncomfortably away from mine and was focused on Taneshia, who seemed to be healing, albeit slowly compared to me. "Once again," I said, "I'm left with a choice. Follow the law to the letter and allow them to escape, or go skirting the edges and do what's right. My agency wants me to just walk away. Should I do that?"

"No," Augustus said, sullen.

"Hell no," Jamal said.

"You almost seem gleeful about this," Augustus said.

"Oh, I'm as pleased as punch," I said. "As in, I'm as

pleased as if I were punching someone I hate in the face, because it looks like I might be doing that soon. I talked to an old friend about this situation, someone who's familiar with Weldon, and he jokingly suggested I knock him out and drop him in the middle of the North Atlantic, just let him die of the landing or hypothermia and wash up on someone else's shores." Augustus's eyes widened. "I'm not going to do that, obviously."

Augustus shook his head. "No. No. That was not an occasion for use of the word 'obviously,' because that would imply that no one would believe you'd do that."

I sighed. "Yeah. Okay. Well …"

"How do you want to do this?" Augustus asked, and he sounded resigned. "You want to kill them all? I'm actually to the point of being so low I almost believe that's the only way we'll stop them."

I lowered my head. "No. It doesn't have to be like that."

"I think it does," Jamal said.

"No," I said. "Listen. I want them alive. I want them to feel that sick sensation of weightlessness that comes just before the fall. Men like Cavanagh and Weldon deserve to be broken and humiliated for what they've done."

"You honestly think they'll see the inside of a cell?" Jamal asked.

"You're damned right they will," I said. "We're going to hang what they've done around their necks like a sign. We're going to find a way to get the press to turn on them like the sharks they are, chum the waters with enough truth that not even the most head-up-their-ass reporter will be able to ignore it—"

"They can ignore an awful lot," Augustus said.

"Not this," I said. "All their friends are going to abandon them." *And I know what that feels like,* I didn't say. I wanted Weldon and Cavanagh to feel it, too.

"Will that make you happy?" Augustus asked. He was watching me, looking for an answer that would satisfy.

"It won't make me sad," I said. I wanted to say something reassuring, something that would repair the damage of having seen two of his personal heroes fall in as many days. Maybe three, if you counted me. I didn't count me as one of his heroes, though.

I did count me as fallen.

"These men are snakes," I said. "And snakes don't show themselves as snakes, or even necessarily believe they're villains. When I first met Sovereign, he was in disguise as a teenage boy with a crush on me."

Augustus's eyes were glazed, wide, with his mouth slightly agape. "Whut?"

"That didn't make the news," Jamal said.

"There's a lot that doesn't," I said softly. "So … the lab. If we're lucky, maybe we can find something there to tie them to it, and if not, then at least we—"

A loud tone sounded in the room. Augustus fumbled and snatched up his phone, staring at the faceplate. He held up the screen and I saw the words, "Cavanagh Tech," underneath the number. He answered and held it up to his ear. "Hello?" He paused, blinked, and then said, "Um … okay."

"What is it?" Jamal asked, edging closer.

Augustus stared straight ahead. "They asked me to hold for Mr. Edward Cavanagh."

I stared at him. "He's making you wait on hold before your climactic conversation? What a dick."

"The hold music is …" Augustus frowned. "I think it's … 'Black Horse and Cherry Tree.' Damn! It is."

"If this doesn't prove he's the villain, I don't know what will," I said, looking at Jamal. Jamal just nodded.

"Hold on," Augustus said and pushed the speaker phone button, holding it out in the middle of all three of us. The song played, nearly causing me to grind my teeth.

"Hello, Augustus," came a voice as the song blissfully clicked off. "It's Edward Cavanagh."

"Yeah, I … heard your secretary or whatever announce that," Augustus said, meeting my eyes. "What can I do for you, sir?" I couldn't tell if Augustus was just playing it cool or if he was really that polite.

"I feel like we need to have a face to face," Cavanagh said. His voice sounded exactly like it did on TV—smooth, youthful, exuberant, with some real energy coming off it. It would have been infectious if I hadn't known he was up to his neck in testing some nasty stuff on human beings and then disposing of their bodies.

"Uh … what for?" Augustus asked.

Cavanagh chuckled. It didn't sound like an evil laugh, which meant he clearly needed to practice. "I think we can just leave that aside for now, can't we?"

"Not sure what you mean," Augustus said. He wasn't a good actor.

Cavanagh sighed. "You're a smart guy, Augustus. Do we really need to play games?"

"Maybe I'm just giving you a little room to deny," Augustus said. "We are on an open line, after all."

"We are indeed," Cavanagh said. "But no one's listening, and I doubt you've got a tape recorder handy, but … we should meet. You and me. Your friends, too, if they want to."

I felt my eyes get wide, and watched Augustus's do the same. "Uh huh," he said. If my brother had been here, he would have been screaming, "It's a traaaaaaaaaaaaaap!" I restrained myself from doing it, but only barely. "That doesn't sound like something I should do if I want to live a long and healthy life."

"You have no idea what I've done for you," Cavanagh said, and there was a rustling on the other side of the phone. "How much I've tried to help you over the years. But there's other things you don't have, either. Like … any hope of escaping this state alive. The cops are after you, Augustus. They're planning to shoot to kill after that thing at your house. They think you killed a lot of people, that you masterminded a metahuman terrorist attack."

"I'm sure they came to that conclusion totally organically," Augustus said with a fair helping of sarcasm.

"Doesn't matter how it happened," Cavanagh said. "What matters is how it's going to finish. Personally, I'm hoping to see you walk out of this one. Look, I know you, man … you're a hero. I want to see you become the hero Atlanta needs. We're not anywhere near a point where that can't happen. Nothing has occurred here that will keep you from being that guy, from having a long, exciting career doing what you want … getting what you want. I can help you clear your name. And I think you know I've got friends with pull, friends that can see this all cleared up. You can be the man, Augustus. Your friends can walk out of this—the cops can end up thinking you're all heroes. This is not a problem. It's an opportunity if you're wise enough to come talk to me. We can come to an understanding."

Augustus looked at me and mouthed the words, "You can't be serious." But he didn't say that out loud. "That certainly seems like a better alternative than getting shot like a dog in the streets …"

"No one wants to see that happen," Cavanagh said, and damn, he was smooth. "No one. Everyone I've talked to about you knows that you're a bright young man who'll make the right choice. Come talk to me. Let's straighten this out."

"Just me?" Augustus asked. "By myself?"

"Of course not," Cavanagh said. "You can bring your friends, too. We should all talk."

Augustus cringed. "Where were you thinking?" He kept the cringe out of his voice, though.

"I've got a facility," Cavanagh said. "It's not too far from you. I suspect you know where it is." Augustus looked to Jamal, who nodded before Cavanagh continued. "Come on down, we'll meet in person. I think we have a lot to talk about."

"How can I be sure you'll be there?" Augustus asked.

"I'll be there," Cavanagh said. "One hour. Look forward to seeing you." He hung up without another word.

Augustus fiddled with the phone, making sure it was hung up before he spoke. "That dude is going to try and bushwhack the hell out of us, isn't he?"

I thought about it for a minute. "It's totally possible he's decided he'd rather buy you off, at least for now. You did sort of go through his massive meta army, which—remind me to ask him how managed to get that many of them in one place. That's pretty much unheard of these days."

"So we're going?" Augustus asked.

"Oh, I wouldn't miss it for the world," I said.

"You realize he's going to stack it all against us," Augustus said.

"Damned right," Jamal said. "He's not going to be there, but what he'll have waiting for us is going to come at us hard."

Augustus looked pensive. "You think he was lying about the cops being after us?"

I pulled up my phone and loaded my news app. Right at the top of the page was a grainy picture of Augustus. "Nope," I said, and showed him.

"How'd you get out without a mention?" he asked, frowning at my screen.

"Clean living, I guess," I said then smirked. "They must not have seen me enter the fray through the smoke."

"How are we going to do this?" Augustus asked.

"Like heroes," I said, looking at Jamal, who did not meet my eyes. "You up for that?"

"I'll do what I can," Jamal said. "But no promises. Some fool comes at me hard, I'm not going to hold back the lightning."

"No holding back," Augustus agreed. "But that's not what makes a hero. Not when you're outgunned like this."

"No," I agreed. "But if we get Cavanagh or Weldon

alone, we spare their lives and find a way to make them twist for this."

"You can … count me in on this," Taneshia said. I hadn't even noticed her get to her feet. She had her back to us, and her wound was almost entirely gone.

"Damn!" Augustus said. "You—"

She came around and her eyes were dark with fury. "You better not even give me one second of that crap about keeping me safe, Augustus Coleman, or you'll be trying to figure out how to unlock every muscle in your body from lightning-based convulsions. Jamal may not have figured out how to control his lightning … but I have."

"Four against … I don't know, an army?" I stared at each of them in turn. "How do you like those odds?"

"Who you calling odd?" Augustus said, and he had a faint smile.

"You," Taneshia said, limping over to us. "Hell, this whole thing is odd. The three of us, and …" She looked at me, "her … together? On this? It's all crazy. What would Momma say?"

Augustus's face hardened, the slack lines gone in an instant. "She'd say if they've done wrong …" Any look of lightness in his eyes was now gone, long gone. "… we should go get 'em. And that's exactly what we're going to do."

45.

Augustus

Getting to the lab was half the fun. Sienna flying with us in some sort of human chain was an interesting way to go about it. Taneshia was still hurting, and she was last on the chain. Holding her up wasn't exactly taxing for me, and it didn't seem to bother Jamal above me. We probably looked like the world's weirdest bird if anyone saw us, crossing the moon in silhouette, stacked one holding on to another like we were ready to drop each other as bombs.

"It's right there," Jamal said as we overflew an industrial building that probably wasn't a tenth the size of the Cavanagh factory where I worked. It looked old and worn, and it had a faint smell coming off of it like sulphur. A massive silo loomed on one side over a square, boxy main structure. We were flying slowly, a fractional amount of the speed Sienna had displayed in the time I'd flown with her before. We started to descend with a slight jerk, losing altitude quickly.

"Whoa!" I called in slight alarm.

"Sorry," the answer came from above. She didn't sound strained, exactly, but she didn't sound calm, either. "I'm not used to flying with all this extra mass. Kinda unwieldy." We steadied out, coming in for a landing just below a catwalk in a loading dock area. There was another, smaller silo off the main building, and I wondered what it contained. Maybe human beings for all I knew.

Taneshia dropped first, about ten feet off the ground. She rolled and cleared the landing area, and I followed right after. Jamal landed with a grunt five feet from me, and I heard Sienna's feet come down just between me and the loading dock. The night air still had the day's humidity, and even though it was a little cool now, I felt like I was still sweating, and not from carrying Taneshia, either.

"Here we are," I said, trying to find a way to lighten the tension. Nobody seemed all that happy to be walking into this particular trap. We'd talked about a few different strategies, maybe leaving someone outside to listen in. But the truth was, anyone outside of a hardened building like this would have to take a few minutes to get in if we got in trouble, and that didn't seem as smart as just matching our strength against theirs.

I mean, we were standing with the most powerful metahuman in the world, after all. That seemed like an odds-evener to me.

"Now …" Sienna said, "… how do we get in?"

And then the answer appeared.

The loading dock door in front of us rattled as it began to rise. We all stood there, waiting to see what happened. A pair of black dress shoes appeared first, followed by giant legs, and finally by the face of a man as humorless as any I'd ever met.

"Hey, Laverne," I said. "What's up?"

"Come in," Laverne said, not taking the bait on my question. It left a little tension. "You can keep any weapons you have."

"Was planning to anyway," Sienna said, "but thanks."

That made me feel a moment's relief. After all, if Cavanagh was planning to hit us hard in an ambush, he'd want us unarmed, right? Maybe this was going to be a discussion.

I hoped.

Laverne shut the door, leaving the chain pull rattling as he strode away from it. I started to follow after sharing a look with Sienna, Taneshia and Jamal, and we fell into a line. I could feel the electricity as I brushed past Taneshia. The nervousness showed on her face.

We walked through massive automatic doors into a beautiful stainless steel facility that was totally at odds with the run-down look of the building from outside. The doors whooshed closed behind us with a mechanical finality that I found uncomfortable. The place was lit up like midday and it looked sleek as hell. Even the floors were steel, and glass lab rooms were visible on either side of me.

We walked down a long row of labs and under metal catwalks. I watched above us for any sign of people. There was none. This place was quiet, like they'd sent all the help home. Which made sense, I supposed. You don't really want to get into a throwdown with super powered folk with a bunch of potential casualties all around you. That's just bad HR practices.

We headed toward a room at the end of the long chamber. I could see Mr. Cavanagh in there, waiting, arms crossed in front of him. He was alone and looking at a computer. It wasn't exactly an office, though. It looked more like a storage room, with some kind of massive tanks on the wall.

The glass doors in front of him swished open as we approached, and I caught a hint of something slightly putrid in the air as he looked up to greet us with a tight smile that didn't appear to be feigned. "Augustus," he said, like he was greeting an old friend. "I'm so glad you came."

"Yeah," I said, looking around. "It's a real impressive facility you've got here."

"I know," he said, looking around. "This is the first time I've been here. I really regret that now. I would have liked to have been more involved in this project, but … I just couldn't be."

"It's always good to keep your distance from felonious activity," Sienna mused.

"Necessary evil, I'm afraid," Cavanagh said. "But I'm not here to talk to you about regrets."

"Tell me you're here to confess," Sienna said, "and save us all lots of time and trouble."

Cavanagh sighed. "I'm here to explain. Now, I'm told—by the company stock price bump every time I hold a meeting like this, where I get to go into detail about what we've done and why—that my explanatory style has a wonder all its own."

"Has anyone ever told you how humble you are?" Sienna asked.

Cavanagh let himself grin. "If you'd done what I've done, the word humble wouldn't even be in your vocabulary."

"A remedial reading course could fix that problem right up for you," Sienna said. "I'm assuming you skipped that day in favor of attending the Egomania 101 lecture?"

"Please," Cavanagh said, still smiling, still charming, "I *started* egomania at the graduate level." He waved a hand and looked at me, seemingly seeking understanding. "She's trying to get a trap to spring. But I'm not here to trap you. I'm here to show you the brighter tomorrow that we've been building. Which is what a leader—a hero—"

"A raging egomaniac," Sienna added.

"—is supposed to promise," Cavanagh went on, undeterred.

"A brighter tomorrow based on human experimentation?" Jamal asked, cutting into the conversation.

"All of the wonder drugs of today were tested on humans at some point," Cavanagh said. "Every last one. The difference here is … this particular leap forward could only be tested on humans. Because no other animal on earth possessed the genetic potential that we were looking to unlock."

I watched Sienna's forehead and nose wrinkle. "You … tell me you didn't."

Cavanagh smiled at her. "We did. It took … years. Years of lab time, before we even thought about trying it out on another human being. But you know what? Once we did, it worked exactly as we thought it would. Perfectly. It doesn't work a hundred percent of the time, but when it works …"

"You mind explaining what you're talking about?" Taneshia asked, watching the subtle interplay between Sienna, whose face was frozen in a pained look, and Cavanagh, who looked triumphant.

"Haven't you asked yourself why you developed your powers when you did?" Cavanagh looked at her, then Jamal, then me. "I'm guessing none of you have metahumans for parents. But the three of you, all developing powers together, with seemingly no genetic link. That's extremely unusual."

"Like having ten metas in your private army that you can just deploy seemingly at will," Sienna said quietly. "There are only some six hundred left in the world—"

"It doesn't have to be like that," Cavanagh said. "Not anymore. Now, with what we've done here, the possibilities are unlimited."

"Oh my Lord," Taneshia said, and I could tell she'd gotten it.

"You didn't," I said.

"I did," Cavanagh said, eyes agleam. "I really did. I discovered the secret of metahuman powers in human DNA … and now we can unlock the door and use it at will."

46.

Sienna

"Ohhh, great," I said, laying it on with the sarcasm. "I've been wanting another super-powers war. Because I got to the one out on the street just a little too late to scratch the itch I've been having for the last couple years."

"You're afraid," Cavanagh said, prompting me to give him my best "You idiot," look. "It's okay," he said. "You're a control freak. You've got a goddess complex. I get that. That's me, too. I understand. You're afraid you'll lose the handle on the situation, that you'll no longer be relevant."

"I would be overjoyed to be irrelevant," I said, more than a little annoyed at this cocky prick. "But I think, unfortunately, I'd be more relevant than ever, and that troubles me."

"You're missing the silver lining for the cloud," Cavanagh said. "Think about this. Disease, injury … they'll be gone overnight. It'll be an awakening. Most people will go to bed and sleep peacefully, and when they wake up the next day they'll be something different. They'll have power over their lives in a way they never had before, but really, it'll be the same story. Society won't fall apart because the biggest difference will be in the small scale—that ability to heal that we've never had before, that ability to ward off sickness. A cure for cancer? I've discovered it, and it's already in genes of every person with powers." He pointed at Augustus. "You're the future."

Augustus looked at him hard. "Did you test this on me?"

Cavanagh gave him a slight nod. "I did. On you and your family. Clearly your mother didn't—"

"Why me?" Augustus asked, looking suddenly outraged.

"Haven't you always wanted to be somebody?" Cavanagh asked, his voice soothing. "Haven't you always wanted to stand head and shoulders above others? To have something special to differentiate yourself from the herd? You are a special young man, Augustus. I put you in my management program because I saw it. You have the hunger to do great things—like me."

"So you tested this—this stuff on my family?" he asked. He wasn't taking the news well, but he was accepting it better than I would have.

"Yes," he said, "about a year ago. We added a few parts per million of our compound to your house's water supply under the guise of being the water company. It doesn't have to be ingested, but that helps. A year later, your brother, your best girl—"

"Excuse me?" Taneshia asked. "I'm not his girl."

"—and you are all metahumans," Cavanagh said.

"But not his mother," I said, wanting to know the answer to why almost as much as I wanted to punch Cavanagh in the face.

Cavanagh hesitated for the first time since we'd come into the room, no slick answer easily accessible. "We're finding a percentage of people—about a quarter—that simply don't respond to the treatment. It's possible their genetics aren't predisposed to accepting the unlock. Like … there's no key for them. We call them passives."

"Gah," I said, rubbing my forehead. "So you want to give superpowers to seventy-five percent of the population of—what, the U.S.?"

"The world," Cavanagh said. "This is a global community

now."

"Have you not ever picked up an *X-Men* comic?" I asked. "Because leaving twenty-five percent of the population without defense against these shiny new powers seems like a formula for disaster."

"You can't just put an anchor on human development because there might be some people who don't use them responsibly," Cavanagh said. "But then, I should have expected this regressive attitude from you; you already have powers, after all. Wouldn't want to upset the balance."

"Yeah, I think the world becoming unbalanced is a great idea," I said. "Because turning a randomly selected subset of people into weapons of mass destruction makes a ton of sense. You realize that there are some metas who have the ability to explode with the force of a nuclear bomb? Try to imagine giving that power to a person who—I don't know, has the ideology of a Hitler but lacks anything but fringe nut support for his ideas. I've heard of metas with chemical abilities, too. Think of the damage one of them could cause if they snapped into a psychotic rage. Whole cities could get wiped off the map. Mass destruction or even the annihilation of humanity could become the province of individuals with a grievance."

"Whereas today we reserve that particular right for only the largest governments," Cavanagh said. "I'm strangely uncomforted."

"This is a terrible, terrible idea," I said. "You can't do something like this without at least pondering the consequences first."

"I can," Cavanagh said. "I absolutely can." His face twisted. "It's going to be my legacy, in fact. I'm an idea man, see, like Edison. I just keep churning them out—ten, a hundred, a thousand—until I find one that works."

I sighed, and stared him down. "Well, you've tried to kill us, like, a hundred different ways now. Maybe for your next attempt you should change a sign so that it leads us over a cliff? Maybe that'll be the one that works."

Cavanagh grinned. "I think … just maybe … I found something better."

"You have to realize I will fight you to the death to keep you from unleashing this plague on the world," I said.

"Oh, I realized that was a possibility," he said and looked at Taneshia, then Jamal, and finally Augustus. "Which is why we're here, in a steel facility without any concrete or dirt or stone nearby for Augustus to play with. And why I've got these canisters leaking a very small amount of gas," he waved a hand to extend to metal containers stacked in storage racks all around us, "that will explode if either of our lightning bearers or our lady of the flames cause so much as a spark." He gestured to the area around us. "No dragon in here, either. You try, odds are good things will explode. And those light-based nets? I'm not so sure they won't set off a boom as well—which is fine for you." He looked at me and smiled tightly. "You might walk out of this alive. But me and the kids won't." He took in Augustus, Taneshia, and Jamal with the wave of a hand.

"Why don't I just kill you now?" I asked, feeling my blood run cold.

"You could," he said. "You absolutely could. Break my neck, I'm done. But … then you won't know what I've got lined up to disperse the treatment to the whole city of Atlanta. Which, I believe, is something you're afraid of?" He smirked and walked in a line in front of us like a visiting lecturer. "This doesn't have to go bad. We can all still—mostly—get what we want. I want to make the world a better place. Always have."

"Your vision of it, anyway," I said.

"This is a great equalizer of power," Cavanagh said. "Don't be such a nagging parent. Look how these three have done with power."

"Umm, one of them has been murdering people," I said. "Kennith Coy, Joaquin Pollard and Roscoe Marion were not accidents."

Cavanagh frowned. "Really? That's—well, that's …" He looked annoyed and shot an irritated look at Laverne before turning his gaze back to Jamal and Taneshia. "Thanks for screwing up my point, asshole. Who did it? No, never mind, it doesn't matter. This is going to happen, but we can all benefit from it. Augustus," he said, looking right at his intended target, "I know you want to be somebody. I know you want to climb the ladder of the world, go to college, get your own little slice of the American dream. You can still do that. I can help you. I mean to help everybody I can. To make it possible for more people to help themselves than ever before. We have an obligation to put an end to sickness, to disease, to pain—"

"This is going to cause more pain," I said, looking straight at Augustus. I felt like I was in a war for his soul, and I couldn't let it go unargued.

"You need to think like a hero," Cavanagh said. "Heroes save the world, but she treats the world like it's past saving. All she wants to do is hold the status quo in place because she benefits from it."

"You know I don't," I said darkly, letting a little of the pain I'd been bottling up for months spill out. "If I could change the world right now into a better place, a place where there was no hurt, no sickness—I wouldn't do it. Because I saw that vision, and it was the same vision that Sovereign offered—a scorched and barren surface."

"People could be better," Cavanagh said.

"Not this way," I said. "People are getting better, generally, a little at a time. Less war, less murder—these things are happening right now, just slowly."

"It could happen all at once," Cavanagh said. "It could be a revolution."

"Revolutions usually involve a lot of bloodshed and frequently don't result in much stability for a long period after they start," I said. "A lot of innocent people will die. Maybe more than would have from sickness and injury that you're touting."

"You're not certain," Cavanagh said. "You're speaking in hypotheticals."

"So are you," I said. "This is human nature you're going against. The natural desire to conquer, to fight amongst ourselves, to lord it over our neighbors and divide based on our differences. Now you want to give us a whole new set of differences." I stared right at him. "And you've been willing to kill people to make it happen. That tells me everything I need to know about you."

"Just like you've been willing to kill people to protect the way things currently are," Cavanagh said quietly. "And that says everything about you. You'll never change. You'll always be someone who holds humanity back out of fear."

"Fear keeps you from walking off a cliff," I said.

"Fear keeps you from learning how to fly," he said.

"Enough," Augustus said, and he shook his head, looking weary of the never-ending argument. "Just … enough."

"You're in the middle of this," Cavanagh said, "and I'm sorry for that."

"You want me to choose, right?" Augustus said.

"I did," Cavanagh said. "But that was before I found out that she," he nodded at me, "was going to end up being the stickler on this. Unfortunately … that means you're going to have to remain my leverage." He smiled tightly. "Unfortunate, but … omelet, eggs … you see where I'm going with this? I'm sorry."

I heard the door open behind me as the click of a pistol hammer sliding into cocked position at the back of my head sounded loud as an explosion. A half dozen people walked into the room and surrounded us, standing with the glass lab windows at their backs. Metas all, I knew from looking at them, from the way they carried themselves. Laverne may have had a pistol at my back but this was the coup de grâce, the cherry on top—the overwhelming force that Cavanagh needed to put an end to us once and for all.

47.

Augustus

I watched Laverne Dobbins put a gun to the back of Sienna Nealon's head, and my mind worked fast. "If he fires that, it's going to set off the gas, isn't it?" I asked, turning my eyes to Cavanagh.

Cavanagh was a damned statue, eyes bereft of his typical amusement. "Maybe. But even she won't survive that shot."

"Along with you," I said. "Along with us." This whole thing was out of control. Not for a minute was I excited to fall in line with Cavanagh's plan. It wasn't the democratization of power that had me bothered. It was the idea you could just take people and fiddle with their genes against their will. Experiment on whole communities and countries? With some drug he'd tested on homeless people that he'd pulled off the streets. "How'd they die?" I asked, solemn, staring right at him.

Edward Cavanagh blinked. "Who?"

"Those people who ended up in Flora Romero's yard," I said, glancing at Jamal. He was taut like a string pulled to its maximum. My brother was usually a low-key guy, but I could see that being in this situation wasn't enhancing his calm.

"Like I said, sacrifices have to be made to pull us forward," Cavanagh said. "You can't build a new and better world right there in the old one. You have to clear some space first."

Talking wasn't going to solve this, but hasty action wasn't going to end it very well for anyone. I knew for a fact that there was no dirt anywhere nearby. Cavanagh had seen to that, and whoever his cleaning crew was, they were good. The minerals in the steel that made up the walls was something unnatural, too, something I couldn't get any kind of a hold on with my powers. I reached out, and then I felt something I could actually influence and realized exactly how much of a miscalculation Edward Cavanagh had made.

It was big.

"You were my hero, man," I said to Cavanagh, and he cocked his head at me like a dog listening to its master but not understanding. "That day you and Mr. Weldon took a picture with me was the best day of my life."

Cavanagh's expression changed to a pained look. "I'm sorry that has to remain the high point, Augustus, I truly am. I doubt you'll understand, but by doing this, I'll be a hero to millions more just like you."

That was even more crushing. "So much for being special," I said, turning my head.

"Hopefully you'll be one of the last to die before we change this little world," Cavanagh said. "That'll just have to do."

I chuckled, mirthless. "I actually am special." I reached out and felt for what I needed. I caught a glimpse of Laverne reaching back with the gun. He was about to punch Sienna in the back of the head. I locked eyes with Cavanagh. "Maybe you unlocked the power, but I'm going to be the one to use it to stop you."

Cavanagh froze. "You think you can outwit me?"

"Oh, I dunno if I can defeat your stunning brilliance," I said, drawling. "But I reckon I stand a decent chance against a genius who forgets that the primary ingredient in glass is *sand*."

I blew out the computer monitor screen right into his

lower back and hauled on the big windows that surrounded the entire lab room we were standing in. I didn't have full control over the elements of the glass, but I had enough of a grip on them I could use them clumsily to do what I wanted. I ran a hard channel right through every meta in the room except Sienna, Jamal and Taneshia, and funneled those shards into them. I didn't pull them hard enough to shred them to pieces, but I watched them all scream and dance as the glass, busted down to fine bits, tore them up in seconds.

It was messy.

It was nasty.

It was like something Sienna Nealon would have done. Except I tried not to kill them. It was tough.

I paid special attention to Laverne Dobbins, funneling most of the glass I sent his way right into his hand. I heard him scream and the pistol dropped. I watched Sienna take a few steps back from him, clearly unwilling to jump into the grinder I'd created around him. I thought about continuing the process, maybe setting up little cells for each of them in the middle of a sweeping tornado of the glass, but just steering it like I had was taking a lot out of me, so I let it rest and slumped against a counter, took a breath.

"Damn," Taneshia said. "That was …"

"Special," Sienna said, looking right at me.

"Always knew I was going to be somebody," I muttered. "Didn't bother me that no one else believed it."

The sound of tinkling glass reached my ears, and I turned my head to see Cavanagh jump through the window into the next room. "Augustus!" Jamal shouted, and he was leaping after him.

I shot a look at Sienna. She was staring at Laverne Dobbins, who was clutching a bloody hand and looking right back at her with absolute fury in his eyes. I hadn't been doing this long, but I had a feeling they were about to throw down. "I got this," she said, waving me off. "Go get Cavanagh, will you?"

"I'm all over that," I said and tore off after Jamal. He and Cavanagh were already out of sight, running through a side door and into the night.

48.

Sienna

"Not gonna lie," I said, looking at the big man. "I like kicking the crap out of guys like you. Watching your pride fall to new lows as you get beat by a girl? It makes me feel better about the current state of my life." His hand was bleeding from a dozen cuts, but he didn't seem to notice that or care. Which was fine by me, because after the incessant frustration of the last few days, I was looking for an emotional release.

"I don't think you've ever fought anyone quite like me before," Laverne said. I was all set to come back with a Shirley joke when he started to grow. His shirt started to distend, his sleeves ripping along his biceps as his already enormous muscles bulged with strength. His neck muscles grew neck muscles, and his eyes got tiny by comparison. "You have no idea what you're in for," he croaked in a furious voice.

"Oh no, so frightening, it's a … it's a … a *Hercules*," I snarked and watched him blink in surprise, his shoulders going slack as he deflated. "Whatever will I do?" And I launched myself right at him, slamming a fist right into his nose.

It was such a relief to finally be punching someone in the face who truly deserved it.

49.

Augustus

I was after Cavanagh, running into the night. The ground was a little slick, the exterior lights of the lab reflecting dimly off the hard asphalt surface. I saw a puddle ahead from the rain two nights earlier and saw it rippling from being recently disturbed. I wondered if Jamal or Cavanagh had splashed their way through it on the way by, or if the heaviness of their footfalls had just set it to rippling.

I could hear them both pounding against the pavement ahead of me. Cavanagh was laughing in the night, an almost gleeful sound, as he tore off at meta speed. I guessed he had been using his own product.

I saw a flash around the bend ahead and knew that Jamal at least had run around the enormous silo that stood like a hundred-foot cylinder just in front of me. The lightning flashed left, so I sprinted right, trying to catch up with them on the other side. I wasn't hopeful that Cavanagh was going to do something as stupid as double back around in the circle so he could run straight into me, but I figured if Jamal had the one side taken care of, I'd take care of the other.

Oh, Jamal. I hoped he wasn't going to do anything we'd both regret. Though I was honestly more worried he'd do something that only I would regret at this point.

I sprinted around the giant silo and caught sight of Jamal

a hundred feet ahead. He and Cavanagh had really pressed that head start. Or maybe they were just in better meta shape than I was. Either way, I hustled to keep up and watched Jamal shoot lightning at Cavanagh again. It looked like it missed, dragged down to the earth by something, an unnatural curving of the arc of electricity. Beyond the two of them, a helicopter waited in the distance, Cavanagh's ever-present escape route. Just in case that failed, I guess, there was a brand new BMW sitting just this side of the helicopter.

Cavanagh halted, spinning around to look back at us. He was only a couple hundred feet shy of the helicopter now. I'd say he was grinning madly, but there was too much calculation in it to call it that. He knew what he was doing, all the way down the line. Jamal threw another bolt at him and it curved away, grounding out uselessly against the pavement.

"I start to wonder if these powers don't speak to our personality in a way," Cavanagh called out to us. "Augustus is the strong, earthy type, grounded. He's got the heart of an old-school hero. But you," he pointed to Jamal, "you're a live wire. Impulsive. Angry. Reckless, jumping like a current from whatever conducts you."

"What does your power say about you, then?" Jamal asked.

"I'm the thing that brings you down," Cavanagh said. "I'm inevitable. Inescapable. That constant well of unlimited strength. The never-ending thing that you just … can't escape."

"You look like you're trying to escape right now," I said, shuffling into place at Jamal's shoulder.

"Just angling for a little breathing room," Cavanagh said. "I like to have some space to work."

"You're not the first maniac to demand some lebensraum," I said, stepping forward, "But you'll—"

He lifted his hands like a conductor. "Shhh … you don't go crowding a black hole."

I felt the world shift underneath me, felt pure force land

on my back and drag me down. I watched the same thing happen to Jamal next to me, smashing his lips on the pavement. It was like ten thousand tons landed right on me, and I couldn't evade it, couldn't shake it, couldn't get away.

"And that, gentlemen, is what heroes deal with—the weight of the world on your shoulders," Cavanagh said. "Everyone always gives credit to wind, water, earth and fire as the avatars of nature, but that's so flawed. Modern science recognizes more forces in this world than that, and I've got the most powerful at my command …

"Gravity."

50.

Sienna

"… And this is reason number eight hundred and twelve why you shouldn't mess with me." I hammered big boy one last time in the face, watched his eyes droop, his eyebrow trailing blood down it. He slumped, drool oozing out of his mouth. I'd beaten him into near unconsciousness and let my powers work him into a painful stupor more than I usually did.

Ahhhh. I felt better.

"Holy hell," Taneshia breathed behind me. I looked over to see her standing at a strange angle. I guessed her back was still bothering her. "You just … I mean … that was … is he still alive?"

"Oh, yeah," I said, kicking Laverne lightly with my shoe. His face showed zero reaction. I surveyed the others in the room, the ones Augustus had showered in glass. "I think this trap didn't quite spring the way these guys figured it would."

Taneshia looked everything over once, almost comically. "You can say that again."

"Come on," I said, clapping a hand on her shoulder lightly as I passed, "let's go help Augustus and Jamal."

51.

Augustus

I could taste the grains of dirt from the asphalt as Edward Cavanagh mashed my face into the ground. I could feel the crackle of the electricity as Jamal started to panic next to me, the faint hints of it running between us. It was weak, and born through the moisture left by the rain days earlier, but I could smell the ozone it left in its wake, like water evaporating off a summer sidewalk.

The grains of rock were not my friends as they pressed against my cheek. I felt blood well out as Cavanagh pushed me harder to the earth. I'd always heard people talking about the man keeping you down. I'd always tried to ignore that as best I could. Because I was Augustus Coleman, dammit. I was somebody. I was going to make it. I was not going to be denied!

Now I had a literal man holding me down, and that did not sit very well with me. The weight was getting so heavy that the breath was being forced out of my lungs, oozing out of my lips in a low rasp. I could see his legs as he plied his trade, slowly turning me and my brother to paste. The pain was increasing now, and I'll admit—I was starting to panic.

But panic was good. Whenever I'd panicked before in a fight, things had happened. Ideas presented themselves. New options opened themselves up.

Necessity was still the mother of invention.

And I was about to show this dude just how nasty of a mother she was.

I reached out and felt the ground beneath his feet, the pebbles that were tarred into the asphalt beneath him. My guess was that he hadn't heard about this yet. Laverne didn't seem like the sort who wanted to share the excruciating details of his failures. And it had definitely been Laverne wielding that shotgun, I was sure of it now.

I felt my skull start to buckle under the gravitational pressure and squeezed my hand tight as I grasped for those rocks beneath Edward Cavanagh's feet. I could feel them, I could touch them with my powers, and all I needed to do was apply enough force to—

Set them loose.

They exploded out of the ground in a much lower arc than the last time I'd used the power. I was in control this time, and I meant to keep Cavanagh alive. He screamed in pain, and I watched his legs buck as his fancy pants legs shredded under the impact and he hit his knees.

The pressure on my back released in a sudden, wonderful sense of lightness. I could breathe again in one explosive, joyful intake of air. I gulped down hungry breath after breath, watching the spots fade from my vision as I tried to force myself up on one elbow, then another.

By the time I looked up, Cavanagh was already to the helicopter. He was hurrying in, the door open. He let it thump closed behind him as he started frantically pushing buttons inside. The engine made a noise as it started up, the rotors slowly beginning to spin, gathering speed as they came around faster and faster.

"I would have gone for the BMW." Sienna spoke as she landed, extending a hand toward me. "Need help?"

I thought about it for only a second before taking her hand and letting her drag me to my feet. "I wouldn't turn it down."

She helped Jamal to his feet as Cavanagh's chopper blades spun faster and faster and started to rise in the air.

"I'm going to smoke this fool," Jamal said and raised his hands.

"No!" I said but got drowned out by Sienna, who slapped his hand down. Jamal gave her a look, of course, and she gave it right back.

"He killed Flora," Jamal said quietly, and the fury in my brother's voice was unmistakable even under the sounds of the helicopter engine whirring in the night.

"And he'll pay for it," Sienna said.

"Damned right," I said, lifting my hands. "I think the mountain's about to come to him—maybe settle right on top of his helicopter."

Sienna sighed, loudly and comically, entirely for effect. "Boys, boys. There are easier ways." She shook her head at us chidingly and started walking toward the chopper. Her steps were slow and measured, even as the skids rose off the ground and Cavanagh started to get away.

"He's—!" Jamal said, pointing.

Sienna just waved us off, walking over to the BMW. She ran a hand along its hood, gripped it tight with both hands, and then LIFTED THE WHOLE DAMNED CAR INTO THE AIR. She chucked it right into the helicopter, and I watched the blades slap against the car's body and frame, shredding it and itself in some glorious destruction that I was hard-pressed to look away from until the shrapnel started flying. Then I ran.

I was expecting an explosion, a bang, and I ended up getting a whimper. Jamal and I stood back as Sienna floated into the wreckage, the engine of the helicopter already spinning down, trashed. The car was in pieces, part of the chassis laying across the bubbled front of the helo like a Tinkertoy someone had left on top of the contraption.

When she came back around, Sienna had Edward Cavanagh in her grasp, his head lolling back and his body limp.

"Is he …?" I asked, pointing. The night was quiet save for the sound of sirens coming from somewhere in the distance.

"He'll live to stand trial," she said and dumped him in a pile at our feet. "Won't he, Jamal?" She looked at my brother, and he turned his head to avoid my gaze.

"Guess we'll see," Jamal said, but he couldn't hide the little bolt of electricity that ran down his arm as he said it. "But I won't be doing it here." He locked eyes with me. "Got to go, brother."

The words, "You don't have to," died on my lips. There was pain in his eyes, and I knew he didn't regret Roscoe or Kennith or Joaquin. "Where are you going to go?" I asked instead.

"I'd like to go anywhere but here," he said and turned his attention to Sienna. "What about you? You going to stop me?"

She took a long breath and sighed. "You going to kill anyone else?"

Jamal's lips pressed together tight for a minute before he answered. "I don't know. I don't aim to."

"That's a start," she said and lowered her head. "Go on. Get out of here. Don't let me catch you breaking the law again."

My brother stood there in silence for a moment and gave me one last look before he ran off into the night. I listened to his footsteps disappear into the dark, and I wondered if I'd ever see him again.

52.

Sienna

Detective Marcus Calderon made my life easier, thankfully. He could have been a real prick about the whole incident, could have doubted every word I said, but instead he listened with guarded skepticism while Augustus, Taneshia and I told the whole story.

"So … Cavanagh kidnapped people through this unauthorized lab and experimented on them to create powers?" Calderon asked, looking about as long suffering as any guy I'd ever seen.

"With the aid of Cordell Weldon and all his organizations," Augustus said, the red and blue police lights flashing across his face.

Calderon leaned back against the police car he'd been standing next to. "I'm going to need so much antacid to make it through this night. I'm going to need to drink the whole bottle and then chew the little pills like they're breath mints." He shook his head.

I was almost afraid to ask the follow-up question. "So … do you believe me?"

He looked at me, once again, like I was an idiot. "It's an insane story, accusing two of the most powerful men in the area of absolute corruption and greed in the course of attempting a Nazi-like genetics experiment that nobody noticed." He sighed. "Of course I believe you."

"Well, okay then," I said and felt a small sense of relief. "What do we do?"

"How do we contain Cavanagh if he's got these powers?" Calderon asked. "Seems to me that if the man can affect gravity, we're not going to be able to put him in a conventional cell."

"I've already called for transport," I said, "but … this one's unique. I've already got a call in for an injectable version of suppressant, because I'm not sure our standard containment unit will be able to hold him."

"When does that show up?" Calderon asked, looking at Cavanagh's limp and unconscious form.

"I don't know," I said and felt a nervous rumble in my stomach. "I think my agency is still deciding whether or not to fulfill the request."

Calderon gave me the eye. "You really did step in it, didn't you?"

"All the way up to the knee, at least," I said. "Maybe even to the hip, this time."

"Mmhmm," Calderon said, shaking his head. "Cordell Weldon and Edward Cavanagh. You don't aim small."

"Heroes don't punch down," I said and felt Augustus's very uncomfortable gaze settle on me. "At least not very hard. Or something. I heard that once. Probably while I was punching someone on the ground."

Calderon put a hand around my upper arm and gently led me away from Taneshia and Augustus, who were watching every word between us like they were expecting something. I let him because it was kind of cute. "Let me handle the press?" Calderon asked, eyeing me. I wasn't quite sure how to take that expression.

"They're all yours," I said. "How are your superiors going to take this?"

"The governor has directed the Georgia Bureau of Investigation to lend a hand," Calderon said. "Which of course pissed off the mayor and the council, including Weldon. No one quite predicted that. I hear the feds are going to land on Atlanta's side, but it's becoming quite the jurisdictional fight. Until that settles out, though, the governor is in charge and seems to be more on … your side, let's say."

"How do we go after Weldon?" I asked, throwing a mental thanks to Senator Robb Foreman for keeping his word to me.

Calderon shook his head. "Won't be easy. Any chance your boy here would like to confess?" He bumped Cavanagh with the toe of his wingtip, nudging him as if he were testing to see if he was still alive.

Cavanagh stirred, rolling his head back, his hands cuffed eight times behind him. His drowsy eyes found Calderon's and blinked sleepily. "I'd like to make a full confession. If I'm going down for this … that bastard Weldon is coming with me."

I stared at Cavanagh for a full five seconds before looking to Calderon, whose jaw was down. "Let me, uh … read you your rights, and then we can get this show on the road, if that's all right …?" He glanced at me and then ran for his car, waving at every cop he could find in a close radius, trying to get as many witnesses as he could for this.

I just stood back and listened as Edward Cavanagh spun a story I'd already heard in front of about thirty cell phone cameras while I let my eyes drift over the cars parked nearby. I eventually found the one I was looking for, a black sedan with North Carolina tags, but I didn't approach it or say anything. Why would I? Cavanagh was talking, he wasn't resisting, and everything was coming up roses.

Fifteen minutes later, we were ready to arrest Cordell Weldon.

53.

Augustus

You ever have a hero? Someone you watched from a distance do incredible things, things that made you admire them? Maybe it was taking a principled stand under pressure. Maybe it was stepping in front of a punch meant for the little guy. Maybe it was just calling someone powerful out on a wrong they'd done.

I thought I'd seen Cordell Weldon do those things. But what'd I'd really seen was Cordell Weldon doing what he thought people wanted to see.

I'd gone by his office building before, just to see it from the outside. Nice three-story brick building not far from home, with Atlanta's skyline as a backdrop. The whole city was lit up when we came to Cordell Weldon's office, because it was the middle of the night.

And Weldon's lights were on.

This was only our first stop, though. Detective Calderon had already pulled up Weldon's home address, because we figured he wasn't going to be at work at this hour.

His home address wasn't anywhere near my home address, that was for certain. Dude lived in the burbs, far from the neighborhood. I had no idea. No one I knew had ever mentioned that.

At that point, I wondered if I'd ever known anything

about Cordell Weldon at all, really.

Taneshia and I went in through the front door while Sienna took the back stairs, cops with us every step of the way. They took us along because while Cavanagh claimed Weldon hadn't ever taken any of the meta serum that would give him powers, none of us fully believed him. And I sensed that once they'd heard the story, most of the cops were all too happy to drag Cordell Weldon out into the street with a particular glee. He hadn't always been the kindest to them, after all.

Weldon's assistant wasn't at her desk, and when I busted open his doors we found her under his. Heard a thump under the desk, that's how we knew. When the cops shouted, "Police!" she came scrambling out with her hands up. Sienna and her crew of cops came in through the side door, filing in through the shattered frame.

We had actually caught Cordell Weldon with his pants down in every sense of the phrase, and I wasn't too proud to be amused by it, though Taneshia looked a little embarrassed. Sienna just looked tickled pink. No, really, her cheeks were pink, and there was laughter in her eyes. Rare thing for her, I think.

Weldon looked at us, pure fury embodied in that wiry frame. His eyes, always all business, now were calculating where to direct the lash. "What is the meaning of this?" he asked, keeping one hand below his desk as a couple detectives pulled his secretary out of the room.

I felt a little bad for him, then I saw the picture of him with his wife and five kids, and I didn't feel that bad anymore. "Cordell Weldon," Detective Calderon said, "you're under arrest."

"For what?" Weldon said, standing up as he zipped his pants.

"Conspiracy to commit murder is a good start," Calderon said. "I'll let one of these officers read you your rights, though I'm sure you're familiar with them by now."

"What I'm familiar with," Weldon said, seething, "is a police department that's so petty that they'll take the word of a proven liar like Ms. Nealon here—"

"We have a full confession from Edward Cavanagh," Calderon said.

Weldon paused, appropriately stunned. I gave him about five seconds before he came up with a reply to that.

It only took four. I counted. "If you think I'm going to just stand idly by while that man—"

"A.k.a one of your biggest donors and a close personal friend," Sienna interjected.

"—smears my reputation in the community," Weldon said, "you're fooling yourselves. This is not going to end well for you. You're making enemies here. Powerful enemies."

"I've had some of those," Sienna said loudly. "Of course, mine were the sort that could actually throw fire at you, whereas yours were the sort that could maybe toss a political favor your way, but … hey, we come from different worlds."

The lines around Weldon's eyes grew taut. "You haven't heard the last of me, Ms. Nealon, and you're a fool if you think any of this will stick."

"I dunno," she said and sort of gestured at his pants, "you look like you might be sticky." I blanched and looked away. "Take him away," she said, and I heard a few laughs as they did so, along with an officer reading Weldon's rights to him as the cuffs clicked on. "Hey, Weldon," she said, and he turned in the grasp of the cops. "Remember how you said it doesn't matter what you do, it matters what you're seen doing?" She clucked at him. "You might want to rethink that philosophy, because nowadays … someone's always watching."

"'Someone's always watching'?" I asked her after they'd led him away. I stood next to Taneshia, admiring Cordell Weldon's leather couch in the corner of his office. I was tempted to just throw myself upon it since I didn't exactly have a home anymore, but considering how we'd just found him, I decided against it.

"What's that old Ben Franklin quote?" she asked, thinking about it.

"'Three men may keep a secret if two are dead,'" Taneshia said in a low voice.

"Seems like however many men were involved in this, they kept the secret pretty well for a good long time," I said. "Years."

"It always comes back sooner or later," Sienna said, and the look on her face went resolute, traced with sadness. "Can't outrun the past forever. It's part of you."

"That's grim," I said.

"It's truth."

"I don't know if I agree with that," I said. "What's the point of life if you can't change? Life is change. Otherwise we'd just be hitting the same notes day after day. No," I shook my head, "I don't believe that. I think people can change—if they want to. But," I shrugged, "that's coming from a guy who two days ago was just a normal dude who was going to have his college paid for by an employer that's now probably going to … collapse under the weight of more indictments than the Capone organization."

"I'll believe it when I see it, kid," Sienna said, a little too smug. She was in her patronizing mode again, and she only seemed to pull that out when she was being defensive. But I was onto that game now.

"Hey," I said, catching her before she turned away. The cops were clearing out, heading downstairs, probably radioing for backup for their backup, ready to throw up a cordon and watch the place 'til sunrise so they could soak up some more overtime. "You may fool everyone else," I said, so low that no one else could hear me but her and Taneshia, "but Cavanagh, when he thought he had us over a barrel—he never had *you* over a barrel. You could have dodged that fool Laverne's bullet at any time and just let the lab blow up around you."

Her smug smile vanished. "I—that would have—"

I stepped closer. "The press may not acknowledge it, the newspapers may not print it, hell, maybe no one will ever know but Taneshia and me, but … you saved our lives tonight. You may be too hard sometimes, but you're still a hero."

"I don't …" she let her head sink, unable to meet my eyes, "I …"

"Maybe you ought to let someone save you sometime," I said and squeezed her shoulder. She looked at my hand like I'd imagine a white blood cell looked at a virus: foreign invader! Destroy! Destroy! But she didn't act on that, and a moment later, her expression softened.

"You can't save me from the choices I've made," she said, and there was a dark undercurrent beneath the soft voice. "They're like a wedge that I've driven between me and everyone I know."

What do you even say to something like that? I thought about trying to be serious, but she cleared her expression a moment later, went back to neutral, and I knew the discussion was over. "You know what else comes in a wedge? Pizza and pie, and I want both," I said.

She nodded. "I could eat." She looked at Taneshia.

Taneshia rolled her shoulder, testing out her back like it still hurt. "I'm starving. And I know this great place just down the road from Georgia Tech. They're open all night."

"I'm in on that," I said, following them to the door. I felt a little tweak of regret thinking about Cavanagh Tech and my lost opportunity. That stung. Two years of work for nothing. I sighed and followed them out, though. The sun would come up tomorrow, after all, and there'd almost certainly be some other opportunity that would come along for a man in my situation. A man of my means? No, that wasn't right. Whatever the case …

Something would come along for this *somebody*.

54.

Sienna

I found the black sedan with the North Carolina plates later, after both pizza and pie, about a mile from the precinct. I had a feeling that I was supposed to, because when I was flying over, it was right there, parked down an alley that was blind on two sides.

I descended in a flash, trying to remain unseen. It was unlikely, given the dim lighting in this area, that anyone would be seeing me, but I took precautions nonetheless. A moment after I landed, noiseless, the night air washing against my warm skin, the car door opened and Agent Faraday of the United States Secret Service stepped out.

"You armed?" he asked.

"Always," I said. "You don't even need to ask from now on, just assume I am."

He gave me that wary look, then shook his head and got back in the car. The back passenger side door opened on its own and Senator Robb Foreman of Tennessee stepped out, buttoning up the bottom two buttons of his suit as he did so. Classic gentleman, that one.

"Good evening, sir," I said, carefully walking the line between respect and contempt. Foreman should have been honored; I usually didn't come anywhere close to that line. I was firmly on one side for 95% of my life, so this was a concession.

"Hello, Sienna," he said, not making much in the way of concessions himself. But that was a politician for you; they never wanted to make a concession, especially in speech form. "I know it's summer out, but it sure does feel a lot like Christmas."

"I didn't know you were planning to use your powers to pound on them while they were down," I said, crossing my arms. "I just figured you'd use your influence."

He looked amused. "I don't know how much influence you think I have as a junior senator, but it's less than you think."

"What about as a presidential candidate who just watched the other party take a direct hit to the nuts?" I asked.

"Small-time scandal," Foreman said. "The press won't make too much hay out of this one. Blogs and news media will have a field day, and it'll make enough of an impact to cause a stir around here, but don't anticipate Cavanagh or Weldon's departures to be nationally significant except for the sudden lack of PAC donations Cavanagh will be making. Still and all, I have no complaints."

"Did you …" I wanted to be careful here in what I suggested.

"You know I can't force a thought into someone's mind, Sienna," Foreman said, and I felt heat in my cheeks from the chastening. "I can, however, pull on a very narrow emotional thread—say, someone like Edward Cavanagh's deep-seated feelings of guilt, inadequacy and mommy issues—and make them want to do the right thing by confessing all their sins in the heat of the moment."

"That would explain a few of the curiouser things he confessed," I said.

"That man was a little damaged," Foreman said. "Or so I assume from the state of his emotions."

"Did you know what he created in that lab?" I asked. Foreman shook his head. "Metahuman abilities in a bottle. A serum that unlocks the powers hidden in our genetic code."

Foreman had a slightly stricken look on his face at that, and he looked aside while mopping his brow where sweat was starting to pop up. "Well, that's a genie that's going to be hella-hard to squeeze back into a bottle."

"Ya think?" I squeezed my arms tight around myself. "He was dead set on releasing it worldwide somehow. Fortunately, he confessed that he didn't have the delivery apparatus in place for it yet."

Foreman shook his head. "I don't think I got him to confess everything. There was something else in there, something guarded under a layer I couldn't get through—fear deeper than any ocean. There's more than he was telling you."

"Gah," I said, throwing my head back. It strained my neck, squeezing my spine together. "What could be worse than what he already threw out there?"

"I don't know," Foreman said, shaking his head, "but I suppose you have enough problems to be getting along with as it is."

"Tell me about it," I said. "I haven't even figured out how I'm going to contain Cavanagh. Dude shifts gravity with a thought. I expect he can crunch his way out of any cell we can put him in, so I'm guessing we're going to be feeding him a steady diet of his own suppressant for as long as he lives."

Foreman hesitated there, and he'd been looking like he was ready to head back to the car only a second earlier. "About that …" he started.

"Yeah, I know," I said, feeling a world-weariness settle on me. "It wasn't very … pragmatic of me, was it?"

"Seems like this cat would fall into the same category as the Cassandra in England," Foreman said, "too dangerous to live, at least in Sienna's world."

"Maybe I had a sentimental moment," I said, covering my face out of, I don't know—shame?

"I don't think that's it at all," Foreman said. "That young

man you've been hanging around with—I get the feeling he's been … an influence on you."

I cocked an eyebrow at him. "You make him sound like booze or a teenager's badass friend."

Foreman chuckled, and I'd forgotten what a pleasant sound it was. "Didn't mean it like that. Your emotional state now versus earlier today—it's like night and day. I'm no psychiatrist, but I might suggest that you do something to keep that darkness at bay."

"Oh, yeah?" I asked. "What would you suggest to do that?"

"Hire that fellow for your team," Foreman said, and now he did start walking away.

"I figured you'd come down harder on me for not making the pragmatic decision to kill Cavanagh," I said. "I … didn't expect you to go in this direction. Are you sure you're still the same guy who wanted to blackmail me into taking the government job?"

"No," Foreman said as he opened the door and leaned against it. "I saw things working with you that … changed my view of the world in a lot of ways. Hard-nosed pragmatism can't always win, Sienna." He stared me down. "Killing every single threat to humanity in the most brutal, expedient method possible is the work of an executioner, not a human being. For all your mantra of 'I do what I have to do,' I wonder how many times you've considered that these people you've killed are the lowest sort of scum in most cases. They aren't ambiguous characters. They made choices that made them into the villains, choices that put them in place to kill a lot of innocent people." He shook his head. "No, I don't mourn them for their loss, and I never questioned your decisions to kill when you thought it was necessary." His expression softened just a hair. "I did, however, occasionally worry about what those decisions were doing to you." His lips twisted, and I could almost feel him wanting to say something more. But all he managed to get out was, “Good night, Sienna. And good luck,” before he climbed into the car and it drove off.

“Good luck to you as well,” I said to the car as it went past. I knew he’d hear it.

55.

I said a curiously neutral goodbye to Calderon at the station. He was swamped with paperwork and I understood that. He looked up for a few minutes as I said my piece, something about, “Nice working with you, I’m sorry things sucked for so long, but thanks for believing in me.” I left out any references to our evening together because, well, I doubted he’d forgotten, and it seemed like it would be pointless to mention it now, other than to serve as an unpleasant reminder that things had gotten a bit messed up somewhere along the line. I hadn’t gone home with him expecting anything serious, and I doubted he had, either. One-night stands didn’t translate into romance in my world. I didn’t live in a sunny romcom where the leads circled each other making acerbic comments until they reached that moment when they realized they were desperately in love with the other person. I wasn’t even sure I believed in my capacity to love anymore.

“I’m sorry things got screwed up, too,” Calderon said, nodding along. “You could have gone about it a little better, though, you know?”

I didn’t quite glare at him, but it was close. “Look … I’ll get better at being a delicate detective who knows just where to step if you want to give me lessons.”

“Hell, I don’t think I have enough time left on my clock to pull that one off before I die,” Calderon said, nearly laughing. "Just keep going at it full speed ahead, you'll get to the truth eventually. Might end up in a few more YouTube videos, though."

"That seems inevitable," I said and gave him a wave.

"Look me up if you're ever in Atlanta again," Calderon said. He didn't wink, but I think it might have been implied. For my part, I held in the smile until I made it outside and airborne.

I arced east, heading over the English Avenue neighborhood until I found Augustus's house. The neighborhood was a mess, that much was obvious when I came down in the middle of the street. At least the burned-up cars and fire engines had been hauled away. I felt a deep, serious sense of guilt, looking around at houses without roofs, front lawns that were cratered, houses with holes in the brick like a bomb had gone through the window. It was appalling, the level of damage that Cavanagh's meta army had unleashed here, and it left me shaking my head.

"You look like you're a presidential candidate," Augustus's voice reached me from the shade under the tree on his lawn. He was just sitting there under the somewhat scorched—maple? Oak? What the hell am I, a botanist? He was sitting under it with Taneshia, and his mother was in a folding lawn chair next to them. "Circling the FEMA disaster area, nodding your head with a serious look."

"I'm sorry I'm brought this down on you all," I said, walking tentatively into the shade.

"Oh, you didn't hear?" Augustus asked.

"Hear what?" I asked, looking around at each of them. Momma had a very serene expression on her face.

"It seems Mr. Cavanagh has found himself a heart," Augustus said with more than a little gusto, "and has signed over a large portion of his fortune to assuage his guilt over the destruction here."

"That's … surprisingly generous," I said cautiously. I wondered for about a second how much Foreman had had to do with this, and then I realized—he was probably entirely responsible. Then again, Cavanagh was the sort of narcissistic dipshit who might try and do something like this just to make himself look better in a press that was currently in the process of ripping him up like buzzards working over a carcass.

"I always thought that Mr. Cavanagh was a good man," Momma said.

"Momma, he sent those metas that destroyed the neighborhood," Augustus said.

"*Allegedly*," she said.

"He confessed!"

"I don't think I believe that," she said, shaking her head. "Just like I don't think I believe that Jamal ran off with a girl. You know, a mother would know if her boy was seeing some hussy on the side. I think he just wanted to get away from all this."

Taneshia and Augustus exchanged a look with me. "The timing was suspicious," Taneshia agreed. "But I can't blame him. The neighborhood is going to take time to come back from this, even with Cavanagh's money. And you just know when the word gets out, every scammer for twelve states is going to come running to get himself a piece of that."

"Somebody ought to watch out for people around here," I said.

"I believe I will," Taneshia said. "Or at least, as much as I can while still completing my degree." She elbowed Augustus.

"I believe I will, too," Augustus said too, but with much less enthusiasm. "Without the degree, though."

"I would bet that the University of Georgia would be more than happy to accept a bonafide superhero into college there," I said.

"Oh, yeah?" Augustus said with disinterest. "You think they'd pay for it, too? Because that's the real sticking point."

"Mmm, maybe not," I said.

"Just as well," Taneshia said. "I hate the Bulldogs."

"How about the University of Minnesota?" I asked nonchalantly.

"Nobody likes them," Taneshia said. "Golden Gopher? What the hell is that, even?"

Augustus just rolled his eyes. "You think they'll throw out a free scholarship? They got one for superheroes up there?"

"Yeah," I said, "it's a government scholarship with a work program attached."

"Work program?" Augustus frowned. "What work program?"

"You come work for me at the agency," I said, "and in return we'll pay you and fund your college."

"Whaaaaaat?" Augustus asked, looking at me like he didn't think I was serious. "That's not a thing!"

"It's a thing," I said. "A real, genuine thing that I am making up in my capacity as person in charge of hiring and budgeting for the operations department." I smiled at him. "My team's a little light, and I could use someone around to remind me … what a real hero is like."

"You serious?" Augustus asked, lips open. "You're serious?" He looked at Taneshia. "Is she serious? I can't tell!"

"I'm serious," I said to Taneshia, who looked—not surprisingly—torn.

"She's serious," Taneshia said, nodding. I thought I saw hints of tears in her eyes.

"Oh, yeah, everybody's serious," Momma said. "I miss my television programs. They are way less stupid than y'all."

"Momma, I'm going to college," Augustus said, nodding his head. "Hell yeah, I'm going to college!" I wondered if he was going to stand up on his tiptoes and bellow it out to the world. He didn't, but I sensed it was a near thing.

"I heard about that," Momma said. "Whole damned neighborhood just heard about that."

"Can you just be happy for me for a minute, Momma?" Augustus asked.

She stared at him, and then rose from her chair and put a hand on each of his cheeks and drew him in. Then she looked him in the eyes. "Augustus, you put the community's number one advocate in jail. You landed your boss in the clink and his factory is almost certain to shut down, casting a whole mess of people out of jobs. People who live all around us. In spite of all that … I still think you did the right thing, and I'm proud of you." She kissed him on the forehead. "But I'm glad you're going, because until things get rebuilt around here, people are going to be all manner of irate with you." She looked at me. "When can he leave?"

Augustus looked at me, hopeful. "As soon as he wants," I said. "I'm actually escorting Cavanagh and Laverne back to Minnesota with a few of the others so we can contain them there until trial. The flight leaves tonight at nine from the cargo section of Hartsfield-Jackson."

"I'll be there," Augustus said, and I could see he was swallowing the intense emotions down. "And … thank you."

"Damned right you say thank you," Momma said. "I was worried for a minute you'd forgotten all those manners I taught you."

I found myself laughing, out loud, in a way I hadn't in a long time, as my phone started to buzz in my pocket. I'd been ignoring my boss for about two days now, and he'd stopped calling. I hadn't heard a peep from him since the story broke about Cavanagh, and I figured this was going to bite me any moment now. Time to face the music, I figured. And the music was probably that damned "Black Horse and Cherry Tree" song.

I stared at the caller ID on my phone, blinking. It was the same simple white lettering as always, but it felt somehow … smaller.

Katrina Forrest. Los Angeles, California, the phone told me.

"I'm going to college!" Augustus called out from behind me. "We need a party! I need a going away party, like nowwwww."

"You do need a party," Taneshia said. "There needs to be some celebrating. And I think the neighborhood would be very happy to say goodbye to you now that you've destroyed everything." They broke into playful laughter.

I stared at the screen of my phone, just blinking at it. Should I answer? Should I let her have it? Unload all the emotional baggage that I'd been feeling for the last few months at this little war of comparison she'd kicked off?

Those questions ran through my mind in less time than it took for the phone to buzz twice more.

"Sienna, you're coming to the party, right?" I looked up to see Augustus staring at me, Taneshia and Momma right behind him.

"What?" I asked, and then my mind processed it. "Yeah. Sure. Of course. Cavanagh and his boys are suppressed, and I can get there in seconds if I need to. Count me in."

"Who's on the phone?" Augustus asked.

I watched the phone buzz once more, and then it stopped, warning me of a missed call. I stared at the screen for another second and just hit the power button, letting it fade to black. "No one," I said, and put the phone back in my pocket. And I went to go help plan the party ... like a normal person.

56.

Augustus

One last thing:
HELL YES! I am going to college!
I am SOMEBODY!
Damned right. Always knew I would be.

Epilogue

Edward Cavanagh
Fulton County Jail

Edward Cavanagh leaned his head back against the hard concrete block and stared at the bars in front of him. The smell of the crappy food was still lingering in the air from dinner. He'd tried a few bites and nearly threw up. It wasn't just unpalatable; it was gross. He'd been prepared for hardship, but he wasn't prepared for that.

Everything seemed a little hazy for him, a little … like the world was in a fog. That was a shame, but not unexpected given he had a full dose of the suppressant in his veins. That little chemical had been an interesting discovery. Of course, coming up with it had been a very natural byproduct of reverse engineering the serum that unlocked powers, but no one had needed to know that the chicken had come before the egg.

Cavanagh wasn't exactly sure what had possessed him to make his confession, but he had his suspicions. An empath, probably. When they'd come to him, when this whole thing had started, they'd warned him about what types of metas there were in basic terms, and in fairly explicit ones when it came to certain, more problematic types.

He'd been warned, and he'd ignored it. But then, playing with the serum hadn't been something he was supposed to do, not yet. The word hadn't come down, after all. That had been his own initiative. His idea. His vision.

And up until the moment when Laverne had sunk him by striking at bait he shouldn't have gone after, his vision was looking better than 20/20.

Cavanagh felt the pressure of the brick against the back of his head as his thoughts swirled half-formed in his mind, coalescing so much more slowly than they would if he hadn't been on the suppressant. He knew it didn't have an actual effect on his cognition—maybe it was just the disturbing change of environment and circumstances coupled with that sick feeling in his stomach—but his mind didn't feel like it was moving very fast. He could hear the heartbeat in his ears, though, the blood rushing through his brain.

The first spike of pain behind his eye was the clue that gave it away. It sent him back to thinking about the list, the list of metas they'd told him about. What did they call the one that could affect your—

Oh—

Oh no—

Cavanagh could feel the pressure build in the front of his skull, and it forced his eyes to roll back in his head involuntarily. It was like someone had a fist in the front of his brain and was squeezing, squeezing until the blood pooled, each beat of his heart building the pressure like an overburdened dam, all the way until it came to a frenzied peak—

Splat.

Cavanagh saw the wash of red hit the wall of his cell out of the corner of his eye as he pitched over. He left a trail of it, but by the time he was on the ground he was only dimly aware of it—or anything else. His consciousness faded to the point where he couldn't hold even a simple thought.

But the last one that crossed his mind was a doozy, though just a little incomplete.

Shouldn't have crossed A—

Location Unknown

"It is done," the voice on the other end of the phone said.

The watcher did not acknowledge the message, merely hung up the phone. It was not his way to acknowledge, merely to receive the report, to operate within the guidelines. Edward Cavanagh had had his guidelines and had chosen to exceed them. That was his foolish mistake, and now he had paid for it with his death. His silence was assured.

The news flickered on the screen, and once more the watcher was treated to an image of the girl, Sienna Nealon. He had been watching her for as long as he had been in this place. Of course she had been involved. She was always involved. Pesky. That was how he would describe her.

But her day would come. And it would be according to the guideline, the day when he would leave the darkness again.

And his first day back in the light would be her last day alive.

Sienna Nealon Will Return in

TORMENTED

Out of the Box
Book Five

Coming September 1, 2015!

Note from the Author

Hopefully this isn't a surprise for you, but that one was another blast for me to write. I can honestly say I'm having so much fun with these Sienna books, and keep coming up with so many ideas. That's a good sign, right? Anyway, this book hinted at some larger things going on in the series, and also at some things going on in the story arc that will cap off in book #6 (Vengeful) as well as some ones that will maybe come to a head in book #7 as well. (That could change.)

I've once again set a release date for book five. I make no promises about doing this for future installments. If you want to know when future books become available, take sixty seconds and sign up for my NEW RELEASE EMAIL ALERTS by visiting my website at www.robertjcrane.com. Don't let the caps lock scare you; it's FREE, I don't sell your information and I only send out emails when I have a new book out. The reason you should sign up for this is because I don't like to set release dates (it's this whole thing, you can find an answer on my website in the FAQ section), and even if you're following me on Facebook (robertJcrane (Author)) or Twitter (@robertJcrane), it's easy to miss my book announcements because…well, because social media is an imprecise thing.

Come join the Girl in the Box discussion on my website: http://www.robertjcrane.com !

Cheers,
Robert J. Crane

ACKNOWLEDGMENTS

Okay, I'll admit it. I've run out of new ways to thank people and make it interesting. I might try again next book.

My thanks to these fine folks, without whom this book would not be possible:

Sarah Barbour, Jeff Bryan and Jo Evans – Editorial clean-up crew.

Adrienne Prevo and Taneshia Pearl for their read-throughs.

Karri Klawiter – Cover by.

Polgarus Studio – Formatting.

My parents, my kids, my wife – For all their help.

About the Author

Robert J. Crane is kind of an a-hole. Still, if you want to contact him:

Website: http://www.robertJcrane.com
Facebook: robertJcrane (Author)
Twitter: @robertJcrane
Email: cyrusdavidon@gmail.com

Other Works by Robert J. Crane

The Sanctuary Series
Epic Fantasy

Defender: The Sanctuary Series, Volume One
Avenger: The Sanctuary Series, Volume Two
Champion: The Sanctuary Series, Volume Three
Crusader: The Sanctuary Series, Volume Four
Sanctuary Tales, Volume One - A Short Story Collection
Thy Father's Shadow: The Sanctuary Series, Volume 4.5
Master: The Sanctuary Series, Volume Five
Fated in Darkness: The Sanctuary Series, Volume 5.5* (Coming in 2015!)
Warlord: The Sanctuary Series, Volume Six* (Coming in late 2015!)

The Girl in the Box
and
Out of the Box
Contemporary Urban Fantasy

Alone: The Girl in the Box, Book 1
Untouched: The Girl in the Box, Book 2
Soulless: The Girl in the Box, Book 3
Family: The Girl in the Box, Book 4
Omega: The Girl in the Box, Book 5
Broken: The Girl in the Box, Book 6
Enemies: The Girl in the Box, Book 7
Legacy: The Girl in the Box, Book 8
Destiny: The Girl in the Box, Book 9
Power: The Girl in the Box, Book 10

Limitless: Out of the Box, Book 1
In the Wind: Out of the Box, Book 2
Ruthless: Out of the Box, Book 3
Grounded: Out of the Box, Book 4
Tormented: Out of the Box, Book 5* (Coming September 1 2015!)
Vengeful: Out of the Box, Book 6* (Coming December 1 2015!)

Southern Watch
Contemporary Urban Fantasy

Called: Southern Watch, Book 1
Depths: Southern Watch, Book 2
Corrupted: Southern Watch, Book 3
Unearthed: Southern Watch, Book 4
Legion: Southern Watch, Book 5* (Coming in Fall 2015!)

* Forthcoming and subject to change

33303486R00181

Made in the USA
Middletown, DE
13 January 2019